DARK PROPHECY

APOCALYPTIC URBAN FANTASY

ANN GIMPEL

Edited by
K.R. SHIELDS
Illustrated by
FIONA JAYDE

CONTENTS

DARK PROPHECY

SOUL STORM, BOOK ONE

Apocalyptic Urban Fantasy
By
Ann Gimpel

**When the dream world spills its murky contents, everyone's worst
nightmares run free.**

COPYRIGHT PAGE

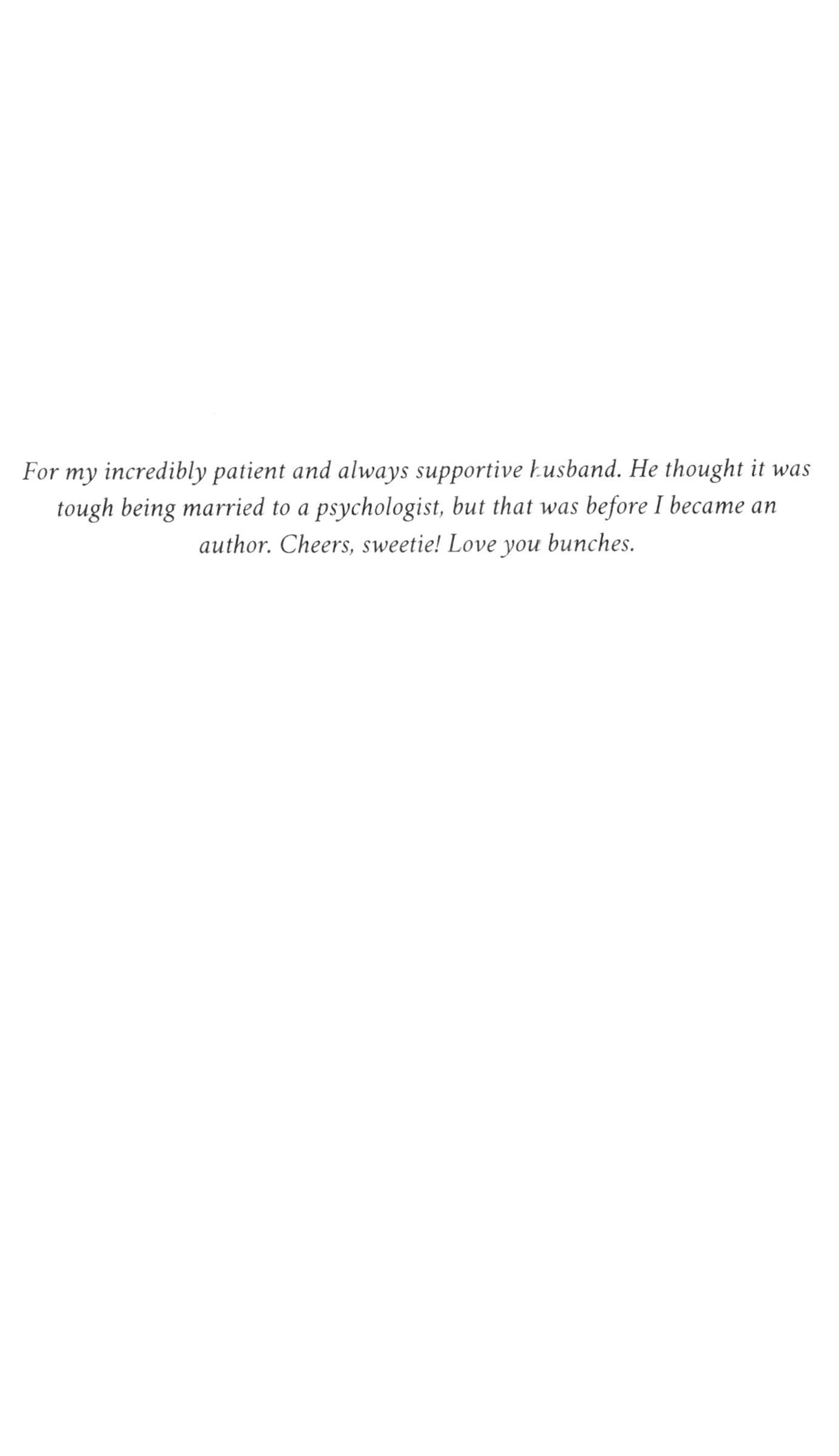

For my incredibly patient and always supportive husband. He thought it was tough being married to a psychologist, but that was before I became an author. Cheers, sweetie! Love you bunches.

ACKNOWLEDGMENTS

I'd like to send warm hugs and thanks to the wonderful women who beta read this book for me. Karen Mikhael, Bridgette Thoroughman, Heather Stanley, Shelly Small, and Holli Greer. I'd also like to send warm thoughts to Fiona Jayde, best cover artist ever. And then there are my author friends who helped with editing. It truly takes a village and I'm so grateful for every single person who's jumped in to support my writing career.

AUTHOR'S NOTE

The *Soul Storm* series is a leaner, meaner revamp of an earlier trilogy. Once I was offered my rights back, I decided these books would be a great place to dip my toes into self-publishing. They're thousands of words lighter and much more tightly plotted. The good news is I've learned a few things in the last four years—at least I think I have. I have no doubt that you, my readers, will let me know if I'm right.

There are many allusions to real places in the *Soul Storm* books. I'd like to add a bit of information about two of them.

Denny Hall:

During the years when I was a student at the University of Washington, Denny Hall did indeed house the Psychology Department and it was said, a ghost or two. It's the oldest building on campus and began providing classroom space to students in 1895. It has truly charming architecture and the college bell tower. The Psychology Department moved to Guthrie Hall, a much newer and far less interesting building, sometime after I left the Seattle area. I far prefer Denny Hall, therefore, in my fictional account, the Psychology Department is still there.

Garland Mineral Springs:

Garland Mineral Springs was a health spa from the turn of the century up until the main lodge, also known as the Garland Mineral Springs Guesthouse, burned down in 1960. In its early years of operation, people believed the waters were curative, and the very ill made pilgrimages there. Supposedly, the mob hid out at Garland in the 1930s. Its last known use was as a Christian retreat. Because of its remote location and wild, untouched beauty, it seemed to be a perfect location for Raven's home.

Remains from about half the cabins are still at the site, but are in serious disrepair. The location is accurately depicted in my novels. A scant ten minute walk from the gate will bring you to what is left of the cabins. The mineral springs are still not very hot, even though they look as if they could be. If you visit, be aware the springs are located on private property.

*L*ara McInnis reads auras and flirts with an elusive ability to foretell the future. Ambivalent about her magic, she's done a fine job sidestepping most of it. After several patients—and a student or two—describe the same cataclysmic dream, ancient evil bursts its bounds, and she can't ignore her power anymore.

Trevor Denoble shields his secrets with a stunning body and a boatload of British charm. The airline he works for folds. Lara's changing into someone he barely recognizes, and the rest of his carefully crafted life isn't in much better shape.

Living in a world teetering on the edge of anarchy, Trevor and Lara face painful decisions. Her burgeoning paranormal ability scares the hell out of him. Meantime, she does her damnedest to survive her magic in a world gone mad. A world where the rules have changed and there's no one left to trust.

CHAPTER 1

*L*ara McInnis uncrossed her legs and sat straighter in the ginger-colored, overstuffed chair taking up most of one corner of her cozy psychotherapy office. Long years as a therapist made it easy to hold a neutral expression. Less easy was latching onto enough energy to support her quarreling clients. What she really wanted to do was tell Bethany Beauchamp to dump her bastard of a husband and get on with her life.

Lara nodded encouragingly at Bethany, but the woman ducked her head and lapsed into silence. Big surprise since her husband never shut up, cataloguing her faults as if they pleased him and clicking them off one by one on his fat fingers. Lara searched for an opportunity to intervene before things got any worse.

"Mr. Beauchamp," she murmured, voice pitched purposefully low so he'd have to stop talking in order to hear her.

"What?" He sounded irritated, his tone scratchy from too many cigarettes and a sour disposition. "You interrupted me."

"Sorry, but I was interested in what you were saying, and I didn't quite catch that last part before I *interrupted*. Might you be so kind as to repeat it for me?"

Ken Beauchamp tossed his shoulders back and rearranged mouse-brown hairs that had fallen out of place in his too-careful comb over. He patted his short, chubby legs encased in expensive suiting, turned, and looked right at her with close-set blue eyes. Broken blood vessels along the sides of his nose suggested an intimate relationship with alcoholic beverages.

"We pay you quite well. The least you could do is be attentive," he complained, an unpleasant whiny note in his voice.

She nodded, offering a silent invitation to speak to her rather than to his wife, who looked exhausted. Bethany's eight-month pregnancy dragged at her tall, slender frame, and dark smudges under her hazel eyes detracted from her showgirl beauty. Light auburn hair fell in limp curls to her shoulders. Though only in her early thirties, today she looked ten years older.

After a short pause Ken took the bait. Rather than repeating his last statement as requested, he started in on Lara. "Well, *Doctor*, you've been late for our appointments twice out of the ten we've scheduled. None of the things you've suggested work, and our marriage isn't any better than it was the day we walked in here." He sat back in his chair, a smug smile on his florid face.

"Which things have you tried?" It became more and more difficult to keep her features pleasant. She detested Ken Beauchamp and suspected his wife felt much the same. Stealing a glance at her other patient, Lara noticed Bethany had begun to cry, her face contorted in silent grief. Lara handed her the box of tissues she always kept next to her chair. "Mr. Beauchamp?" she urged. "What things have you tried? I need to know so I can work with you to figure out what might be more effective."

Or so I can find an excuse to refer you to another therapist.

Ken's face reddened even more. "I'm sure we've tried some of them," he said defensively. Shifting his bulky body around in his chair, he shot his wife an intimidating look. "Beth, the good doctor here is asking what we've tried."

Bethany withered under her husband's knife-like stare. Her crying escalated, and she choked on the word, "N-nothing," as she buried her face in her hands. Outside of her strangled sobbing, the corner office, morning sun streaming through leaded-glass window panes, was absolutely silent.

Lara leaned forward, her gaze shifting from Ken to Bethany. "It's like I told both of you when you first came here, I can't fix your marriage. Only you can do that. For there to be *any* improvement, you have to be willing to listen to one another. We're nearly at the end of today's hour, but frankly there's not much reason for you to spend your money coming week after week, just so I can listen to you argue and try to referee. Go home and have an honest discussion this morning while everything's still fresh. Figure out if you really want to continue seeing me. If the answer is yes, call me and come on back next week. Otherwise..." She let her last words hang in the air, realizing she hoped she never had to lay eyes on Ken Beauchamp again.

"Uh, here." Ken rustled around in an inner jacket pocket and came up with a well-creased piece of paper that he shoved her way. "Sign this."

Lara flipped it open, scanning the few lines. *Damn the man.* He'd been court-ordered to attend marriage counseling and hadn't told her. Neither of them had. Fuming, she hastily checked the box verifying attendance at ten sessions, signed the document, and handed it back.

"You should have told me, Mr. Beauchamp. We might have done things a bit differently." *We sure would have, since I never accept court-referred clients.* He just looked at her as he snatched the paper, a feral smile adding a malevolent note to his already-unattractive face.

"Thank you, Dr. McInnis." Bethany's voice was still clotted with tears as she planted her feet beneath her ample belly and then struggled to her feet. Lara stood and held out her hand; Bethany latched onto it like a lifeline. The two women looked at Ken, who hadn't made the slightest effort to leave his chair. He was chewing on his lower lip, his face the color of a boiled lobster.

Acting on impulse, Lara let go of Bethany's hand and gestured to her. "I'll just walk your wife to the ladies' room, Mr. Beauchamp, so she can put some cold water on her face. She'll meet you at the car."

Pulling the office door open, she exchanged a meaningful glance with her receptionist. "Arabel, could you please see Mr. Beauchamp out?"

Without waiting for a reply, she took Bethany's elbow and pushed her into the hallway. As soon as they were safely out of the office, Lara turned to her client and murmured, "He hurts you, doesn't he?" Her voice was the barest of whispers as she remembered the little she'd been able to drag out of Ken about his obscenely violent childhood.

Another tear leaked from one of Bethany's eyes as she mumbled, "I, uh, can't, um, shouldn't…"

They'd reached the bathroom and were both inside the tiny enclosure. Lara regarded her patient intently, with well-honed inner senses. Bethany maintained an edgy silence, the ragged, darkened edges of her aura radiating a gloomy melancholy. Probing with her psychic side, Lara suddenly knew much of what the woman was unwilling to divulge. And then—as was often the case when she used her gift—she wished she'd left well enough alone.

Reaching into a pocket of her plaid wool skirt, Lara pulled out a pen and one of her cards, scribbling a number on the back. "If things get bad, make an excuse, any excuse. Tell him you're going for a walk. Bring your cell phone and call this number. They help women like you."

Bethany's hand snaked out and she took the card. A frantic look washed over her. "But what if he finds the number?" she whimpered and tried to stuff the card back into Lara's hand.

"It doesn't matter. They won't talk to him." Lara laid a hand on Bethany's arm. "Keep the card. You need to get to your car, so he doesn't react further. Maybe you could come in and talk to me by yourself."

"He'd never let me." Dull voice matching her dead eyes, Bethany let herself out into the corridor and walked toward the stairs with the awkward gait of the very-pregnant.

Back in her office, Lara stopped at Arabel's desk. "Who else do I have today?"

Hooking her thumb out the door, Arabel asked, "What's up with them? The mister, he seemed pretty put out. For a minute there I didn't think I was gonna git him out of the office."

"You know I can't discuss patients with you, dear. At least we have to pretend we don't talk about them." Lara smiled fondly at the elderly African-American woman who'd been her sole office help for over twenty years. Arabel was dressed in her usual white blouse, navy gabardine skirt, and black flats. An ancient maroon sweater hung over the back of her secretarial chair. Hair in a modified mostly-gray afro, she had a piquant sense of humor. Quick temper sparked from her nearly black eyes.

"Humph…" Arabel bristled, her mouth twisted into a frown. "You know I got nobody I'd be tellin' anything to. Never have."

"Sorry, sorry. Didn't mean to hurt your feelings." Lara held out a conciliatory hand. "Truce?"

Arabel cocked her head to one side, and the corners of her mouth twitched as she clasped Lara's hand. "Truce. Never could stay mad at you. Not for long, anyway." Turning back to the computer, she brought up the day's schedule on the monitor. "David Roth cancelled, so you're free till one thirty. Then you got folk packed in here till close to eight."

Lara walked around the desk so she could look at the screen. She loved what she did, but today's schedule was too jam-packed even for her. She glanced at her watch. "I'm going to swing by the gym and then grab some lunch. Call me if anything comes up."

"You got it." Arabel's voice followed Lara into her office where she grabbed her purse and her cell phone, locked her client file drawers, and let herself out the back door.

Her office was in an old, pale blue Victorian on Seattle's Capitol Hill. She'd bought the building for a song ten years before because someone thought there were problems with the foundation. There'd been some structural deficiencies, but they'd proven relatively trivial to fix. Split into four offices, her building was home to an architect and a CPA on the first floor, and herself and a psychiatrist on the second. She walked through a carpet of leaves that had fallen off the Madrona trees lining East Avenue, heading for her nearby BMW.

As she drove, Lara thought about the Beauchamps. She'd spent an unusually long time—at least the first five sessions—gathering a history from them. One problem was Ken's reticence to disclose much of anything. Persistence and caginess had paid off, though, and he'd told her far more than he meant to about the French-Irish gang-affiliated father who'd turned him out as a child prostitute at the age of eight. His mother had abandoned the family when he was so young he had no memories of her at all, just oodles of anger that Lara suspected he generalized to all women—including her. By contrast, Bethany's meager life story tumbled out with very little prodding. Not that hers read much better than her husband's.

Fears for Bethany nagged her. "What if they want to come back?" she asked herself softly. "Should I see them?" Pulling into the parking lot for her fitness center, Lara knew she'd turn *that* question over in her mind as she moved through her workout. Once she lost her objectivity—and any empathy she'd tried to develop for Ken had long since evaporated—it became progressively more difficult to work with clients. She'd learned some hard lessons over the years, including that it was usually better to cut the cord sooner rather than later.

"Hi, Tony!" Lara dropped her membership card onto the glass countertop, snagged both key and towel from the tall, well-sculpted front desk attendant, and headed down lushly carpeted stairs.

"Have a good workout, Doc! Power's on today, so all the machines are available." Tony's throaty voice trailed after her.

Lara gathered her longish coppery hair into a snug ponytail. She was just pocketing her locker key when her phone trilled a Bach Etude. Wrinkling her forehead in irritation, she stuffed the key back into its hole, retrieved the phone, and barked, "Dr. McInnis," without bothering to look at the screen.

"Hey there, Lara. It's me." Trevor's clipped British accent was like a balm. Her long time, live-in lover rarely called during the day, and a prickle of concern moved down her spine.

"Sorry to bother you, love," he went on, "but the power's off again, at least on Queen Anne Hill." He paused a beat. "Thought you'd want to know."

She gripped her phone hard enough it cut into her hand. "Again? But that's the third time since, let's see, last Wednesday. How long did they say this time? Or did they? Or did you even call? What about the food in the freezer?" She stopped abruptly because her voice had become unnecessarily shrill. "Sorry," she muttered. "I'm just worried, that's all."

"I know, I know. That's why I called you." Another hesitation. "Guess I'm worried too, and I just wanted someone to talk to."

She closed her eyes, summoning an image of him with his Nordic features and summer-blue eyes. He was a flight attendant for KLM airlines, which meant he only worked about fifteen days each month. She'd met him ages ago on a return flight from Europe where she'd been completing the last leg of her analytic training at the Jung Institute in Zurich. Exhausted from a grueling six weeks of seeing patients, she'd been half-asleep in her narrow airline seat, and he'd brought her tea and cookies. Lara wasn't quite sure how it happened, but he'd come home with her that night and they'd been together ever since. Those first few years were more than a bit rocky. She'd run screaming from their home a time or two, so she wouldn't kill him on the spot. But something indefinable—she still didn't truly understand what it was—always drew her back.

Lara sank into one of the wicker chairs in a corner of the locker room with apprehension tugging at her. "What do you think it means? Have you any idea?" There was a very long silence, so long she finally asked, "Trev, you still there?"

"Yeah, Lara, I am." His accent was more pronounced, so she knew he was debating whether or not to give voice to his thoughts. Finally, he blurted, "I think we're really running out of oil this time. Not like all those other times when the government stock-piled it and then released it after the price sky-rocketed. You wouldn't know about this, since you're such a news-phobe and I gas up the cars, but it was really hard to find petrol last month. Damned near impossible, actually.

"If what I suspect is true, everything that takes oil to run will eventually go tits-up." He paused to draw a frazzled breath before adding, "We might have been all right here in the northwest with all our hydroelectric power, except the rest of the country's been draining juice off our grid to compensate for *their* shortages. Our state lawmakers have been kicking up a fuss in D.C. Anyway," his voice was brusque, "I'm cooking what I can from the freezer. We'll talk more about this when you come home. If you get any breaks today, consider the pros and cons of moving away from the city. Whoops, my cell's ringing, love. See you tonight."

She slipped her phone back into her locker, walked toward the aerobics room, and jumped on one of the elliptical trainers. She wanted to come to some decision about Bethany and her husband, but the conversation with Trevor kept intruding.

Damn it. He hung up before I could react to that whole doomsday scenario he laid out. Humph! Probably didn't want to give me a chance to talk him out of it. Meantime, I'm supposed to think about leaving the city? Where the hell would we go?

She used her towel to mop sweat trickling down her face and caught a glimpse of herself in the mirrors covering every wall. Staring back was a tall, too-thin redhead with freckles dotting every inch of exposed skin. Her angular face, with its prominent nose and chin, glistened in the reflected light, and her dark brown eyes were pinched with worry.

Moving to the treadmill, she set it for six-and-a-half miles an hour and ran hard for ten minutes. Gasping, she backed off the speed, while increasing the angle. Ten more minutes and she abandoned the machine in favor of water from the drinking fountain. Three sets at the squat rock and twenty pull-ups completed her workout, and she trotted toward the locker room and showers.

As she toweled off, she felt animated and dynamic, her problems with power outages and the Ken Beauchamps of the world temporarily pushed to a back burner. *Nothing like a few endorphins,* she told herself, inhaling deeply. As she made plans to get a smoothie-to-go with extra protein powder from the small on-site restaurant, she contemplated the afternoon's lineup of patients.

Out of the six who were scheduled, there was one analytic client, two angry teenagers: a cutter and a bulimic, another couple, and two lonely, middle-aged women, one depressed, the other anxious.

Too bad it's unethical to introduce patients to one another...outside of a therapy group that is. Lara chuckled softly. She loved doing analytic work, but there weren't many who really wanted to delve that deeply into themselves. Not to mention the cost. She picked up her smoothie, a tofu bar, and some green tea before heading for her car. The sun, an elusive phenomenon in Seattle, was nowhere in sight, and it was raining lightly. While not cold, the day held some of the crispness typical of mid-October. Her phone chimed again but she ignored it, figuring she'd be back at her office in less than five minutes.

"TELL me what goes on inside you before you start cutting?" Lara took in the overweight seventeen-year-old sitting catty-corner from her, arms and legs covered with a network of fine, white scars from years of self-mutilation. Caren would have been attractive, with her silky black hair and porcelain skin, were it not for the miasma of absolute misery emanating from her like a spider's web set to trap the unwary. The girl had been coming to therapy for a month, but was steadfastly unwilling to divulge anything.

"I suppose I could tell you, but I don't really want to," the teenager grumbled. "You don't care about me. You see me because my stepmother pays you. This is nothing but a fucking waste of time." Folding her arms across her chest, she stared defiantly at Lara.

Lara watched Caren intently. She squirmed in her chair, before gluing her gaze to the floor.

"Caren, would you look at me, please?" Lara made her tone as non-confrontational as possible.

"Why?" The girl sounded sullen.

"Because I want you to see I'm telling you the truth when I say I do care about you. You've had a perfectly rotten life, and you have every right not to trust anybody."

Caren risked a sidelong glance at her. "How do you know anything about my life? I haven't told you very much."

Lara was silent for several seconds. Even without her ability to read auras, she'd have been able to figure out a likely script for Caren's early life: molested, physically abused, and emotionally neglected. "What we really need to talk about is a plan so you have something to do besides carving on yourself when you feel bad. Once we come up with that, we can talk about anything you'd like."

"Can I take a bathroom break?"

Lara nodded. "Second door on the left outside of my office." Watching the teenager leave, she wondered if she'd made a mistake. *What if she has razors with her and cuts herself in my bathroom? How do I explain* that *to her parents?* Lara made a conscientious effort to breathe. She glanced at her watch and decided to give Caren five minutes before going after her.

While Lara waited, she summoned her elusive ability to predict future events, but came up dry. Damn, but it would be convenient to find a shaman who could teach her about her psychic abilities. "Yes, but first I have to be willing to tell people I can do those things," she muttered. "I've always been afraid they'd cart me off to the loony bin."

With just ten seconds to spare, Caren sidled back through the door. She had a mulish look on her face, and Lara knew her young patient would bolt if given the slightest excuse.

"Thanks for coming back," Lara offered, attempting to soothe the alienated girl.

"Thanks for trusting me to leave." Caren resettled herself in one of the comfortable chairs across from Lara. The barest of smiles ghosted across her face and she took a deep breath. "This is really hard to talk about."

"I know, but nothing you say leaves here."

"That's almost not the point," the teenager mumbled, twisting in her chair. "Talking makes it hurt more."

Lara nodded. As she looked at Caren, scenes flashed quickly, one after the other: a woman holding a small screaming girl and doing unspeakable things, brutal beatings, cigarettes pressed into tender flesh. Lara closed her eyes and sucked down a surreptitious, ragged breath.

"Yes, it does hurt to talk about it," she agreed. "But that's the only way out. If you keep everything bottled up inside, you'll just keep cutting. The first part is always hardest. After that it won't be quite so bad."

"How can you know?" Caren risked a sidelong glance at her.

"Because I've done this for a long time." Lara paused. "And I've got no reason to lie to you."

Caren raised crystalline-blue eyes. Lara saw a scared little girl, living behind teenaged bravado, desperately wanting to trust someone, anyone, but frightened half out of her mind at taking that first, small step. After a very long time, Caren began hesitantly, in a voice so low Lara had to strain to hear. "It feels like I have to cut, or something terrible will happen. I fight it, but I always lose."

"What do the voices that live in your head tell you?"

"How do you know about *them?*" Caren sounded rattled. Fear flitted across her face, and she folded her arms protectively across her chest. "I didn't tell you."

"Because everybody who cuts has voices that tell them things, before they tell them to cut. It's okay to talk to me about them. The voices don't mean you're crazy."

Caren closed her eyes and dropped her head back against the chair. One tear escaped, rolling down the girl's pale face.

Time dripped past. It was impossible to force anyone to reveal their secrets. Clients had to come to an inner juncture where they believed the pain of disclosure would be worth the risk. Fleetingly, Lara thought about how lonely and isolated the teenager was. *Just like me when I was her age.*

"Dr. McInnis?" Caren's voice was thready, almost not there at all.

"Yes, dear."

"You said everybody who cuts has voices telling them things. Have you helped other people like me?"

Lara nodded, then realized Caren couldn't see her because her eyes were still closed. "Yes," she said simply. "I have."

"Did they stop cutting?"

"Some of them did."

The girl seemed to consider this. She opened her eyes, shiny with unshed tears, and looked pleadingly at Lara. "You must be telling me the truth," she said in a choked voice.

"How can you tell?" Lara smiled gently and she hoped, encouragingly.

"Otherwise, you'd have told me all your other stupid, fucked-up cutter patients got well."

"You're not stupid or fucked-up."

"Yes, I am. Fat and ugly too." Caren was struggling not to cry.

"That's what the voices tell you, isn't it?"

Caren nodded miserably and gave in to a flood of emotion.

"It's all right," Lara murmured. "Cry. This is a good place for your tears. Here're more tissues. I think you're courageous. Maybe we can re-program those voices to say good things."

Caren shook her head vehemently. "Nothing good. Never." She choked out the words between sobs.

"Take a few deep breaths," Lara urged and waited for the girl's emotional storm to subside. "Now I want you to listen, just listen. None of what happened to you was your fault. And it doesn't matter how I know." Lara held up a hand to still Caren's protests. "You were a child. None of those things happened because you were fat or ugly or stupid. They happened because your caregivers were sadly damaged…"

CHAPTER 2

*H*ours later, Lara let herself out of her office, reached back in to activate the alarm, and then locked the door behind her. Arabel had gone home at six. Normally her receptionist left a note if there was something she needed to communicate. Tonight there hadn't been any notes because there weren't any patients she needed to call. But there had been a few zucchinis from Arabel's lovingly-tended garden. Lara was grateful, both for the organic produce and for the lack of patient-related affairs to attend to. She was tired and hoped nobody had a crisis that evening.

She double-checked the pager that lived clipped to her belt. As she moved away from the front door of her building, she stumbled. The outside light was out—when had *that* happened?—and it was very dark in the shadows of the cavernous front porch. She made a grab for the railing to steady herself and took a tentative step toward the street.

"Stop right there," a familiar harsh voice boomed from behind her.

"Mr. Beauchamp. That *is* you, isn't it?" Alarm ricocheted through her, but she knew intuitively it was important to hide her fear. "What do you want?" Though she aimed for nonchalance, her voice sounded thin and shaky. *Is it Ken? Aw, Jesus, who else could it be?* She closed her eyes, gathering data from an unseen realm she knew well. Once her energies were focused, she discerned his twisted energy field throbbing against the darkness. *Better the devil you know* flashed through her mind. *Not necessarily* came close on its heels, as she realized, with a sinking feeling, that Ken Beauchamp really was dangerous. She'd known it the first time he walked into her office, but drawn in by his wife's soft helplessness, she'd ignored her concerns, compassion overriding common sense.

"I want to talk. No, don't turn around." The man's voice held menace as it sliced into her tumbling thoughts.

"What do you want to talk about, Mr. Beauchamp?" With effort, she kept her voice steady. "Surely whatever it is can wait until tomorrow. You really do need to call my office and make an appointment." *There, that seems like about the right amount of bravado.*

"What did you tell my wife today? When you were in the bathroom. You'd better tell me the truth."

"Are you threatening me? Because if you are, I'll call the cops and have you thrown off my property." Anger was rapidly displacing her fear—or at least coexisting with it. She reached a hand into her bag in search of her phone.

"That wouldn't be smart, Doc, not very smart at all. Take your hand out of that purse."

Ken Beauchamp's voice was mild, but an ominous undertone chilled her. Sweat gathered in her armpits and dripped down her sides. *Think!* she commanded herself. *There's got to be a way out of this.*

"Well, *Doctor*?" Ken's voice oozed sarcasm, with undercurrents of something darker and far more primal. "I asked you a simple question. Answer it and we can both go home."

What was he doing? Lara dug deeper with her hyper-honed senses. His breathing seemed…uneven. Was he getting off by intimidating her?

Something clicked ominously. The snick of a gun's safety mechanism? What else could that cold metallic snapping sound possibly be? Fighting fear that threatened to paralyze her, Lara asked,

"How's Bethany, Mr. Beauchamp? She's all right isn't she?" Despite her concerns for herself, Lara was suddenly frantic about Bethany.

"That's none of your business anymore. We won't be back. I just want to know what you told her today."

"Why is that important to you?"

"I ask the questions around here." *Yes*, Lara thought as she listened intently, he was practically panting. *Oh shit, this guy's a pervert on top of all his other less-than-stellar attributes.* She flirted with flying down the porch steps and trying to outrun him, except she had dress shoes on and her heavy shoulder bag. What if he really did have a gun? She hadn't heard the metal click again.

A car pulled to the curb in front of her building and she started, heart beating like a mad thing. *Christ, is it one of his henchmen come to help out?* Practically moaning aloud, she wondered what Ken Beauchamp had in mind for her.

Lara choreographed pulling her phone and wallet out of her bag and making a run for the small business district several blocks away, dress shoes and all. Then the car door opened and she saw Pete Schneider, the psychiatrist who shared the second floor of the building with her.

"Dr. Schneider," she screamed. "Over here."

"Lara, what is it?" Pete slammed his car door and rushed toward her, apprehension stamped on his familiar face.

Lara stumbled as Ken Beauchamp pushed past her, loped down the steps, and launched himself into the darkness between the street lamps. She caught the glint of something shiny clutched in one of his hands and heard a zipper close as he rushed away.

I was right. That bastard was actually working on himself while he interrogated me. And there *had* been a gun. What else could that sparkly thing have been? Nausea rushed through her, and she was afraid she might vomit.

"Who was he?" Pete held out his arms to steady her. "What was all that about? My god, Lara, you're shaking. What happened?"

Her legs buckled under her, and she slumped to the painted porch floorboards, gasping for air, her stomach roiling. Pete sank down next to her, still offering the comfort of his arms.

"One of my patients." She forced words out with a tongue that didn't want to work anymore. "Threatening me. Getting off on it. Thank fucking God you showed up here, or I—I'm not sure what he might have done to me." She had a hard time talking around the golf ball-sized lump blocking her throat. Pete sat with her, rubbing the back of her shoulders and making soft, soothing sounds.

"Can't swallow," she managed breathlessly.

"Relax, Lara. It's just *globus hystericus*. It'll get better once the adrenaline backs off. Here." He pushed her away from him so he could look at her face. Securing her wrist, he took her pulse. "Do you want me to call Trevor? Would you like me to follow you home? Or do you want to go inside and call the cops? Not that those choices are mutually exclusive, mind you."

"No cops. Client confidentiality." Lara's voice sounded garbled to her. "I always wondered what that man did for a living. He left that part blank on my patient registration form. Pah! He's got to be involved in something illegal. It was just so…casual, the way he accosted and threatened me. Normal people can't do that." She shuddered. "I want to go home."

"Do you think that's a good idea? If he *is* some sort of criminal, aren't you worried he's lurking out there somewhere, and he'll just follow us?"

She considered, and then discarded, the possibility. "I'm not sure why, but I don't think he'd do that." An uncontrollable laugh bubbled up, shrill with a crazed edge. "I feel really weird, Pete. Please, just help me get home to Trevor."

Her phone jangled in her purse. Rooting through her bag, she drew it out, looked at the caller ID screen, and touched the answer key. "Hello, Trev. Yes, I know I'm late. Something unexpected happened. Tell you about it when I get there." *Because I can't stand to talk about it now.* "Don't worry, I'm with Pete. He's going to follow me home." She listened for a few moments. "No, you don't need to come. Be there in twenty minutes."

"That might have been an over-ambitious time estimate." Pete's voice was subdued. "Let's see if you can stand, first." Grasping the porch railing, he hauled himself upright a bit awkwardly, and then extended a hand. Gripping it, she stumbled to her feet. They were close to the same height, but his body, thickened by chronic inactivity, had lost much of its once-youthful flexibility.

"I'm not feeling quite so shaky anymore," she said, breathing in the damp night air as she met his worried gaze.

Pete nodded. "I need to run upstairs for a second. The reason I came back here is I'd forgotten a patient's file. There's a court hearing tomorrow, and I don't feel very prepared. Will you be okay, or do you want to walk back upstairs with me?"

She scanned the night. *Nope, nothing there. Why wasn't I this vigilant before I walked outside my building in the first place? If I had been ...*

"Lara?" Pete was looking solicitously at her. Worry crinkled the corners of his green eyes, and his silver hair was mussed where he'd raked his fingers through it.

"I'll be fine here," she answered. "Just fine. He's gone—at least for now."

Pete eyed Lara, opened his mouth to ask how she could possibly know that, and then shut it again. Turning, he unlocked the ornate front door, killed the alarm, and flicked on a switch. The tiny lights of the entryway chandelier mimicked a medieval candelabrum as he trod heavily up the stairs.

"I still think we should put in an elevator," floated down to her.

Lara took three more deep breaths. Yes, that really *was* better. Pete had been on the verge of asking her how she could possibly have known Beauchamp wasn't still out there when she'd sent a mental obfuscation designed to silence him. She didn't want to lie to her colleague about the psychic ability she'd been born with. The skill, or gift, or whatever it was, worked better when she was paying attention.

She'd been lost in thought while closing up her office for the night.

In particular, she'd been thinking about an analytic client and a dream she'd shared with strong archetypal elements. Most disturbing was that the patient's dream was very similar to one of her own.

"Ready?" Pete's voice interrupted her reverie.

"Yes, maybe you could drive me to my car and then follow me?"

"Sure. Get in." Pete loped ahead and pulled the passenger door of his car open. He drove a BMW that could have been a twin to hers, except it was a slightly darker silver.

Driving the familiar route from Capitol Hill to Queen Anne where she lived, Lara thought about the strange withdrawn aunt who'd raised her. Mary Tyler knew what people were thinking and was able to read both auras and the future, at least some of the time. About all Aunt Mary had told her—once she figured out Lara could do the same things—was to not tell people she had *the sight*. "They just might lock you up," she'd cautioned, and Lara took her seriously.

She drove automatically, lost in thought. As she pulled up in front of the rustic, twisting, twenty-five steps leading to her home, she scanned the street for a parking spot and maneuvered the BMW into the closest one half a block away. *Should have bought a house with a garage,* she thought for the thousandth time.

Lara stepped out of the car, feeling bruised and vulnerable. Pete drove past her and pulled into a red zone half a block away. He strode back to where she stood, not wasting any time.

"You'll get a ticket," she protested. "They're death on illegal parking around here."

"I'll chance it." Pete smiled. "If I have to I can always tell them I had a patient near here with an emergency."

She hit her clicker one more time, just to be sure her car was locked, then hoisted her bag over her shoulder and trudged up the street to her front steps.

"I really do love your house," Pete stopped to catch his breath halfway up the stairs, "but I've often wondered why you picked one that's so hard to get to. What happens after you're old? You two won't be able to live here anymore."

Lara stopped climbing and inclined her head over one shoulder. "Talk to Trevor. He thinks we're running out of oil, and we're all done for anyway." Three more risers and she stepped onto her front porch. The elaborate wrought-iron porch light blazed, so the power must have resurrected itself at some point. "Come on in for a few minutes, Pete. I'm sure Trev has something made for dinner."

"Nah, I'll just say hi, and then I've got to go. I still need to review that case before tomorrow." The front door swung inward, framing Trevor in lamplight from the interior of the entry hall. Shadows played over his worn green woolen shirt, faded jeans, and sheepskin slippers. His perfect features were a study in concern as he pulled Lara into his arms.

"Are you sure you're all right?" he demanded while motioning to Pete from behind Lara's back. "Come on in, old man. Good to see you. Thanks, oh bloody hell, more than thanks for rescuing Lara from whatever happened. She didn't tell me much, but I know something went on. Heard it in her voice. Wish I'd been there," Trevor said wistfully, but with steel beneath his words.

"Miss your old street fighting days in Amsterdam, eh?" Pete laughed indulgently.

"It was actually Carlisle." Trevor laughed too, but he didn't seem amused. "I just work out of Amsterdam."

"But you have a Dutch surname." Pete sounded puzzled.

"That's simple enough." Trevor kissed the top of Lara's head and let her go. "My family was Dutch. They migrated to farm country in northern England during the early eighteen hundreds. Enough of this. How about a bite of supper?"

Pete shook his head. "No. Like I told Lara, I have work to do yet tonight. Thanks for the invite, though. Assuming I don't break my neck getting back down those stairs of yours, I'll see you both another time." With a smile and a wave, he disappeared into a night that had turned foggy and damp.

Pulling the door shut behind them, Trevor held Lara at arm's length and examined her closely. "Are you sure you're all right? Come on in here where I can get a good look at you. You have to tell me exactly what happened over supper."

The last thing she wanted was to relieve the tense moments outside her office, but she didn't see any way around it. Dropping her heavy bag in its customary spot next to an antique armoire, she followed Trevor into the interior of their Craftsman home, her low heels clicking on the hardwood floor.

MUCH LATER THAT NIGHT, Lara lay in Trevor's arms. Drowsiness pulled at her, and she thought she might actually find respite in sleep, something that often eluded her when she was upset.

"I really think you should tell the police." Trevor's voice jarred her.

"We've been through that," she protested sleepily. "I won't see the Beauchamps anymore, and that will be the end of it. I'll send them a referral letter tomorrow."

"You don't know you won't see them again. Or do you? Is that sixth sense thing of yours working here? If it is, why didn't it tell you someone was lying in wait to ambush you?"

She rolled over to face him and propped her head a bit higher on the down pillows. "Don't you think I've asked myself that over and over? What's the point of having psychic ability—or whatever it is I've got—if it doesn't even alert me to danger?"

"Good question." He drew her close, his voice rumbling against her hair. "I'm sorry. You're knackered, and I'm keeping you awake. Do you have patients tomorrow? I never can keep your bloody schedule straight."

"No patients tomorrow. Wednesday's my class at the University."

"Sleep, love." Trevor didn't sound the least bit sleepy. "We can talk more in the morning. I'm going to get up and read for a bit." He kissed her tenderly, stroking her back and neck affectionately. "See you in the morning."

"Love you," she whispered. Sleep claimed her before he even left their bedroom.

◌

"Lara, Lara." Trevor shook her gently. "Your pager's going off. You left it in the front hall with your bag. I wouldn't have heard it, but I'd snuck down to the kitchen for a bit of a snack."

"Mmph…" She had a hard time resurfacing from sleep. "What time is it, anyway?" She opened one eye the barest of slits.

"Around three."

"And you're still up?"

He shrugged helplessly. "I've buggered my sleep cycles permanently from all those trans-Atlantic jaunts. You know that. Anyway, here's your pager. Wait just a minute and I'll get your phone. Guess I wasn't thinking or I'd have brought it along." Rising from where he'd been seated on the edge of their king-sized bed, Trevor disappeared out the bedroom door. His slippers slapped against the risers as he descended two flights of stairs.

Their house was an architectural delight with five floors, each offset slightly from the one below. Their bedroom was in the middle, on the third floor. The fourth and fifth floors held their studies, her sewing room, and Trevor's wood shop. The first and second floors were designed like a split-level, and contained the kitchen, living area, dining room, library, and a laundry. The majority of the walls, and some of the ceilings, were glass. Those that weren't were either natural wood or stone. *That* was why they'd been willing to deal with the reality of the twenty-five stairs—and no garage.

Lara reached behind her and switched on a muted light in the headboard, pushing several books out of the way in the process. She peered at the small number flashing on the front of her pager. Recognition was instantaneous. Her eyes flew open, and the last vestiges of sleep departed about the same time Trevor reappeared holding her cell phone.

He looked closely at Lara and frowned. "What is it? Or who is it? Guess you know the number."

"It's the back line to the King County Sheriff's office," she said holding out her hand for her cell phone. "I hope to hell it's not as bad as I figure it must be for them to call me at this hour. Jesus, maybe one of my patients committed suicide." *And left a note blaming me.* She punched numbers into her phone as she spoke. After a momentary pause for someone to pick up at the other end, she announced herself. "This is Dr. McInnis. You paged me."

"Sorry for the late call, Doctor. I'm Sergeant Nelson." The hollowness in the phone line indicated the call was being recorded, just like all calls in and out of every law enforcement office in the country.

"Yes, Sergeant. What can I do for you?"

"Dr. McInnis, we got a call tonight from Lakeshore Terrace. A neighbor reported the couple next door was making a lot of noise—none of it good. We dispatched officers to the scene, and they interrupted quite the domestic violence squabble. Aw hell, it was more like a knock-down, drag-out fight."

The sergeant sighed heavily, breath whistling through his teeth. "Bottom line, Doctor, the woman was very pregnant and pretty banged up. The officer who intervened called an ambulance to take her to University Hospital. When one of the nurses in the Emergency Room went through the woman's clothes, your card was in her pocket. So I figured she was one of yours, and you ought to know."

Lara took a deep breath. "Are you going to tell me her name, Sergeant Nelson? You know I can't tell you anything about any of my patients. And I don't understand why you woke me up just yet. Maybe you could clarify that part for me too." Silence stretched between them. She envisioned the beleaguered law enforcement officer considering how to phrase his request to maximize the possibility of securing her cooperation.

"The woman is one Bethany Beauchamp. She says she wants to go home, and she's refusing to press charges against her husband. We can't do much if we don't have a victim complaint. Worse, she claims she fell down their stairs, started screaming because she was worried about her baby, and her husband never laid a hand on her. Supposedly, he rescued her by breaking her fall."

Lara understood exactly what he wanted. "You were hoping I'd get up, get dressed, jump in my car, and talk some sense into her," she muttered dryly, with an incredulous snort. "Look, Sergeant, you understand domestic violence as well as I do. If she's that frightened of him, she's got good reason to be, and there won't be much I can do to convince her to file a complaint. Not if she thinks she'll end up dead next time."

Another lengthy silence. "Dr. McInnis, you didn't see her. I have. The woman has four broken ribs, a collapsed lung, and a broken nose. Both of her eyes are black and someone pulled out big hanks of her hair. No way in hell she did that falling down some stairs. The doctor who examined her says there's evidence of other physical abuse, some of it years old."

Lara felt ill. She debated whether to tell the officer about her earlier run-in with the likely attacker. In the meantime Trevor, who was once again perched on the edge of the bed, mouthed something at her.

Glancing his way, she recognized the words, "…tell him what that sodding bastard did to you."

She pinched the bridge of her nose between thumb and index finger and squeezed her eyes shut. "Okay, Sergeant, I'll consider going in to see her, but not until morning. With all those injuries, they'll be keeping her for a while. Did you say University Hospital?"

"Yes, ma'am, I did. Sorry again for waking you." The line went dead.

"You are not going, and that's final." Trevor took the phone out of her hand. "Look at me, Lara."

Wearily, she opened her eyes and locked gazes with Trevor, fielding the heat in his burning blue eyes with irritation of her own. "But I can't just ignore her," she protested. "She's my patient."

"She didn't call you," he pointed out. "She's not asking for help."

"That's a technicality." The corners of her mouth twitched in spite of how ravaged she felt.

"Well, what about that Tarasoff thing?" Trevor looked determined, his jaw set in a hard line.

"That was a California law."

"Yes, but isn't there something like that here?"

"Sort of… But I'd need an actual threat to a reasonably identifiable victim so I could warn the victim and the police. I don't have any of that."

"Yes, you do. He threatened *you*. Bollocks, Lara, didn't you tell me you thought he was wanking off whilst he was interrogating you? What kind of sick fuck does things like that?"

She nodded bleakly and drew her brows together into a frown. "Yes, I certainly agree he's pretty disturbed. And I am sure that's what he was doing, but I didn't actually *see* anything. It was dark, so at least that part would never stand up in court. Besides, it would be my word against his. Pete didn't actually see or hear anything. Ken split as soon as he pulled up. Look dear, let's not do this. Why don't you come to bed and we can try to sleep for what's left of the night?"

Trevor walked to the bedroom door and doused the hall light. Discarding his robe and slippers, he pulled his nightshirt off its hook, slipped it over his head—tousling his blond hair in the process—and got into his side of their large bed. Meeting in the middle, they hugged each other. "I'm sorry, love," he murmured. "There're just so many things I'm worried about right now. The world seems all pear-shaped. I really do think this oil thing is going to bugger us, and now there's a demented creep threatening you. I don't like any of it. The worst part is there's nothing I can do but stand by and watch, whilst everything goes tits-up."

"Nobody likes feeling helpless," she agreed a bit prosaically.

"Oh for chrissakes, Lara, stop being a therapist. I don't need you to interpret my feelings."

She winced. *Of course he was right.* "Sorry," she mumbled, her face buried in his shoulder. "Sometimes it's hard to turn it on and off. At least I didn't ask if you'd had any dreams," she added in a small attempt at humor.

Lara pushed back enough to look at him in the cloud-shrouded moonlight streaming through the windows. Without quite understanding why, she asked abruptly, "When do you leave for work again?"

He cocked his head to one side as he thought. "Not until Tuesday, next. And then I'll be gone for about a week or ten days."

"Maybe I'll go with you. There are some of my old instructors at the Jung Institute I'd like to talk with. I haven't been back there for close to five years. I could stay at the flat in Amsterdam for a couple days and then catch a train to Zurich."

"That would be nice." Trevor pulled her body back against his. His warmth relaxed her, and her eyes shut of their own accord.

"Yes, it would," she murmured before sleep claimed her once again.

CHAPTER 3

"More coffee?" Trevor stood over her, pot in hand. Glancing up, she wondered if he took Peter Pan pills. At times, particularly in the morning, he still looked heartbreakingly young, hair slightly awry, dimples aglow and the lightest dusting of freckles on his fair skin. Perfect teeth nested between the strong line of his cheekbones and jaw. It took a far closer look to pick out the network of fine lines starting around his blue eyes and the strands of gray intermingled with his blond curls.

"Actually, what I'd like is more of you. Think we could manage that sometime later today?" She smiled in what she hoped was a come-hither way.

"Ah, my mum warned me about wenches like you!" Trevor's broad smile got even wider, and he ran his tongue suggestively over his upper lip. "Wanton hussy!"

"All the better to rob you of what meager virtue you still have left." She laughed. "I do love you, Trevor. Artemis—or maybe Aphrodite— truly was looking out for me when she put me on your plane twenty- two years ago. Pour me more coffee so you can sit back down."

After Trevor settled into his chair at the glass-and-chrome table in their kitchen, he reached across it and lifted Lara's chin, forcing her to look at him. "Are you going to visit Bethany?" he demanded.

"Haven't decided yet. I've been waiting to see if anything comes to me when I try to look into the future, but the mirror's a bit cloudy this morning. Maybe I pissed off some goddess."

She grimaced ruefully. "Honestly, Trev, I don't understand it. I've never had this much trouble using my gift. It's fickle and stubborn, but it generally gives me what I need. Then there's an odd dream of mine that's almost the same as one a patient had." Taking a couple measured breaths, she cleared her jumbled thoughts. "That's why I want to go to Zurich."

"Did you tell them about *the sight?*"

She nodded. "Sure, Jungians are nothing if not mystics at heart. They believe in astrology and precognitive dreams and all that mumbo-jumbo. It's what attracted me to depth psychology in the first place." She sipped her coffee, and scenes from her years at the Institute played through her mind.

"I think I will drop by the hospital. No, let me finish." Lara held up her hand to still the protests rushing to his lips. "You're welcome to drive with me if you'd like and wait in the visitors' lounge. That way you'll be close by. Afterward, you can drop me in front of Denny Hall and I'll teach my class. Maybe after that, we can go out for a nice dinner."

When he looked at her, relief was written all over his face. "Give me ten minutes, and I'll be ready to go. After last night, I wonder if I'll ever be comfortable again if you're not where I can see you."

While she waited for him, her thoughts turned to her class. She'd been quietly pleased when the Dean of Psychology—an old friend of hers from her own graduate school days—called a few years before asking if she could offer a graduate seminar in depth psychology. As he'd explained it, the University of Washington Psychology Department was heavily research oriented. He thought it would be a plus to offer at least a taste of analytic training to those graduate students planning degrees in clinical psychology. Over time, the seminar had morphed into six different classes spread over a two-year curriculum.

Better get my notes. Lara carried her dishes to the sink and flew up the stairs to her top floor study. Rummaging through a filing cabinet, she pulled out her material on dreams and archetypes and pawed through it, selecting the fifth lecture in the series.

Two floors down, she brushed her teeth and pulled a multi-colored sweater out of her closet. A quick glance out the window made her wrinkle her nose at the gray rainy day. In deference to the weather, she donned a pair of green-striped socks. Wriggling her toes into the soft wool, she luxuriated in the feel of the fuzzy fibers, before stepping into a pair of soft leather boots.

"Lara? I'm outside." Trevor's voice drifted up the circular staircase. "I'll prune a few of the flowers whilst I'm waiting."

"Be there in a second." She stopped in the front hall long enough to stuff her lecture notes into her over-sized shoulder bag so they wouldn't get wet. Halfway out the door, she stopped.

Damn it!

"Sorry, Trev. I forgot a couple things."

She ran back to the bedroom to retrieve her phone and pager. The phone's message light blinked reproachfully. "What's wrong with me?" she sputtered. "I'm usually not this irresponsible." She trotted back down the stairs, while she scrolled rapidly through her messages.

"Finally." Trevor furled his brows and set a pair of garden shears on a low table.

'No kidding, huh?" She waited on their front porch, crowded with potted herbs and buckets of pink and red rhododendrons, while Trevor locked the house and set the burglar alarm. "Let's take my car," she suggested and gave him a quick kiss before starting down the steps to the street.

"I'll drive," he offered.

Nodding, she hit the clicker twice, opened the passenger door and got in, handing the keys across to him once he was in the driver's seat.

It was a small luxury to have someone else deal with the Seattle traffic, which had been getting worse for years.

If gas is as hard to get as Trev says, why aren't fewer cars out and about?

She leaned against the soft leather of her seat and let her eyes close. She hadn't gotten nearly enough sleep last night, and it was bound to catch up to her sometime.

The edges of her vision grayed out. Recognizing the onset of a psychic event, she emptied her mind. A jarring scene pummeled her senses, and her hands balled themselves into tight fists with a will of their own. Her nails dug uncomfortably into her palms, but she couldn't uncrook her fingers.

The scene grabbed her with such shocking immediacy, she forgot about the pain in her hands. Bethany lay before her in a narrow hospital bed, her face bruised almost beyond recognition. The lump of her stomach tented the bed covers, and the sheets fluttered when the infant kicked his comatose mother.

A shadow fell across Bethany's form. Though Lara tried, she couldn't identify its source. Bethany's awkwardly-pregnant body began to buck, almost as if she were in the throes of an epileptic fit. A red stain spread through the sheet stretched across her swollen abdomen. Crimson liquid—blood?—dripped onto the floor, creating a rapidly growing rivulet. One of the bedside electronic instruments wailed like a stricken banshee, and a nurse rushed into the room, impeding Lara's field of view.

Then, like it always was with her sendings, someone—or something—decided she'd seen enough, and her vision faded back to the interior of her car.

"What did you see?" Trevor asked tightly, his fingers clenched around the steering wheel as he drove. Her link to the unseen world unnerved him—badly.

Lara opened her eyes and shook her head to clear it. "I'm not sure," she managed after a pause, while she sorted through her vision. "Bethany's in serious trouble, though. She may be dead by the time we actually get there, or in such bad shape, they'll never let me see her."

Lara felt the hot prick of tears just behind her lids. Why hadn't she realized what Ken Beauchamp was capable of? If she had, maybe his wife could have escaped his ire last night, and then... *Stop it. This is not my fault. I offered appropriate support to a distraught client. Don't make more of this than it is.*

Yes but a different inner voice was implacable. *I'm supposed to be able to spot the crazies. Why was I so blind to this one? Dragging Bethany into that bathroom was really stupid. All it did was drive Ken into a jealous rage.* Her thoughts shifted focus. *That poor baby if it even survives. What rotten luck to be born into that wretched home.*

"We're not far," Trevor took Lara's hand. "Look, dearie, I may not have *the sight*, but you're beating yourself up over this thing, and I think you should stop." She nodded wordlessly, still fighting for control.

"Here we are then," he announced as he crimped the wheel and pulled smartly into a space labeled Physician Parking.

She was out of the car before he even had the key out of the ignition. Pulling her bag from the back seat, she stuffed her phone and pager into it and set off at a jog for the emergency entrance with Trevor close behind. Lara yanked the plasticized card that identified her as University teaching faculty with hospital privileges out of her pocketbook. She stopped at the admitting desk and flashed her ID badge at the ward clerk.

"I'm Dr. McInnis," she said breathlessly. "A patient of mine, Bethany Beauchamp, was brought in here last night. I'd like to see her, please."

"One moment, Doctor." The haggard looking clerk manipulated the mouse and brought up something on her computer screen. With practiced eyes, she scanned the list of occupants in the ER. "We seem to have moved her to the ICU, Doctor. Do you know where that is?" Lara nodded and turned away, ready to head down the long passageway that would take her to intensive care, when the clerk added, "She's critical, Doctor. They may not let you see her."

Lara walked over to Trevor, who'd been hovering near the double glass doors that marked the entrance to the Emergency Department. "She's in ICU," Lara said softly. "Follow me. It's quite a way from here down that corridor to our right."

Trevor captured her hand, and the two of them moved rapidly in the direction she'd indicated. Rounding a corner, she tugged at his hand and said, "This way."

She presented her identification at the nurses' station for Intensive Care and repeated her request. A young blonde nurse glanced at her, empathy in her greenish eyes. "I don't think Mrs. Beauchamp is up to any visitors just now."

A harried looking house officer ran past and shoved his way into the open-architecture ICU behind the nurses' station. "Which one?" He was breathing hard as he looked back over his shoulder.

"Bed E, Doctor." The nurse turned back to Lara. "It was good of you to stop by to see your patient, but we're fairly busy here this morning. If you want to wait, you'll need to go to the visitors' room just down that hallway." She pointed with one well-manicured, pink-polished nail. Her voice held a note of finality. Arguing with her would be pointless.

"Can you at least save her baby?" Lara held the nurse's eyes until the younger woman looked away, uncomfortable—and unwilling—to discuss patient issues.

"Um, I don't know, Dr. McInnis. I still hope we can save them both. Now you really do need to leave. There's just not room for you to stand right next to the nurses' station."

Lara had been trying to peer around the young woman to see into the ICU, but the way things were arranged, it wasn't possible. Recognizing defeat, she turned and walked slowly back to Trevor.

"WOULD you like another cup of coffee?" Trevor opened the car door for her. Lara had been silent during the several minutes it took them to exit the hospital.

"Sure, Trev. That would be nice." She looked at him; his shoulders sagged and his lips were pressed into a thin, worried line. "We have at least an hour before my class starts so, yeah, coffee would be wonderful. How about the little place up on University Avenue? They've got that Kenyan blend you're so fond of. Or they did, anyway. Seems like the last couple times I was there, they were out of a bunch of stuff."

She gritted her teeth, her face drawn with worry. "I should call Arabel and warn her to keep the office door locked." Lara pulled her phone out of her bag. Once her receptionist answered, Lara described her confrontation with Ken from the previous night, as well as what happened to Bethany. "So, unless you're expecting someone," Lara's voice was uncharacteristically sharp, "keep that door locked, okay? I don't want anything to happen to you. Oh yes, you might warn Neil and Robert."

"Thought they'd gone to Australia," Arabel said.

Lara thought about her downstairs office mates, the architect and the CPA. Two unattached gay males, they'd finally discovered one another after working side by side for years. "You're right, of course." Lara blew out a tight breath. "This trip was sort of like a honeymoon for them. It's good they're gone so they don't have to deal with all this craziness." She disconnected, shut her eyes, and tried not to think about Bethany, but it was a losing battle.

"We're here," Trevor said.

"So we are. Sorry I haven't been better company," she murmured apologetically and opened her eyes.

"Never mind that," he said and walked around the car to open her door. "Maybe they'll have some of those cinnamon buns you like so well."

"Thanks for remembering." She offered him a weak smile as she led the way into the small café.

"Do you really think she's going to die?" Trevor pitched his voice low so he wouldn't be heard over the din in the crowded coffee shop.

"If she does, will you feel differently about reporting that husband of hers to the police?"

Lara opened her psychic side, but no more visions came. She was aware of a familiar inner emptiness, though, that never presaged anything good. Catching Trevor's gaze with hers, she inclined her head ever-so-slightly. "She was on her way out when we were at the ICU. It's why that doctor raced past us. We must have just missed the nurse with the crash cart. To answer your other question, I have no idea what I want to do about reporting Ken."

Trevor draped an arm around her shoulders and squeezed lightly. "Let me know if there's anything I can do. You take these things hard. Sometimes—hell, most of the time—I don't understand why you chose psychology. There's so much unhappiness."

"You're right, but I can't imagine doing anything else."

He cupped the side of her face in his hand. "You have the most amazing eyes, Lara. Deep, dark, mysterious. I swear, they reflect the entire gamut of human emotion."

"See?" She quirked a brow. "I did chose the right profession. I may be a repository for people's pain, but I'm right where I belong." She hesitated, her thoughts focused inward. "Once I knew I had psychic ability, I considered how to maximize it. Psychology was a logical choice. I considered medicine, but I didn't think I could stand knowing ahead of time which patients would die."

The sting of tears was there again, just behind her eyes. One spilled over and found its way down the right side of her face. She wiped her cheek with a sweatered sleeve and murmured, "Thank you for offering to help. If I wait, I'll figure out what I need to do about Ken. That vision I had earlier... They often come in twos and threes." Her voice petered out, and exhaustion dragged at her. *The sight* was like that. When it intruded, it drained her.

"Will you be all right to teach?" Trevor sounded worried. He tightened his arm around her shoulders.

"Sure. It's a good group, and it will take my mind off the rest of today." She snuffled, blowing her nose. "I do love analytic psychology.

It's a treat to be able to share it in this day and age, where everything has turned into a soulless, evidence-based wasteland. Medicine—and psychology too—used to be part science and part art." She smiled wryly at him. "Thanks to managed care, the art part is pretty much dead. If there's not a placebo-controlled, double-blind study out there somewhere that proves something works, no one will reimburse you for it."

She disentangled herself from his half embrace. "I'll stop by the ladies' room. Meet you outside in a couple minutes."

CHAPTER 4

"...So if the goal for the Seeker is searching for a better life or a better way, can anyone tell me about a historical figure that personifies this archetype?" Lara looked expectantly at the eleven graduate students scattered about the faculty lounge. She'd wanted a more intimate atmosphere for her lecture series. After a bit of reluctance, the Dean agreed to let her use this room.

"Telemachus searched for Odysseus," Rachel Smith offered, brown eyes glowing in her ruddy face. Lara nodded approvingly, and then looked at the group, silently soliciting another example.

"Well, if the Seeker responds to the call of spirit," Michael Baldwin ventured, twisting his slender fingers together, "Wouldn't Jesus have been a Seeker too?"

"Absolutely," Lara agreed. "Part of what drives the Seeker archetype is a yearning for the unknown. Most would agree Jesus charted a journey through mysterious waters. What happens if we ignore that inner call?"

"Is there some sort of shadow manifestation?" Christina Yee, shyest of the group, asked hesitantly.

"You're on the right track. Can you say more about that?" Lara felt drawn to the timid young woman.

Christina colored, her pale Asian skin developing a rosy tint. Impatiently, she brushed fine black hair out of her face and looked at Lara. "Hillman said our pathologies are sent from the gods. It seems to me if we deny the Seeker, we might end up with runaway ambition, phony perfectionism, and just maybe, inability to commit to anything…even when we want to."

"Very good, Christina!" Lara was impressed. The quiet Chinese woman had a razor-sharp mind that only occasionally came out to play.

"What about the transcendence and death link?" Natasha Romanova asked in her broad Russian accent. Her white-blonde hair was caught up in a thick queue at the back of her head. "Those brave women who were killed on Lenin Peak have always tugged at my heart. Did someone not memorialize their deeds in a poem?"

"Yes, Natasha, they did." Again, Lara was awed by her young students. "Adrienne Rich. We read it last year." Glancing at the clock, she noted they only had fifteen minutes left. "We've spent more time on archetypes today than we usually do. Did anyone bring a dream they'd like to share?"

A man's hand shot up. "I did."

"Go ahead, Ryan." Lara settled back into a comfortable chair, hands clasped beneath her chin.

Nodding, he withdrew two sheets of paper from his notebook, stood, and cleared his throat. As he began to read, Ryan shifted nervously from foot to foot, his lanky limbs moving with a mind and purpose of their own. "I'm asleep outdoors under some sort of huge leafy tree. I wake up because I feel cold and there's a strange old woman, wearing a long black robe, standing against the tree looking at me. Her hair is white-blonde and so long it brushes to the ground. She's holding some sort of staff in her hand, and her eyes are the bluest eyes I've ever seen…"

Lara squeezed her eyes shut. *It's the same dream. The same one my patient and I had.* She shivered and tried to swallow, but her throat was dry as dust. Forcing herself to open her eyes, Lara sat ramrod straight as Ryan told a tale she knew only too well.

"…I feel frightened, but I don't know why. The old woman doesn't say anything, but I know she wants me to follow her. She waves the wand, or staff, or whatever it is, and the ground on the other side of the tree just sort of caves in. I'm not sure how I stay on my feet, but I follow her to the other side of the tree. The tree, Dr. McInnis, it's absolutely immense. I've never seen a tree like that in real life." Ryan cleared his throat again. "I don't want to follow her—the witch or whatever she is—but it seems as if I have to. She points down into the hole and I see rough earthen steps spiraling downwards." Ryan paused, looking up from his papers to the rest of the class. Sweat beaded on his forehead, and he mopped it with a sleeve.

"It's all right, Ryan." Lara's voice was as soft and soothing as she could make it. "We all want to hear what happened next."

Forehead furrowed, he pulled the second sheet of paper out from under the first and went on reading, his fingers twitching the corners of the pages. "I start down the steps. I'm afraid I won't be able to see, but after a few turns I realize there's a subterranean source of light. I'm feeling a little less frightened, but I'm still pretty uncomfortable. The old woman is right behind me, blocking the way, so I can't go back. Eventually, I come to the bottom and start down a curved hallway. It has a dirt floor and a low ceiling, and there are shiny things studded into the walls. I step on something soft and hear a faint cry. Feeling panicky again, I bend down to pick up what I crushed. It looks like a small animal. When I hold it under one of the lights in the wall, I can see that I—I've killed it."

Ryan was rolling and unrolling the edges of his papers. He didn't really need the pages. He'd memorized the dream…as had she.

"The old woman snarls at me to be more careful, so I really slow down. When I see another tiny creature, and I pick it up and put it in my jacket pocket. Pretty soon all my pockets are full, but the crone tells me we're almost there and to keep going. So I start handing her the animals, because I've run out of room."

Ryan stopped, looking embarrassed. A blush spread upward, from his open-neck shirt to his hairline. "It was, uh, sort of nice being surrounded by all those little bodies. Really soothing. Anyway," more throat clearing, "the passageway ended. There's this shovel leaned up against a wall, and the crone tells me to dig, so I do. Every once in a while one of the creatures falls out of a pocket, and I have to stop and put it back. I'm getting tired, and my back and neck are starting to hurt, when I look into the hole and see something golden. I pull it out and it's a conch shell. It's really heavy, and as I hold it in my hands, it uncoils and a small black woman crawls out, seats herself cross-legged in my cupped hands, and glares at me."

"That's all. I'm done." Ryan fell into his seat. Looking across at Lara with tortured eyes, he croaked, "What does it mean? It frightened the crap out of me."

"Stop and think, Ryan. And breathe. A couple deep breaths would help a lot right about now. What do you know about the dream? We've covered many of the symbols."

Ryan dropped his notes and clenched his hands together. He struggled to take cleansing breaths as she'd suggested. "The underground part, that's the unconscious, isn't it?" he asked in a strained voice. She nodded, waiting. "Am I killing some part of myself by not being careful?" he finally blurted. "Or is it some kind of message from the collective?"

"I don't think this is so much about you, Ryan, but it may be something from the collective. Unfortunately, we're all but out of time for today. When we meet next week, we can start the class with a discussion about your dream. In the meantime, I'll give it some serious thought. The rest of you," she waved her hands in a broad swath, "think about it too. Figure out which parts resonated for you and write them down. Read the material about the Orphan archetype."

Rather than leaving, everyone sat motionless in their chairs, mesmerized by the powerful dream material.

Clapping her hands smartly together, she said, "Come on. Up and out of here. You'll all be late for your next class—if you have one." She stood, slipped on her sweater, and picked up her heavy shoulder bag. Fishing through it, she felt for her phone and flipped it off the silent setting. Lara tugged it to eye level and glanced at messages that had come in while she was lecturing as she walked out the door and down several flights of stairs.

A message with Sergeant Nelson's name on it set her heart pounding and she waited until she was outside to read it.

Her silver BMW waited outside Denny Hall in Trevor's favorite no parking zone. Reaching across the interior of the car, he pushed the passenger door open for her. "Hey, Lara. How was class?" And then he looked closely at her, and his smile faded. "What happened?"

"That dream again," she growled through clenched teeth. "One of my students had the same goddamned dream I and my patient had. What the fuck is going on?" She shoved her bag heavily into the back seat and settled into the car. "Oh yes, and Sergeant Nelson texted me. Bethany's in a coma."

"How is that different than where she was this morning?"

"I don't know. Remember I didn't see her this morning, except in my vision. I suppose she might have been in a coma then. It was hard to tell."

Pulling away from the curb, he asked, "What do you want to do? Is there somewhere in particular you want to go, or is home okay?"

"Do we have something for dinner there?"

He nodded. "There are leftovers from last night, but if you're tired of quiche I can make something else."

Lara glanced at her watch and scrolled hastily through the rest of the messages on her phone. "It's only a little past four o'clock. We could swing by the hospital."

"Or the precinct..."

Lara's breath whistled as she exhaled sharply. "You still want me to file a complaint?"

"Yes. And I want you to get a restraining order. Look what he did to his wife. Mental stuff is your bailiwick, love, but don't you think he just might blame you if his wife and kid crump?"

"Oh." She frowned, considering his statement. "Yesterday, it seemed as if he might actually *want* to be rid of both of them, but you're right. He's unhinged enough he might figure it was all my fault for meddling." She shifted uneasily in her seat and grabbed the seat belt she'd not yet hooked into place. "All right. The police station wins. I'll file a report."

"And ask about a restraining order?"

Jesus, you're relentless. "I'll see what the officer taking the report recommends," she conceded. "I think I'd actually have to file something with the Court to get any sort of order."

He pulled into one of two empty parking spots in front of the Forty-Second Street precinct and opened his door. "No, Trev. You have to stay here."

"Why?"

"You can come into the station house and wait, but you can't go in with me when I talk to the officer because I'll be disclosing confidential information."

Nodding, he shut the heavy car door. "I would rather stay out here," he agreed. "More comfortable." He flipped on the audio system and Joan Baez's haunting soprano filled the car, singing of lost loves and departed dreams.

She reached over and gave him a quick kiss. "Back soon, I hope. Maybe, if it's not too late, we can still check in at the hospital before we go home."

After introducing herself, and telling the desk sergeant what she wanted, Lara settled onto a hard wooden bench that had been shoved against walls painted a dreary industrial tan. Metal steelcase desks, filing cabinets, and scuffed linoleum floors added to the bleak demeanor of the place.

What a depressing environment. Not even a plant to liven things up.

"Dr. McInnis?" Lara looked up, surprised to hear her name called so quickly. "Follow me, please." An officer with a blond crew cut, rumpled uniform, and highly polished service shoes beckoned to her. He looked young, maybe late twenties or early thirties, but his eyes were far older. Reflections of the seamy side of humanity that he dealt with on a daily basis clouded their otherwise clear blue color. He held out his right hand. Lara shook it, and the man smiled slightly. "I'm Sergeant Brandon Nelson."

"From last night?"

"Yes, from last night."

Lara walked beside the sergeant down a long hallway that was, if possible, even more depressing than the waiting area had been. "Why are you still working?" she asked conversationally. "Wouldn't your shift have been over with this morning?"

"Yes, except we're short right now. In here, please." The sergeant motioned her through a door. The interview room was small with a table, two chairs, and no windows. Outside of a telephone on the table, nothing else occupied the claustrophobic space. Sergeant Nelson pointed to one of the chairs. Once Lara settled into it, he took the other and positioned a clipboard with a form on it in front of him. "You wanted to file a report?"

"Yes, but could we close the door, please? The matter concerns one of my patients."

Nodding, the police officer stood and pushed the door shut, then returned to his seat. He looked expectantly at Lara, pen in hand.

"You know the case you called me about last night?" she asked. Sergeant Nelson inclined his head. "I'm afraid there's a bit more to it." She was surprised at how nervous and uncomfortable she felt. *Never mind about that. Just need to open my mouth and start talking.*

"…and then my office mate, Doctor Schneider, pulled up, and Mr. Beauchamp practically threw himself off my porch, he was in such a hurry to get away," she said, finishing her story.

"Let me be sure I've got this straight." Sergeant Nelson looked directly at her. "Ken Beauchamp was lying in wait for you on the front porch of your building when you left work last night. He threatened you in vague terms to tell him what you'd discussed with his wife earlier that day. You think he had a gun. And you thought he was masturbating while he questioned you."

Lara nodded, "Yes, that's all correct."

"What'd you discuss with his wife?"

"I can't tell you that, Sergeant. I believe I can only disclose the bare minimum I need to about my patients. I can't see how my discussion with Mrs. Beauchamp is relevant."

Sergeant Nelson looked up from his clipboard, an exasperated expression on his face. "Look, Dr. McInnis, if you know something about the perp—oh, excuse me, Mr. Beauchamp—abusing his wife, that would be helpful information. Particularly in light of the fact her condition is deteriorating. You did get my earlier message? Well, since then the doctors on the case are discussing whether to simply go in and take the baby."

Lara dropped her gaze to the battered metal top of the small table. Previous occupants of this room had carved graffiti into its nondescript top. "She didn't actually tell me much," Lara finally said. "It was all by inference. But it turns out he was court-ordered into marital counseling, which likely means he'd hit her before. I didn't know about that part until yesterday." She hesitated before adding, "Normally, I don't accept court-ordered clients."

The police officer's shoulders sagged. "That's the way it always is," he snapped. "The vics clam up until they're dead, and then the creep who did them gets away with it. I'll have staff do a search of court records, though. Who knows? Maybe something I missed will turn up."

"Do you think I need a restraining order?" Lara asked, recalling Trevor's concerns.

Sergeant Nelson looked at her. "Not a bad idea," he replied crisply. "You'd be better off getting a sidearm and taking it out to the range to practice." His blue gaze drilled into her. "If Beauchamp kills you, there's no one around to complain he's violated the order, now is there?"

The sergeant stood. "I'll have the clerk draw something up. You can pick it up here tomorrow, but you'll need to take it to the Court Clerk's office to have it signed by a Judge." The phone on the desk jangled loudly, jarring her.

Sergeant Nelson made a grab for the receiver and said, "Yes?" He listened for a few moments, and then replaced the phone in its cradle. "Please wait," he told Lara and left the room.

After he'd gone, Lara stood and wandered aimlessly around the windowless cubicle. *Wonder why he wanted me to stay? Maybe there's some new development about Bethany.*

"Dr. McInnis." Sergeant Nelson came back in the room, accompanied by another cop. "This is Detective Ramson." The older white-haired man held out a hand. As Lara gripped it, she noted the unflinchingly straight set of his spine and a pair of chilling brown eyes.

"Have a seat, Doctor," the Detective motioned her back into her chair, commandeering the other for himself, while Sergeant Nelson remained standing. "There's been an incident," he began.

Lara's guts twisted as she waited to hear Bethany had died.

"An accident was just reported near your office. Is that silver BMW out in the parking lot yours?"

"Yes, but what does that have to do with—?"

Detective Ramson held up a hand to stop her. "I did a bit of research. Your office mate, Dr. Schneider. He drives the same kind of car."

"It's the same model, but his is a darker gray than mine." Uneasy feelings battered her, and she felt as if she were being sucked into the hungry maw of a vortex. "Why? D-did something happen to Pete?" Her voice was a strangled gasp.

"We won't be sure until the coroner's done, but his car is a smoking ruin. With someone that's likely to be him in it."

Lara's eyes filled with tears; her heart squeezed painfully in her chest. Images of a smiling Pete swam through her mind. He'd always been such a good friend and a supportive colleague. Blindly rooting through her bag, she pulled out a tissue and dabbed at her streaming eyes.

"…Dr. McInnis." The detective had said something else to her, but she'd missed it.

She looked over at him, biting her lower lip. "I'm sorry. I wasn't listening."

"Given what you just told Sergeant Nelson, we think whoever did this was probably targeting you. Since your vehicles are so similar, they mistook his car for yours. You'll want to be extremely cautious. In fact, if I were you, I'd take a vacation right about now."

"Maybe it wasn't a mistake," Lara said. "If Beauchamp's behind this, he might have targeted Pete. He's who interrupted him last night, and why Beauchamp took off without doing anything beyond threatening me."

The detective steepled his fingers together. "I see. Interesting angle."

Her insides were suddenly all sharp edges, as if they were made of jagged glass. Every breath became a struggle. She wanted to curl up in a tight little ball and howl.

The sight. Why didn't it warn me?

Because I wasn't the target—not this time.

The periphery of her vision narrowed. For a long dizzy moment, she thought she might faint. Forcing herself to her feet, she shook her head from side to side. "Can I leave now?" she asked in a garbled voice she scarcely recognized as her own.

The detective exchanged a meaningful glance with the sergeant before coming to his feet. "Yes, Doctor, of course you're free to go. We'll contact you once we know more. Did Dr. Schneider have any family that you know about?"

Lara shook her head and fought to talk around the lump in her throat. "No. He never married. He was an only child, and his parents died years ago." She paused. "He was a really good doctor. His patients loved him. I don't think there was room in his life for anything else."

With her shoulders bowed under an impossible weight that wanted to flatten her, she walked between the two law enforcement officers, pulled the door open, and plodded out of the room.

CHAPTER 5

*L*ara practically fell into the car. "Oh my God," she said, gasping for breath. "Pete's dead. Someone blew up his car. The cops think whoever did it mistook it for mine, but I think Beauchamp killed him because of last night. Shit, this is all my fault. I've killed one of my closest friends."

Snuffles gave way to heart wrenching sobs, and she let Trevor gather her into his arms. Holding her awkwardly over the car's console, he stroked her hair and murmured wordless comfort as the story poured from her in disjointed bits and pieces.

"This wasn't your fault. Not really." He said after a time. "You couldn't have known."

"But it is," she insisted. "I'm the one who accepted that…criminal into my practice."

"You didn't know," he repeated.

"Yes, I did. I got sucked in by his wife and didn't pay attention." Lara was adamant. The pain of loss, liberally mingled with guilt, cut deep into her soul. Pushing away from Trevor, she blew her nose again.

She sagged against the leather seat in a boneless, nerveless heap, but she'd no sooner closed her swollen eyes than a vision claimed her,

51

and all she could see was Bethany. The bruising from earlier had spread. Every inch of exposed skin was either green or purple, except around both eyes, where her normally translucent skin was black.

"Dr. McInnis." Bethany called to her. "Dr. McInnis, they're going to take my baby. Don't let Ken have my baby. Help me. Please, help me. He told them to take the baby and let me die." Bethany's voice was contorted by sobs. The vision was so real Lara reached out her hands, expecting to be able to touch her patient. As the image faded, she clutched helplessly at empty air.

Trevor's lips had thinned as he watched her. When she opened her eyes, she saw apprehension etched deeply into the planes of his face. "It's okay," she whispered, her voice quavering.

"Oh no, it's not. What did you see this time? This rutting psychic thing of yours is getting worse."

"The visions come in twos and threes," she croaked, trying to reassure herself they wouldn't be endless. "We have to go to the hospital. Now. Bethany told me they're planning to take her baby. She believes they've given up on her."

Lara dug through her purse, coming up with her phone. She scanned her contacts list and quickly entered a number. "This is Dr. McInnis," she said. "Is Dr. Morgan available? It's an emergency."

"One moment, Doctor. I'll see."

Lara clutched the phone. *Please, please let her be there.*

Helen's crisp, no-nonsense voice cut through the line. "Lara, what on earth?"

"Helen, there's no time for long explanations, but I need you to go to the ICU and monitor a patient of mine, Bethany Beauchamp." Lara took a deep shaky breath. "I'll be there in fifteen minutes or less. I don't care what you have to do, but intervene so both of them have a shot at living."

"On my way." Helen's matter-of-fact voice was soothing. "Ask for me at the ICU desk when you get there."

"Who was that?" Trevor notched the car into gear and drove out of the precinct parking lot.

Lara glanced up from forced, but largely ineffective, efforts to scroll through the messages on her phone. She was having a hell of a time concentrating on anything. "Helen Morgan. She's the head of the OB-Gyn Department for the hospital. I know her because I do a class every year for her residents about postpartum depression and postpartum psychosis."

"Well, that was a stroke of luck. Positively brilliant, actually." He looked over at her and his eyes narrowed with concern—and fear. "Are you going to tell me about your vision?"

Lara laid down her phone. "I told you pretty much all of it." Reaching over, she stroked his woolen jacket sleeve. "Maybe you should take a cab home from the hospital. Not much point in you waiting around for me. Doesn't seem to be safe for you—or anybody else—to be anywhere near me." Two more lonely tears dribbled down her cheeks. She dabbed at them, grim desolation settling over her like a winding sheet.

"What if the husband's there? No, I'm staying where I can keep an eye on things." He looked so determined, she decided not to push it.

"Ack! I need to call Arabel. Got to warn her. Christ, I should have done that the minute I heard about Pete." Lara grabbed for her phone again. As soon as she heard the beginnings of 'Dr. McInnis's office,' she interrupted. "Arabel. Thank God you're okay. You've got to go home."

"What's wrong, Doc? You sound awful. I don't generally go home till 'bout six."

"Did you hear an explosion earlier?"

"Sho did, but I was on the phone arguin' with one of them insurance companies trying to git us paid, so I didn't think much 'bout it. Heard lots of sirens, though."

"Pete's car blew up. It's likely Beauchamp did it. Either he mistook it for my car, or Pete was the one he wanted to harm." Lara had to stop, gather herself together, "You've got to get out of there while it's still daylight. Maybe you should call the cops to have them check your car."

"That poor lamb. You sure he's dead?" Arabel's voice broke, and Lara heard muted sniffling. "Don't you worry none 'bout me. I took the trolley today. Generally do on Wednesdays. I will lock up and go home. Think I'll stop by the church and light a candle for poor Dr. Schneider on my way."

"That'd be a really nice thing to do. Text me to let me know you got home safe. Okay?"

"I'll call and leave you a voice mail. My thumbs is too big to hit them tiny keys."

"So are mine, but I ignore it. Thanks, Arabel. I'll see you tomorrow."

Lara spent the remainder of the short ride to University Hospital returning messages from her phone and grieving for Pete. When she and Trevor got to the ICU, she asked for Dr. Morgan and told the middle-aged nurse manning the desk that the doctor was expecting her.

"Lara? Oh, there you are." A short woman with steel-gray hair pulled back into a severe bun, strode out of the ICU. Hazel eyes twinkled behind gold-rimmed spectacles, and a white lab coat with Helen Morgan, M.D. emblazoned on a pocket, stretched across her ample bosom. Noticing Trevor, Helen asked, "Who's this?"

"Uh, my husband. He's just worried about me. Trev, why don't you go to the waiting room? It's right down the hall."

Trevor had other ideas. Holding out his hand, he smiled brightly and said, "Trevor Denoble, Dr. Morgan. Nice to meet you."

"Nice to meet you too, Mr. Denoble." Helen shook his proffered hand warmly. "Lara is correct, though. You can't stand here, and you do need to wait somewhere."

"Okay, I can take a hint. I'll be in that visitors' room."

As soon as he was gone, Helen took Lara's arm. "Follow me, dear. We need to talk."

Settled in a small anteroom, Lara looked at her old friend. "How bad is it, Helen?"

Helen Morgan cocked her head to one side and looked right at

Lara. "It's strange," she began. "There's no reason I can see from any of the imaging studies why Mrs. Beauchamp should still be unconscious. Since I don't think she's in any danger, there's no reason to do an emergency C-section like the husband is requesting. So we're holding off on that, at least for now. What can you tell me about this?"

Holding Helen's direct gaze, Lara replied, "She's an abuse victim… domestic violence. Her husband threatened me last night." Lara fought against tears rising behind her eyelids. Words stuck together and refused to leave the safety of her throat. *Got to pull myself together. I can cry later.* She swallowed hard, willing herself to go on. "I'm pretty sure Bethany's husband killed Pete Schneider earlier today with a car bomb. If he didn't mean to kill Pete, the only other explanation is that Beauchamp mistook Pete's car for mine."

Helen raised perfectly arched brows over her spectacles. "Doctor Schneider? The psychiatrist from your building?" Reaching over, she touched Lara's hand. "I'm so sorry. Have you filed a police report? That's why your significant other is here, huh?"

"Yes to both questions. Could I see Bethany? It would only be for a few minutes." Lara raised grief-stricken eyes to Helen, pleading for access to her patient. "The husband's not here is he?"

"Not now. But he was earlier, and I suppose he could always come back." Lips pursed in a thin line, Helen Morgan picked up a nearby phone and entered four numbers. "If Mr. Beauchamp shows up, tell him his wife's in the middle of a procedure, and we'll come get him when it's over. Do not allow him access to the unit."

She slammed down the phone. "Come on." Following a circuitous route, the two women entered a back doorway into the west wing of the ICU, only a few feet from Bethany's bed. Tiptoeing forward, Lara reached out and took one of Bethany's mottled, nearly transparent hands in hers.

As she stroked the unconscious woman's bruised hand, Lara spoke to her in a low voice. "Bethany, Dr. Morgan here is my friend. She says you're not going to die. There's no reason for you to still be unconscious, except you don't want to face Ken. I'll help you. I promise. You don't have to go back to your husband. We'll figure out a way to keep you safe. You reached out to me so I know you want to live."

"You can't stay much longer." Helen spoke softly. "Having you here at all is a violation of hospital policy." Lara nodded, but when she tried to withdraw her hand, Bethany's fluttered and clung to it.

Noticing, Helen nodded and bent close to Bethany's ear. "I'm Dr. Morgan. I'll be right back to talk with you." Straightening, she beckoned to Lara. Once they were safely out in the corridor, Helen stopped abruptly. "That poor woman. I need to get back in there. Can you find your own way out?" At Lara's nod, Helen looked pointedly at her and asked, "Do we need to post a police guard and keep the husband out?"

"That would be wise," Lara replied, meeting Helen's discerning gaze as she thought back to Ken's recent push to save the child while jettisoning his wife. Likely so she couldn't testify against him.

Pete's face, the sardonic smile, laughing eyes, and silver hair she'd never see again in this life, filled her heart. *I'm sorry, Pete. I'm so sorry. You have no idea how much I'll miss you.*

"If we do that, it probably increases the danger to you," Helen said gently.

"Yes, I know. It's a risk I'm willing to take. How much more danger could I possibly be in?" Lara spoke briskly to manage her tumbling emotions. "Would you call me when you know something? I want to visit her once she's awake. I can get her situated at a battered women's shelter when she's recovered a bit, but not here in Seattle."

"Sure, dear. Will do." Helen stepped forward and gave Lara a quick, hard hug before bustling back the way they'd come.

CHAPTER 6

*L*ara and Trevor fought rush hour traffic as they headed for home. "She's going to be all right, Trev. She squeezed my hand," Lara said for the fourth time. She slumped against the seat, eyes closed, relief spilling through her. In an odd way, Bethany living might assuage some of the biting loss of Pete's death.

"Yes, love, I get it your patient's likely going to survive. I am sorry about Pete. Really liked the bloke." He patted Lara's shoulder. "What about tomorrow? Did you ask the police to swing by your office every hour or so to check things are all right?" He paused. "Actually, I liked the cop's idea about leaving town."

She tapped the screen of her phone and brought up her calendar. "Hmm, tomorrow's not too bad. I only have five patients. The morning is pretty much free."

When she glanced up, Lara gasped, "What the hell? It must be another power outage." As she watched, a chiaroscuro blanket fell over Queen Anne Hill, dousing every source of light except moving vehicles. The darkness spread from Queen Anne toward the freeway. "How are we going to get home? There must be twenty stoplights between here and our house."

Trevor drummed his fingers on top of the steering wheel. "Maybe we shouldn't go home," he ventured. "Usually these things don't last all that long. How about if we try for a bite to eat?"

"Ach, I'm not very hungry."

"Know what you mean. I'm not especially hungry myself, but it would be good for both of us to eat something. 'Specially you. You're too thin." After a brief silence, he added, "I know you're grieving for Pete, but nothing either of us can do will bring him back."

She closed her eyes and tasted the bitter swell of tears again. Swallowing hard, she looked out the car windows. "Thanks. Pete always really liked you." She searched her heart for the right thing to do. Pete wouldn't have wanted her to don sackcloth and ashes.

Finally, she said, "We could head over the bridge to Bellevue. It's far enough away, maybe they have power and we could find a restaurant." Trevor just nodded and drove. Brakes squealed behind him as he cut someone off to pick up the proper exit.

"It won't help if we get into an accident." She aimed for supportive rather than critical, but didn't do very well.

"You want to drive?" Trevor sounded terrified. In that moment, she realized how much the power outages had affected him. Now there was Pete's murder added to the mix.

"You're doing fine. I'm not being a therapist, but do you want to talk about… Well, about anything?"

He sighed, and his shoulders slumped. "I don't know. It's not like we can actually *do* anything about any of this. So maybe there's not much point in talking about it, either."

"Earlier you said you wanted me to think about somewhere we could escape to if things got really bad here," she pressed. "To be honest, I haven't had much in the way of time to think about anything, but we could kick some ideas around now or over dinner." She paused a beat. "Actually, I'd welcome a diversion away from Ken Beauchamp."

"It's not just the power." Trevor stole a glance at her. "I haven't said anything, but the natural gas went out last week. I had to relight the oven and water heater pilots. Petrol's been none-too-easy to find, either. I had to wait in line for close to an hour to fill the tank today. It took virtually all the time you were in class." He snorted. "You never pay attention to the news, but there have been riots in other parts of the country."

She stroked his right hand, resting in his lap. "Have you talked with any of your friends in Europe? Are things just as bad there?"

"This is the right exit, isn't it?" Trevor squeezed her hand. "Yeah, I've talked to quite a few of the people I know in Europe and the U.K. It's frightening, Lara. They've started rationing petrol all over Europe. China's had to shut down over half their coal-fired plants—"

"What's the link with oil there?" Lara cut in, puzzled. Recognition dawned. "Ah, they don't have any more oil, so they've been using coal exclusively and pollution got so bad that…"

"…lots of people—millions—died. Everyone has worn respirators to go outside for months now," Trevor finished for her. "Riots are an inadequate term for the civil unrest there."

Panic reared up, mingling with her grief. Trevor was correct she ignored current events as much as possible. Could things really have gotten so far out of hand while she wasn't looking? "It's so overwhelming, I'm having a hard time absorbing what you just said." Her voice was strained.

"It's not particularly important against the backdrop of an end of civilization scenario but yes, that was the right exit. Go up Eighty-Fourth until it dead ends, and then…"

"Got it. I'm sure things will start looking familiar here in a moment. Bollocks! There aren't any lights here, either."

"Let's at least wait until we get to downtown Bellevue before turning back."

They drove in silence for the next several minutes. The roar of the BMW's big engine was soothing, until Lara reminded herself how dependent they were on fossil fuels. After that, the luxury car just sounded greedy. As soon as they came over the lip of a hill on Old Main Street, things were normal again. Lights, blessed lights, shone as far as she could see. Trevor blew out a breath, and she wondered how long he'd been holding it.

"Is that fish place okay? At least it's pretty close," he asked.

"Sure, Trev. Wherever you want is fine with me."

THE WAITER DROPPED their check on the table. "I trust your dinner was satisfactory?" he inquired a bit unctuously.

"Quite good. Thank you." Trevor extended his hand for the leather bi-fold. Glancing inside, he pulled out his wallet and placed a few twenties on the table.

Lara made an effort to smile. "It *was* a good dinner. We should come here more often. It's not actually all that far. You were right about us needing to eat something." Guiltily, she realized she hadn't thought about Pete for most of their meal. It seemed wrong to enjoy anything, on any level, with him gone.

It's not. Remember what I've told my patients all these years.

"We didn't figure very much out, did we? In spite of an hour's worth of conversation." He smiled back, but his eyes looked sad and worried.

"No. We didn't. But we did ascertain neither of us knows shit about farming, or animal husbandry, or any sort of a back-to-the-land adventure."

"That doesn't mean we couldn't learn," he pointed out. "I'll check some books out of the library."

Lara's phone trilled its Bach Etude. Rifling through her bag, she pulled it out and looked at the screen. The incoming call was from a private number. Her finger hovered over the screen for long seconds before she tapped the answer button and said, "Dr. McInnis."

"Well, well, well, I got lucky, Doc. Didn't think you'd pick up your phone."

"Who is this?" She kept her voice steady and professional because she was pretty sure she already knew who it was.

How the hell did he get my private number?

"You know who I am. In fact, right about now, you're probably wondering how I got your number," the voice drawled.

Lara didn't wait to hear more. She punched the end call button with trembling fingers.

"Who was that?" Trevor drew his brows into a harsh line.

Her heart tripped into double rhythm. Her face was on fire, but the rest of her felt icy cold. "Ken Beauchamp. He didn't tell me his name, but I'm sure it was him." The phone rang again.

"Don't answer it," Trevor hissed. "Better yet, give it to me." He held out his hand.

"I'll just turn it off." Switching the phone to its silent setting, she dropped it back to the bottom of her bag. "Are you ready to go?"

In answer, Trevor pushed back his chair. It made a loud scraping noise, and some of the other diners looked at them, apparently concerned something untoward was about to intrude on their pleasant dinner experience. The waiter hurried back over.

"Are you all right, sir?"

"Perfectly fine. We were just leaving."

"Very good, sir." The waiter shepherded them toward the front door, positioning his body between them and the other patrons.

"Sodding bloke!" Trevor growled as soon as they were outside. "All I did was push my chair back a bit too abruptly, and that bloody waiter treated me as if I were *persona non grata*."

He reached into his pocket for the clicker, pushed it, and the BMW chirped merrily from its parking space across the street. "Are you going to see if that arsehole left you a message?"

"I can check. Why do you want me to?"

"I think we should see what he had on his mind. If he could get your cell number, he may very well know where we live too."

Lara paled. She hadn't thought about *that* possibility. Ken hadn't followed her and Pete back to her house the previous evening. Or had he? A part of her balked, finding it impossible to believe it was only last night when Pete had rescued her. As she thought of him, she said one more sad farewell to her old friend.

While they drove down Lake Washington Boulevard, she pointed. "Look. The lights are back on. At least here."

"Yes, that's how it's been. There'll be a day when they don't come back on though, and we need to be better prepared than we are." He busied himself with coaxing the car onto the northernmost of two floating bridges. "That's what the dream's about, love."

"How do you know about it?" Shock waves rocked her. Even her fingertips tingled. "I told you about a dream several people—including me—have had, but I never told you what was in it." Her voice cracked, and she cleared her throat.

He looked sheepish. "I figure it's the one with the tree and going down into the ground and gathering up all those little animals. Isn't that it?"

"Yes, but how do you know about it?" She inhaled some saliva, choked, and started coughing.

"How else? Because I've had it too," he explained patiently.

"Why didn't you tell me?" Her voice was deathly quiet.

"Because you seemed so upset, especially when that student of yours shared the same dream in your class today. It's not like I've been holding out on you. I just had the damned thing last night, uh, no, night before."

"Oh." Lara's voice almost wasn't there. Pulling out her phone, she glanced at the time and the message indicator. It was closing on eight o'clock, and there were three new voice messages. "I need to call Zurich," she said. "But it's too late. Or rather, too early. There's either an eight or nine hour time difference, so that would mean it's four or five a.m. there."

"Who do you want to call?"

"Doctor Tueller, my primary control analyst when I studied at the Institute."

"How do you know he's still alive?"

"Well," she admitted, "I don't. He would be dreadfully old. But if he's not, there's bound to be someone who remembers me."

"It's a nine hour difference," he said, validating her earlier guess. "You could probably call around eleven tonight."

"Still pretty early. Dr. Tueller's well past ninety. When you're that old, you sleep quite a bit. I'll try first thing in the morning. And Trev, if you want to look for a little farm somewhere, well, that's all right with me. We're bright, capable adults. There's no reason we can't figure out how to raise vegetables and milk cows."

"Goats, Lara, goats. Or sheep. Cows give way too much milk for two people. I see you have some messages," he persisted, retreating to his earlier concern. "Aren't you going to listen to them?"

She closed her eyes. Searching inwardly, she summoned her gift, but nothing came.

"What are you doing?" He sounded irritated.

After a bit, she opened her eyes. "Trying to cheat," she admitted. "I thought if I could scare up a bit of *the sight*, perhaps I wouldn't have to actually listen to the messages. That's not how it usually works, though. The visions come to me when they come. I've never really had any control over them."

Trevor exited the freeway. Turning down a side street, he parked under a streetlight and held out his hand. "Give me the phone. We need to hear what this blighter wants before we go home. I don't want to walk into a trap." Silently, Lara handed him her cell. "Is the code still 1497?" he asked.

"No, it's always been 1492." She laughed, but there wasn't any humor in her. "It's the year Columbus discovered America. I've told you that before."

"So you have." Trevor raised the phone to his ear and listened. Color drained from his normally-rosy complexion, and he dropped the phone into his jacket pocket.

"Well?" she asked, after waiting through at least five minutes of silence. "Are you going to tell me, or do I need to listen for myself?" Panic ricocheted through her, and she regretted the brandy and French roast she'd had to finish off her dinner. Her stomach churned, and she laid a hand over her midsection to calm it.

Trevor transferred the cell phone from his pocket to the center console. Turning to face Lara, he took a deep breath. "The guy never actually gave his name. He said not to bother to try to trace the call. He also said things would go worse for you if you brought in the police, although he called them by some other slang term I wasn't all that familiar with." Trevor stopped, swallowing with difficulty. "That man is pure evil. He had this hideous laugh. I'm not superstitious, but it sounded like something unearthly."

"Does he know where we live?" Lara felt nauseated. Her mouth flooded with saliva, and she wondered if she was going to be sick. Just in case, she reached over and pushed the button to roll her car window down.

"He didn't say. He made a point, though, that he was going to get you. Just like he got Pete. And when he came for you, there'd be no way of predicting it. Or something along those lines." Trevor touched Lara's shoulder, stroking it tentatively. "Maybe we should just check into a hotel."

"I am *not* going to let that bastard chase me out of my own home." Lara was surprised by the rush of anger that buffeted her. "We have a burglar alarm that rings down at the police station. They could be there in five minutes if we needed them. Would you like to walk for a bit?" she asked abruptly, groping for the button to roll her window back up. "I'd feel better if I was moving. I'm stewing in my own adrenaline."

"Fine by me." He got out of the car. Tucking a hand under her elbow as she emerged from her side of the BMW, he glanced at her multi-colored sweater. "Do you think you'll be warm enough?"

"Sure. It's not particularly cold out, just damp."

They walked in silence for several minutes. "Now we have another reason to move, don't we?" she asked.

"That's one way to look at it." He shrugged, shivering slightly. "I think we'd have enough money, but we'd have to sell our house, and no one's buying much of anything right now."

"There's that money my aunt left me," she pointed out. "Remember that discussion we had a few years ago where I wanted to invest in gold, and you wanted to buy real estate?" He nodded glumly. Treading carefully, she softened her voice a couple notches. "Anyway, it's more than doubled. There's something over a million dollars in that account now. If the bottom doesn't fall out of the gold market, like it did with everything else—"

"But that's yours."

"Look, Trev." She plucked his hand from under her arm and threaded her fingers in with his. Despite being out of the weather, his fingers were cold. "What's mine is yours. Always has been. We decided not to get married because we didn't want children. Otherwise, what we have is just like a marriage. You can't be sure about the house. If we priced it low enough, someone would pick it up. How'd your hands get so cold?"

"I don't know. I've been feeling chilled ever since I listened to that manky blighter."

"Did he leave all three messages?" She was curious if he'd run out of recording time and kept calling back to harass her.

"No. Just the first one. The other two had numbers attached to them. Figured it might be patients of yours, so I didn't listen to them."

She wondered who the other calls had been from.

Then her thoughts turned to the children Trevor hadn't wanted. She'd been disappointed once she discovered how intransigent he was around that particular issue. *Why didn't I try harder to change his mind?* She struggled to resurrect those many-years-ago conversations, but nothing came beyond a vague sadness.

Fog rolled in off Lake Union. It was damp and redolent of oil from the boats that hauled goods back and forth from distant places. "I've walked enough," she murmured. "I'm a little chilled myself, now that I think about it."

revor built a fire in their living room woodstove, and they sat on a buttery-soft leather couch watching the flames burn and sharing snifters of brandy.

"I've been thinking about moving and a bunch of other stuff too," Lara said after a lengthy, but companionable, silence.

"What kind of other stuff?" He draped an arm around her.

"How it might be to leave my practice and our comfy urban life. I've thought about Pete too and how unfair his death was."

Trevor tightened his hold on her, but didn't say anything.

"I'm not convinced we have to leave quite yet," she added and swallowed a little brandy. "From what you've said, there's plenty in the media to suggest a Gotterdammerung is brewing out there. But there haven't been any riots here. Not yet anyway."

"Why don't you ask your muse? Or whoever, or wherever, your visions come from?" Trevor pulled Lara closer. "I really do think that's what the dream means. I've already told you that."

"But I'm the psychoanalyst," she objected weakly, "and I'm having a hard time interpreting it. So I don't see how you can be so sure." She snuggled deeper into his arms.

"Maybe you're too close to it. It will be interesting to see if you can raise someone in Jung-land to ask, though. Ready for bed?"

"Sure." Turning her head slightly, she sought his lips with her own. He closed his mouth over hers and stroked her back. Her body responded with shocking immediacy. *This is like wartime. Proximity to death intensifies life for those who are left.*

He curved a hand to cup her breast, and she stopped thinking. As their kiss deepened, electric currents shot along her nerve endings, sharp and sweet at the same time. Moaning softly, she slid a hand under his sweater, desperate for the feel of his bare skin.

"Ye cannae e'en bide until Ah gie ye up th' stairs, lassie?" Trevor, who could ape any accent, morphed into Scottish, with a hint of a Cockney overtone. Pulling away, he slipped his sweater over his head, then began tugging at hers.

She thought about Pete, who would never make love with anyone again, and hesitated. "I don't know—" she began. "It seems disrespectful."

"If Pete were here, what would he say to us?" Trevor asked softly.

"That we should take advantage of every moment we can. He never was one to wallow in guilt. " She took a breath. "Earlier, I was thinking we were like survivors during a war. That's why there are so many war-time babies. People fuck a lot to remind themselves they're still alive."

He laughed. "Glad there's a precedent. Come here, love," he coaxed, reaching for her. A roughened edge in his voice betrayed his arousal, and he winked seductively. Sliding out of her cardigan, Lara quickly undid the buttons of her finely-textured silk blouse, the cooler air of the room a counterpoint to her overheated skin. Her nipples pebbled into sensitive peaks and ached for his touch. Moisture slicked her thighs. When she was down to her bra, Trevor gathered her close.

"I can take care of that," he murmured and reached around to unhook the flimsy garment. "So beautiful, my lassie, my love," he murmured between kisses, his breath making an odd catching noise in his throat.

Desire, strong as she'd ever felt, caught her unawares. It was potent and heady, like a fine wine, obliterating her misgivings. Moving up from where he'd been kissing her breasts, Trevor's gaze met hers, hot and hungry and warm and loving, all at the same time. That look ignited something primitive and their bodies tumbled against one another as they yanked clothing out of the way. An emptiness at the core of her screamed for him, and she pulled him on top of her, frantic for the touch of his skin against hers, for his hardness inside her.

Hot, intense sensation spun through her, pulled her outside herself as she melted into him. From a distant corner of her mind, she heard herself cry out, as wave after wave of heat pounded through her.

Trevor's solid weight on top of her and the warm dampness beneath her brought the world back into focus. Wriggling slightly to reposition herself, she laid a hand on either side of his face and kissed him tenderly.

"Mmm… We should do that more often." Trevor's voice held the seductive undertone it always got when sex had been very, very satisfying for him.

"Yes, we should. Wonder why we don't?"

"You're the analyst."

"Not right now I'm not." She laughed, deep and rich. "Right now I'm just your lover."

Trevor kissed her lazily, exploring the interior of her mouth with his tongue. She could feel him beginning to harden again where he pressed against her. Pulling away from what was turning into an ever-more-insistent kiss, she smiled at him. "Let's finish this in bed."

Trevor pushed himself up on his arms and slid one leg off the sofa. Ambling lazily out of the room, he called, "I'll set the alarm," over one shoulder.

Lara's gaze followed him through the semi-darkened room, until he was lost from sight in the downstairs hallway. She realized how much she loved looking at him. He never worked out, yet, he could easily have passed for a model with his sleekly muscled form—all shoulders and slim, boyish hips with a high tight butt.

That was how he'd prevailed on the children issue and likely others as well. He'd charmed her with his beautiful body. Smiling a bit ruefully at the ease with which he'd always been able to divert her, she got off the couch. She'd love to blame the arid, loveless wasteland of her childhood for her spinelessness, but she knew better.

No one to blame but myself. If I were really being honest, I'd examine my own ambivalence about being a mother.

She met Trevor at the foot of the spiral stairs. Leaning into him, she took his hand, and they walked up the steps to their bedroom.

THE CHIME of the cell phone's alarm wakened her. Groping sleepily toward her nightstand, Lara pulled the phone to where she could see it and tapped the dismiss icon before the alarm disturbed Trevor. He often didn't sleep well at night, so early morning slumber was important for him.

Shaking her head from side-to-side, she tried to clear her sleep-addled brain, but she still felt like she was sleepwalking when she padded barefoot into the bathroom and flipped on the sink taps.

As she did nearly every morning, she soaked a washcloth, dipped her head forward, and buried her face in the warm, soothing terrycloth. She still felt groggy and figured a full shower would finish waking her, so she pulled off her nightgown and stepped into their deep Jacuzzi tub, where she lost herself in steam and the cucumber-lavender scent of her soap and shampoo.

After drying herself and wrapping a plush towel around her hair, she peeked into their bedroom. Trevor was still asleep. She watched for a few moments as an errant ray of sunlight played over his boyish features. The corners of her mouth tipped upward. Children or no, Trevor was a jewel.

He'd always hidden something from her, though. Gaps in his aura, and a wall he could throw up so fast it made her head spin, clued her that whatever it was ran deep. She'd guessed long ago something unspeakable had happened to him as a boy, but she'd never gotten him to talk about it, despite many lovingly-crafted invitations.

Lara pondered waking him. She wanted to call the Institute, and Trevor's facility with languages would prove useful if whoever answered the phone only spoke German. "I can always get him if I need him," she murmured. Tiptoeing back into their bedroom, she quietly donned an old pair of sweats and her slippers and walked out the bedroom door, tugging the door shut behind her.

She brewed coffee and sat at the kitchen table with a printed transcript of the dream nearby to read to Dr. Tueller, if he asked. She was practically certain he would. That's how she'd been trained. She could almost hear his thickly accented German voice instructing her. "Always write them down, Lara. It is the details that will give you what you need to help your patient. You will forget them if you do not commit them to paper. Psyche can be slippery, and she guards her secrets well."

Feeling unaccountably anxious, Lara picked up the landline handset to dial, then stopped. "Better have it handy," she muttered and rushed up half a flight to the small library adjacent to their spacious living room to get her English-German dictionary. Back at the table, she punched in the numbers for the Jung Institute. The phone rang, once, twice.

"*Guten Morgen. Jung Institut,*" A female voice said.

"*Guten Morgen. Kann ich spreche mit Dr. Tueller. Es ist Dr. McInnis,*" she said uncertainly, consulting the dictionary. Her studies at the Institute had come in six week blocks at six month intervals. She'd never been there long enough to master German. It hadn't helped that nearly everyone spoke a different dialect.

"*Nur einen Moment,*" the woman said. "*Ich werde jemanden finden, der Englisch spricht.*" Lara relaxed a bit. Good. The receptionist must have recognized how bad her German was, and she was going to find someone who spoke English.

"May I help you?" The man's accent was heavy, but Lara didn't think he was German. Possibly Austrian, or even from northern Italy.

"Yes, thank you. I would like to speak with Dr. Tueller. Is he still there?"

"Were you a patient of his?"

"No, he was my primary control analyst when I trained there."

"Ah, Dr. McInnis, was it? I am sorry to be the one to have to tell you this, but Doctor Tueller died about two months ago, a few days shy of his ninety-fifth birthday. He worked until just before he died." The stranger's voice held a touch of awe. "Doctor Tueller saw two patients that last night, bid us all a good evening, and retired. When the housekeeping staff went to rouse him the next morning, he had passed peacefully during the night."

Silence settled between them. Lara supposed it was to allow her an opportunity to digest the sad news. Sitting in her cheery kitchen, she thought about her old mentor and friend and felt saddened she hadn't made an opportunity to tell him goodbye, nor to reiterate how much their time together meant to her. "I'm sure he knew," she spoke softly.

"Dr. McInnis? What was that you said? I did not hear you. Was there something someone else here could help you with?"

"I wanted Doctor Tueller so I could tell him about a dream," she said and then felt foolish. Of course that would be why she wanted to talk with him. Starting over, she explained, "Lately, one of my patients, one of my students, my husband, and I have all had the same dream. It's archetypal and I need help deciphering what it might mean."

There was another lengthy silence. So long she began to wonder if the man with the accent was still there. Finally, he cleared his throat. "I am Dr. Himmelschaun. While we have been speaking, I retrieved the records from your training here out of our computer database." Sounding pleased with himself, he continued. "This is something new for us, this computerization. I am not so young to be easily familiar with it." He chuckled softly.

"In any event, those who trained you are either no longer with the Institute, or are with Dr. Tueller, on the far side of the veil. I would be pleased to discuss your dream with you, but I have an appointment in ten minutes. Could you be so kind as to call back at eight this evening?"

"What time is it there?" she asked, checking the kitchen clock on their Jenn-Air range.

"Three in the afternoon."

Doing some quick math, she concluded Trevor had been right about the nine hour time difference. "Certainly. Would I use the same number?"

"Yes."

"Talk with you then, Dr. Himmelschaun. Thank you." Lara hung up.

"What'd they have to say?" Trevor breezed into the kitchen, dressed in faded blue jeans and a torn T-shirt advertising KLM Airlines. "I assume you must have called the Institute. Not much of anyone else you'd be talking with this early unless one of your patients had a crisis. Plus that," he flicked the open dictionary with an index finger, "is a dead giveaway."

Lara stood and went to Trevor, holding out her arms for a hug. He obligingly drew her close. "That doctor you wanted must be dead, huh?"

"How'd you know?" Drawing back, she stared at him. "Is *the sight* catching?"

"No, love. You just have this subdued look, so I figured…"

"You're right." Lara didn't care for the tone of her voice. It sounded just as dead as Anton Tueller. Returning to her seat, she gulped half her coffee searching for a quick pick-me-up. When she set the mug down, her hands were trembling.

"What's wrong?" Trevor pulled a chair up right next to hers.

"I don't know. I figured Dr. Tueller might be dead. He was awfully old. But the person I spoke with told me everybody who trained me is either dead or has left the Institute. I guess I'm feeling bereft and lonely."

Trevor patted one of her hands, but held himself silent, giving her space to keep talking.

"I don't usually talk about it," she said, "but the work I do is quite isolating. I never had much of a family of my own, so the professors at the Institute became my family. It's like I've been orphaned all over again."

"You have me. We're a family." Trevor kept hold of her hand. His aura looked odd. Unusual colors flashed through it as he comforted her.

She tried to smile, but failed. "Yes, dear. I know. I was thinking how fortunate I am to have you in my life earlier this morning. But it is lonely without any extended family," she said wistfully. "That was one of the things I loved about the Institute: a sense of belonging to something. Most of them saw the world the way I do. And they accepted I have *the sight* without question."

"Did you find out anything about the dream?"

"Not yet. I did speak to another doctor there, though, and he said he'd go over it with me, but he didn't have time now. I'm supposed to call him back at noon. Oh crap." Reaching for her phone, she pulled up her calendar. "Damn. I have a noon patient. I'll have to re-schedule her." Flipping to her contacts list, she retrieved a phone number and dialed it.

"Maryanne? It's Lara McInnis. Sorry it's so early. Hope I didn't wake you. I wouldn't ask except there's a bit of an emergency and I need to move your noon appointment…" Finishing with the conversation, Lara laid the phone down.

"Want some breakfast?" Trevor held the door to the refrigerator open and was perusing its contents, likely seeking inspiration.

"How about if we go for a run? It's early yet. We can cover a few miles and then stop at that little breakfast place you love over on Comstock."

He groaned. "Run? You can run circles around me. Not so good for my manly ego." Grinning at her, he sifted his fingers through his blond locks, making them fluff up around his face. "But sure, I'll go. It was the breakfast that clinched it, though. Don't expect I'll suddenly become the workout partner you've always dreamed of."

CHAPTER 8

"What does your day actually look like?" He panted as he tried to keep up with her effortless runner's stride.

"Patients at one, two, four, and five. If I can squeeze it in somewhere, I'd like to dash over to the hospital to see how Bethany's doing."

Trevor stopped dead. "That is *not* a good idea. Promise me you won't do that."

Realizing he'd stopped pacing her, she turned and trotted back to him. "The hospital is full of security personnel." She tried for a conciliatory tone. "I'll be safe."

"You have to get from your car into the hospital," he pointed out. "And then back again. If you want to go, let me know when and I'll come with you."

"Okay. Can we get going before my heart rate drops?" She sprinted down Queen Anne Avenue, turning hard left up a side street to climb a steep hill. Nearing the top, she recognized the sensory shift that presaged one of her sendings.

Oh shit. Not again so soon.

She looked for a place to sit before her visual field tunneled down to nothing, but all she saw were office buildings, with the occasional older home tucked in between. A stone bench caught her eye and she dropped onto it, panting, just in time. Moments later, a vision swept her away.

She was back at the Jung Institute, seated in the informal parlor, sipping strong black tea from one of their priceless porcelain cups. A cheerful fire blazed in the open fireplace, and some of her old teachers were gathered around. As was common with her visions, conversation eddied around her as if she weren't there. The group spoke their native Swiss German, but she was able to understand them perfectly.

"We will have to let that one go." Anton Tueller's busy gray eyebrows were drawn together into what Lara had always called his "troubled" look.

"It is a shame, really." Mary Louise Von Franz also looked distressed. "It is not just the dreams, Anton. There is something unsettling about Himmelschaun. Almost as if he is a devil. There was that problem with a female patient of his too. Times have changed. Such things are no longer accepted. Ach, Jung. I miss him so. I wish he was still with us. He would know what is best here." Miss Hannah nodded agreement. As was usual, she sat right next to Dr. Von Franz.

"I will tell him tomorrow." Anton straightened his bent shoulders. "It will not be easy, but it must be done."

The vision receded. As soon as she opened her eyes, Lara found herself staring at a very upset Trevor, who squatted in front of her. "Lara? Thank bloody Christ. I didn't know whether to disturb you or leave you alone. It was another of those sodding sendings, wasn't it? What was it this time? Your patient again?"

Fighting the disorientation that always followed her trips to the paranormal world, Lara shook herself hard. "Come on, Trev. I'll answer your questions over breakfast. I need coffee." She stood, shook out her legs, and loped downhill toward the little crepe place that had lured Trevor out of their home. Ten minutes later, breathing hard because she'd pushed herself, she stood in front of the *Creperie* stretching out her hamstrings and quads. When Trevor caught up, there were red splotchy places on his cheeks from the effort of trying to pace her.

"I don't see how you can run that fast," he gasped, sucking air into his oxygen-starved body. "Even if I did this more, I don't think I could keep up."

"Stretch a bit," she suggested. "That way you won't be as sore later."

He mimicked her motions. "That's hard too," he complained. "Can we eat now, oh dominatrix of my heart?"

"Love it when you talk dirty to me." She winked broadly and pulled the café's door open.

Seated at a small corner booth, sharing a savory vegetable crepe with a yogurt-herb sauce and buttered crumpets, she revealed the contents of her vision. "Guess I won't bother calling him back. Might as well save the long distance charges. That's why Psyche sent me those images. To keep me safe."

"How do you know they come from Psyche?" Trevor sounded intrigued in spite of his general discomfort with paranormal phenomena.

It was her turn to look uncomfortable. "I don't. But they have to come from somewhere. She seems the most likely source."

"I think you should call him back, as scheduled."

Lara's eyes widened and she frowned. "But why? You don't want me anywhere near the hospital, at least not by myself. Why would you want me to call someone back who's a fraud at best and might quite possibly be dangerous?"

"He's a long way from here. There's an ocean betwixt us. It might be interesting to see what he has to say. You never checked those other two messages did you? There might be even more at this point."

Unclipping the phone from her belt, she glanced at it. "No more messages, but I will see about those others." After a time, listening and pushing buttons, she glanced up. "Excellent news! Helen Morgan called, and Bethany's out of her coma. She asked if I could drop by to see her today and arrange for shelter care. The other call was Sergeant Nelson. He wanted to let me know about Bethany too."

The lights in the restaurant flickered. "Not again!" Trevor looked around. "At least we got our breakfast whilst they still had electricity."

As Lara sipped her vanilla latté, the lights stabilized. She let out a tense breath, called a waiter over, and requested he box up the remains of the crepe and crumpets.

"Whilst you're working today, I'll start hunting for an area where we might relocate. In case things get worse." Looking hopefully at her, he murmured, "You're on board with that, aren't you?"

Am I really comfortable with that? Can I pull up roots, stop being an analyst, and become something like a pioneer?

What happens if I don't have a choice?

Reluctantly accepting she wouldn't still be working if the world ran out of oil and the power quit for good, she finally looked at Trevor with a resolute expression on her face. "Yes, Trev. I want you to at least do some spade work. It's always good to have options, and if we wait too long, they might get taken away from us."

He looked deadly serious, his brows scrunched into a thick line. "Thanks for believing in me. I know I'm not prescient like you, but I have this unsettled feeling we're on the edge of a precipice, and if we don't do something different we're going to be swept away." He colored, and then mumbled, "Sorry, that sounded pretty bloody dramatic."

She reached across the table and took his hand. "There are lots of ways for Psyche, or whatever, to reach out to us. Maybe this is some sort of paranormal event, or maybe you have a finely tuned sense of the future. Whatever it is, though, we shouldn't discount it. Time to jog back home?" She smiled brightly and crinkled her nose.

"Can't we call a cab?"

"Come on. It's less than two miles. We'll be home in twenty minutes."

"You might be. It'll take me at least thirty since it's uphill."

"Do you really want to call a taxi?"

"No, I guess not. I probably should get a bit more exercise, especially if we're going to buy a farm." One corner of his mouth turned down. "You know that childhood you're always nagging me about? I suppose I've mentioned it, but I grew up on a small farm in northern England." He pushed back his chair and stood, dropping twenty-five dollars on the table.

"Yes, I did know about the farm. You've told me about it before. Just never very much." She looked at him, her forehead creased in thought. "Didn't you say you don't know anything about farming last night over dinner?"

"What I said was I don't know much. And I don't." He grinned apologetically. "I chose not to mention how much work that farm was. The five of us worked our butts off from before dawn until after dark."

They exited the restaurant and jogged toward home at a moderately slow pace.

"Are they still there? Your family, I mean?" She was curious. Trevor was estranged from his family, though he'd steadfastly refused to give her enough details for her to understand quite why. And he never talked about them.

"Don't know."

"Are you ever going to tell me what happened? It can't be much worse than the way I lost my parents."

"At least yours died."

She considered that. His answers were short and clipped, which meant he didn't want to talk. At last she said. "Whenever you're ready, I'd like to hear about it. If you're never ready, well, that's okay too."

CHAPTER 9

*L*ara parked the BMW on the street right in front of her office. It was a two-hour parking zone, but sending Arabel out to move the car, moving it herself, or even getting a ticket, was preferable to having a long walk between her vehicle and the relative safety of her building. She stared intently up and down the quiet tree-lined boulevard. Against all the inner exhortations she could muster, her previously benign street had developed sinister overtones.

"Stop that!" she spoke firmly to get herself moving. "Get out, lock the doors, and go upstairs. Just like I always do."

Taking her own advice, something she suspected her patients rarely did, Lara got moving. Out of the car, across the street, into the building, and up the stairs. She pulled the oak door of Suite Four open. "Good morning, Arabel." She smiled tiredly at her old friend.

"Mornin', Doc. There's no one till noon today. You're early."

"I need to talk with you about something."

The elderly woman looked up from her computer screen and turned her warm, liquid eyes in Lara's direction. "Yes, hon, what is it? You sound worried. I can't believe there'd be much more than what you called and tol' me 'bout yesterday, though."

"Oh, Arabel. You've known me far too long. Yes, I *am* worried. And sad. You see, something else did happen yesterday."

By the time she finished talking, Arabel's face had turned somber, and her brows were drawn together like a thundercloud. "What you tol' me 'bout Bethany is chillin', just chillin'. Him wantin' to murder her and run off with that innocent babe. What kind of Daddy he gonna be? You tell me that. All night long I thought 'bout poor, poor Dr. Schneider. Didn't git much sleep. I'm really gonna miss him."

"Yes, me too. What Ken tried to do is hideous, shocking. Thank God I knew Dr. Morgan."

"Think I should go to my car and get my gun?" Arabel asked, her voice so quiet Lara wasn't sure she'd heard right.

Eyes wide with surprise, she managed to choke out, "I didn't know you owned a-a gun."

"No, sweetie. Why would I tell you? That neighborhood I live in, down lower Capitol Hill, well it's gotten worse and worse what with all them drug dealers, homeless, and other trash. So I got me a gun about five years ago and learned how to use it. Even took them classes to git a permit to carry it." Arabel looked up expectantly, and then added, "No way I'm leavin' before you tonight. I'll stay till you're done, then we'll go down together. You and me."

Lara fought a quick, hot surge of tears as she bent and hugged the receptionist who'd become her friend. "Thanks, Arabel. Thank you very much. Yes, that gun's probably not a bad idea."

Arabel hugged Lara back, patting her and whispering wordless comforting sounds. "There, there, honey. We'll git through this. You turned him in to the cops and they'll git him sooner or later. If not for you, then for that poor woman he beat up. And for Dr. Schneider." Arabel got to her feet and peered through the windows behind her desk. "Still drizzlin' out there?"

"Yeah, a bit. I've got an international call I have to make at noon. I rescheduled Maryanne for tomorrow. By the time you get back, I'll be in my office on the phone."

"No problem. You just lock the door behind me. I know what to watch out for." She turned away from the window and quirked an eyebrow at Lara. "After Daddy got hauled off to fight in the war, rest of the family was tossed off the farm. Guess they figured we wouldn't be much use sharecroppin' without him. I spent a whole lotta years livin' on the bad side of town."

Lara smiled fondly at Arabel. "I'd love to hear more about how you grew up. If you'd like to tell me, that is."

"Humph." Arabel snorted as she pulled on her sweater. "Things was pretty awful back then. But if we ever git us some spare time, we can talk 'bout the Deep South seventy years ago." Retrieving her bag out of a bottom drawer, Arabel let herself out the door.

After turning the deadbolt, Lara hung her coat on the coat tree, poured herself a cup of the strong black tea Arabel had brewed, and settled into her comfortable therapy chair. According to the clock on the opposite wall, she had five minutes to compose her thoughts.

Could she pull off pretending she knew nothing about the events that must have presaged Dr. Himmelschaun's egress from the Institute many years before? How the hell had he managed to talk his way back in after he'd been asked to leave? Lara shook her head sharply. She had lots of questions, but not much in the way of insights.

"Let's see," she mused, "Mary Louise died in nineteen ninety-eight, but Miss Hannah's been gone since nineteen eighty-six." Did the fact that they were all alive in that vision mean anything? Once again, she wished desperately there was someone who actually knew something about paranormal phenomena, who wasn't some sort of New Age quack. Embarrassment flooded her as soon as the thought paraded across her mind, and she bit her lower lip. Wisdom lurked in odd places, and she needed to look harder to find a teacher—and be far less picky.

Lara reached for her landline and dialed.

"*Guten Abend. Jung Institut*," an androgynous voice announced.

"Um, good evening." Too late, Lara realized she'd failed to bring her English-German dictionary. *Not much I can do about that now.* "*Ich spreche kein Deutch.* I have an appointment to speak with Dr. Himmelschaun. This is Dr. McInnis."

"Ein Moment erfreut, werde ich ihn finden." The telephone line reverberated with the nondescript sound signifying she'd been put on hold. Lara thought the person said they were going to find the doctor. She hoped they understood when she mustered up enough German to tell them she couldn't speak it.

"Dr. McInnis?" Dr. Himmelschaun's carefully modulated voice came through the fiber optic network.

"Yes, thank you for taking my call."

"You mentioned a dream. Do you have it in written form so you can read it to me?"

She closed her eyes. This was so like her analytic training, she began to relax in spite of herself. "Yes, I do." Picking up her notebook, she began to read. "The dream starts with…"

Fifteen minutes later she was done. Lara dropped the pages into her lap and waited, anxious to see what he would say. Minutes dripped by, the silence stretching so long she finally asked, "Are you still there?"

"Ja, um yes, I am still here. I am thinking." More silence. She checked the clock. Only twenty minutes until her first patient was due to arrive. She decided to give Himmelschaun five more minutes before pressing the matter and focused on her breathing to relax. Despite her comfortable chair, her muscles felt like blocks of concrete.

"This is a very curious matter, Dr. McInnis, very curious. I can, of course, present you with a standard interpretation, but I am sure you could have done that yourself. The reason you called here is because of the shared nature of the dream. That is correct, is it not?"

Lara nodded, then realizing he couldn't see her, she answered, "Yes, that's right."

"This will not make you feel any better, Doctor, but there are others here who have had a similar dream. We too, are struggling to make sense of why so many are having the same dream."

She narrowed her eyes at the unexpected information, and her heart rate accelerated. Finally, she managed, "Do you think it has something to do with the collective unconscious? Jung believed the psychotic got stuck there, and that's why there's such commonality to their delusional material. Could this be a psychic representation of some sort of mass craziness escaping from the collective that will eventually overwhelm the planet?"

"But those who have had this dream are not psychotic. At least not here," he pointed out, his voice blandly neutral.

"That's not exactly what I meant." She thought quickly. *Did he purposely misunderstand me? Or is this some ploy on his part?*

Even though she was playing with fire, she pushed the point and asked, "Why would we presume the severely mentally ill are the only ones who get sucked into the collective? Think about all those visions Jung had that presaged the coming of first World War One and then World War Two."

A muted chuckle came through the lines. "Why did you call for assistance, Doctor? It would appear we trained you quite thoroughly."

Lara wanted to scream at him for being dense. What the hell kind of analyst was he? Instead, she explained carefully, "Because there's no one else I can talk with. I didn't train at the Jung Institutes here, and they're pretty much closed societies, especially to those who studied in Europe."

"Yes, yes. I had heard that, but I was not so sure I believed it. If you would like, please feel free to return to us. You could join the group that is dissecting the meaning of this shared experience."

Something in the innocently-worded invitation made the small hairs on the back of her neck stand on end and set her teeth on edge. He clearly wanted her back in Switzerland. Why? Surely not to lend her mind to an academic discussion. She could do that via email and the telephone.

"Dr. McInnis?" he persisted. "When might you be returning to us?"

"I'm not sure." She aimed for a nonchalant tone. "I have a full practice, and it's difficult to take time away from it."

"Of course, of course. Surely you take some vacation time. You could plan to spend it here."

"Thank you, Dr. Himmelschaun. I'll consider it."

The compulsion blasting through the phone lines, lessened. "Certainly. If you have any more dreams to share, please call me. I work every weekday. And I am in residence here."

"How long have you been there?"

"Why do you ask?"

"Because I don't remember you from the years I trained there, or from workshops I took after my training, so I was wondering when you affiliated with the Institute."

"I was here before your time, left for a bit, then returned a few years ago. Is there anything else I can help you with today?" He cleared his throat, the sound dismissive.

He's the same one, she thought triumphantly. "No, Doctor. Thank you again for taking my call."

"Goodbye, Dr. McInnis. We will talk again, I'm sure." The line went dead.

When she placed the phone back in its cradle, the receiver was damp because she'd broken out in a cold sweat. There was something menacing about the unseen Dr. Himmelschaun, who'd unknowingly corroborated he had to be the same analyst Dr. Tueller chased off. How had he managed to muscle his way back in? Something horrible must have happened in Zurich since her last visit.

She'd never return to the Institute now, and a sad, slow tide washed over her. *Need to pull myself* together. *My client will be here in just a couple minutes.* As if on cue, the intercom buzzer rang, and Arabel's soft southern drawl announced the arrival of her patient.

Lara pushed the ottoman she'd been resting her feet on off to the side and got to her feet. Opening her office door, she beckoned to Gary. "Thanks for being on time. Come on in."

He scuttled past her, clutching a bottle of mineral water. Slightly built, with cropped blond hair, he was dressed in his usual tan slacks and long-sleeved dress shirt. Gary had a severe case of social anxiety, coupled with agoraphobia, and Lara knew how difficult it was for him to leave his house. Their first ten sessions had been on the telephone. This was only the third time he'd actually been to her office.

"How are you doing?" She eyed her uneasy patient, who sat perched on the edge of a chair, nervously pulling at his fingers and staring at the floor.

"Not good. I almost didn't make it today."

"Tell me what happened."

Gary coughed, then opened his ever-present water bottle and took a swig. "I knew we had our appointment coming up, see. I mean, it's at the same time every week. Last night I started thinking about the drive across town and how I might not make it. And then I thought about having one of those spells where I can't breathe, and having an accident, and…"

"…by the time you got up this morning, your anxiety was out of control." Lara finished for him.

He nodded miserably. "Uh, yeah."

"You did manage to drive here, though. Nothing happened, because here you are."

"I had to pull over three times and do that thing you taught me where I breathe into the paper lunch sack," he protested, his voice shrill with outrage. "That doesn't feel like *nothing happened*. It was perfectly horrible. Maybe I should go back to taking Xanax again. At least then I got some relief."

Lara tried for eye contact, but her patient couldn't look at her for more than a few seconds. "You could do that," she agreed, "but isn't that why you came to me in the first place? Because the drugs weren't working anymore? You told me you were taking too many and felt like a zombie all the time."

"You have too good of a memory," he mumbled. And then he did look at her with eyes that were deep hazel wells of unhappiness. "How long is this going to take?" he demanded. "I want to be like everybody else. I just want a normal life. Maybe I should come more often. Would that help?"

"The thing that will help most is practicing the tools you and I have talked about." Reaching over, she briefly touched her patient's hands gripped together in his lap. "You're a forty-two year old man, Gary. You've had this problem since before you went to college. It's not unrealistic to expect it to take a bit of time before it becomes less intrusive."

"Yes, but how long?" he persisted, still managing to hold eye contact with her.

"That's very good," she said encouragingly. "You've managed to look at me for several minutes now."

"You didn't answer my question."

"How long it takes depends on you." She smiled gently. "I'm not trying to sidestep your question. If you force yourself to go outside the comfort zone of your home every day—even if it's only to get a cup of coffee from Starbucks—you'll get better far more quickly. If you manage to go to a couple places most days, say for coffee and to the store, I'll bet you won't need me anymore in just a few months."

"I've tried that before, and things got worse."

"Yes, but you were taking Xanax or another of the benzodiazepines. They're notorious for only working for a little bit of time, and then you have to take more to get the same effect, and then they don't work at all. Plus, they have the unfortunate side effect of making you depressed."

"Boy, did they ever," he agreed. "Why didn't anybody warn me about that?"

"Side effects don't happen to everyone. One of the big downsides of managed care is you're in and out of the doctor's office in about seven minutes. Your practitioner doesn't really have the time they need to tease apart what's going on with you, especially for psychological issues." Lara stopped talking. She wanted to escape the slippery slope of psychiatric medicines, which she saw as a bane, eliciting cruelly false hopes from patients who swallowed them by the bucketful.

"Let's review the things you can do for yourself," she said brightly.

"Then we're going to make a schedule for you to follow. It's more work up front, but over the long haul you'll find this far more empowering than the Band-Aid those pills offered."

Over what remained of their session, she mapped out a daily schedule, memorializing it on a yellow-lined pad. "If you want to squeeze in an extra session, we can do that. Maybe just a thirty minute pep-talk would be enough."

"That would be great." Gary smiled shyly at her. "There's something about being here. I don't feel quite so tied up in knots inside."

"That will just keep getting better. I promise." She smiled back, noticing he really did have lovely expressive eyes with lush dark lashes. Maybe, with a concerted push on his part, he might actually find the companionship he craved. She suspected loneliness had driven him out of his house and into her practice. Loneliness and desperation. Standing, she tucked the newly-constructed worksheet into an envelope and handed it to him. "Give Arabel a call for a short appointment between now and next week. Okay?"

Gary stood. With his gaze on his shoes again, he held out a tentative hand for her to shake. Lara beamed at him as she captured his hand between both of hers. "See you soon." Opening the back door of her office that led directly into the hall, she watched for a moment as he trod heavily down the long hallway.

She shut and locked the door before sitting at her desk to jot down what they'd talked about. If she didn't stay on top of them, client notes piled up. At least so far, she placed her handwritten notes in the clients' files because she'd always done it that way. Maybe someday, she'd switch the office over to electronic records.

Or not.

Certainly not if Trev and I end up leaving Seattle for points unknown.

CHAPTER 10

Several hours later Lara wrote the last of the day's notations in her client charts and locked her filing cabinet. When she opened her door, she saw Arabel reading a novel while waiting patiently. "How'd things go out here this afternoon?" Lara asked. "Was it much trouble to move my car?"

"Moved it twice between patients. No tickets. We did git a couple hang-up calls." Arabel closed her computer down. "But that's not all that unusual. People think they want to come in, but then they change their minds soon as they hear me say 'Dr. McInnis's office.' I did look outside a couple times—even went out and wandered round the buildin'—but I didn't see nothin' out of the ordinary."

"Any calls I need to return?"

Arabel consulted her steno pad. "No." Anticipating Lara's next question, she added, "Tomorrow looks a lot like today. Nothin' in the morning, and then six patients between noon and seven. Here hon, brought you a couple more zucchinis and an eggplant."

Lara smiled. "Thanks, Arabel. Trev always raves about the vegetables from your garden. He says they're better than anything he can find anywhere else. Ready to go?"

Arabel dragged an oversized handbag out of the bottom drawer of her desk. Slipping into a light jacket, she slung the long purse strap over her shoulder and patted the heavy bag that obviously held her firearm. "Yep. Ready."

Lara yanked open the outer door and looked up and down the corridor. "I hate this," she muttered under her breath. "I hate being scared."

"I know what you mean, honey. Me too. But you wasn't brought up in the ghetto like me. I don't remember *not* bein' scared till I got away from there when I was 'bout twenty."

Lara patted Arabel's arm. "Thanks for being here. It means a lot that you stayed so I wouldn't have to leave by myself."

"Don't mention it, Doc. If somethin' happened to you, I'd have to find me another job. And I like this one fine." Arabel chuckled.

"Even if it *is* self-serving on your part," Lara grinned at her employee, "I still appreciate you being here."

As she drove from Capitol Hill home to Queen Anne, Lara gazed at the comforting lights of the Seattle skyline and wondered if there'd been another power outage during the afternoon. She'd forgotten to ask Arabel. She glanced at her phone, settled in its pouch on the console between the front seats. All the email and message lights were lit. Damn! She'd meant to check the phone before she left work, but she wasn't about to scroll through it while she drove.

It felt like another lifetime when she'd had that vision and talked to Dr. Himmelschaun. An involuntary shiver coursed down her back. "Like a ghost walking over my grave," she muttered, turned the car onto her street, and hunted for a parking spot. Finally giving up on something close, she parked a block and a half away, double-checked the BMW was locked, and trotted toward her house, looking anxiously over her shoulder as she clutched her purse close to her body.

"Jesus fucking Christ." She exhaled sharply. "Guess I need my own gun, or a big dog or something." The fine drizzle that had begun midday hadn't let up, and she brushed damp strands of hair off her forehead with her free hand.

Lara bounded up the steps to her hillside home, unlocked the front door, and let herself in. Dropping her bag in its usual place, she heard a soft snuffling sound and then a small yip. "What the hell?" she looked around, trying to locate what she'd heard. "Trevor?" she called. "I'm home."

"In the kitchen."

She rounded the corner and ran into a gate stretched across the kitchen doorway. Before she could react, a small furry form leaped to its feet, threw itself at the gate, and barked in a high-pitched puppy voice.

"Oh, you precious little thing, you." Morphing into baby talk, she bent and scooped up the young dog. "Ooof, you're heavier than you look, yes you are, sweetums." Lara cradled the puppy against her and stepped carefully over the dog gate. "Are we babysitting for someone?" she asked curiously.

Trevor blushed, a very unusual occurrence. "Er, no, Lara. I'm afraid he's actually ours."

Still holding the pup, she sat on one of the kitchen chairs. "What? But how are we going to do that? You can take care of him while you're here, but what are we going to do while you're working? I can't very well take him to my office, and he's far too young to be left alone. You did say it was a 'he' didn't you?"

Lara had always wanted a dog. She stroked fluffy puppy fur and cooed nonsense at the bundle in her arms.

Trevor shut off the gas jets on the range and pulled up an adjacent chair. "That's just it," he blurted, looking uncomfortable. "Looks as if I've lost my job. KLM called today to tell me they can't get aviation gas. Or maybe they can get it, but it's quadrupled in price. Anyway, they can't continue to operate, so they've laid the lot of us off. Just like Northwest and American did a couple months ago. I called and left you a message."

"Sorry, I haven't had a chance to check the phone."

"It's been all over the Internet too. Guess you didn't look at that, either?"

She glanced up, startled by the strong accusatory undercurrent in his voice. "Sorry again, dear. No excuses, but I had patients all afternoon. Look, Trev, we should be all right. I'm sure this must have been a shock for you, though. You've worked for them for, what, twenty-five years."

"Twenty-seven." Trevor's voice was muted.

"Do you get anything like severance pay?" *Oops.* She shrank at the crassness of her question.

"Yeah, because I've been there for so long, they said something like fifty thousand Euros."

"That's great, Trevor! That will go a long way. Really. It's a bit more than seventy-five thousand dollars."

"Yes, but I liked my job," he protested bleakly.

When she looked closely at him, his eyes were red and she wondered if he'd been crying.

"I'd rather have that than the money," he went on. "After they called, I went out and got a paper and spent some time looking at the want-ads, but I couldn't picture myself in anything that was available. Truthfully, there wasn't all that much to pick from. So I was feeling quite sorry for myself and went shopping." He looked chagrined. "That's how Gunter got here."

Lara still held the little black puppy that had fallen asleep in her arms. "It's a good name," she murmured. "He looks like a small German Shepherd. Is that what he is?" Trevor nodded. "I'd like to set him down. Is that his bed over there?" Trevor nodded again.

She walked across the kitchen and gently placed the twenty pound bundle on soft quilts. Then she made her way back to Trevor, sat on his lap, and threaded her arms around him. "It really will be all right, dear. I always struggle when you're gone. So it will be lovely to have you here, especially now that there's all that trouble with Ken Beauchamp. And the Institute—"

"But I have to do *something*," he interrupted. "I've worked all my life, love. I'd feel like dead weight around here if I didn't have something to do besides housework and cooking."

Recognizing he didn't want to hear reassurances from her, Lara held him and let him talk.

After a long while, he said, "Thanks for listening. This doesn't actually seem as terrifying as it did before you came home." Glancing over at the puppy, he added, "He'll give me quite a bit to do for the next few months. Haven't had a dog since I was a boy, but if you put a lot into them at the front end, it pays off over time." Gunter stretched and whined softly. "There's my cue! Get up, love, I need to take him out before he has an accident."

She heard him say, "Good boy," a couple times from the back yard, and then the two of them were back in the kitchen with the puppy cavorting around on the tile floor, his puppy claws slipping and sliding on its slick surface. When a flick of his back paw upended his water dish, Gunter looked momentarily surprised by the impromptu shower. Then he started playing in the spilled liquid with his oversized front paws. Laughing, she stepped over the gate, walked to the linen closet, and plucked a bath towel off the neatly folded stack.

"I'll get him," she said and wrapped the damp wriggling puppy in the towel. "Why don't you mop up the floor? How's that dinner? Is it fit to eat, or does it need more cooking?"

"Oh, it just needs a bit of a re-heat." He turned the stove's two front burners on low and pulled a mop from the corner behind the stove.

Settled at the glass and chrome table in their stainless steel and granite kitchen, Lara pushed her plate away. "That was wonderful. You really are a gifted cook. Good thing too since I can barely boil water." She smiled fondly at him over the top of Gunter's head.

"You shouldn't hold him all the time. You'll spoil him." Trevor half-smiled back at her.

"But he's still a baby. It's all right to spoil babies. Isn't that right, snookums?" She kissed the air over the top of Gunter's soft head.

"What do you think we should do about the flat in Amsterdam?" Trevor asked abruptly. It was the first time since before supper he'd alluded to anything related to his KLM job. Mostly, they'd spent their mealtime discussing Lara's concerns about what might have happened in Zurich.

"When's the lease up?"

"Not for a couple years. I took it long term to save a few hundred Euros a month. I wasn't so worried about that, though. What are they going to do to us all the way over here if we request to be let out of our agreement? I'm more concerned about my things. It's looking like it might be difficult to get over there to box them up. And harder still to transport them back here. I suppose they might have to come by ship."

She dredged up a mental picture of exactly what was in their waterside Amsterdam apartment. "Books and clothes," she murmured absently. "What else is there?"

"Not much that's yours," he agreed, glancing at her sadly. "But that was my home before I met you. There are things I can't replace: photographs, my diplomas, and the few things I have from my family."

"Is there a friend who could pack them up for you? Surely there's got to be someone you trust living in Amsterdam."

"I already thought of that. I suppose I might try my cousin." He frowned. "I rather got the impression when I was talking to Mr. Smythe from KLM that things are far worse in Europe than the international news suggests."

"Did you try to reach your cousin?" she persisted.

"It was so late there when Smythe called I thought I should wait until tomorrow. Here, let me get those." Trevor pushed himself up from the table and carried their few dishes to the sink.

"At least let me help, since you cooked."

"No, Gunter's comfy. If you get up, you'll disturb him."

"I thought you were worried about spoiling him." She laughed softly. "Um, Trev," she spoke to his back.

"What?"

"I need you to work on something for me." Lara laid the small furred bundle on the floor. Gunter shook himself, padded to his replenished water dish, lapped noisily, then began crunching on puppy kibbles.

"I'm listening." Trevor arranged the last of the pots in the dishwasher.

"I need to find a psychic." She was irritated when her face heated, and she knew she was blushing.

"What! Did I just hear you ask me to find you a fortuneteller?"

She walked up behind him, wove her arms around his waist, and laid her head against the back of his shoulders. "I need someone who can teach me more about *the sight*. I don't understand it. I can't control it, and frankly, it's starting to frighten me. It wasn't so bad when I only had a couple episodes every few months. But Jesus, I've had, what? Three or four in the last couple days. Auras are one thing. They help me read my patients, but these visions are quite another. I need help. I've thought about looking myself, but I scarcely know where to begin."

"You think I do?" His voice held a note of incredulity. He turned around and hugged her hard, then picked the puppy up for another tour of the back yard.

"Do you think it would be all right for Gunter if we settled in one of the studies, or the front room?" Lara stood in the back doorway watching Trevor and the pup, who was batting clumsily at a large leaf.

"Sure. I got a kennel for him. I'll bring the box and pop him in it, along with a toy or two. Where do you want to be?"

"The front room. I'll get a fire going." Lara stopped at her bag to rescue her lonely cell phone with its bevy of unattended messages. Before she scrolled through them, she bent to light the fire Trevor had thoughtfully laid sometime earlier. Dry cedar kindling crackled and caught, filling the room with its piquant scent. She was still standing in front of the fireplace, staring into the whirling flames, when Trevor came into the room with Gunter tucked under his arm.

"Here," he said, handing her the puppy. "I'll go get his crate."

Lara sat on the sofa. Perched on her lap, Gunter started chewing on her sleeve. She ignored his needle-sharp teeth that occasionally grazed her skin and flicked through the messages on her phone, typing responses where she could.

Trevor, an inveterate gadget person, thought the phone would help organize her over-crowded work life. Though she'd never told him, for fear of hurting his feelings, she actually hated the multi-tasking phone.

Off on an internal tangent, Lara grinned. Jung would roll over in his grave if he knew about the electronic era that allowed people to share their innermost ramblings in incoherent blog posts on the Internet. She tried to remember the last time she'd actually gotten a handwritten letter, or even one typed on a word processor, and couldn't. All communications nowadays came in the form of email or text messages.

Everybody's into instant. No wonder people are so unhappy.

Trevor turned a large plastic crate sideways and slid it over the hardwood floor. Opening the wire mesh door, he tossed puppy chew toys and a couple biscuits inside. Next, he coaxed Gunter off of Lara's lap and onto the faux sheepskin lining the kennel.

"You shouldn't let him chew on you," he told Lara, flicking a finger at the wet places on her sleeves. "Sets a bad precedent. His teeth will be a whole lot bigger when he gets the next set."

She grinned. "Yeah, guess you're right about that. Where will he sleep?" Having finished with her phone, she laid it on a side table.

"In the box. I'll move it to our bedroom, so I can hear if he needs to go out. They do better when they sleep in the same room with you," he explained. "It eases the transition from the puppy pile, where he had lots of company, to being with us."

"I got an idea while I was sitting here." Lara fitted her body against him once he stretched full length atop the lounger that was part of their sectional sofa. "The University of Washington Psychology Department has a psychic phenomenon section. That means there's got to be at least one professor who knows something. Maybe I'll start there."

"Rather than with 1-800-Psychic?" Trevor winked at her, his Peter Pan-ish enthusiasm seemingly restored, at least to some extent.

"Yeah. Hey, kill that light, and let's watch the fire."

"Better enjoy it. That last cord of wood cost almost five hundred dollars."

"You're kidding." She stared at him, aghast.

"People are using it to heat their homes now that oil and electricity have gone up so much. Caveat emptor—"

The shrill jangle of the telephone interrupted him. Lara grabbed the handset. "Hello?"

"Dr. McInnis. I was thinking about our conversation from earlier today, and I had an idea or two. I hope you don't mind I've called you back."

Jesus Christ, it's Himmelschaun. Pulling abruptly away from Trevor, she sat up. "How did you get my home telephone number? Isn't it the middle of the night in Zurich?"

He laughed. Rather than conveying mirth, the sound was ominous. "Your telephone number is a part of your student record here, Doctor. And yes, I do keep unusual hours." There was a pause. "Are you interested in hearing my ideas, or would you prefer to call me back when you're better prepared to have a conversation?"

"Sure, Dr. Himmelschaun, tell me what you thought of." She forced an unnatural brightness into her tone. Trevor looked pissed. He drew his eyebrows together into a frown, uncurled his body from the lounger, and sat next to her.

"Certainly. Certainly. Since it appears you might have difficulty arranging a trip to Zurich, I thought I might come to the States. I assume you are still living in the same place we have noted in our records. As you know, it is always preferable to discuss dream material in person."

Fear soured her belly. She gripped the phone receiver so hard it cut into her hand. "That's very kind of you, Doctor, but I don't need any further assistance with that dream. There's certainly no need for you to travel thousands of miles." Hurrying on before he could say more, she added, "It's quite late here. My husband and I were just getting ready for bed."

"Just so. Well, think about my offer, Dr. McInnis. It has been years since I have left Europe, and I fear travel will become more difficult—if not impossible—in the months to come. And *liebchen*, I have been thinking of you as well as that dream." Something creepy, malignant, and repulsive crawled beneath his cool, accented tones like a slimy beast.

Anger, hot and fresh, raced along her nerves. *The gall of him. What's he trying to do, seduce me?*

"Just so we're clear here. I am not your *liebchen*, and I do not want you to visit me. In fact, I'd prefer it if you never called me again." Without waiting for his reply, she slammed the phone in its cradle. She locked gazes with Trevor, and her body shook from head to toe with a mixture of fear and anger.

"The Zurich guy?" he asked. At her nod, he went on. "He's planning a trip over here just to see you?"

"That about sums it up." Her voice was tight, and then relief sluiced through her. "Thank the goddess for small favors. I wasn't thinking straight there for a moment. He doesn't have *this* address. We bought this place fifteen years ago. They have our old address on file, so even if he comes all this way—and I can't believe he'd do that uninvited—he wouldn't be able to find our home."

"Yes, but he could certainly look up your office address. It's in the phone book," Trevor commented dryly, poking a gaping hole in her theory that Himmelschaun wouldn't be able to locate her.

"Why the hell would he want to come here? What does he want with me? That wasn't just a phone call, it was a fucking proposition. Wish I knew why they kicked him out of the Institute. That might help a lot. Ach, I never should have called him back today."

She lurched to her feet and turned first one way and then another to stretch the tension out of her body. Her hair, loosened from its clips, swirled around her body, floating up and down with a mind of its own.

"Come to bed. It's unlikely he'd be able to get here. Not much of anyone left flying trans-Atlantic routes right now." Trevor smiled crookedly, probably in an attempt to lighten her bleak mood.

"Isn't that fortuitous? Guess there's a silver lining to the oil crisis after all. Do you need help with the pup?"

"No. I'll take him out, and then you can entertain him whilst I huck the box upstairs."

With feelings of foreboding so strong they rocked her to her core, Lara gathered her phone and pager, then trudged wearily up the stairs, hoping sleep wouldn't be as elusive as she feared.

CHAPTER 11

She was roused from the depths of a dream that scattered like a fine mist in the face of Gunter's frantic barking. "Trev?" she mouthed sleepily, reaching out to poke gently at him. "Does that mean he needs to go out?"

"I just took him out." Trevor sounded very much awake. "He did everything, so I don't get it. Except I thought I heard a thumping sound coming from outside. Maybe that's why he's fussing."

Lara came awake instantly. Her heart pounded hard against her chest, and the dregs of sleep fell away like the petals of a rotten rose. "Christ. You don't suppose it's Beauchamp." She reached back to switch on the headboard lights.

"No! Leave them off." His voice held a prickly edge. "If that is Ken—or one of his buddies—out there, it's best if he doesn't think we're awake."

"Did you call 911?"

"Uh-uh. Didn't occur to me it might be your deranged patient until you just suggested it. But I can now." Trevor reached for his phone, a twin to the one he'd bought her, and punched in the emergency number, flipping the phone onto speaker so Lara could hear too.

"What is your emergency?"

"Possible burglars."

"Address."

Trevor rattled it off.

"Please wait." There was a short pause before the operator came back on the line. "Officers are *en route*. Do you want to stay on the phone?"

"Not if I don't have to."

"Understood. Call back if you need to before the officers arrive."

Gunter continued to bark and whine. "Poor thing," Lara murmured. "He must be terrified because I sure am." She slipped out of bed, wrapped a robe around herself, and then bent to let the small dog out of his box. He quieted as soon as she opened the kennel door. Cuddling the puppy close, she returned to her warm nest under the covers. Heart thudding loudly, throat constricting, she stared into the dark, straining to hear something.

"Trevor, do you still hear whatever it was you heard?"

"No," he said shortly. "Look, I'm already dressed. I'm going to go down so I can be there to let the police in."

"Be careful," she whispered, and then they both heard the unmistakable sound of breaking glass. Her airway narrowed further as fear clawed her. "Lock us in," she hissed, gesturing frantically at the door. "Call 911 back and tell them someone's in the house."

Hysteria trod just beneath the surface, an uninvited companion. Sweat beaded on her forehead, and she clung to the puppy as a hedge against a world whirling out of control.

Before she was even done speaking, Trevor had their door locked and was back on the phone.

"Officers should be there in less than two minutes, Mr. Denoble. Please remain on the line. Your alarm system tripped at the station, but officers were already on their way."

Footsteps clomped up the creaky spiral staircase. It sounded as if the intruder wasn't even trying to be quiet. Trevor held a finger over his mouth in the universal signal for silence. Gunter whined nervously. The footsteps paused at their level.

Whoever it is, they have no idea how this house is laid out. Lara tried to reassure herself. *Most people would assume we slept on the top floor.* Thank fucking God Trevor had the presence of mind to stop her from turning on any lights. Her heart was thrumming like a tripwire; more sweat dripped down her sides. The smell of her own fear reached her nostrils as she stroked Gunter soothingly, reassuring the puppy so he wouldn't bark again and give away their location.

The night illuminated outside their window. She saw the red sweep of lights and heard the squealing brakes of an emergency vehicle as it careened to a stop. Masculine voices rose as police officers raced up their stairs.

"Stupid damned people." She heard one officer cursing. "Who would choose to live in a place like this?"

Their unwelcome visitor had obviously heard the commotion too. Lara could imagine him searching for an escape route that didn't necessitate going back downstairs into the waiting arms of law enforcement. If he got very lucky, he'd find the fire escape city building codes had demanded they install half a dozen years ago. Lara held her breath, waiting.

The hallway window creaked in protest at being shoved open. The metal rungs of the outside ladder clattered as someone threw themselves down the fire escape.

"He's gone." Trevor flung the door open. "I'm going to see which window he broke and let the law in."

Throwing the covers back, Lara murmured, "Good doggie," to Gunter. As she stood, dizziness swept through her and her stomach balled into a knot. Lara ran into the bathroom and threw up what was left of her many-hours-ago supper.

The vertigo eased almost immediately. She splashed cold water on her face, then swished some around in her mouth to remove the fetid taste of her own sickness. After a hefty swig of mouthwash, she discarded her nightclothes in favor of sweats. Picking up the puppy, who still cowered in the welter of covers, she pushed him gently back into his box, then went down the stairs, stopping to latch the fire exit window on her way.

When she saw the stained glass side panel from their front door—one of a pair that had been hand-crafted in Italy—lying in shards on the hardwood floor, Lara felt sick inside. She knew they'd never be able to replace it.

Oh come on, she thought, irritated by her own superficiality. *If that glass is the only thing I lost tonight, I got off cheap.* Voices buzzed from the living room, and she followed the sound.

"Dr. McInnis?" one of the two blue-uniformed officers standing in the front room glanced her way.

"Yes. Thanks for getting here so soon. Did Trevor already tell you the guy went down the fire ladder?"

"Yes, an officer gave chase. He's still out there, but he thinks he lost the suspect. Unless we'd brought dogs, there are just too many places here on Upper Queen Anne where the perp could hide until after we leave."

Lara felt cold again. She hadn't considered the possibility their intruder might try again. *Jesus, am I ever naïve.* "Did you get a chance to read the report Sergeant Nelson took from me yesterday? Uh, no, the day before."

"Yes, ma'am. It came over our wireless on our way here."

"I haven't gotten to the Clerk's office yet to actually file the restraining order, but can't you do something, even before I get that done?"

Who am I kidding? I haven't even picked it up from the precinct yet.

"Not if we can't catch whoever it was. TROs are only worth the paper they're printed on if we actually catch somebody violating them," he explained patiently.

"Could you at least drive by here a few times between now and morning?" Trevor asked. "Home Depot's not open for another three hours, and then I'll need some time to remove the last of that glass and put up plywood."

"We'd planned to cruise by every half hour." The younger of the two officers informed him. "Do you have a gun in the house?"

Gunter, apparently deciding he'd had more than enough of being left alone, howled piteously. "I'll just run up and rescue him." Trevor turned to leave the room. "And no, no guns here."

"Too bad," the other officer frowned. "When you live in a location like this, that's not so easy for us to get to, you need to have a gun. Something you've practiced with so you might actually be able to hit a moving target."

Trevor trotted down the stairs holding the puppy just as the officers were preparing to leave. The young officer, Sergeant Boyd according to his badge, smirked. "He'll be useful, but not for quite a few months."

"He did bark and warn us." Lara looked pointedly at the sergeant.

"Well, that's about all he'll be good for until he's grown. Young Shepherd, isn't it? They're great dogs. Good choice." And then the officers were gone.

"I'll take him out." Trevor walked heavily across to the laundry room.

"I'll heat some water. Chamomile tea might taste good right about now." Her stomach still felt queasy. Spooning some rice, left over from an earlier meal, into a small bowl, she blitzed it in the microwave. As she stood over the tea kettle waiting for the water to boil, she nibbled on the rice. By the time Trevor and the puppy came back inside, she'd brewed two cups of pale, fragrant tea. She stirred honey into hers, then placed both on the table. "You were out there for quite a while."

"We were playing Sherlock Holmes." He pecked her on the cheek before sitting next to his tea. "You didn't put anything in mine, did you?" he asked, sniffing suspiciously at his cup.

"I know better than that after all this time."

He glanced fondly at her. "I was looking for footprints next to the fire ladder, and I found them. I could see the trail our guy made in the soft dirt. And then a second set of tracks that I figure were from our buddy in blue."

"Do you think it's safe to even consider going back to sleep?" Lara felt she'd asked a purely rhetorical question, since sleep seemed the most distant of possibilities. Her eyes were dry and scratchy, and a faint taste of sickness lingered in her mouth.

"If you want to try, I can stay down here with Gunter," Trevor offered. "You have to work tomorrow. All I have to do is fix that window."

"Thanks." She tipped the dregs of her tea into her mouth. "I know I should try, but my nerves feel pretty frazzled."

"Why don't you put on that meditation disk you have?"

"Thanks! What a good idea, dear. Brilliant, as you'd say. I'd actually forgotten about it." She got up from the table. After bending to kiss Trevor and ruffle Gunter's puppy fluff, she walked slowly up the stairs to their bedroom.

She thought about the many patients she'd seen over the years who'd been victimized and flinched. The sense of violation flooding through her—no, make that drowning her—was actually far worse than she'd imagined it would be. She shook her head when she recalled the meaningless platitudes she'd mouthed to her patients.

"I feel goddamned helpless," she muttered. "Part of me wants to hide, and the other part wants to strike out at something, except there's nothing but emptiness."

Lara crawled into bed. She located her headphones, turned out the lights, and started the relaxation CD, shooing the ghosts of Beauchamp and Himmelschaun away.

I will not let either of you get to me. Beat it. Scram.

She turned up the CD player and sank into the sound of rain on a windy day.

CHAPTER 12

The good morning trill from her phone jarred her from sleep. Once she shut off the alarm, she rolled over and pulled her dream journal and pen from the nightstand. Clicking on a small book light, she faithfully transcribed what she could recall of the odd, other-worldly landscape the cell phone's alarm had cut short.

She and Trevor had been in Amsterdam wandering the streets, but something horrible happened, and the elaborate system that kept the sea at bay in Holland was failing. Everywhere they turned, they were confronted with knee-deep water. Wherever the water touched her, it burned. Dead sea birds and other small marine life floated on the murky surface of the hungry sea.

"My, that's dark," she mumbled. "It has to be linked to the other dream. And the burglary. And being stalked by that madman from Zurich. My God, maybe the world we know—or at least my world—really is ending."

Feeling hopeless, she rolled out of bed. Would their life hang together long enough for this dream journal to join all the others ranged high on a shelf in her study? She plodded slowly into the bathroom and turned on the shower. As the hot water jets pummeled her body, her head cleared, but she didn't feel much perkier. It wasn't merely last night, but the entire week that had been perfectly wretched.

Back in the bedroom, she stood in front of her tumbled closet with a towel wrapped around her wet hair, surveying possibilities. She'd never been much of a clotheshorse and settled on a black wool suit with a teal silk blouse. A pair of black leggings and flat-heeled, polished pumps completed what she hoped was a professional-looking outfit. She combed out her damp hair and blew it dry before heading down the stairs.

Gunter started barking with his shrill puppy voice, in anticipation of her imminent arrival, the minute she started down the risers. As she passed her ruined front door, she noticed Trevor had swept up the glass.

"In here. Breakfast's about ready."

The minute she stepped over the puppy gate, Gunter jumped on her, snagging her stockings with his sharp little claws. "Damn!" she snapped, but when she looked at the small dog's eager face, and felt his pink tongue licking her, her anger bled away. "Okay, sweetie," she said and picked him up.

"Has he been out?" she asked Trevor.

"Yep, about ten minutes ago." Dark smudges rode beneath Trevor's clear blue eyes, and his jaw was set in a tense line.

"Guess you didn't get any more sleep?"

"Oh, I got a bit. Me and the pup laid down on the couch, but it wasn't the same as snuggling up to you," he said gallantly. "Felt like I slept with one eye open. It would've been a piece of cake for that sodding bastard to come back. House wasn't even locked properly. He could've waltzed right in."

After she filled a plate with the omelet-esque dish on the stove and some diced fruit, she carried both puppy and food to the table. "Coffee?"

"In the carafe behind you."

"I'm going to have to set you down so I can eat," she explained to the puppy before putting him on the tile floor. Gathering a cup, cream, and sugar, she poured herself some French Roast. Sniffing appreciatively, she said, "Mmm. Thanks. Looks great. Did you get a chance to call Europe?"

He settled himself at the table. "Since I wasn't sleeping much anyway, yeah, I called one of my friends from the airlines. I decided that would be better than my cousin. Anyway, she said she'd help. Problem is it's been years since I've really looked through what I have there, so it was damn near impossible to describe what I wanted Angelique to gather together. I did tell her where to find a key, though. And she said she'd call me whilst she was working if she had questions."

"That sounds pretty good." Lara eyed him with concern. "You seem really glum. Still depressed about the job, huh?"

"Of course I am. Who wouldn't be? Let's not forget the bloody break-in." His usual good humor was conspicuously absent, his voice tones bitter. "I'm sorry." He dropped his head into his hands. "It feels like my life just went balls-up, that's all. I don't know what I'm going to do. If that wasn't enough, the power went out again last night for over an hour. I feel helpless, and I don't like it."

She nodded compassionately. "I understand. I felt the same way before I went up to bed. Like no matter what I do it won't make any difference. It's not a good feeling. Try to get some rest today after you've figured out a fix for our door panel."

She fished a couple more forkfuls of egg into her mouth. "It feels stupid and shallow, but I'm just sick about that stained glass door panel. We had those commissioned to celebrate our tenth anniversary."

"How could I forget? I was flying out of Milan then, and I found the little shop that made that phenomenal glass." He looked even more depressed. Draining his cup, he poured more coffee then asked, "What do you have lined up for today?"

Gunter whined. He'd walked to the puppy gate and was scratching at it. "Quick learner!" A wan smile spread over Trevor's face, and he jumped up to take the puppy out.

When he came back, she was piling her dishes in the sink. "I'm going to start at the University to see if I can find someone to talk with. After that, I have patients most of the afternoon. I should be home around seven. And you?"

"That door will be secure by the time you get home. I'm going to research where we could move. It'll probably take months, by the time we settle on a location and then I go look at things."

The lights flickered. Both of them stared in horrified fascination as the light fixture over the sink wavered again, then winked out.

"Bollocks!" he swore softly. "Bloody bollocks! We might not have all that much time." He spun her around to look at him. "Lara, I think we need to pull all our cash out of the bank. We can turn it into gold or something. I never paid much attention to economics when I studied it in school, but aren't banks the first thing to go?"

"I never studied economics at all," she reminded him gently. "But yes, I believe you're right. Banks are usually a bellwether. It's not like lots of them haven't gone under already. Even I know that, newsphobe that I am. The gold from my aunt's money is in bullion in an exchange traded fund. We probably need to liquidate that too, at some point. What's at the bank feels more pressing. I'll do what I can to start the process to close out our account. It will probably take them a couple weeks after I file the request. The bank's in the University District, though, so at least it will be convenient."

She thought for a moment. "You'll have to sign too, since it's a pretty radical move. I'll call my broker to see what I have to do to extricate the gold out of the ETF. Bye, dear. See both of you tonight."

She picked up her shoulder bag, making sure her pager was still clipped to the strap. Fortunately, it wasn't blinking, but her phone certainly was. Cursing Apple for making a device that dogged you worse than a pager ever could, she let herself out their front door.

Squinting against the unexpected glare, she pulled dark glasses from her purse, while looking across Elliott Bay at the Olympic Mountains. Seattle was stunningly beautiful in the brilliant sunlight. Lara shelved her troubles for a moment and breathed in the crispness of the morning, before starting down the steps to the street.

It didn't take too long to drive the few miles to the University. Lara stood in the lobby of Denny Hall, surveying the information board. It wasn't easy to read in the dark foyer, lit only by sunshine filtering through the double glass doors. Not finding what she needed, she climbed the stairs to the floor where the graduate student office was located.

"May I help you?" A pleasant looking young woman asked, looking up from a book she was reading on developmental psychology.

"I'm not sure." Now that she was here, Lara felt uncomfortable even broaching the topic. "Who teaches the Paranormal Psychology class? There is one, isn't there?"

"There certainly is, and that would be Roxanne Dykstra." The student receptionist smiled and flicked a thick strand of auburn hair over one shoulder. "Would you like to know where her office is?"

At Lara's nod, the receptionist consulted her laptop screen, scrolling through menus and sub-menus. When she looked up, her blue eyes glowed. "You *are* in luck. She has office hours right now." The girl grinned engagingly. "I'm lucky too because my laptop still has two hours' battery capacity left. Would you like me to call Dr. Dykstra and tell her you're on your way?"

Lara gathered herself together. She'd hidden the psychic part of herself for so long, the thought of revealing her secret to a stranger felt less than appealing. "Yes, please," she murmured, burying her ambivalence. "My name is Lara McInnis."

"The Dr. McInnis who teaches Jung here?"

Lara's face heated. "Yes, that would be me."

"I'm really looking forward to taking your class. That is, if they accept me into the graduate program. They don't take too many of their own undergrads, as you probably know." She winked conspiratorially, before adding, "I should be fine. I have an inside edge."

"And you are?"

"Oh." The student colored. "Sorry. Didn't mean to be rude. I'm Martha, Martha Christian."

"Nice to meet you, Martha. Now where is Dr. Dykstra's office?" The corners of Lara's mouth twitched as she smothered a smile. "I'd watch those inside edges, especially if they wear pants."

Martha's lipstick pink mouth flew open, and she giggled nervously. "Thanks for the advice, Dr. McInnis. Next floor up, number 357."

Lara mounted a set of stairs and located her objective easily enough. She walked through the open door to Room 357 and stopped dead just past the threshold. Mouth agape, she stared at a panoply of arcane symbology. Statues, carvings, mobiles, and wall hangings, all representing some aspect of either an ancient or New Age belief system, filled the airy space.

"Can I help you, dear?" A diminutive older woman looked up from a desk Lara hadn't even seen, since it was tucked away toward the back of the large hexagonal office.

"Dr. Dykstra?"

"Yes? Can I help you?" The little woman, long gray hair hanging loose, got up from her chair. She wore a quantity of silver jewelry set with colorful precious stones. Merry gray eyes twinkled at Lara. "It's a little overwhelming at first, isn't it? But the energy is perfectly balanced. I simply added things until it felt right."

"I do recognize the mythological symbolism," Lara murmured, not wanting to appear a total rube.

"Of course you do. You teach the depth psychology seminar. At least that's what Martha said. Sit down, sit down. I'll get you a cup of something refreshing." Roxanne Dykstra bustled over to a tea kettle perched on a hot plate under one of the many windows. "Here you go, dear. Lucky for us this hotplate runs off D cells. I found it at a garage sale eons ago." Handing Lara a charming porcelain cup shaped like a lotus blossom, the other woman dropped into an easy chair and motioned Lara to take the one opposite. "Now, what do you seek?"

The question was so unusual Lara started. Not what do you want?

Or how can I help you? But what do you seek? "Would you mind if I closed the door?" Lara met the other woman's unusual pale gray eyes, set off by an over-abundance of turquoise eye shadow.

Dr. Dykstra looked closely at Lara. "No, I don't mind. In fact, I'll close it. That way I can put out a sign letting students know I really am in here. It is my office hours, you know."

Sitting back down in her floral chair, Roxanne leaned forward. "Just spit it out, my dear. Sometimes it's easier that way."

Lara squirmed. She set her tea down, then she picked it back up. "Oh, hell," she fumed. "Look, I feel quite the fool here. I've had this, um, thing—this sort of psychic ability—ever since I was really small. It's become more and more intrusive lately, and I don't know what to do with it. So," Lara managed to scrape her gaze up off the floor and actually look at Roxanne, "I guess I'm searching for someone who can teach me something about *the sight*." Laughing nervously, she added, "I suppose that means I'm seeking a teacher, to answer your question."

"I think I know someone who could help."

Disappointment swept through Lara. "I was hoping you might be able to. Help me, that is. It's not easy to talk to people about this. Seems to make them just as uncomfortable as it makes me."

Roxanne reached out and took one of Lara's hands. "I wish I had paranormal abilities, my dear, but I don't. You need someone who can help you learn to manage what you have, and that wouldn't be me. I'm sorry." Lowering her voice, she went on. "We're living in an unusual time. Many of us expected things to deteriorate a few years from now." Noticing Lara's raised eyebrows, she shook a finger at her. "Now, now. You came here because you wanted to learn things. Cycles of time are very real. If your Jung could come back from the land of the dead, I suspect he'd tell you the same thing. Now, where was I? Oh yes, we thought we had more time left, but the climate change and oil shortage issues are escalating far more rapidly than we suspected they would. If you read—and I'm sure you do—you must know we're losing entire species of animals every day. They can't migrate fast enough to find a suitable temperature."

"Does that mean you think the reason my psychic ability is becoming more apparent is because there are some sort of dynamic—or demonic—forces out there escalating things?"

Roxanne stared hard at Lara. "No. I didn't say anything of the kind." Her voice had an edge to it. "What I did say was we seem to be at the end of a major cyclical progression, and many have predicted the end of life on Earth coincident with the closure of that cycle. I said nothing about demons. Where did you come up with that?"

Lara shrugged, feeling uneasy. "Probably pure projection on my part. I've, uh, had my own personal demon here of late and it's colored how I see just about everything." Unbidden, she launched into an abbreviated version of the saga with Ken Beauchamp, though she didn't mention him by name. She was surprised, but unable to rein herself in, when she found herself confiding her omnipresent sense of guilt and loss around Pete's death.

Roxanne listened intently as the minutes clicked by. *Yes,* Lara thought to herself. *That's one thing we psychology types all do well: listening.* When she was done talking, silence stretched through the room. Even the arcane symbols seemed to have leaned closer of their own volition so that they too, could absorb her story.

"That's quite a tale," Roxanne said at last. "I can see why you'd be troubled. Being stalked is devastating. I'd love to tell you I see some sort of connection between the mess we've made of the planet and your problems with that madman. But I'm afraid he's just a garden-variety sociopath, and unfortunately, you've become his latest target. Would you like the name of a woman who has abilities I think might be similar to yours?"

Nodding mutely, Lara stood and walked her cup back to the collection next to the tea pot. Doctor Dykstra rose as well, went to her cluttered desk, and scribbled a name and telephone number on the back of one of her cards. "Come by again. I enjoyed our little chat. And I want to know what you think about Lillian." Handing her the card, Roxanne ushered Lara to the door of her office.

Lara bid the professor goodbye, thanked her for listening, and retreated to her waiting car. Mildly embarrassed by how quickly her tale of woe had escaped her, she understood she needed a few therapy sessions. Who could she talk with? Her old analysts at the Institute weren't there any longer. At least that's what Himmelschaun said.

Lara stopped at the bank, surprised to find it open, since the electricity was still off in the University District. The lighting inside was dim, probably powered by generators. After she'd made her request, the young teller looked at her with startled eyes and then asked to see two more forms of ID.

"You want over three hundred thousand dollars in *cash*?" The teller sounded incredulous, and her fingers tapped a staccato rhythm on the faux wood of her desktop.

"Yes, you heard me correctly." Lara pushed several pieces of paper through the small half-window. "I thought your computers might be down, so I brought copies of last month's statements with me."

The teller riffled through the pages, then said, "One moment please." When she returned to the window, an older gentleman was with her.

"Dr. McInnis." The bank manager looked stunned—and annoyed— as he shoved her bank statements back through the window. "You will have to have Mr. Denoble, co-owner of these accounts, come by here to sign, assuming he is in agreement with your withdrawal request. I, of course, am advising you against such a large withdrawal. Banks are still the safest place to maintain one's savings."

"Once Mr. Denoble signs, how long before I can close out this account?" Lara was becoming impatient. The bank manager, with his bald head and ill-fitting suit, epitomized the officious type who'd always irritated her. He'd completely lost sight of the fact she was simply requesting her own funds.

"Seven days." Consulting a calendar, he coughed and clarified, "That would be next Friday. Assuming Mr. Denoble signs in a timely fashion."

"Thanks." Lara signed her portion of the account surrender forms and turned to leave, checking her watch as she walked out of the bank. It was only ten thirty. She had plenty of time to visit Bethany and still make it to her office in time for Maryanne at noon. First, she called Trevor, sketching out what he needed to do at the bank.

Already feeling guilty about what she planned to do next, she extricated herself quickly from the call. *I'll tell him later*, she promised herself. *That way I'll be home safe. He might be angry with me, but at least I'll be done with it.* There'd be no more trips to University Hospital after today.

Next she dialed Helen Morgan. "Helen? It's Lara. I've got a half hour or so here. Would this be a good time to visit our patient?"

She made arrangements to meet Helen in her upstairs office in the obstetrics department and drove to the medical center. By the time she got to the physician parking lot, her conscience was raising hell.

I promised Trevor I wouldn't do this, at least not by myself.

I won't be alone, I'll be with Helen.

Despite her logic, a niggling sense of wrongness pricked her. She didn't know if it was guilt or an unusual awareness from her psychic side, but it bothered her so much she strode to the small security shack and asked the guard if he'd be so kind as to walk her into the hospital.

After a short trip to the obstetrics department that was so uneventful she felt foolish, she knocked on Dr. Morgan's door, noticing the hospital lights were operational, but dim.

Another generator. It made sense. Hospitals had a boatload of equipment that had to run or patients would die.

"Come," Helen called in response to Lara's knock.

Pushing the door open, she walked into the familiar space, crowded with textbooks and journals that spilled onto the floor. "Hi, Helen. How is she?"

"Scared. Did you find somewhere for her to go yet?"

"No. To be honest, I haven't even tried. Mostly because I didn't know when she'd be ready to leave. We, ah, had a break-in last night..."

"…and you think it's the husband?" Helen fixed Lara with steely eyes. "Do the police know?"

Lara nodded. "Yes to both."

Helen made a clucking sound. "Maybe you could call your receptionist so she can get to work on a shelter placement. Bethany's actually good to go now. I can't keep her in the ICU much longer, and she's not safe out on the floor."

"May I use your phone?"

Helen turned it around and pushed it toward Lara, who dialed her office number. When Arabel answered, Lara described what she needed, reminding Arabel of the Yakima and Wenatchee shelters.

"I'll have found somethin' by the time you git here," Arabel said in her cheerful drawl.

Lara pushed the phone back to the only clear place on Helen's desk. "Sorry. I should have gotten to it sooner. In fact, I should've visited yesterday."

"No matter. Let's go and see her now."

Bethany looked worse than when Lara had last seen her. The bruising had deepened and spread, but her eyes were open and they overflowed with tears when Lara walked to her bed. "Dr. McInnis. Thank you for saving me."

Lara patted her hand gently. Only one IV remained, and it was on the other side. "I didn't actually do all that much, Mrs. Beauchamp. But I am glad you're awake."

"I dreamed you, and then you came and helped me. I told you Ken was trying to have them take the baby by C-Section and get rid of me. I don't know how you did it, but you heard me and you came." Bethany wiped at her face with the sheet. "Dr. Morgan says you have somewhere safe for me—well, for us—to go."

"Do you have family anywhere?" Lara asked kindly. "I can hunt for a shelter near your family if you'd like."

"Oh, no." Bethany clung nervously to Lara's hand. "That's the first place he'd look. No, I have to disappear, at least until after I have the baby. Then I can probably disguise myself. You know, dye my hair and lose myself in a big city."

"You could tell the police what he did to you. Then he'd go to jail, and you wouldn't have to spend the rest of your life looking over your shoulder." Lara gentled her voice gentle to mask the harshness of her message.

"It wouldn't matter. If he was locked up because of me, one of the other ones would just do me."

Helen, who'd been listening off to the side, came close to the bed. "Young lady. Are you trying to tell us your husband's involved in organized crime?"

Bethany nodded mutely. Taking in a breath, she looked up at her two doctors and said, "This is my own fault. I knew what I was getting into. I wanted the fancy house and to not have to work. I just didn't know how bad it would be actually living with him." Tears rolled quietly down her disfigured face. She looked pleadingly at Lara. "You know how bad my childhood was. Never went to school past the eighth grade. I'm still not quite sure how it happened, but I ended up with a bastard who was worse than my father." She shook her head dolefully.

Squeezing Bethany's hand, Lara glanced surreptitiously at the ICU clock. She felt torn. The same childlike innocence that had drawn her in when she'd first met the woman was still in play. "Bethany, I'm sorry but I've got to leave. I'll let Dr. Morgan know just as soon as I've found a shelter placement for you. Right now I'm looking in eastern Washington."

"That's not far enough." Bethany sounded terrified.

"You can start there. The shelters network with other places. If staff where you are feel you're not safe, they'll make arrangements to move you. It will be all right." Lara released the woman's hand. "I'll keep tabs on you, no matter where you end up."

"Would you? That would mean so much to me. It's like we have a special bond, since you came to me in my dream."

Lara walked to the door of the ICU with Helen. "I feel a bit odd asking this," she admitted, "but could you cal. Security to walk me to my car?"

"Don't know why you'd feel odd about that." Helen sounded tense. "If it was me, I'd do the same thing. I expect to hear from you before the end of today with a place for that poor woman. Besides," she added voice lowered, "we've got to get her out of here. Security's noticed quite a few odd things, and they actually intercepted a homemade incendiary device in one of the hospital's laundry bins yesterday. Got lucky, someone's Seeing Eye dog started barking like crazy. Turns out the dog had failed bomb-sniffing school at TSA. Anyway, he sure earned his biscuits here."

An involuntary shiver coursed down Lara's spine. "Don't worry. I'll call even if I haven't quite found something, just to let you know what progress I've made."

"Thanks," Helen said softly. "I'm worried, and I hardly ever feel that way. I just keep thinking about Dr. Schneider, and my blood runs cold."

Lara turned to look at her old friend. Helen's lips had pressed into a harsh line, as she talked about the bomb.

"Yes," Lara muttered through gritted teeth, "I'm scared too. Ken's into bombs. It's how he killed Pete."

CHAPTER 13

"I'm going to count backward now, beginning with ten. After you wake, you'll remember everything we talked about…" As Lara invoked the litany to guide her hypnosis patient back from the other side, she thought about how well Ruth had done. Hypnosis was a hit or miss proposition for weight control, but she'd managed to shed nearly a hundred pounds.

Stretching in her comfortable chair, Ruth grinned at Lara. "Thanks, Dr. McInnis. I really do feel like a new woman. And I absolutely love hypnosis."

"You're the one who did all the hard work. I've just been sort of a cheerleader. If you like the trance state, why don't you look into that meditation tape series I told you about?"

"I'll think about it." Ruth gathered her things. "Do you think the power's going to come back on today?" she asked, sounding worried.

"Wish I knew. Guess I'll have to deep-six my evening office hours if we revert back to kerosene lanterns." Lara tried to make a joke, but it didn't seem very funny. "You're about done with me, Ruth. But if you want to come back, make an appointment with Arabel on your way out." Lara stood and ushered her patient to the door.

Once she'd finished her notes, Lara found Arabel, feet up on the window sill, reading a psychological journal. "Hmm. *Journal of Comparative and Physiological Psychology*? Surely there are some others I get that aren't quite so dry."

"There's an interestin' article in here, though." Arabel looked up at Lara from where she'd dragged her secretarial chair over beneath the window. "It's about how maybe there's some other strain of humans with psychic abilities who came from another place."

"You found that in there?" Lara felt incredulous. "Sounds like something from *Science Fiction and Fantasy*. Boy, I'm glad it's Friday, aren't you?" Stretching luxuriantly, she reached for the ceiling and rotated her torso from side to side. "How does next week look? Did we get confirmation on a place for Bethany?"

"Hope there's power by next week." Arabel sounded exasperated. "I brought the laptop. Can't leave it on, though, 'cause I'll drain the battery. Next week is pretty full, but your Wednesday is open as usual. Shelter in Wenatchee said they'd be glad to take Bethany and her baby. I called that doctor friend of yours to let her know." Arabel stood and walked to her desk to close everything up for the week.

"Did Dr. Morgan say there was a way to get Bethany to the shelter?"

"Yeah. She said a friend of hers was going to drive her. Tonight, I think. I'm sure glad she's gittin' away from that bastard she's married to. He always gave me the creeps."

Impulsively, Lara hugged Arabel. Concern nagged at her as she held the older woman. "Do you have a way to cook things with the power out for so long? And stay warm? I know you have your garden, but—"

"Oh, honey, I'll be fine. Just fine. I got me a woodstove, and I'm a fair hand at cookin' on it. It's how I grew up. Garden's still got vegetables in it. You ought to know that." She looked at Lara a bit reproachfully. "I'm still bringin' you things."

"You're probably better off than we are," Lara replied wryly. "Ready?"

"Yup." Arabel pulled her bag out of its usual drawer.

When Lara yanked open the front door of the office, the hallway was practically dark. Peering into the gloom, fear gripped her, tightening her stomach. The beginnings of a sudden headache throbbed dully behind her right temple.

"Let me go first." Apparently sensing the same unseen danger, Arabel drew her gun and took Lara by the arm.

She stared in macabre fascination at the shiny steel-blue death machine clutched so easily in Arabel's large-fingered hand. Lara tried to steady herself, but it was a losing proposition. Finally, she tore her gaze away and locked the office door.

"Did anything happen today while I was in session?" she whispered as the upper tumbler fell into place.

"No, hon." Arabel spoke in a normal voice. "But pays to be safe and it's dark in here. If they don't git that 'lectricity problem fixed, I don't think we ought to work past five next week. Days is gittin' shorter."

"Ssht." Lara willed her ears to preternatural sharpness. *Did I hear something? Was that a footstep? Damn carpet's too thick to hear anything.* Utter silence surrounded the two women.

"Come on." Arabel urged. "We're sittin' ducks up here." Pulling Lara along with her, she ran for the stairs Part way down, Lara turned—sure she heard something behind them. Stumbling slightly, she caught her ankle bone on one of the risers. The *thunk* reverberated through her leg like an electric shock.

"Damn!" Pain shot through her ankle, but she kept going. Once they were in the downstairs hall, Arabel threw the front door open, shoved Lara through it, and turned to drop the deadbolt into place with her key.

"How's your foot?" Arabel turned to look at Lara. The older woman was panting.

"I crunched my anklebone bone against the steps. It hurts, but I can walk on it. Do you really think someone was in there with us? I'm practically positive there was, but maybe I'm just being paranoid and over reactive."

Arabel nodded. "Nothin' I can put my finger on, exactly. But it just didn't feel like we was alone. You felt it too, didn't you, Doc?"

She nodded. "Yeah, I felt it too. Well, whoever it is—if there really was someone—is locked in, unless he can figure out where to come up with a key." It had been Pete's idea to use a double locking deadbolt, requiring a key on both sides, as a security measure. Poor Pete. Her heart ached for him—again.

Arabel looked somber. "Gonna be a long weekend in there. Bet he breaks a window."

"That'd trip the alarm system, except we were in such a rush to leave we didn't set it." Grim-faced, Lara pulled her phone out to dial 911. In response to the brusque operator's voice asking for details about her emergency, Lara explained she thought there was an intruder in her building. The dispatcher told her to wait in her car with the doors locked.

"I'll wait with you," Arabel volunteered.

"You don't have to." Lara felt contrite.

"I'm stayin' and that's that."

The two women settled themselves in the car, and Lara relayed what had happened the previous night at her house. Once she was done talking, she rubbed her aching head and rotated her sore ankle.

"Shit," she muttered. "Trevor. He'll be worried about me." Scrabbling for her phone again, she called home.

"…ran into a problem here." After describing their frightening exit from the nearly-dark building, she reassured him she was safe with Arabel—and Arabel's gun—in her locked car, and that she'd be home just as soon as she could.

"Doc, look there!"

Lara stared at the side of her office building. The figure of a man was just disappearing over the low hedge between her office and the next building. His dark clothing blended into the falling night.

"That settles it," she told Trevor. "Someone was definitely in my building." She repositioned the phone between her shoulder and ear, feeling sickened and outraged by the invasion. Her head just kept pounding. "The guy must have picked a lock or something. I still have to wait for the cops, so I can secure whichever door he opened to get out of the building."

"How do you know he didn't break out a window?" Trevor's voice vibrated with tension. "I think I should come down there."

"I don't know how he got out, but if I can't relock the building, I'll have to call out workmen. I can't leave it open all weekend. There're client files in there."

"I'll be there as soon as I can."

"No, Trev. Don't come. It's really hard driving with the street lights out and traffic signals working off generators. The police just pulled up. I'll call you as soon as I know something."

Lara opened her car door. Arabel stowed her weapon in her purse and got out too.

"Ma'am? What was the problem?" The sandy-haired officer who spoke to her was tall and trim. He looked tired, with deep circles under bloodshot blue eyes.

"I'm Dr. McInnis. I own this building and have an office here. Someone was in the building tonight. I think he was waiting for me, but we hurried out and locked him in. Then we saw someone leaving, so I don't think he's in there anymore." Lara sounded lame and flustered, even to herself. "Anyway, I need to lock up. The dead bolts lock from both sides and—"

"Never mind, ma'am, I get the picture." The other officer, older and bald, interrupted her. "We'll just go have a look-see. Give me your key so we can lock the place back up, if it's lockable."

Silently, Lara handed her office key to him and watched as the two cops trotted smartly over to the front door of her office.

She walked to the other side of her car, opened the passenger door, and pressed the catch on the glove box. Grabbing a bottle of Ibuprofen, she shook three into her hand and swallowed them dry.

"That bad?" Arabel's soft voice was soothing.

"I've got a horrible headache. It started in the hallway outside the office." Lara sucked on the insides of her cheeks to gin up enough saliva to move the pills along.

The officers were headed back. The younger of the two handed her key over and said, "Looks like he let himself out the back door. Must've picked the lock, 'cause there wasn't any damage. We did a walkthrough before we locked things up. No one in there. Let me get your names. Do you always keep evening hours by yourself, Doc? Who was your last patient and when did they leave?"

When they were through with her, they started in on Arabel. "Do you work with the doctor? What do you do for her?"

Lara stood on the curb listening to the cops quiz Arabel. A wave of weariness washed over her, and she swayed on her feet.

"She's tired, officers." Arabel reached a supportive hand toward Lara. "And she got a long drive home. Maybe you could let us leave. Not much more to tell you anyways."

The haggard looking sandy-haired officer shrugged. "Guess you're right, ma'am. We'll be sure to check on that Ken Beauchamp. Seems like the sooner he's off the streets, the sooner you two can rest easy. Drive carefully. This power outage is a real mess. You might want to consider installing an alarm system in that building."

"Got one. Thanks for the reminder. I need to set it before we leave." Lara smiled wanly at the officers. Turning to Arabel, she added, "Thanks for staying. Don't forget your purse."

"Just gittin' it, Doc. Call me after you get home, so's I don't worry."

Lara blushed, feeling like she was about sixteen. "Thanks for caring about me," she murmured.

"Don't mention it, hon." Hoisting her bag onto her shoulder, Arabel hugged Lara, and then crossed the street to her blue Toyota Avalon.

Lara sighed bleakly and trooped up the stairs to engage the building alarm. She got back into her car, locked the doors, and fired the engine, while thinking about Arabel. *So that's what it feels like to have a mother. Pretty nice, actually.* Fumbling for her phone, she called

Trevor to tell him she was on her way, too worn-down to care she wasn't supposed to use her cell and drive at the same time.

~

LARA STRUGGLED to eat the pasta with burgundy sauce Trevor had made for supper. Her head still ached dully, and her stomach felt torn up from the Ibuprofen. Or maybe it was cumulative stress burning a hole in her guts. Gunter, who'd greeted her with typical canine abandon, was curled up on her lap while she pushed the food from one side of her plate to the other. "Did you get by the bank?"

Trevor looked at her strangely. "You already asked me that. Twice. Lara, you don't have to eat if you don't want to."

As they sat in the candlelit kitchen, the lights flickered abruptly a couple times, and then the power lurched back on, filling the kitchen with the hum of their many appliances.

"Gee, you don't realize how noisy they all are, do you? Or how much power they're pigging up," Lara mumbled. She laid the sleeping puppy on the floor, wrapped plastic film over her half-eaten plate, and stuffed it into the fridge.

"What'd you find out from the University?" Trevor asked, moving dishes off the table to the granite sideboard. "You've been pretty quiet since you got home."

Turning to face him, she said, "I suppose that's because I have a confession to make." As he looked at her, bafflement crept over his handsome features. Lara forced herself to keep talking before she lost her nerve. "I went to the hospital today. I hooked up with Dr. Morgan, and I saw Bethany. And now I'm done with it. I found her a place to go. Helen's figured out how to get her there. I'm really sorry. I didn't want to deceive you, but I was already there, and Helen wanted to get her out of the hospital, and—"

"But you promised me." Trevor's voice was deadly quiet. "All you would have had to do was call. It only takes twenty minutes to get over there, even with the traffic snarls."

"I don't have any excuses. I'm sorry. I figured you'd be angry."

"And you didn't fucking care! Bloody hell, Lara. I don't know what to say to you." His face blotchy with rage, he stomped out of the kitchen. She heard the front door slam a few seconds later. When she ran out onto the porch, she heard the clop of his shoes running down the stairs.

"I suppose it's about what I deserve," she groaned. "He's right, I *did* promise. I was so wrapped up in that whole psychic thing, I didn't think to call him soon enough."

No, an implacable inner voice reminded her. *I did call him. I didn't tell him because I didn't want to have to wait for him.*

The puppy walked up behind her, snuffling and whining. Slipping past, he began lurching his way down the uneven front steps, tripping over his ungainly front paws as he tried to follow Trevor.

"Oh no you don't." She caught him up, lecturing sternly about what happened to errant puppies that left home too soon. She trudged through the ornate front door with the puppy in her arms, and her thoughts turned to the previous night. When she looked at the plywood, she cringed.

Feeling perfectly miserable, she wandered through the house, still carrying Gunter until she could deposit him on the small grassy area in the backyard. The puppy squatted immediately, and then sniffed at a toadstool. She watched the small canine for a bit before ushering him back into the house.

Desperate for something to do, so she wouldn't have to think, she scraped pots, pans, and plates, piling them in the dishwasher. There wasn't quite a full load, but she figured she'd take advantage of the power while it was on.

She'd just clicked the dishwasher on and was folding the dishtowel when she heard the snick of a key in their front door. Still clutching the towel, she ran for the entry hall, heart in her throat.

Had he only come back to tell her goodbye for good?

"Trevor, oh Trev, I'm really, really sorry. I know I made a mistake. I never wanted to hurt you. You're the best thing that's ever happened to me and the sweetest, most considerate—" Overcome by emotion, she couldn't talk anymore. Lara flung herself at him and twined her arms around his solidness.

Seizing the opportunity afforded by the open puppy gate, Gunter padded out from the kitchen to see what the commotion was all about and added his whines to her sobs.

"Of course I came back. It's my home too, isn't it?" he said with a crooked grin, ever the understated Brit. "All right now, Lara. I was just angry. I'm not feeling all that useful right about how. No job. Girlfriend doesn't seem to need me."

"Oh, but I do," she said, her voice muffled against his shoulder. Gunter pushed his little body between them, nipping at their ankles. "Hey there," she protested and pushed away from Trevor to reach the pup. "No biting!"

"Here, I'll take him. He just needs a toy. They're pretty oral at that age." Pulling a chew toy out of his jacket pocket, Trevor popped it in the puppy's mouth. Easily diverted, Gunter flopped down, chomping eagerly on the rubber bone.

"Why'd you have that in your pocket?" Lara raised her eyebrows questioningly.

"Because I was playing with him before you got home," he said and smiled at her.

"Would you like to come sit with me?"

Trevor nodded, and she grabbed his hand and headed for the living room. Gunter's box was already in a corner near the fireplace. Trevor lured the puppy into it with treats.

"Holy crap. I forgot to call Arabel." Lara clapped a hand to her head. "I don't know what's happened to me today. It's not like me to be so inconsiderate and forgetful."

Lara groped for the landline handset and dialed her receptionist. In the midst of her apologies for not calling sooner, Arabel interrupted her to say, "It's okay, hon. I knew you was all right."

"That's curious," Lara said as she replaced the phone in its cradle. "She seemed to know I'd gotten here, even without me calling her."

"Well hey, maybe she's got the same thing you do." Trevor crooked a finger at her. "Come over here next to me. There's a lot to catch up on. Did you find someone who could help you at the University?"

"Yeah, I got a name, Lillith, no Lillian."

"What did she say?"

"I didn't actually talk to her. Not yet, anyway." Snuggling in next to him, she summarized her visit with Roxanne. Gunter had fallen asleep in his crate, his small body curved around a puppy toy.

"Are you going to try to reach Lillian?"

"Yes, but not tonight. It's past ten. She's probably asleep." Shifting around, Lara pulled off her watch and dropped it on the coffee table. Next she kicked off her shoes, drew her legs up onto the sofa, and tucked them beneath her. "You did a good job on that side panel. Looks weather tight, even if it's not very aesthetic."

"The best part is that it's screwed in from this side, so unless that bloody blighter shows up with a jig saw, it would be really hard for him to get through it. We need to talk about a couple other things, though. You asked me about the bank, but I didn't tell you much, except that I'd gone.

"I met up with Mr. Serious there, and got a lecture—same as you did—about what a bad idea it is for us to withdraw our funds. He was really nosing around. Asked all kinds of things about what we were planning to do with the money, like what we wanted it for, and did we want to sit down for a talk with a financial advisor?

"I could have throttled him after the first five minutes. After ten, I politely asked for the papers I needed to sign." Trevor tightened his arm around Lara. "I swear to God, I thought for a moment he was going to refuse. I wasn't sure what I was going to do then, besides calling you, that is. After this really tense moment, he threw a paper at me and pointed to where I should sign. When I gave it back to him, I asked for a copy of my signed request. He snarled that he'd mail it to me, but I told him I'd wait whilst he copied it. Then he told me, in the most patronizing tone of voice imaginable, they couldn't copy anything with the power out."

"What'd you do?" Lara was intrigued.

"I told him to get another blank that he and I both signed. He took one original, and I took the other. People did manage to conduct business before the invention of the copier."

"It was smart of you to get a copy. Wish I'd have thought to do that. It's odd he was so protective. You'd think it was *his* money the way he was acting. I suppose the reason he let me off so easily was he told me you had to come down. Maybe he figured this withdrawal thing was my harebrained idea, and being the man, you'd never agree to it." Lara inhaled sharply. When she rubbed her temples a bit gingerly, she realized her headache was almost gone.

"It's like the world's gone crazy, Lara. I suppose lots of people have closed out their bank accounts. Maybe the bank will have a hard time coming up with all that cash we've asked for. Who knows?

"No one is nice anymore, or even particularly civil. You don't do the shopping, so you don't see it, but the grocery stores are a nightmare. Lots of things are out-of-stock, and people fight over what's left. One of the things I did today was wait in line at a filling station for over an hour to fill up my Benz and two ten gallon petrol cans. Bloody hell, people screamed at me whilst I filled the cans. Like I didn't have a right to more fuel than would fit in my tank. The attendant at Costco stood between me and a couple chaps who wanted to pound me into the dirt."

"Do we need to buy a gun?" Lara thought about the weapon Arabel carted along with her. Next, she revisited her lifelong antipathy for violence and wondered if she could actually bring herself to kill someone, even if her life were in danger. A frisson of fear skittered down her back like a small unwelcome animal with unpleasantly sharp claws.

"Have you ever fired one?" Trevor looked quizzically at her, and Lara shook her head. "Well, if you get a large enough gauge, you don't have to be a particularly decent shot. But they've got quite a kick to them."

"I guess that means you have?" She twisted her head to look at him.

He nodded. "When I was a boy, we hunted some for game with shotguns. Often as not, that was all the meat we had."

"Are you ever going to tell me about how you grew up?"

"You never told me very much about your childhood, either," he countered.

"Maybe we can have a show-and-tell session sometime soon." She laughed hollowly. "Guess neither one of us likes to think much about our humble origins. We should go to bed, Trev. It's late and neither one of us got enough sleep last night. Did you set the alarm?"

"Yeah. I've got some ideas for how we can invest that money in property. If the bank actually turns loose of it, that is."

Her eyes were hot and gritty, the lids heavy with exhaustion. "I'd love to talk about it, but could that conversation keep until morning?"

"Guess it's my turn to be sorry now, love. You're completely knackered. Here, let me help you up. I'll let Gunter out and bring his box upstairs."

"Thanks. I always did need more sleep than you."

She dragged herself up the two flights to their bedroom. Lara dropped her clothes in a heap on the floor, pulled an old nightshirt over her head, and fell into bed, thinking guiltily about her unwashed face and unbrushed teeth for the ten seconds or so before she fell asleep.

CHAPTER 14

They wakened to a blissfully sunny fall day in Seattle and decided to have breakfast outside in their back yard. That way the puppy could cavort around without them having to watch him so closely. The late autumn sun was unusually warm on Lara's skin. It felt good, and she wasn't in a hurry to go anywhere.

Time passed as they chatted of this and that. Lara eyed Trevor. "Gosh, it's closing on noon."

"So?" he grinned at her. "There's still coffee left in the pot. Never mind it's the third one."

"This would be as good a time as any." She quirked an eyebrow at him across the small rattan table.

"For what? It's a lovely day, but we have neighbors. We need to go inside for anything amorous."

"Ooch! You Brits. You're about as subtle as a typhoon. No, Trev. I really do want to know about your family. Won't you tell me, please? You've always circumnavigated my questions. I've told you about how my parents dumped me with Aunt Mary when they went off to find themselves at that ashram that didn't allow kids. And how they ended up getting killed in a car wreck before they could come back for me.

I'm not sure who was more upset—me or Aunt Mary because she was stuck with me."

Trevor folded his arms on the table, laid his chin on the back of his hands, and looked at her with eyes that had turned painfully serious. "I've never told anybody."

"Why not?" Reaching across the small space, she caressed one of his forearms. "Things tend not to hurt so much when we talk about them."

"Stop being a therapist." He drew his brows together, darkening his features.

"It's true," she persisted. "I'm not just saying that. I've built a career —and my life—around it. I believe it really helps Psyche to heal and become whole when we haul our demons out of the closet. They never look quite so bad in the light of day."

Trevor closed his eyes. "These ones will." He was silent so long after that, she thought he'd ignore her request as he'd done so many times before, but then he started talking.

"I was oldest," he began in a strangely broken voice. "There was Lizzie who was three years younger, and then Robbie who was a year younger than her. My parents hated one another. Fought like cats and dogs, they did. Dad beat Mum, but she hit him back. And they'd drink, mostly till they passed out. Good thing we were so poor, else they'd have been at the bottle every night. As it was, they only drank when there was a wee bit of extra money, maybe a couple times a week."

Lara watched Trevor as he talked. His eyes remained closed, as if it were too painful to look at her. His accent became broader, like it always did when he was really stressed. "It wasn't your fault," she said softly. "You were just a child."

"You haven't heard it all," he snapped. "In fact, I've barely begun. This is hard enough. For Christ's sake, do not psychoanalyze me. Don't be a therapist. Don't coo over me or make nice compassionate statements." Opening eyes that were blue pits of pain, he stared intently at her.

She took a deep, startled breath. "All right. I won't say anything. I'll just listen. Promise."

He closed his eyes again. "When I was about ten, Dad beat Mum so bad he broke her back. She couldn't walk very well after that, so I had to take over caring for Liz and Robbie. Mum got real bitter. She wouldn't let Dad back in her bed, so he took to visiting the whores, and bringing them home. One night, Mum poisoned one of them. I was maybe twelve by then. I still remember gathering up the little ones and herding them out to the barn so they wouldn't see that woman writhing on the floor vomiting blood. We could still hear her screams, though, even from outside. I don't know if she died or not." He stopped talking. Emotional turmoil roiled through his aura, turning it nearly black. Lara ached to reach out to him, but held herself back.

After a few moments, he began speaking again, haltingly, as if he were struggling to find the words. "After the ambulance carted the whore off, I was the one that had to scrub up the mess whilst Mum and Dad hurled curses at one another."

Lara felt sick. She wondered if she could stand to hear the rest of whatever he had to say. *No,* her inner voice was uncompromising. *I asked for this. I cannot tell him how awful it is. He already knows. That's why he didn't want to talk about it.* Sending tendrils of *the sight* outward, she had a sinking feeling she knew exactly what was coming next.

"After that, Dad started in on Lizzie, since Mum wouldn't service him, and she'd made such a mess with that whore. Aw Christ, Lara." Trevor's eyes were open now and filling with tears. "My little sister was only nine years old. I can still hear her screams from when he took her that first time. She was crying for me, Lara. Begging me to save her. I tried to pull him off her, but he outweighed me by six stone. He knocked out a couple of my teeth and bruised me up pretty good. There wasn't anything I could do but hold Lizzie and try to comfort her after he'd finished.

"By the time she was twelve, she was pregnant. The authorities came round. See Liz, she tried to tell them about Dad. But Dad just called her a little trollop. Said she'd gotten herself into trouble with one of the neighbor boys. I think the law didn't want to bother with our family. We were poor, not worth the trouble it would've taken them to tease out the truth of things."

Tears coursed down Trevor's cheeks, and he buried his head in his hands. The sounds coming from him reminded her of a wounded animal caught in a trap, wretched and heartrending. Longing to go to him, but not daring after what he'd said earlier, she waited, willing him the strength to finish. If he could just get through telling her, he'd find some relief. Not immediately, but eventually. Unable to stop them, she felt tears drip down her face too.

He stood and paced up and down the small yard. When he spoke next his voice was muffled since he was wiping his nose on his sleeve. "She hung herself." The anguished words tore out of him. "Lizzie hung herself. She couldn't stand the shame. Dad, he was still having his way with her, whenever he wasn't so drunk he couldn't get it up."

Lara couldn't help herself. Heart breaking for him, she pushed up from the table, walked over to Trevor and held out her arms, but he shook his head. "If I do, I won't be able to tell you the rest." His voice was hoarse, and he looked down, unable to meet her eyes. "Once I'm done, I will never talk about any of this again. Never. Do you understand?"

Nodding mutely, she walked to a spreading maple and leaned against its bole. She found a tissue in one of her pockets, quietly blew her nose, and blotted her still-seeping eyes.

"I was the one who found her out in the barn. I knew she had to be dead because of the way her body looked. See, her neck was twisted at this unnatural angle. I cut her down and tried and tried to breathe life back into her. Whilst I was crying and trying to do CPR—except I didn't really know how—Dad came into the barn and started screaming at me. He accused me of killing Lizzie and trying to cover it up.

"Something inside me snapped. My ears were roaring, and all I could see was this red mist. I straightened up over my dead sister's body, grabbed a pitchfork from off the wall, and I ran right at that bastard who was my father."

Trevor was crying again; huge aching sobs welled out of his soul. "The 'fork cut through him like he was made of paper. I could feel the tines scrape against his ribs, but it just went in so easy. Blood splattered everywhere. My hands were slick with it when I finally let go. Dad was hollering and I ran out of the barn, got Robbie, and we rode our bikes down to the precinct station. I told them what had happened and what I'd done. There was a juvenile hearing a few months later, but they let me go. They sent me to a youth work camp in between. Robbie went to live with one of Mum's sisters. After they released me, I joined the merchant marines. I'd turned sixteen by then, so I was legal to work. I never went back. Robbie writes to me sometimes. I think Mum might still be alive in a rest home in North Cumberland."

Lara left the shelter of the maple, and once again, held out her arms. Her face was drenched with tears as she struggled to contain helpless fury. Trevor fell heavily against her, winding his hands in her hair and saying her name over and over in a broken little boy's voice. "It's all right," she murmured again and again, stroking his hair and shoulders. "Oh Trevor, what a nightmare you lived through. My poor, poor dear. I'm sorry, so very sorry. I'm not being a therapist when I say none of this was your fault. Your parents were monsters."

"But I killed him." Trevor snuffled, his face lost in her hair. "That makes me no better than him."

"Don't you dare compare yourself to that horrible man." Lara pulled back, took his face between her hands, and forced him to meet her eyes, blazing with anger. "You came out of that hellhole a decent, compassionate human being. You did what anyone would have in the same situation. Good God, your poor sister. I had no idea, or I would've pushed you harder to tell me about all this years ago. You've suffered far too long holding yourself responsible for that wretched man and his actions. Your mother wasn't much better. She must've known what was happening to Lizzie, and she didn't do anything to protect her own daughter. Jesus Christ!"

"I reckoned you'd hate me if you knew the whole story." Trevor closed his red-rimmed, swollen eyes, briefly. "My life reads like a goddamned, fucking Greek tragedy."

"No, baby. No, I could never hate you." She stroked his face softly. "I ache for what you had to live through. I'm just so incredibly, terribly sorry. Maybe this can be the beginning of you starting to forgive yourself." Wrapping her arms around him again, she held him against her as tightly as she could. It took a long time before he stopped trembling.

"Come on, dear," she said at length, "Would you like to take a little walk with Gunter and me?"

"Sure, Lara, that would be nice," he said shakily. "Let me run some cold water on my face first."

"I'll get a leash for the puppy," she said. "Meet you on the front porch." She watched him stumble up the back steps and into their house. Dropping her head to her chest, she squeezed her eyes shut in an attempt to obliterate the vision of a young Trevor fighting desperately to save his sister's life. Despite spending years listening to stories of people's pain, she didn't think she'd ever heard anything quite as horrific as Trevor's recitation.

Breathe, she told herself. *Nice cleansing breaths so I can be the partner he needs right now. He took a huge chance sharing all that with me, even after over twenty years. He needs to know how much I love him. And that none of what he pulled out of himself here will make any difference in that love.*

"Jesus Christ," she muttered again, shaking her head. "That's why he'd never tell me any of his dreams, and no wonder his aura had all those dead spots."

"Come on, Gunter," she called to the pup. "Let's go find Daddy."

❧

"…THE Captain on that first ship, he was more like a dad to me than anyone I'd ever known." Now that the worst was out, Trevor was filling in the blanks between when he'd shipped out of Liverpool, and starting work for KLM when he was twenty-three.

"He encouraged me to finish school. So that's what I did when I was off shift. I got correspondence courses and I studied. The other guys, they'd go into town and get drunk and visit the whores, but I wasn't interested." He laughed bitterly. "The straight ones, they thought I was gay. The ones who were gay, well, they just thought I was in denial."

Trevor stopped and turned Lara to face him. They'd made it beyond the end of their street and were heading for Queen Anne Avenue. "You're the only lover I've ever had. I didn't dare tell you when we first met. I figured you'd have thought it odd, since I was past my mid-twenties."

"I'm glad." She hugged him, then bent to untangle Gunter's leash scrunched between them.

"Anyway, since I wasn't buying women or drink, I saved my money. When I applied to Imperial College in London, they accepted me. That's where the degree in International Relations and Linguistics came from. The rest you know. The airline was delighted to hire me since I spoke so many languages and had a four year degree."

As they walked farther from home, the puppy sat down more and more frequently. "We're tiring him out," Lara said. "He's just a little guy. Maybe we should head back. Do you think we should carry him?"

"I'll pick him up for a little bit, but it's good for him to walk. He's nearly nine weeks old. Pretty soon he'll be too big to carry."

As they walked, a thought ran around in her head, nagging for a voice. Finally, she gave in to it. "I think I understand why you were so dead set against getting married," she said remembering the many conversations they'd had on the topic during their early years. "You probably saw our common-law status as a hedge against what you grew up with. And I understand too, why you never told me any of your dreams. You were afraid I'd see something in them."

"You're being a therapist again. I didn't want to pick through my life with you. I never wanted to dredge through the wreckage of my youth with anybody."

"Why'd you finally tell me?" Lara thought she knew, but she was feeling bold.

"Because you'd been badgering me about it for so long, I decided what the hell. If you're going to sodding dump me over this, at least it'll be over and done with, and I won't have to live in fear any longer that you'd somehow find out. That your psychic ability would pluck it out of my head."

Lara gazed compassionately at him. "That's not quite everything, Trev. You told me because you were sick of holding all that inside. Despite the fact it was excruciating to hear the person I love most in all the world relive that nightmare, I'm grateful you trusted me enough to unburden yourself."

Trevor stopped again. Using the arm that wasn't holding Gunter, he turned her face toward his and kissed her long and deliberately. When their lips parted, he said, "I do love you, Lara. Now that I don't have to be afraid anymore of what would happen after you somehow found me out, it finally seems safe to tell you I've wanted to marry you since a few weeks after we met."

Shock widened her eyes, and then unbearable joy whooshed through her. "I'd be honored to be your wife, Trev. I never pushed it because you seemed so dead set against it."

"Even after hearing what I told you?"

"Yes, dear, even after." She kissed him this time until Gunter, sandwiched between them, began to squirm and whine.

CHAPTER 15

The afternoon faded while Lara sat in her study catching up on grading papers. She heard Trevor one floor up, rustling around. Since she was mostly done anyway, she threaded her way up the spiral staircase to ask what he wanted to do about supper. "Wow! What's all this?" she asked, gaping at the disarray.

Trevor stood in the middle of stacks of papers with his back to her. At the sound of her voice, he turned abruptly. "This," he gestured roundly, "is cleaning. I've got stuff shipping from Amsterdam, and I need a place to put it. Plus, if we end up moving, I figure it'd be a good idea to go through things and get rid of a lot of it."

Lara groaned inwardly. She hadn't even begun to think about what it might mean to move. "Good that you're getting a head start," she said, "because you'll probably be the one going through my things too."

"As long as you don't get mad if I throw something away you later decide was irreplaceable."

She perched on the edge of a small beige sofa that butted against a dormer window under the fifth floor's eaves. "Promise." She snorted. "Hell, I probably don't even remember half the stuff I have scattered through this house."

"Wherever we move to, we won't be taking ninety percent of what we own," Trevor said. "We won't need thousands of books to operate a farm. Hell, the books we would need we haven't even acquired yet. What do you want to do for dinner?"

Lara looked around. "However dinner shapes up is fine. Where's Gunter?"

The little dog had figured out the sound of his name because Lara heard a yip from under Trevor's desk just before the sleepy puppy crept into the middle of the room and stretched out his front paws.

"Time to take him out." Trevor scooped up the pup and started down the stairs with Lara close behind. "Back to dinner, so far today we've been lucky. Power's been on. Makes cooking easier. Say, Lara, did you ever try to call that psychic?"

Guilt pricked her. "Not only have I not done that, I left my pager clipped to my bag, and my phone's still in the living room. Haven't checked it all day. Shit, I'll be lucky if someone doesn't turn me into the licensing board for an ethics violation. I can see the headlines now. 'Woman goes on killing spree. When questioned, she claimed it was because she couldn't get hold of her therapist...'"

Leaving Trevor at the junction where one hall led down a few steps to the kitchen and the other up to their living room and library, she recovered her pager. Shutting her eyes for a moment, she willed the screen to be blank...and it was. "Okay," she said to the hallway sprites—or whoever might be listening—"one down, one to go." As soon as she saw her cell phone, her heart fell. Every icon was lit, which meant voice messages, emails, text messages, and instant messages. Who on earth had thought it was a good idea to be so damned available?

She took the phone and pager into the living room. Sinking onto the soft leather sofa, she attacked the voice mails first, pen and pad in hand. There were only two. The first one, from Helen Morgan, said Bethany had been transported to the shelter by helicopter and would Lara please call. The second message was from Lillian. Lara listened to that one twice.

"I hope you won't consider this an imposition, but my friend, Roxanne, said you were going to call me. Since I hadn't heard from you, I thought you might be feeling a bit uncomfortable. Just so you don't have to look for it, my number is…"

While she thought about Lillian and her message, Lara dialed Dr. Morgan. Helen picked up on the first ring. "Lara, that you?"

"Yes, Helen. Sorry it took me a while to get back to you. It's been a tough day."

The doctor snorted, then said, "All my days are tough. Mostly I wanted you to know that Bethany is safe. At least for now. But there was something else."

"What was that about a helicopter?" Lara broke in. "Do you need some money from me? Aren't those pretty expensive?"

Her friend laughed. "Thanks, but it belongs to my daughter. She used to be a military chopper pilot in Iraq. I worried myself silly about her for four years. Anyway, she's done with all that now, and she owns a charter flying service. I asked her if she could help out, and she was more than willing since she's had her own share of, well, the same sort of problems." Helen's voice cracked. "Watch your back, Lara. The husband knows Bethany's not here anymore. He forced his way into the ICU about an hour ago, and then fled before Security could corral him."

"Maybe he thinks she's just been transferred onto the floor." Lara's words sounded hollow to her.

"Not likely. There's more. That bastard held a knife under a nurse's chin—pressed up against her neck—until she told him his wife had been discharged from the hospital. Then he broke her arm like it was spaghetti and somehow managed to elude two armed Security employees."

Lara pushed up off the sofa to go see if the front door was locked. She flicked on the porch light and outdoor floods. "Thanks for letting me know, Helen. I'm not sure what I can do, but I'll let Trevor know, and we'll be alert."

"Call me Monday so I know you made it through the weekend."

Helen's curt voice echoed through the wireless connection. "I have to go, they're paging me."

Lara started to say goodbye, then realized Helen had already disconnected. Making her way back to the sofa, she scrolled rapidly through her messages, deleting some and answering others. She was just finishing up when Trevor and Gunter came into the room.

"He was a good boy," Trevor said, patting the pup's furry head. When he looked at Lara's drawn face, he refocused instantly. "What's wrong? You look like you just saw a ghost."

She told him about her conversation with Helen. Trevor bit his lower lip and glanced at his watch as she was talking. "I think Big Five should still be open," he said once she finished. "I'm going to run down there and get a shotgun."

"Don't you need a permit or something?"

"Not for a shotgun."

"I'm coming too. I don't want to be here by myself right now."

"Looks like we'll all be going, then. Guess we should take your car. The Mercedes roadster's too small for the lot of us."

The Bach Etude from her cell phone startled both of them. Glancing at the caller ID, she saw an international string of numbers. With a sense of apprehension, she pushed the green phone icon. "Dr. McInnis here."

"Well, Doctor, are you feeling a bit better today?" Dr. Himmelschaun's cultured tones raked across her nerves like barbed wire.

"I wasn't feeling badly yesterday. What do you want?" She made her voice brisk, dismissive.

"Just to see how you are. Are you usually this rude to strangers? I tried to help you when you called here with a problem." Mild reproach flooded the fiber optics of the cellular phone system.

"Yes, well, I'm fine. I really have nothing to say to you. Why are you continuing to call me?"

"I always check on my patients—"

"I am *not* your patient," she cut in. "Listening to a colleague's dream does not constitute the beginnings of a doctor-patient relationship. I really need to go."

"Please do not hang up. You are in danger, as is everyone who has had that dream. You need me, Dr. McInnis. It would be a grave error on your part to sever your connection with me."

She ground her teeth together. "We have no connection. Don't call me again. Do you understand?" The line went dead in her hand.

"What do you suppose he wants?" Trevor had begun gathering things so they could leave. "It's unnerving he won't take no for an answer."

"How do you think I feel?" She reached up, pulled her hair into a loose pony tail and wound it into an unpinned bun behind her head. "How did he get my cell number? I didn't use that phone for any of my calls to the Institute, and even if I had my number is blocked. He's stalking me for some atavistic purpose I can only guess at. Shit, between him and Beauchamp I'm so rattled I scarcely know whether I'm coming or going."

"Come on. We're not going to solve any of this standing here."

She followed Trevor out of the house and trailed down the steps, bag slung over her shoulder. Before she got to street level, she peered anxiously up and down their block, searching the shadows for…for what?

I've become a target and I don't understand why. Or what I can do about it.

LARA WAITED in the car to keep Gunter company, while Trevor went into the store. No time like the present for dealing with something she was ambivalent about, so she groped around in her bag until she found her phone, pulled up the call log, and scrolled until she came to Lillian's number.

"Dr. McInnis. I am so glad you called back." The voice at the other end of the line was rich and honeyed.

"How did you know it was me?" Lara felt mystified. "My outgoing number couldn't have shown up on your phone."

"Oh, I just had a feeling," Lillian laughed warmly. Lara could almost feel a soft scented breeze rustle around her. "I'd love to meet you, Lara. Would any time tomorrow be convenient? After four in the afternoon, say?"

"Where do you live? And do you mind if I bring my fiancé?"

"So you're finally planning on getting married. That's marvelous. Good decision the two of you just made." She lowered her tone conspiratorially. "The Winter Solstice is perfect for weddings. Very auspicious."

Lara was gripped by an irrational desire to punch the red phone icon and end the call. *How much does this woman know about me, anyway?* Her palm began to sweat, and she gripped the phone tighter.

"I'm sorry," Lillian said contritely, almost as if she sensed Lara's ambivalence. "That was forward of me. Since Roxanne told you about me, I assumed it wouldn't surprise you that I know certain things. Anyway, there'll be time tomorrow to clear everything up. I live in Magnolia. It's the brick house on the corner of Magnolia Boulevard and West Dravus Street. Shall we say around four or four thirty?"

"I think we can make that." Despite saying the words, Lara was far from certain she'd actually honor the commitment she just made.

"Be sure to call if you change your mind. Bye now, dearie. I'm looking forward to meeting both of you. Oh, and feel free to bring that puppy too. I do love dogs. He'll be just fine here."

When Trevor pulled open the driver's door and reached over the seat to dump the long bag he carried, Lara was frowning at her phone.

"Something wrong?" he asked, continuing on without waiting for her to answer. "I got a twelve gauge, eight shot pump action. Should work fine for our purposes. Got some ammunition too. I was gone so long because I spent time looking at deer rifles. But they didn't have ammo for them—"

"I talked with Lillian." Lara broke into his light-hearted chatter.

"We have an appointment to go see her tomorrow at around four. Unless I decide not to go."

Trevor pulled the door shut, clipped his seat belt, and started the engine. "Maybe you should tell me what happened from the beginning."

Lara leaned back against the seat and shut her eyes. *What exactly had happened?* "I'm not sure, Trev, but it was sort of bizarre. She knows things about me—and some stuff about you too—despite the fact we've never met her. For instance, she knew we'd decided to get married. She even started planning the wedding, picked a date and everything. Somehow she also knows we have a dog."

"What?" He looked stricken. "The weirdness quotient lately's been ridiculous. Sodding hell. I miss normal, whatever *that* used to be."

"Yeah, me too."

He fell silent. When his words came, they had a reluctant feel to them. "I think we should go see her, anyway. If she's truly clairvoyant, or prescient, or whatever, it seems she's your best hope of learning more about your psychic side."

"I suppose you're right." Lara chewed on her lower lip. "If we met up with clairvoyants every day, it'd feel less peculiar."

Gunter, apparently feeling left out of the conversation, yipped his agreement from his crate in the back seat.

"Did you take him out, Lara?"

"No. Guess we ought to do that before we head home."

Trevor had just pulled out of the Big Five parking lot. He circled around and pulled back in. "Yes, we should. He'd be happier."

BACK IN THE car and headed for home, Lara's phone rang. Glancing at the screen, she noticed it was from a private number. With all her inner senses sounding klaxon warning horns, she answered her cell.

"Hey, Doc. Didn't think you'd pick up, but it was wise of you not to ignore me." Ken Beauchamp's unmistakable voice slithered through the phone and clutched at her stomach, leaving threads of fear in its wake. "Where is my wife, *Doctor*? You must know. If you're as smart as I think you are, you'll tell me, and then I won't have to hurt you. Or that pretty-boy Brit boyfriend of yours."

"Actually, I don't know, Mr. Beauchamp. And I don't appreciate your threats." Lara aimed for a casual nonchalance, but knew she was failing since her mouth was dry as dust.

"You're lying, you fucking slut. Where is Bethany? She's my wife. She's carrying my son, and I want both of them back."

"Then you should have treated them better." The elusive anger she sought to lend her some backbone finally showed up. Grasping at it, she used the energy to end the call. Lara turned the phone off, her fingers trembling so badly she could barely push the buttons.

"Maybe we shouldn't go home tonight." Trevor's voice sounded strained. "We're all here. We could check into a motel. I'm still feeling pretty wiped out from this morning." He sighed deeply, and a bit shakily. "Actually, I'm not sure I can take another tense night at home listening for untoward sounds."

"Oh, I don't know—" She paled, and then a vision slammed her against the soft leather of the BMW's front seat. Ken Beauchamp was in their house. As Lara watched in macabre fascination, he shoved something under their bed, pulled it out and double-checked a dial on the strange-looking device, then pushed it back into place. Next he pulled back the quilts on their carefully made bed while stroking the front of his pants. Lara saw the bulge of his excitement.

No! she screamed, except no sound came out. *That's our bed. Don't you dare.* The vision held her, riveted. She couldn't get away from it. There was no place to go. She couldn't even block out the disgusting scene by closing her eyes, since they were already shut.

He pulled his cock out, gripped it in his right hand. A drop of semen gleaming on the end of it dribbled onto her bedding as he fondled himself with well-practiced efficiency. It only took a few strokes before he ejaculated onto their sheets. Grinning in satisfaction, he pulled the quilts back into place, zipped his fly up, and strode out of their bedroom.

The scene shifted abruptly to the Jung Institute. "Hah! I knew I could capture you if I waited until you dropped into a vision state. Your records here told me everything I needed to know." A white-haired man with a pasty complexion, wearing an old-fashioned black suit with a bow tie, stood in front of the ornate fireplace in the front parlor. He was tall, stoop-shouldered, and had a small paunch. Bottomless dark eyes held hers. "You have changed little since you studied here," he said silkily, and licked his lips suggestively.

I've got to get out of trance, she thought frantically. *How do I do that? If I let this run its course, he'll never let me go.* She tried to move her body. While she felt herself thrash in the seat, the man she assumed must be Himmelschaun remained stubbornly present.

After a time, he smiled slightly, displaying yellowed uneven teeth. "I can come to you any time I want to from the shadow world. Never forget that. Next time I call, I expect you to talk with me. There are things we must discuss." As abruptly as he'd materialized, he was gone.

When she came back into herself, the car wasn't moving. She pried her eyes open and fought bewilderment left in the wake of her sending. Trevor rested his head on the steering wheel, his hands balled into fists.

"Are you all right?" she gasped. "Did we have an accident?"

He lifted his head and turned to gaze at her. Fine lines carved by worry etched into the corners of his eyes. "No, not an accident. I thought I should pull over, though." He swallowed hard, his throat working with emotion. "You were having one of your spells. It was obvious you needed help, except I didn't know what to do. I parked because I didn't want to split my attention betwixt the car and you. You were battering yourself against the seat, Lara, and screaming. Ach, it felt like I was small again and trying to help Lizzie." His voice broke and he drew a deep, shuddering breath. "For God sakes, tell me what happened."

She had an almost-overpowering desire to urinate. Glancing around, she saw they were in a Safeway parking lot. Pushing the car door open, she said tightly. "I've got to find a bathroom. If I don't, I'll wet my pants."

As she stood in the harsh iridescent lighting of the supermarket bathroom, Lara splashed water on her face after she'd washed her hands. Her crotch was damp because she hadn't quite made the toilet in time. She still felt wobbly—and absolutely furious—from what she'd seen. Desperately frightened too.

What if something like that happened while I was driving? Or in session with a patient? Taking a shaky breath, and then another, she waved her hands under the hot air blower, then headed back outside. She found Trevor, with Gunter on a leash, exploring the grassy perimeter of the nearly-empty lot. The puppy raced to Lara, tugging on his tether and barking excitedly.

"I was about to go in there and get you." Trevor reached for her hand with his free one, but she waved him off, bent, and fondled the little dog, cooing to him.

"Do we need anything?" she asked. "Store's pretty empty. Not much there to buy, but not many shoppers either." *Guess I don't want to talk about what happened. What a lame diversion I just suggested.*

Trevor shook his head. "Nope. I stocked up a couple days ago. Tell me what you saw, please. Is it safe to go home? Or do you even know?"

She scrubbed her hands down her face before answering. "I think Beauchamp put a bomb under our bed, so we need to call the cops. They can take the bomb, or whatever it is, somewhere and dismantle it. Assuming it hasn't already blown our house to bits. And that creep jerked off on our sheets." She shuddered. "He is just such a nasty, dirty, horrid pervert." Riddled with disgust, she recalled the self-satisfied look on Ken's moon-shaped face as he'd tucked his dripping penis back into his pants.

"If that's the worst he did to the house, we got off cheap," Trevor said, mirroring the thoughts she'd had a couple days before about their ruined stained glass panel.

"He must've called me from our house." She was beginning to think more clearly. "So even if I told him what he wanted to know, he'd already planted whatever's beneath our bed."

"Come on. Let's go." Trevor tugged at her arm. "You need to call the police, and we need to get home. I want to be sure that bloody arsehole didn't damage anything."

"There's more," she muttered.

He looked shocked. "How could there be? What you just told me is bad enough."

"Yeah, I thought so too. Himmelschaun must know something about psychic states. He showed up right after Ken faded away, dragged my astral self to the Institute, and threatened me."

She dropped her head into her hands. "Christ, it's not safe for me to have visions anymore, except I have no control over them. If he can lie in wait for me like he just did and commandeer my consciousness when I'm vulnerable…"

Lara raised her head slowly; her tormented gaze sought his. "I am so fucking screwed," she said in a strained voice. "I've never been this frightened in my life, and I don't know what to do about it. There's nowhere to run where I can get away from any of this." Her eyes burned, but tears were out of the question. Anger simmered, fraying her nerve ends and filling her with a twisted energy. For the first time ever, she understood on a visceral level how one human being could kill another.

Yes, I'd do just about anything to get rid of those two bastards.

"Let's go home, Trev. One problem at a time. At least we can *do* something about the bomb and our sheets."

CHAPTER 16

*H*ours later, the last of the bomb squad was departing. Lara had stripped everything off their bed before the cops arrived, which was expeditious because they'd ordered her out of her bedroom, chastised her for going in there in the first place, and barred her from further access. The police, appearing other-worldly in their bomb suits, had looked at her as if she were mad when she'd told them exactly where to find the bomb. *Well, perhaps I am,* she thought.

After being exiled and rebuked, she ran into Trevor on her way down the stairs with her arms piled high with bedding. "Crikey, Lara. All you really needed to wash was the sheets. He didn't come on our quilt, did he?"

"No, but they took the sheets. Said they needed them for DNA analysis." Impulsively, she heaved the mass of cloth in her hands over the stair railing. It fell down the center of the spiral staircase and landed with a splat in a heap on the first floor.

"Trevor." Her eyes burned into his. "If we hadn't paid twenty-five hundred bucks for the mattress, I'd burn it and buy another. It's going to take some doing for me to get back into our bed after seeing what he did to it." Furious at the universe, she stomped down the stairs to collect the laundry.

Trevor trailed after her, shaking his head. "Here, let me help you."

Her temper cooled as quickly as it flared. When they reached the first floor, she stepped over the rail and handed heaps of bedding to Trevor. "Sorry," she mumbled. "I'm just edgy."

"You have every right to be," he replied. "I'm not at my best either, right about now. Lucky the power's not out. It'd be tough to wash all this by heating water on the stove and pouring it through a wringer washer like we did when I was a kid."

"You never told me about that. Sounds like you'll have a far more complete skill set than me if we trade all this," she swung her arms wide, "for a simpler life." Lara rolled her eyes, still feeling out of control.

"Come on, wench, let's at least get the mattress pad going in the washer. I know those sheets they took were your favorites, but we do have others." Trevor smiled at her, his exquisitely blue eyes glowing like exotic pearls.

The detective who seemed to be in charge waylaid them in the laundry room an hour later. "Might I have a word with the two of you? I'm Detective Archer." The tall, spare blond officer held out his hand. His men, in their bulky outfits, had already left.

"Of course." Lara pushed her hair out of her eyes. She'd spent most of the time the officers were rooting through her house ferrying clothes from the washer to the backyard clothesline. She was on her third—and hopefully last—load. "Just let me get this quilt on the line. Trev, why don't you take the detective to the front room?"

"Sure." Trevor motioned to the man. "Right this way."

Lara joined them and settled on the sofa across from the detective. Gunter, worn out from the excitement of so many strangers in his home, was curled up in his box making little bleating noises in his sleep.

"So, Doctor, could you tell me how you knew there was a bomb here so precisely you could even tell us where it was? Did the perp call and threaten you or something?" The detective skewered her with curious blue eyes.

Lara felt heat rise from her chest and sweep over her head. She forced herself to look at Detective Archer. "Ken Beauchamp did call me," she admitted, "but that's not how I knew about the bomb."

"Would you care to explain that statement?" Detective Archer looked tired. "The sooner I understand what happened here, the sooner I can leave."

Nothing for it but to tell him. She inhaled sharply and ground her teeth together. "This will probably sound odd to you," she began, "but I've had psychic abilities ever since I was a child. I had a vision, and I saw Beauchamp in this house pushing the bomb under our bed and masturbating on our sheets."

Lara held her breath and gripped the sides of the sofa so hard her knuckles whitened, as she stared apprehensively at the policeman, waiting for him to shoot her a look reserved for crazies.

The detective raised his eyebrows. While he did look mildly surprised, he didn't seem shocked. "I thought it must have been something like that," he said. "Either the perp threatened you very specifically, or you knew via some other route." He hesitated. "Guess you don't tell anyone much about the paranormal stuff, huh?"

"Does it show?"

Detective Archer smiled. "Yes, Doctor, it does. If you held onto those couch cushions any harder, the stuffing would start spilling out."

Embarrassment heated her face even further, and she uncurled her fingers, placing her hands demurely in front of her.

"Now, if you'd done that to begin with, you probably could have gotten away with telling me most anything." The detective grinned. When he smiled, it made his otherwise austere face almost handsome. "You must know we use psychics in police work. That means we believe in what you can do."

"I didn't know that." Trevor, who'd been quiet, sounded intrigued.

"Don't you two ever watch that thing?" Archer gestured at the large television mounted on one wall.

"Oh sure, we watch DVDs," Trevor replied. "But we don't have a cable or satellite subscription. Never have."

"Smart." Detective Archer rose to leave. "Bunch of junk on there. I don't watch it because it reminds me too much of work. Eh, what am I thinking? I can't leave yet." He sat back down abruptly, his forehead creased in thought. "There's a good likelihood Beauchamp is somewhere in this neighborhood, watching us move his baby out of your house. Fire-setters and bombers, they all like to be around to bask in the glory of their handiwork when it goes off. Or spreads, in the case of fires. That bomb had a remote switch, so he would've needed to be close by to tell when you got home. Anyway, I'll bet he's still out there and mad as hell right about now. It'd probably be a good call for the two of you to go to a motel for the night."

Trevor looked questioningly at Lara. "I suggested that earlier."

"Does Ken Beauchamp have a criminal record?" Lara stood and paced up and down the spacious living room. "I have a right to know."

The detective snorted. "Not exactly."

"What does *that* mean?" She looked keenly at him, seeking the truth.

"It means he's part of the Hernandez family. He's been implicated in things from running guns and whores to selling drugs and fixing horse races, but we've never been able to get any charges to stick. Maybe all that will change now, since we actually got a sample of his DNA."

Archer balled his hands into fists and drew his lips together in a thin line. "The modern legal system is *not* on our side. The Hernandez family always makes sure Beauchamp has the best attorneys, and so far he's ended up with a slap on the hand. Or he walks. They take care of all their operatives that way. It's not unique to him."

Lara thought about the court-ordered marriage counseling, furious all over again that she'd been duped into providing what she never would have, had she known the truth of things at the outset. "There's a University Hospital employee who could identify him. Dr. Helen Morgan told me he attacked a nurse and broke her arm."

"We know. We've already taken a statement from her. But now we can't find him to haul him in."

"If you're so sure he's in this neighborhood, why don't you search with dogs or something?" Trevor got to his feet. "It's starting to rain. I'm going to pull that wash off the line and start some of it in the dryer. Back in a minute."

"Does that mean I can't talk you into leaving, at least for tonight?" The detective watched Lara as she trod heavily back and forth.

"I don't know," she snapped irritably and felt contrite the second the words were out. "Look, it's not you. I'm just really, really tired. We didn't get much sleep the past couple nights. Hey," she looked questioningly at him as an idea took shape. "Could we have something like a rent-a-cop here between now and morning? He could stay downstairs."

"They're pretty expensive."

"I can afford it. Is there someone I can call?"

"How about one of my off-shift officers? They moonlight, and at least I'd know you were in competent hands."

"Fine. Could you arrange it, or would I need to call?"

"I'll get someone for you. And I'll stay until they get here." Detective Archer pulled his cell phone out and tapped its display.

"Excellent. I'll run and see if Trev needs help with that laundry."

Detective Archer looked up from his phone. "You do that. I'll be right here."

Lara pushed their back door open against a brisk wind. A storm had blown in quickly, and rain pounded on the windows in big splattery gouts. She was worried the linens would be so wet even the dryer wouldn't have them done in time for bed. "Trev?" she called, hunting for him.

"In the laundry room," he said.

She dragged the rest of the linen off the line and found him. While they arranged damp items waiting for the dryer, she said, "No way all this stuff will get dry. Let's make up the bed with a couple old quilts and call it even. I'm exhausted, but we should eat something before we go to bed."

"What about the motel?" He furled his brows at her. "Now it's not just me who thinks it's a good idea."

"Archer's getting us a rent-a-cop for the night."

Trevor raised his eyebrows another notch. "Hadn't thought of that one. Maybe it's a smart compromise."

"Why don't you see if the pooch needs to go out? I'm going to throw a Thai Cuisine dinner in the wave. What do you want?"

Trevor made a face. "Not frozen mank, that's for sure. Don't worry about me. I'm not very hungry. Haven't been all day. I'll just have a quick bowl of muesli with some yogurt and blueberries."

"Sounds like girl food to me."

"Even if the girl in the house doesn't like it?"

"Ick, yogurt tastes like boiled snot. I'll check on Detective Archer before I handcraft my gourmet supper." She trotted out of the room.

One of the long-running jokes between them revolved around Lara being an abysmal cook. Before Trevor entered her life, if meals weren't frozen, canned, or pre-prepared, she didn't eat. Her early experiments with cooking convinced her she had absolutely no knack for food preparation.

She found the detective stretched out in a corner chair with his feet up on an ottoman. When he saw her, he quickly placed his feet back on the floor and muttered, "Sorry."

"Make yourself comfortable," she urged. "That's why there's a cover on that foot-stool, so you can actually use it. Did you find someone to play guard for us tonight?"

"No," he replied tersely. "I haven't. Everyone I called is either working another job or tied up with their families. So I guess it will be me. I ordered a pizza. Hope that's okay with you two."

"Did you get enough to share?" she asked hopefully. "If not, where'd you order from? I can call and add to it."

"Giovanni's," he said, and the corners of his mouth twitched into the barest ghost of a smile. "I probably didn't get enough for two—or three—so if you want something, you'll need to call them."

Lara smiled back. "Let me see if Trevor wants pizza. He might, if he knew it was an option." Loping back toward the laundry room, she practically ran into Trevor with Gunter's leash in hand.

"Whoa, why the hurry?"

"The detective is staying. He ordered pizza. It sounded good to me, so I thought I'd get some too. Do you want any?"

"Does that mean Detective Archer is our rent-a-cop for tonight?" When she nodded, he replied, "That's good. I like him. Seems like a really solid bloke. Sure, pizza would be great. Where'd he order from?"

"Giovanni's."

"Brilliant! Let's get a large of that one with the whole wheat crust, pesto sauce, feta, mushrooms, and tomatoes."

"Done." She gave him a thumbs up and went to get her phone.

After polishing off three generous slices of pizza, chased by Fat Tire Amber Ale, Lara fell asleep the moment she adopted a prone position. While the mattress pad had dried, there hadn't been time to pop anything else into the dryer. It continued to rain, so there was little hope of using the outdoor clothesline for assistance. Besides, clothes never dried hanging outside at night in Seattle, even when it wasn't raining; it was just too damp.

Wrapped in the coverless duvet and another old bedspread, Lara woke once to utter blackness, snuggled closer to Trevor's warmth, and drifted immediately back to sleep. The next time she awakened, light from a quarter moon shone through one of their windows, and Gunter was whining softly. "Trev?" She reached across the bed, hunting for him.

"I'm here, Lara. Be quiet." She heard the click of shells being loaded into their new shotgun.

Slipping out of bed, she padded noiselessly to where he stood next to the large dormer window. "What?" She barely breathed the word.

"Went down to take Gunter out. Heard something when I was coming back up the stairs."

"Did you use the radio Archer gave us to call him?"

"I tried. But he didn't answer."

"When you took the pup downstairs, did you see the detective?"

"No, but I didn't go through the living room."

"What exactly did you hear?" Before Trevor could answer, Gunter began barking. The shrill sound punctuated the night like bullets.

Even young as he was, the dog had far more acute hearing than either of them. Suddenly cold, she ferreted a fleece robe out of the closet and wrapped it around herself. Lara knelt in front of the puppy's box and opened the door. The small dog practically leaped into her arms, but at least he stopped barking.

Two gunshots rang out, followed by the sharp boom of breaking glass.

Cursing her over-active sympathetic nervous system and sensitive bladder, she tucked the puppy into their bed, and then hurried into the bathroom to pee. When she came back into the bedroom, she whispered to Trevor, "What do you think we should do?"

"Wait," he snapped. "We wait. Not much point in calling 911, since they're already here."

"What if Archer's hurt and can't call for back-up?"

"If nothing happens in the next five minutes, I'll take the gun and make sure he's all right Dawn's not far off. I've got the shotgun trained on the door. If it opens, I'll blast whatever comes through it. Get back to bed where you can keep yourself and the pup out of the way."

The unmistakable sound of footsteps mounting the risers filled her ears and Lara dove back into the bed, holding Gunter close. The tableau from a couple nights ago, when they'd listened to the stairs creak while Beauchamp hunted for an exit, replayed like an unsolicited grade B movie.

Her heart pounded in her ears, and she had to pee again. The footsteps drew closer. They were only a few steps away from the level of their bedroom. She tried to swallow, but didn't have any saliva.

"Dr. McInnis. Mr. Denoble. Open your door, please. I'm hurt, but he's gone. Think I winged him."

Oh, thank God. Thank God. Not Beauchamp. It's not his voice. Relief swept through her so dizzying she had to shut her eyes as she fought to orient herself.

Trevor cracked their bedroom door, shotgun still at the ready. As soon as he verified it really was the detective, he clicked on the safety and lowered the gun, pulling the door fully open.

Brad Archer had a hand clapped over his shoulder. Blood welled between his fingers. Lara certainly wasn't an expert, but it looked like a serious wound to her.

"Do you want me to call an ambulance?" she asked. Lara tossed back the covers and stood, still giddy Ken Beauchamp wasn't in their house any longer.

The detective shook his head. "It's a clean wound," he said through gritted teeth. "Bullet went right through my shoulder. Just needs to be bandaged. I called the station. One of our medics is on his way over to do some first aid." He sat heavily on a chair in their bedroom. "The K-9 unit is on the way too. I'm sure I shot that bastard. They just need to track the blood trail and we'll have him."

"You hope," Trevor muttered.

"Our home's been turned into a war zone." Lara spread her hands helplessly.

"Yes, it has. I may not have the whole story, but I think I got most of it from that report you filed with Sergeant Nelson a few days ago. The way Beauchamp sees it, you've stolen his wife and child, and he's waging war against you to get even. You won't have any peace so long as he's at large." The detective winced, shifting positions. A trail of blood dripped onto the hardwood floor. "I hate to tell you this, but it's better if you know. Even if we manage to apprehend Beauchamp, you'll still be targeted by others in the Hernandez family out to avenge their fallen comrade."

The front doorbell rang. "Must be my men." Detective Archer stumbled to his feet. Where he reached to steady himself on a nearby wall, he left a bloody handprint. "Sorry," he said, eying the stain. "Cold water and vinegar should take care of it."

After the detective left, Lara turned to Trevor. Her body shook from delayed shock and fear. "Hold me, please."

He gathered her into his arms and ran his hands up and down her back. "Let's get some more clothes for you."

"It's nerves," she managed through chattering teeth. "Too much adrenaline. What I need is to go out for a run, but I can't do that with Beauchamp on the loose."

"How about a hot shower? That should help. I'll take one with you. It'll be like the old days right after we first met."

She smiled weakly at him. "I do love you, Trevor, but sex is the last thing I need right now. I'm still grossed out by him jerking off in our bed."

Trevor pulled her closer. His heart beat solidly beneath her ear, and she took comfort from the sound. "I don't want sex. I'm still dealing with reliving all that stuff I told you yesterday. As long as I left it stuffed in a little locker in the back of my mind, it didn't bother me so much, but now… I'm not sure I could make love to you, even if you wanted to. What I had in mind is a nice hot shower, with the body jets turned up high. Sound appealing?"

"More than appealing. It sounds wonderful. We should have plenty of time while they dress Archer's shoulder." She pushed their outer bedroom door closed, then turned and took his face between her hands. "If you feel like talking more about what you told me yesterday, I'd be glad to listen. Sometimes it helps to say the words a few more times. If you can do that, the painful part of the memory lessens. And you stop blaming yourself." She kissed him lightly. "Think about it. It's an open offer."

Gunter whined from amidst their tumbled covers.

"I'll put him back in his box," Trevor said. "He was just out before things went to hell, so he should be okay for at least an hour."

Lara shrugged out of her robe, leaving it in a pile on the floor. She skirted past Trevor and turned on the taps in their over-sized tub. The green-veined Italian marble darkened as water bounced off its shiny surface.

Over the roar of the shower jets, she thought she heard, "About that offer, Lara. I'll consider talking more about what happened. Truly, I will."

CHAPTER 17

The three of them sat in the living room nursing coffees. Brad's shoulder was wrapped in a sling and swathe, and the tense lines in his face had softened. Gunter ran from one side of the room to the other chasing a ball. He'd bat it, and the ball would careen off a wall or a piece of furniture. Then the pup yipped and bounded after the toy again.

When the detective's radio crackled, they all jumped. Even the puppy stopped what he was doing and held his head quizzically to one side, one ear akimbo. Detective Archer snatched up his radio. "Archer here."

"Suspect apprehended. You got him good, sir. Right through the thigh. He's lost a lot of blood. Requesting secure transport to Harborview Hospital."

"Understood. Transport approved."

"You got him?" Lara was incredulous. For a moment, she felt ecstatic, then she remembered the officer's earlier pronouncement. "This doesn't mean we're out of the woods."

"You've probably bought yourself a couple days' grace." The detective sounded gruff, and Lara assumed his shoulder was killing him. "If Beauchamp dies, you'll be in a world of hurt. If he just goes to

167

federal prison, you'll be in somewhat better shape. Depends what else the family has on their plate. You may be small potatoes if they've got bigger fish to fry." He chortled. "Sorry about the food analogies. I'm not at my best right now. No sleep and my shoulder hurts like hell."

"Bastard's probably too mean to die. Like my Dad." Trevor looked shocked after the words spilled out, but a small spurt of happiness swept through Lara. The unintentional slip meant he was starting to heal. Being able to talk about the man who'd terrorized him—out loud and in mixed company—was a strong first step.

"I've got to get back to the station." Detective Archer hauled himself to his feet. "Keep the doors and windows locked. Keep that shotgun of yours loaded, and the alarm system on—if you can separate out the internal beams from the ones linked to the doors and windows. And hey, thanks for the coffee."

They sat with their coffees for a long time after the detective left. Gunter was sleeping, tipped over on his back, legs spread, vulnerable pink tummy showing. "At least he's feeling safe," Trevor observed, grinning ruefully. "Too bad it's not contagious."

Lara snorted. "I feel like I've been run over by a truck. Maybe we could go back to bed for a couple hours and then catch brunch somewhere. Or an early supper, depending how long we sleep."

"Why don't you run on up?" Trevor suggested. "Once Gunter stirs, I'll take him outside. Then I want to sweep up the glass from that side window and fit some plywood into the hole. Good thing there's some left. Oh yeah, and there's the rest of the bedding that needs drying too." He cocked his head to the side, listening. "Come to think of it, I haven't heard the dryer for a while now. Think I'll see if that duvet cover's done. Funny I wouldn't have heard the buzzer."

Lara leaned her head back against the couch cushions. She'd just closed her eyes when she heard Trevor spit out a string of expletives. "What the hell?" she muttered and dragged herself off the couch to see what was wrong.

"Bloody sodding fuck. Goddamn power's off again," drifted up from the laundry room.

She sank back onto the cushions. "Oh," she mumbled, giggling irreverently. "Is that all?" Losing the electricity seemed trivial compared with their other problems. By the time Trevor came into the living room with the duvet cover draped over his arm, her fit of giggles had morphed into a full-blown laughing jag.

"I fail to see the humor in having to hang this sopping lump of fabric over our dining room table," he said as he stood there awkwardly, trying to keep the wet edges of their bedding off the hardwood floor.

"It's not you or the laundry." She laughed so hard tears streamed down her face. "I don't give a rat's ass about the electricity anymore."

"Not quite sure I understand." Trevor looked mystified.

"I need sleep," she gasped finally, realizing she was treading a fine edge of hysteria. Swiping at her tear-damp face with the back of one hand, she lurched to her feet and helped Trevor spread the duvet cover before stumbling dazedly toward the stairs.

When she opened her eyes, sunlight streamed through the bedroom's west-facing window, so she knew it had to be midafternoon. Maybe even later. Reveling in having had several uninterrupted hours of sleep, she looked over at Trevor's side of the bed. He was dead to the world, head resting on one arm, mouth slightly ajar. Curls framed his perfect face, and blond stubble covered his unshaven chin. As she watched him sleep, she grieved for the tragedy of his early life.

A muted yip from the crate told her Gunter needed to go out. Moving as quietly as possible so she wouldn't bother Trevor, Lara crept into the bathroom and hurried through what she needed to do. When she came back into the bedroom, Trevor sat on his side of their bed pulling on his sneakers. "Dog needs out," he said fuzzily.

"I'll take him. I'm already up." She scooted her feet into a pair of slippers, tossed on a sweater, and bent to open the kennel door. "Come on sweetie," she invited. "Come to Momma." Tucking him under one arm, she headed for the stairs.

Lara flicked light switches to check if the power was still out.

Wonder if the alarm works if there's no power? Once she thought about it, she remembered the system had come with some sort of backup, but it wouldn't last forever. She picked up her phone from the front hall table so she could check messages while waiting for Gunter to do his business.

"Damn!" She clapped a hand to her forehead as she saw a reminder for the appointment with Lillian. "We've got time, yet," she said half aloud. "It's only a twenty minute drive to Magnolia." As soon as Gunter was done, she raced back up the stairs. The little dog, frightened of climbing the open risers, yowled piteously at the foot of the staircase.

"Trev!" Lara shot back into the bedroom. "You've got to get up. We have that appointment with Lillian. Maybe she can help me figure out how to keep Himmelschaun out of my trance states."

"Oh yeah, that. I'd forgotten."

"Well, so did I. The only reason we didn't miss it entirely was that damned phone, and the reminder I put in the calendar."

A satisfied smile spread over his face. "I knew the phone would be a big help to you. It'll only take me five minutes to throw on some clothes, love. Then I'll be ready to go."

Lara pawed through her drawers. Selecting a pair of jeans, she snugged into them, following that choice with a multi-colored blouse and a black cashmere shawl. Hurriedly pulling on some socks, she scuffled around in the bottom of her closet and found an old pair of black leather boots. After brushing a fine layer of dust off, she slid her feet into them. "Got to get back to Gunter," she said and ran down the stairs to comfort the unhappy puppy.

"Have you thought more about leaving Seattle?" Lara was through catching up with her phone—again. They were just crossing the Magnolia Bridge, so they had a few more minutes for conversation.

"Do you want to stay here in Washington?" he asked.

She rested her chin on one fist and considered his question. "I don't know," she murmured finally. "I suppose I figured we'd stay here. It would make it easier to move if we didn't have to go very far." She hesitated a beat. "To be honest, I was hoping we could buy something and set it up sort of like a summer house. Then if things did get worse, we'd have a place to go. Otherwise, we could just use it for little getaways."

"I'd thought the same thing," he agreed, "at least about the location aspect. But eastern Oregon might work well also. Basically, we need to be close enough to the crest of the Cascades to have a ready source of year-round water. We'll need at least some sun so we can grow things, which means locating east of the crest.'

He glanced over at her. "Look Lara, I know you don't want to leave. Hell, there're all those patients of yours to be dealt with. Not to mention your students. Wherever we choose, you need to plan on us being there for the long haul—and being self-sufficient—because that's how things seem to be shaping up."

"Maybe some government will figure something out," she offered feebly. Never an aficionado of current events, she struggled to recall something she'd read on the Internet. "Aren't they culling through shale in Canada, or burning sugar cane in Brazil or something like that?"

Trevor laughed. "I love you, Lara. Yeah, they're doing a bunch of things, but it's all stuff they should have done twenty or thirty years ago. We're badly behind the eight ball here, and at least from what I've read, there's no way we can ever catch up. No matter how you slice it, our modern way of life is all but buggered. The only ones who shouldn't be affected much are third world countries where they still live at a subsistence level. Things will get worse there too, but it won't be as noticeable."

She drew her brows together. "I need to mull this over. So far I've got lots of questions, but not many answers." Lara tried to connect the recurring dream, Himmelschaun's threats, and Trevor's pronouncements of gloom and doom. She didn't care much for any of the scenarios that popped up, each one grimmer than the last.

"Corner of Dravus and Magnolia Boulevard?" Trevor cut into her bleak thoughts, sounding irritated. "I've made three transits of this misshapen block, and I still can't find the bloody house." He pulled the BMW to a stop, backed up so he'd be the requisite twenty feet from a stop sign, and turned off the engine. "We need to get out and walk. I don't think we'll find her house any other way."

"Okay. I'll get the pup. There're only four corners and she did say it was a brick house." Lara popped the hatch and opened Gunter's box. He wriggled happily, but had learned to sit reasonably quietly until the leash was clipped to his collar.

Lara lifted the puppy to the ground and glanced at the neighborhood. The houses all looked as though they'd been built in the nineteen forties or fifties. Each was unique and well-kept, with manicured lawns and attractive landscaping.

"Ready?" Trevor held out his hand for the puppy's leash.

"Sure. I'll stop gawking. I don't think I've been in this part of Seattle before. It reminds me of a more prosperous version of Queen Anne."

"Her house has to be over there," Trevor said, pointing to what looked like a tree-filled lot. "None of the houses on the other three corners are brick."

"There's nothing there but trees," Lara protested, peering closely in the direction he'd indicated to get a better look.

"Maybe we need to be closer to see. If she's a witch, don't they all have that Gaia-esque connection?"

"First off, Trev, I don't know what she is." Lara dredged up what she knew about Gaia, primordial Greek goddess who personified the Earth, before adding, "I don't really know all that much about Wicca, but I certainly see a connection between Gaia and the natural world. Sounds like you might know something, though."

He shrugged. "The whole Druid thing was still pretty active in rural England—and Scotland—when I was a boy. Probably still is.

Look there." Trevor squinted through the thick trees, shading his eyes with a hand. "I see a house, and this path should take us there." Gunter pranced eagerly, pulling at his leash. The thick undergrowth seemed particularly attractive to his sensitive nose.

"Should we sprinkle bread crumbs?" Lara laughed, but her introspective mood from earlier hadn't dissipated.

"I'm surprised you'd come up with that rather than Ariadne's thread." Trevor laughed too. "Come, lassie. You can see the house from the street, so we'll be safe enough, even without crumbs or thread." He took hold of her arm. "Wonder which we'll find? A witch, or a minotaur?"

As they entered the heavy evergreen growth, a heady aroma enveloped them. No wonder Gunter was so excited. The odor was redolent of delicate wildflowers and rain-wet grass.

"Smells heavenly in here," Lara said. She reached the house and its heavy, carved wooden door. Raising her hand to knock, she stopped, captivated by runic symbols in the door itself. "I recognize some of these." She turned to Trevor. "Jung had symbols that were a lot like these scattered around the Institute. When I asked about them, I was told they were duplicates of the symbology carved into his tower at Bollingen."

The door swung open. "Welcome to Forest House. You're right on time. I'm Lillian. Please come in." Yipping furiously, Gunter tugged hard at the leash in Trevor's hand. Lillian squatted, and the puppy threw himself into her arms.

While Lillian fussed over the dog, Lara looked closely at her. Of medium height, with a slender build, her bright red hair fell in thick braided plaits, with small blue flowers and little winking jewels mixed in. Her hair had to be long enough to skim the floor, since the braids fell below her knees. The woman's eyes were a clear jade green. They looked almost unnatural, like smooth, polished marbles. Her milky skin was covered with freckles of every size, shape, and color. Golden earrings set with semi-precious blue stones bobbed up and down as she petted the puppy.

With a radiant smile that displayed very straight white teeth, Lillian looked up at them. "What a nice little fellow he is," she said. "You'll find he was a good choice." Whispering something in Gunter's ear that earned her a chin-licking, Lillian gently eased the puppy out of her arms and regained her feet. "Come in," she invited again.

"These symbols on your front door remind me of similar ones I saw in Switzerland," Lara said. "Do they hold a particular meaning?"

"Of course, but that would take far too long right now. Perhaps when you come again we can discuss runic representations of the goddesses, natural forces, and the zodiac. I fear we have far more pressing matters requiring our attention." Lillian stepped back inside her home and crooked a finger at them.

Once she crossed the lintel, Lara gaped at the interior of the house. The structure had been built around multiple trees that rose through the floor and grew through carefully-crafted spaces in the raftered ceiling. The house was composed of scattered alcoves, rather than actual rooms, and it extended as far as she could see.

"Lovely home," Trevor murmured diplomatically. "I don't know as how I've ever seen anything quite like it."

Lillian threw back her head and laughed. Peal after peal of bright mirth reverberated through the leafy domicile. "No, sweetie, I bet you haven't." When she looked at Trevor there was something Lara didn't quite like dancing behind her green eyes.

"I've made tea," Lillian said. "Follow me."

Lara, Trevor, and Gunter trailed after their hostess, wending their way through tree trunks. Unusual patterns were embedded in the floor tiles, with more of the arcane symbols arranged in groups.

Lara opened her mouth to ask about them, then closed it again. After they'd been walking for a good five minutes, she began to wonder just how large the house was. In addition to the odd floor, they passed numerous paintings and carvings all depicting some aspect of mythology, Druidism, Wicca, and other spiritual things she could only guess at. At last they came to an alcove that looked like an Old English drawing room. Upholstered chairs with comfortable pillows were arranged in a circle. In the middle sat a generous table with a copper tea kettle, cups, and a plate of sugared cookies.

"How big is this house? It seems enormous," Lara ventured as she settled herself into one of the soft chairs.

"Well now, that's hard to say." Lillian winked as she handed steaming cups of tea around. "Some days it seems far too large, and others a bit too small. It does best if I take care of the trees and don't pay much attention to the house."

Lara looked keenly at Lillian, her professional senses on edge. Was the woman deranged? Something about her was truly disconcerting. Lara thought back to her meeting with Roxanne Dykstra. Surely the professor wouldn't have recommended Lillian if there were something wrong with her.

Lillian reached out and touched Lara's knee as if divining her thoughts. "There's an entire dimension out there that you know very little about, my dear. This house is a living creature. I am merely its custodian. That's why I didn't give you any street numbers. In the first place, there aren't any. But mainly, the house lets those find it that need to be here. Others see only a forested lot."

Trevor stared at Lillian, clearly working to absorb what she'd told them. "I wondered why at first there was nothing there, then suddenly there was," he mumbled half to himself.

"Have a cookie to go with that tea." Lillian smiled charmingly at him, and Trevor reached obediently toward the bone china plate piled high with rich looking treats.

It's almost as if she has him under some sort of spell, Lara thought. "Why did you want us to come here?" Her question was a bit brusque, but she felt decidedly uncomfortable in the tree-lined gallery. As if they sensed her disapproval, the trees began soughing, their branches tossed by an unseen wind.

"Stop that!" Lillian's spring-like voice turned harsh, and the trees quieted immediately.

"Oh my." Lara put her cup down and swallowed hard. She glanced at Lillian and said a bit too brightly, "Thank you for the tea and all, but it was a mistake for us to come here. If you'll just point me in the right direction, we'll be on our way." Standing, she reached for her shoulder bag.

"You stop that too." Lillian looked pointedly at Lara. Without knowing quite how it had happened, she found herself in her chair once again. "It probably feels as if you've dropped in on a Lewis Carroll tale, but you should've started studying to support your psychic side thirty years ago. That you have waited until you are practically menopausal—and are ambivalent about it even now— doesn't bode particularly well for you. Nonetheless, we shall have to play the game where the pieces have fallen."

Lara glared at Lillian and sputtered, "How dare you talk to me like that? I've gotten along quite well, thank you, for forty-six years, without doing anything for that part of me."

"That's the spirit, my dear. I wondered if you had any gumption to you." Lillian laughed again. "Women today, especially you career-oriented ones, have turned into such sheep. Never an opinion that might fly in the face of your colleagues, or the latest research article. Don't you worry," Lillian waggled a long-nailed index finger at Lara, "we'll fix all that."

"Sounds like what I tell my patients." Lara found herself smiling almost against her will. "Maybe you missed your calling. Except the mantra in psychotherapy is the patients fix themselves."

"With a little help from the good doctor? Enough banter. Come closer you two. I've watched what's been happening to you. That horrid man is out of the game for a bit, but he'll escape from the hospital three days from now."

"How could you possibly know that?" Trevor interrupted, setting down his tea and cookie. Lara saw his jaw tighten.

"I have my ways, dear. There's the pool and the crystal ball." Glancing at their shocked expressions, she threw up her hands. "All right, all right. Look, children, just for a bit here, might you suspend your preconceived notions about how the world works? I need to tell you things, and it's important for you to believe me. Could you simply listen?"

Lara nodded once. After exchanging a pointed glance with her, Trevor followed suit. Gunter inveigled his way back into Lillian's lap. "*He* trusts me," she pointed out. "Dogs and children. They always know the truth of things. Now where was I? Oh yes. That man that's been complicating your life. His companions will create a diversion and spirit him out of the hospital next Wednesday. They plan to smuggle him out of the country, so I think you'll be safe from him at least for the present. I've tried to scry whether his associates will create more trouble for you, but I've not had any success. I will keep trying, however. As to that other man—"

"You mean Himmelschaun?" Lara broke in, frowning.

"Oh, is that what he's calling himself now?" Lillian cackled unpleasantly. "Yes, the one masquerading as a psychotherapist in Switzerland. He's far more dangerous than Ken Beauchamp. Before you leave here I have an amulet for you, and we will practice what you must do to keep him out of your head. It was fortunate that he seemed unprepared to do more than threaten you the other day."

She shifted in her chair, rearranging the dog in her lap. "The work you do. The depth analytic work, not the rest of it, has great importance. Dreams come from Gaia. You've been puzzled by the dream with the tree. Many of us have had that same dream recently. You and I must sit and map it out, but not today. I understand Gaia's perspective. You understand it from the perspective of the collective unconscious and Jung's voluminous writings. Perhaps we can find the truth of things somewhere betwixt the two. I'm convinced, as are some of my fellow practitioners, that there are answers in that dream, which point to the direction we must take if we are to maintain any life at all on Earth."

"What do you think about the electricity and oil problems?" Trevor asked cautiously.

"What do you think about them?" Lillian shot back.

"I think we're buggered. We've wrung every last drop of resource out of this planet, and now she's had it with us."

One corner of Lillian's mouth turned upward. "Not far off the mark, young man. If you weren't already taken, I'd find a place for you in my bed." Throwing back her head, Lillian laughed again. This time it held a throaty seductive sound that could lure men to their deaths.

"Wait a minute." Lara raised her voice to make herself heard above Lillian's chortles.

"Don't get your feathers ruffled. There's honor among witches, even though urban mythology paints us far differently. I'd never lift a charm to lure that lovely man away from you, no matter how much I might want to."

Lara wasn't sure if the reassurance made her feel any better.

Lillian looked at Trevor and narrowed her eyes thoughtfully. "You were raised by Druids, weren't you?"

"Not exactly. There were Druids in the neighborhood, but not in my home."

"But you went to some of their celebrations, didn't you?" Watching the blush spread upward from Trevor's neck, she chuckled again. "Scared the hell out of you, did they? Well, never mind. Doesn't matter a twit now."

Lillian stood. The golden torc around her neck gleamed in the flickering light from a number of kerosene lanterns. "Let's see," she murmured. "Where did I put those?" Sidling to a respectable stack of books, she scooped them up, walked to Lara, and dumped them in her lap. "You need to take these home. Start reading in the order I've arranged them."

"What are they?" Lara asked. How the hell would she free up the time to wade through the thick stack of books and numerous loose papers?

Lillian looked annoyed. "You need to learn about your gift. It *is* a gift, you know, not something to disregard. If you don't learn to control and focus your abilities, they'll push you in increasingly uncomfortable directions. You read Stephen King's book, *Carrie*? It's a fictionalized account, but you get the idea.

"On a slightly different, but related track. Those million or so women who were burned or hung as witches between fifteen hundred and eighteen-fifty? Most of them really did have psychic ability that had escaped their control."

Lara fidgeted as she thought about her most recent vision, and the way it came on with no warning. "All right," she agreed cradling the books. "I'll start reading these."

Lillian beamed. "Good. A wise choice. Now, we must do something practical. Young man." She nailed Trevor with her unsettling eyes. "Wander betwixt the trees for a bit if you please."

As if it were a hypnotic suggestion, Trevor rose, losing himself among the boles of the nearest trees.

"He'll be fine, my dear," Lillian said in response to Lara's worried look. "Here." She pulled a large moonstone on a golden chain from one of her pockets and handed it to Lara. "Slip that over your head and come sit next to me." Gently placing the puppy on the floor, Lillian pushed the table aside. When she did so, Lara saw it had been hiding a pentagram woven into the thick fibers of a rug.

"Within the circle?"

"Yes, dear. The circle will protect us." Lillian sat cross-legged and gestured for Lara to sit directly across from her so their knees touched.

"What are we going to do?" Lara asked, riding herd on nervousness.

"I will coax you into trance. After I do so, Gradoxst will appear, but I will be there too." She chuckled. "A bit of a surprise, I might add, for he won't be expecting me."

"Who's Gradoxst?" Lara felt mystified. This just got deeper and deeper.

"That's Himmelschaun's real name. He's an ancient demon of the Goblin ilk. It's unfortunate, but scarcely accidental, that he gained a toehold with the Jungians. If memory serves, they threw him out once, but he managed to convince some of the weaker ones he'd done nothing wrong, so they allowed him to return to preserve harmony. Those living at the Institute were arguing bitterly over him." Grimacing, Lillian continued, "That's the way his kind works. They sow discontent and distrust, turning one against the other."

"I wondered what happened." Lara shook her head, feeling dismayed.

"Hush," Lillian instructed and placed an index finger over her lips. "He's so arrogant it never occurred to him we still know his whereabouts. Close your eyes, still your breathing, hold the amulet in your right hand."

Lara dropped immediately into her unseen world. Shock roiled through her at how fast it happened. When she glanced around, she recognized the library at the Institute. A peculiar warmth radiated from the moonstone still clutched in her hand.

"Ah, Doctor. What a pleasure. I assume this means you've reconsidered your earlier antipathy toward working with me." Himmelschaun materialized about twenty feet from her. He held both hands out invitingly, a cunning smile on his face.

"I thought we could at least discuss it," Lara said, adding sugar to her tone to buy herself time. Where was Lillian?

Was I naïve to trust her?

Himmelschaun spun around, cursing in archaic German. Lillian, albeit a shimmery, nearly translucent version of her, stood in front of an antique bookcase filled with an untidy welter of old leather-bound volumes. "What does this mean?" he growled.

"It's been a long time, Gradoxst," she replied prettily, a predatory smirk on her face.

"What is this name you are calling me?" Himmelschaun's face paled. He plucked nervously at the frayed edges of his black suit jacket.

"Simply your given name, *Gradoxst*. Has it been so long since you've heard it you no longer recognize it?" Lillian stared fixedly at him out of narrowed eyes. "And now Lara McInnis knows your true name as well. You will not—"

"*Sie haben mich für einen anderen verwechselt, störend Sie Hexe.*" His voice boomed ominously, drowning her out. As he spoke, he lifted both hands, his fingers weaving together. A loud explosion rocked the library, and he vanished in the aftermath of a sudden flash of red light.

Lara came back into herself to the sound of Lillian's soft chanting. She released the moonstone and asked, "What did he say, there at the end? Can it really be this easy to drop into trance and control where I go, what I do there, and how I leave?"

Lillian twitched her nose, and her lips curved upward in half a smile. "He said I'd mistaken him for someone else, and he called me an interfering witch. Odd he dropped into German. I'd have expected Gaelic.

"In terms of your question about trance states, it will not be easy, but it is doable. Read those books, my dear. You've not seen the last of Gradoxst. He can be very stubborn, that one." Laying a hand on each of Lara's crossed knees, she continued talking. "Listen closely. Should you fall into trance, hold tight to the moonstone and call for me. It will be some time before you're strong enough to extricate yourself should that demon-spawn reappear. And he will."

"Who is he? You called him a demon."

"I told you, he's a Goblin, born from Cailleach's cauldron eons ago. He's other things too, which makes him exceedingly dangerous." Lillian twisted from her cross-legged position on the rug and focused her gaze at the trees.

"Young man, return to us," she called out. As if he'd been in stasis, awaiting her command, Trevor emerged from the trees, wandered over, picked up his tea, and sat down, a beatific expression on his face.

"I'll visit you soon." Lillian glanced at what Lara thought was a wrist watch. Once she got a closer look, the object was actually a backlit collection of astrological symbols arranged in a circle. Lillian pushed something and the watch's inhabitants rearranged themselves into a hexagon. She looked up, a strange intense smile on her face. "Would next Tuesday evening work?"

"Don't see why not," Trevor said. "Lara's usually home by eight."

"Actually, I'm not scheduling anyone past five o'clock until this power thing sorts itself out," Lara said. "That means I'll be home by six-thirty."

"Excellent! I'll just take your pup out for a second, then you'd best be on your way. It's quite late." Lillian stood, still holding Gunter, and walked toward a nearby wall with a door standing open.

Lara did a double take. "I don't recall seeing that wall—or the door, either—before, do you?" She looked questioningly at Trevor.

"This is an odd place, Lara. I wouldn't make too much of what your eyes tell you."

Lillian was back in just a few minutes. "You really do need to get yourselves home," she said. "The door's right where I just took your puppy."

"That's not the door we came in," Lara protested.

"You'd be surprised." Lillian smiled knowingly. "Have a nice evening, children. Don't forget your books. Keep the amulet around your neck. Oh, and Lara, it'll take a bit of time for the amulet to become familiar with your energy, but once it does you'll notice things."

"What sort of things?" Turing toward Lillian, Lara felt mystified—and apprehensive.

"Hard to say, child. It's different with every owner. Pay attention, though, and I'm sure you'll figure it out." Lillian inclined her head slightly before shooing them toward the door.

Right door or not, it deposited them on the path that led to the street. Lara was quiet as she clutched her shoulder bag and the stack of books and monographs. The moonstone felt tickly and warm nestled between her breasts. She tried to make sense of what had just happened, but her mind was too full of the evening's experiences to form coherent thoughts.

Trevor lifted Gunter into his box. Then he opened Lara's door for her. "It's pretty overwhelming, isn't it?" he asked softly, his voice tinged with wonder. "She was right about Lewis Carroll. Tonight's as close as I've ever come to having an Alice-in-Wonderland experience. I had a peek at my watch just now. We were with Lillian for over five hours. It only seemed like about thirty minutes whilst we were in there. And those trees… I could lose myself amid them for a hundred years. Do you want to put the books in the back?"

Nodding, she pulled the back door open, and carefully laid the dusty volumes on the floorboards of her car. "Better drive carefully," she murmured. "The sky will likely fall in if anything back there gets out of order."

"I have a feeling anything from *that* house is more than capable of rearranging itself." Securing his door and seat belt, Trevor started the car just about the time his phone started ringing. "Damn! Lara, could you get that?"

Fishing around in Trevor's jacket pocket, she snagged his phone.

"Is Trevor there?" a heavily accented woman's voice asked.

"Yes, just a minute." Lara held the phone out to him. Raising his eyebrows questioningly, he took the phone, while maneuvering the car to a curb.

"Hello? Angelique. Nice to hear from you." Trevor listened intently for several minutes. Switching to Dutch, he went on, "*Nee, dat klinkt prima. Je hebt het geweldig gedaan, vind ik. Hoeveel ben ik je schuldig? Geen enkel probleem. Ik maak het geld morgen over via PayPal.*" Dropping the phone back into his pocket, he slipped the car into gear.

"She got your things packed up?"

Trevor smiled. "Yes, she's an efficient one. I'll have to wire her some funds tomorrow. Now all I have to do is talk the landlord out of that long term lease."

"I thought you'd already done that."

"I started. There's a bit more to be done. Don't worry about it. Do you want to talk about what just happened back there?" He waved a hand over one shoulder.

"I'm not sure." She raked her hands through her hair before

looking at him. "We do need to talk about it soon, but I don't know if I can right now. My thoughts are such a jumble, likely anything that came out of my mouth wouldn't make any sense."

He stroked her hand. Whistling what sounded like an old Gaelic tune, he guided the car through Seattle's dark, deserted streets.

CHAPTER 18

$\mathcal{L}$ara woke Monday to a gray drizzle. She girded herself for another day of patients and rolled over looking for a morning hug, but Trevor had already gone. After a quick shower, she slid into a long black wool skirt, pale mauve silk blouse, and the black cashmere shawl from the previous day, since it was still draped over the back of a chair.

Was last night even real? What would have happened if I'd been raised by someone besides Aunt Mary? Someone who actually knew something about what I can do with my gift?

She checked her pager, relieved she hadn't slept through a summons that came in during the night. Settling on a riser near the bottom of the stairs, she scrolled through messages and returned calls, before heading to the kitchen.

"Morning, Trev. Mmm, looks wonderful. How long have you been up anyway?" Lara petted an excited Gunter who'd left a trail of urine droplets in his haste to greet her.

"Whoops!" Trevor dampened a cloth at the sink and wiped the floor. "He'll get over that as he gets older. I just had him out. How's your day shaping up?"

"Just got a call from Arabel. She came in early to do some

rescheduling so we wouldn't be working after dark. Anyway, my entire morning cancelled. I have patients at two, three, and four. So we could eat this marvelous breakfast, let it digest for a bit, then go for a run." She smiled hopefully at him.

He groaned. "Ugh! My legs are still sore from last time."

"They'll get better. All you have to do is make a commitment to do it more."

"As long as Arabel is switching things around, why don't you have her clear Thursday and Friday? We could take a long weekend. Since I couldn't sleep, I went online and checked out maps and real estate listings. We ought to take a look at the Ellensburg and Leavenworth areas. They're a good place to start, since they're close."

"But that would mean I might not make enough this month to cover the mortgage on the office building. I've had a bunch of cancellations, other than the two from this morning. The damned insurance companies are six months behind paying me, which doesn't help. And my malpractice insurance just went up again."

"We have enough money." His voice was gentle. "We'd have enough even if you never worked again." Trevor laid their plates on the table. Returning with two steaming cups of coffee, he sat down. "It must be your deprived childhood that makes you think we're always on the brink of starvation."

She grinned at him. "Now who's being a therapist?

"Maybe it's catching. I've had twenty years watching you to bone up on how to do it."

"Okay, I'll clear the end of the week," she said and grabbed her phone. When she hung up a few minutes later, he smiled.

"See, that wasn't so hard. What'd Arabel have to say?"

"That I should take more time off."

"Well, you should."

"I'll take it under advisement." Lara rolled her eyes. "Once we finish eating I'm going to get out of these clothes since I won't need them for a few hours. After that, we need to talk about Lillian and that house of hers."

He nodded and picked up his fork. For the next few minutes, the only sounds in the kitchen were the clink of silverware as the blueberry waffles and fruit compote disappeared off their hand-fired ceramic plates.

"Another stellar meal, dear. There's whole wheat flour in those waffles, isn't there?"

Looking up from his plate, Trevor mumbled, "Thanks," from around a mouthful of food. "Yeah, I've been trying to sneak more fiber into things. You done?"

"Uh-huh, but don't toss the coffee."

"I wouldn't dare."

Trading her work attire for sweats and jogging shoes, she looked out the bedroom window. It was still raining, a slow drizzle that dampened spirits as well as bodies. Pawing through a drawer, she found a lightweight waterproof jacket with a hood. Slinging it over her arm, she went to find Trevor. The kitchen was empty, but her coffee mug, newly filled to the brim with a perfect blend of whipping cream, raw sugar, and French Roast, sat steaming on the counter. She took an appreciative sip, then walked through the laundry room and pushed the back door open. Trevor was tossing a small ball for the puppy. Gunter barked wildly every time it got away from him.

"Shouldn't he be picking it up and bringing it back?" she laughed.

Trevor glanced her way. "Not if we don't train him. Retrieving doesn't come naturally to this breed, but hunting does. That's what he's doing right now, learning to track and hunt."

"Come on, Gunter." Trevor snapped up the ball. The little dog cocked his head to one side before trotting obediently toward the back porch. Trevor rubbed him down with an old towel and then opened the door for all of them. Unlike the front deck, the back porch was deeply recessed under the second story of their house, a plus given nearly three hundred rainy days each year.

Trevor dried his face and hair. "How about the library?" he suggested. "It's cozy in there."

"Well?" she inquired as soon as he sat down. "What did you think?"

Trevor looked at the floor. He seemed to be picking his words carefully. "Lillian and her house are why I didn't sleep very well," he finally admitted. "That woman was right when she guessed I had more than a passing acquaintance with Druids. Maybe it wasn't a guess. Who knows? I grew up in a village with a local wise woman—euphemism for witch—who sold herbs for whatever ailed you. She had an eye for the young men, and there were always tales."

He fell silent. Lara encouraged him to keep talking by prodding, "Tales of what?"

Looking uncomfortable, he picked up the threads of his story. "Tales of blood rituals. Animal sacrifices. At least I assumed it was only animals. When the village girls started their periods, there were rituals around that too. Then there were all those festivals: Samhain, Imbolc, Lughnasadh, full moon celebrations, solstice and equinox celebrations." He cleared his throat. "And Beltane."

Color stained his face, and he glanced sidelong at her. "If I wouldn't have been so scared—living with what I lived with, sex made me ill—I'm sure I'd have lost my virginity during Beltane. The women, married or not, picked a likely boy and took off with him.

"But that doesn't have much to do with Lillian. Do I think she has magical powers? Yes, I do. It's all bloody unnerving. I'm not at all comfortable with her showing up here tomorrow night. You probably didn't have a chance to look at anything she gave you, huh?"

"Actually I left everything in the car. But I am wearing the moonstone." Plucking it out from under her top, she dangled it from its chain. Guilt about the reading material nagged her, now that she'd been reminded. "I'll just run down and rescue the books and all. Be right back."

Mildly out of breath from running up their steps, she started to push the front door open when writing on the plywood panel drew her gaze. Her eyes widened and she gasped. Someone had used a marker to scrawl "We'll Get You Fucking Bitch" onto the wood. Her heart pounded against her chest. They'd been here! Sometime during the night, because she was certain that ugly message hadn't been there when they'd come home yesterday evening. Shoving her head through the door she screamed, "Trevor!"

He was there in an instant. Mutely, she pointed at the plywood. "Bloody hell!" He pounded on the wood with a fist. "Must've happened last night. That means someone actually came up our steps —whilst we were asleep." He jerked his fingers through his blond curls before curving a hand beneath her arm. "Come on back in. No point standing out here."

"How about that run?" she growled. "Doing something feels a lot better than sitting around worrying. Dissecting last night can wait." She wiped her suddenly damp hands on the sides of her exercise pants.

"Sure, I'll get my shoes and pop the pup in his box."

Five minutes later, they were jogging downhill. Lara's mind raced trying to figure out who could have posted that threat, since Ken Beauchamp was in the hospital. *Will this nightmare ever end?* "I'm sorry," she said, glancing at him.

"For what?" He panted, trying to match her pace.

"Not screening my patients better. This is my fault. I still feel responsible for Pete too. We're nowhere near done with our talk about Lillian. Hell, maybe this run was pure indulgence." Tears were very close to the surface. The amulet thumped against her breastbone as she ran. An infinite sadness radiated from its smooth surface.

Could it possibly mirror my feelings? Was that what Lillian meant when she told me I'd notice things?

"Don't be absurd, Lara. There's no way you could've known about Beauchamp or Himmelschaun. You've just gotten lucky all the years you've had a practice that the only other crazies were suicidal, rather than out to get you."

She shuddered, remembering her earliest training days as a graduate student in the long-since-abandoned state mental hospital system. After a close call in a dark hallway where an old lobotomy patient had jumped her from behind and thrown her to the linoleum floor, she'd been much more cautious. "Humph," she grunted. "The suicidal ones haven't been much fun either."

"Yeah, but at least they only hurt themselves."

She wasn't so sure about that, since she still harbored painful reminders of the handful of patients who'd ended their lives, in spite of her best efforts. The worst had been a brilliant, tortured twenty-year-old, dead by her own hand in a locked psychiatric ward. Lara shook her head sharply from side to side to clear the image of the young woman's face, but once summoned, it refused to leave. "I need to go faster," she mumbled. "Run at your own pace, and I'll circle back to you."

By the time, she was by his side again, she did feel better. The ghosts of her dead patients had retreated to wherever they lived when they weren't pricking at her conscience. "I'm ready to go home," she said.

He stopped and turned her to face him. Rain-dampened curls fluffed around his face giving him an angelic look. "I had a chance to do some thinking whilst you were gone. I don't trust Lillian's world, but it's mostly because I don't understand it very well. I didn't particularly like what she said about your psychic thing getting out of control if you don't do something about it. What happens if you get one of those visions whilst you're driving? It didn't look to me like you had much warning on Saturday afternoon."

"I didn't," she replied tersely. "I thought about the same thing. I will start looking at those books. In fact, I'll take one with me when I go to the office, just in case I have another cancellation. At least she gave me a way to escape from Himmelschaun if he shows up in one of my sendings again."

"Hope it works," he muttered through clenched teeth.

"Yeah. Me too." *What I really hope is I don't have an opportunity to find out.* She cleared her throat. "While I'm at work, why don't you call the bank to see how they're coming with our cash?"

"I'll do that. I'll also call Archer to tell him about our middle-of-the-night visitors."

CHAPTER 19

"*D*id you bring your list?" Lara smiled encouragingly at Clare Rothstein. The nervous thirty-two year old nodded and groped through two pockets before she pulled out a dog-eared piece of paper and handed it to Lara.

Skimming through the list, Lara smiled approvingly. "These were the only things you checked before you left your house?"

"Yes, Doctor." The mousy diminutive woman licked at dry lips. Raising clear brown eyes to Lara, she struggled to find words. "You said it would get easier, but when I don't check everything three or four times, all I do is worry something terrible will happen because I missed something."

"How often are you leaving your house?"

"As little as possible," Clare admitted. "It takes so long to leave, it's easier to stay." Her hands, red and cracked from being washed over and over again each day, and from cleaning, were clasped listlessly in her lap.

"Are you still having groceries delivered?"

The woman nodded again.

Lara took a few minutes to organize her thoughts. Clare was a classic case of obsessive-compulsive disorder. In the earliest part of their work together, Lara had gone to Clare's home so she could escort her patient outside before Clare engaged in her ritualistic checking of the stove, lights, windows, and doors, and before she'd scrubbed her floors, dusted with antibacterial cloths, and washed everything in the house.

"What do you think you need?" Lara asked gently.

"I don't know." Clare dissolved into tears. "I can't seem to drink enough to make all this go away." She waved an arm around while snuffling noisily into a snow-white handkerchief that smelled of bleach.

Inclining her head, Lara smiled and asked, "Would you like to try a bit of hypnosis?"

Clare's eyes flew open, then narrowed. "What would that do?" she demanded suspiciously.

"If it works the way I hope, it might help you relax. Then you'll be able to stop cleaning so compulsively. It might even be easier to leave the house."

"What do I have to do?"

"Nothing. I'll have you move to that recliner in the corner. Then I'll help you focus your breathing until you feel less anxious. After that I'll make some suggestions you'll remember when you come out of trance."

"That's all?"

"That's all." Lara smiled encouragingly. "This is nothing like stage hypnotism you may have seen in the movies. If you want to think about it, that's fine too. We have about half of today's session time left. We could use the time to refine your list and work on some other techniques."

"Okay, you can try that hypnosis thing," Clare said at last, hope flaring in her eyes.

"Thanks for trusting me," Lara said gently. "If you feel uncomfortable with the process at any time, raise your index finger like this." Lara elevated her right index finger. "When I see it, I'll stop, and we'll go back to where you were feeling better."

"How do I know you'll notice?" Clare's voice trembled.

"Because I'll be watching you as I talk. Now move over to the recliner. I know it's upholstered, but no one's sat in it all weekend, and all the germs are dead since they can't survive for long away from a human body."

~

AT FIVE O'CLOCK, Lara escorted her last patient, an elderly woman dealing with complicated bereavement after the loss of both her spouse of sixty years and her only son, to the office door. "Same time next week?" she asked.

"Not sure why I'm bothering," her patient said in a raspy voice, "but I'll be here. You're the only one I have to talk to." Lara thought about mentioning the senior center or volunteer work again, but decided now wasn't the time.

Once her patient was gone, Lara turned to Arabel. "How's tomorrow shaping up?"

"Them power outages got everyone spooked. But there're still three patients scheduled between ten and one. And then you got that eatin' disorders group at one, so you won't be done till 'bout two thirty. How you doin', honey?"

"Not bad." Lara had told Arabel that the police apprehended Ken, but she'd purposefully neglected to mention the disturbing message scrawled on the plywood next to her front door.

"It's good you're takin' some time with that beau of yours. Any chance you two might make things legal?" Arabel's dark eyes twinkled.

Lara felt herself blush. "Now that you mention it, we might do just that."

Arabel jumped up from her chair and hugged Lara. "Oh, hon, I'm so glad. Have you picked a date?"

"Not exactly. Probably soon, though."

The elderly woman looked closely at Lara and narrowed her eyes.

Divining her thoughts, Lara laughed. "No babies. I'm getting too old for that."

"Guess we just a childless pair," Arabel murmured. "I was hopin' for a little one I could dandle on my knees while you worked. You ready to go?"

Nodding, Lara led the way out of her office. "See you tomorrow." She waved goodbye once they reached the street. The earlier rain had given way to what was shaping up to be a spectacular sunset. In a moment of indulgence, she stood by her car and watched one fluffy cumulus cloud blend with another. Together, they reminded her of a rather rotund unicorn. The moonstone pendant warmed against her skin, almost as if it approved. Smiling inwardly at her fit of fancy, she got into her car and started home.

The minute she rounded the corner of her street, she saw two police cars parked in the no parking zone under her stairs, and her hands froze on the steering wheel. *Trevor. Something happened to Trevor.* She scanned the street for a parking spot, said, "Fuck it," and pulled into another no parking zone right across the street. Leaping from the BMW, she raced for her stairs, taking them three at a time.

She tried her front door. It was open. *That* didn't bode well. Still moving fast, she ran smack into Detective Archer as she propelled herself through the door. "Ooph!" he grunted. "Slow down, Doctor."

"Trevor," she managed. Her heart thudded against her ribs, and she had trouble forming words. "Where's Trevor?"

Understanding spread across the detective's face. "He's fine. That's not why we're here. It's taken us all day to check out the new decorations on your door." Rubbing his injured shoulder gingerly, he added, "That was a direct hit. You couldn't have done better if you tried."

Lara mumbled, "Sorry."

She started to say more, but Trevor came down the stairs with Gunter in his arms. To her horror, she started to cry. Great gasping sobs tore out of her, and she collapsed against Trevor and the dog.

"Lara." Trevor sounded frantic. "What happened? Are you hurt? Move back so I can put the pup down."

"Nah, she was just worried sick about you." The detective smiled. "Guess when she saw our cars out front, she figured something bad had happened."

"I don't understand what's wrong with me." Lara made a grab for her composure. "When I saw the police cars, for some reason I was sure you'd been injured—or worse." She tugged a tissue from her pocket and blew her nose. "I've got to go down and move the car before I get a two hundred dollar ticket for being in a red zone." Dropping her bag in the entry hall, she gave Gunter a perfunctory pat and ran heavily back down the stairs.

What the fuck? she asked herself as she searched for a real parking place. Lara prided herself on her equanimity, and she hunted for something, anything, to explain her meltdown. She clicked off recent incidents on her fingers, starting with Ken lying in wait for her on her office porch last week. By the time she'd maneuvered the big car into a smallish space, she was feeling somewhat better. She plucked her briefcase off the passenger seat and got out of the car.

I have every right to be on edge. More than every right.

Detective Archer and three other officers were just leaving when she got back to the bottom of her stairs. "Did the jerk who wrote that leave any clues?" she asked hopefully, wondering if she should tell them Lillian's prediction about Ken's upcoming escape.

"No ma'am." An officer she hadn't met before answered her. "I'm Officer Christopher, ma'am," he added respectfully.

Tell them, her inner voice urged. *I'll feel really stupid if he gets away and I knew something and kept my mouth shut.* "There's something you probably should know about," she said to Brad Archer.

The detective looked closely at her and raised his eyebrows. "Yes?"

She felt flustered. "Uh, you need to watch Beauchamp's hospital room carefully. I think there may be plans to spring him."

"And you know this how?" Officer Christopher's voice held an uneasy edge.

"It's a long story," the detective replied before turning to Lara. "Are you sure?" he asked.

"As sure as any of this ever is," she replied.

"Do you know when?"

"Wednesday." When she looked at Officer Christopher, he was sidling away from her.

"Thanks for the tip," Archer said, "We'll do what we can." He hesitated before adding, "If you get any more, uh, information, call me."

"Of course. What happens next?" Her briefcase was getting heavy, so she shifted it to her other hand.

"You let us know about anything unusual. Keep the dog in your room at night. He hears better than either of you. Please consider that motel for a few days until things simmer down." Brad Archer held out his hand. Lara shook it. Turning away, she started slowly up the steps to her home.

"What's up with her? How could she possibly…" Officer Christopher's voice faded as the men got into their car.

Trevor and Gunter were in the kitchen. Stepping over the puppy gate, she squatted to hug the squirming dog. "Yes, yes, I've missed you too. What did you do today? Tell Momma all about it." She scratched his ears. "Hmm…that ear's a bit straighter. Guess you'll grow up to look like a Shepherd after all." She stood and went to Trevor, who held out his arms.

"Sorry, Lara. Didn't mean to scare you. Guess I could have called to let you know the police finally showed up here."

"Wouldn't have mattered. I don't answer the phone when I'm driving. How'd the rest of your day go?"

"I did get hold of the bank. Same snarky little git I talked to the other day. He told me our cash would be ready to pick up on Wednesday."

Extricating herself from their hug, Lara slipped out of her shawl, draping it over the back of a chair. "Wednesday's perfect. I teach that day. I figured we'd be all packed and just leave from the University.

We can pick up the money in the morning, and it'll be available in case we find something to buy."

Trevor made a face, looking sheepish. "I did some thinking about that too, and I ordered us a safe. It should show up tomorrow. It's pretty big. I'll bet the delivery guys have fits when they see all the stairs. I told the shop about them, but you know how it goes. Make the sale first, and figure out the rest later."

Lara looked askance at him. "Just how large is our latest acquisition? Why do we need it if we're going to move?"

"Big enough a burglar couldn't cart it out of here. Besides, I plan to bolt it to the wall studs from the inside." He paused. "The way things are going around here, even if we only use it until we leave—and it keeps everything secure—it'll be worth the expense."

"Where are we going to put it?"

"In the space between the kitchen and laundry room. There's that extra linen closet we've never used much, so I took the shelves out today."

She felt tired. The adrenaline from earlier had dissipated, leaving her cranky and listless. "Probably a good idea," she agreed. "We'd be an easy mark with all that cash, especially since we seem to have the Mexican Mafia on our ass. I thought we'd just convert it into gold, but we'll need somewhere to store that too. Is there something for supper?"

"Yup, it's in the oven."

Perking up a bit, Lara realized she did smell something food-like wafting around the kitchen. "Sorry I'm so out of it. I'll get out of my work clothes. By the time dinner's on the table, I'll be ready to eat. Some wine would be good. I could use something to help me relax."

An hour or so later, she pushed her plate away and drained the last of a second glass of Pinot Noir. "That pesto chicken was awesome. How did you make the asparagus sweet and tangy at the same time? In fact, where did you manage to *find* asparagus? I am *so* grateful you like to cook."

He grinned. "So am I. A bloke would starve around here,

otherwise. The asparagus—and a few other things as well—came from that local farmers' market they have every Monday at the foot of Queen Anne Hill. I've pretty much given up finding decent produce in the grocery stores."

The doorbell chimed, and Lara's stomach clenched. Glancing at Trevor, she asked, "Are you expecting someone?"

"No, but it's not the bad guys. They wouldn't ring the bell. I'll go see who's there." Pushing his chair back, he trotted out of the room. Gunter followed as far as the puppy gate. When Trevor stepped over it, the little dog howled his displeasure at being left behind.

"I'm here. Isn't that enough?" Lara scooped up the puppy. "Ooph. You've gained five pounds in the week we've had you. Let's go out, little man." Carrying the puppy tucked awkwardly under one arm, she opened the back door and flipped on the yard lights. Gunter stumbled down the back steps, tripping over his big feet. As soon as he was on the grass, he squatted. "Good boy," she murmured. "Good puppy."

CHAPTER 20

Curiosity about who'd rung their bell drove her back into the house. With a little coaxing, Gunter climbed the steps by himself and made a beeline for the kitchen. Lara followed and found Trevor talking animatedly to Lillian. Gunter sped toward the witch— or whatever she was—and tore at her flowing, multi-colored skirt with his teeth and claws.

"Oh, he's a good little one, he is," Lillian cooed, bending to snuggle the puppy and detach him from her clothing.

"Whatever are you doing here?" Lara blurted. As soon as the words were out, she clapped a hand over her mouth. "Oh my, I'm sorry. That was rude. It's just that you said you were coming tomorrow."

"I was in the neighborhood. As long as I was close, I thought I'd stop by." The lie was both patent and transparent. Lillian looked right at Lara with her unnerving eyes, silently challenging her to make an issue of it.

Lara fought irrational anger that threatened to erupt in hot words. Once she thought she could be civil, she said. "I've had a long day."

Didn't anyone ever tell you it's rude to drop in on people? And then lie about it?

"I gather you're feeling out-of-sorts," Lillian interrupted dryly. "I saw the graffiti outside your door. You're planning to ask me to leave, and I will, but not quite yet. The main reason I dropped by was to ward your house. You two are still in a great deal of danger."

"That was kind of you. To think about us and come by to help." Trevor, ever the gentleman, was opening another bottle of wine. "Can I pour you a drink?"

Lara groaned inwardly. It was actually a relief when Lillian replied, "Thank you, young man, but no. I never touch the stuff. Dulls my senses. Not a good thing."

"What did you mean about warding the house?" Lara sank back into her chair.

"Guess you didn't get any reading done."

Lara leveled her dark gaze at the other woman. "No. I did not get any reading done. I do have the books in the front hall, though, and I was planning to look at the first one before I went to bed."

"Humph!" Lillian pulled out a chair and plopped into it. "A ward is a protection. If someone crosses the ward, they generally live to regret it. If they live at all, that is. Anyway," she wiped her palms together in a back-and-forth motion, "I've already taken care of that. Did it before I even rang your bell."

Trevor's forehead creased in thought. "Is there something we have to do so we can get in and out of the house?"

Lillian rolled her eyes. Peals of mirth rang from her, and Lara's earlier irritation dissipated. Lillian had a childlike charisma, in spite of her almost total lack of social grace. When she finally stopped laughing, she murmured, "Even a neophyte wouldn't be so stupid as to ward a home against its own inhabitants." Looking at Lara, she pointed a finger at her. "Go get the book from the top of the stack that I gave you."

Fighting the irritation Lillian's commands engendered in her, Lara walked dutifully to the entry hall, dug around in her briefcase, and came back with both the book and her phone. "Here," she handed the book to Lillian, "I need to scroll through my phone for a moment. I really should keep it with me all the time, but I can't stand having a permanent electronic sidekick. So I take mini-vacations from it."

"I understand, dear. You go right ahead. It'll take me a moment to find the passages I need."

While Lara caught up with her messages, Trevor cleared the table and put food away. Gunter made himself a nest in Lillian's long skirts where they fell onto the floor.

Lara set her phone down and observed, "He really seems to like you."

"All living creatures are drawn to Gaia. Ready?"

Lara nodded. Something had shifted, because she didn't feel nearly as tired as she'd been an hour ago.

"You need to read this chapter about finding the source of your power. And this one, about using that source to develop personal protections for yourself and those around you." Lillian pointed to sections of the well-thumbed tome, turning down page corners as place-holders.

"Will I understand what it has to say?" Lara felt dubious.

Lillian smiled. "Not the first time. Likely not the second. But if you persevere, you'll eventually glean what you need to know. The book will take care of that part. Actually, this volume is the foundation. Once you've mastered it, the contents of the other books and articles should fall into place far more readily."

Eying Lara closely, she added, "How are you feeling after yesterday?"

Her face heated, and Lara felt chagrined at her own transparency. "I've been trying to not think about yesterday, if you must have the truth of things."

"It would be far simpler, wouldn't it?" Lillian placed a hand atop one of Lara's. "But there comes a time to do what we'd rather not. For you, that moment has arrived, whether you wish it or no." Lillian stood. Her skirts swirled around her. Gunter grunted his dismay at being ousted from the soft, cozy fabric to the cold tile floor. "See, I told you I'd leave."

Lara couldn't stop herself from asking, "Are you planning on coming back tomorrow night?"

"Do you want me to?" Lillian arched a brow.

"We'd love to have the company," Trevor replied quickly.

"What about you?" Lillian was looking—no, make that staring—at Lara.

"Sure," Lara said, meeting Lillian's stark gaze. "After all, that's when we were expecting you." To her amazement, she found she really did want Lillian to come back. As she searched Lillian's timeless face, the other woman nodded at her, an unreadable expression in her unusual eyes.

"You needn't bother to see me out," she said softly and walked from the room.

"I'd best lock the deadbolt and set the alarm," Trevor said after he finished drying the pots and pans he'd used to cook their dinner.

Lara pushed up from the table. Stepping over the puppy gate, she followed Trevor to the front door. "That was odd. Her visit, I mean. Didn't you think?"

"All of this is odd, but we're living in unusual times," he replied. Gunter yowled on the kitchen side of his gate. "Let's move to a room where he can be with us."

"How about our bedroom?" she suggested. "It's getting late, and we can finish this conversation in bed. Besides, I have at least half an hour of reading to do before I go to sleep."

One corner of Trevor's mouth turned upward into a lopsided grin. "I'll bring the pup and his crate along presently."

By the time Trevor crawled into his side of their bed, she'd skimmed both the indicated chapters. Laying the book on top of the covers, she closed her eyes, her forehead furrowed in consternation.

"That bad?" he asked.

She opened her eyes slowly. "Worse. My God, this is really arcane stuff. It's written in something like Middle English, and there're all sorts of references to things I've never heard of. She said this was the cornerstone for all the rest of what she gave me. There must be something that came before this. I tried looking up some of the terminology in the cell phone's browser, but didn't have much luck."

"Maybe that other professor, you know the one who sicced Lillian on us in the first place, would be able to help."

"That's a really good suggestion." She smiled tiredly. "I'll make an appointment with her on Wednesday before my class, assuming she's available then. You were awfully polite to Lillian. Doesn't she bother you?"

"Sodding hell. Of course she bothers me, but if there's one thing I learned growing up with witches, it's best to stay on their good side. Besides, we've got a piss pot of problems here, Lara. We need all the help we can get." He looked thoughtful. "If she can teach you how to control whatever floods you with those visions, I'm all for that too. It wasn't much fun watching you thrash about the car the other day, moaning *no* over and over again. I felt pretty fucking helpless."

Lara reached behind her and placed the book in the recessed headboard. *Maybe, if I keep it close to my head, some of the information might sink in by osmosis.* Double-checking the alarm function on her phone, she turned off her reading light. "I'm sorry," she murmured, stroking one of his hands and turning to face him. "I didn't mean to frighten you, but I don't have much control over what happens when *the sight* takes hold."

"My point exactly. That's why you need Lillian, whether you like it or not," he said, mirroring the witch's earlier statement. "Switching subjects here, you'll need to pull a few things together sometime tomorrow if you're going to be ready to push off Wednesday after class."

"Already thought of that. I set the alarm for six. Instead of a run, I'll get up, shower, and pack. First patient's not until ten. Besides, there's always Wednesday morning."

"We won't have much time then," he replied. "We should show up at the bank as soon as they open. I suspect we'll need to go together, or they'll never hand over all that money. Then we need to come back here to lock it up. Then it's back to the University District for your class—"

Lara chuckled. "What a complicated life we lead. I'm sleepy, dear, come cuddle me." Trevor gathered her into his arms. As she lay cradled against him, listening to the puppy yip in his sleep, she thought she heard something else. Closing her eyes to help her ears hear better, she held her breath. Yes. There definitely was something. It was a low, buzzy, murmuring noise that was incredibly soothing.

"Trev?"

"I thought you were sleepy."

"I am. Be quiet for a moment and listen."

"I don't hear anything but Gunter."

"You have to listen for longer than that, silly." Lara stroked the back of his neck with her hand. Long moments passed.

"Is it sort of like a hive of friendly bees?" he asked softly.

"Yes. You *can* hear it. That means it's not my imagination. I think it might have something to do with whatever Lillian did to protect the house. Or maybe it's the amulet."

"Or there could be a wasp's nest under the eaves outside one of the windows." Trevor pulled her closer. "Your hair smells wonderful, Lara. Like lavender. I always loved that smell."

His hands roamed down her back and cupped her ass. He pulled her closer to him, and she felt him swell against her belly. For the briefest of moments, she started to tell him it was too late, and she was too tired. He kissed her, and she melted into him, tightening her hold on his firmly muscled body.

After long minutes of sweet kisses, he murmured, "Come closer, love. I can't stand any distance between us, none at all." Sparks danced where she rubbed against him, heating her blood. Lara pushed him onto his back, straddled his hips, and drew him in.

Her nipples sent unbelievable sensations shooting through her as he fondled them. Panting, she cried out for him to move faster, faster. Stars circled as the sensitivity between her legs became unbearable. An orgasm spun out of her, leaving her empty and shaking in its wake.

She collapsed in a heap on top of Trevor and heard him say, "Saints preserve us, love, what happened to you? Not that I'm complaining, but you're usually not that ardent."

Raising herself on wobbly arms, she looked at him in the glow from the moon shining through their windows. His dear, familiar face was rosy from spent passion. "I do love you," she said, smiling as she rolled onto her back. "As to the other, I don't know. Maybe it's an extra gift Lillian left for us. You were telling me about the Beltane festival and all."

"That's in the late spring," he protested. "This is October."

"Well, don't they have festivals year round?"

He kissed her tenderly on the tip of her nose. "It doesn't matter, Lara. What just happened between us felt holy to me. Let's not ruin it by talking."

CHAPTER 21

*L*ara dreamt she was on a mountain track, climbing up a steep trail. The day was chilly, and she wished she'd brought more clothes. Coming around a sharp corner, she spied a bear in an enclosure. She felt frightened, but told herself it couldn't hurt her since it was caged. When she looked more closely at the animal, she saw a pink bow tied in its matted straggly fur. Picking up half a sandwich lying by the trail, she pushed it through the bars of the cage, but the bear just looked at the sandwich, and then at her out of sad, dark eyes.

"*Chirrup, Chirrup…*" The phone chimed its morning wake-up song. Groaning, she patted the interior of the recessed headboard until she located the phone and stared at the lighted display. *Ugh! Six o'clock. Whose idea had that been?*

She dragged herself out of bed before she noticed the door to Gunter's crate stood open and Trevor was gone.

When she came out of the bathroom with a towel wrapped around her, he was back in their bed with Gunter who'd scratched the sheets into a little home for himself. Whining happily when he saw her, the pup ran in circles on their quilt. "Hey there lazybones." Lara smiled indulgently as she sat on the edge of the bed to fondle the puppy. "What about my breakfast?"

"I made coffee," he protested. "In fact, I brought you a cup when I came back upstairs. Thought I had me a spot of time since you'd be packing and all." She spied her customary mug balanced atop her dresser. Lunging for it, she sniffed appreciatively, then took several long swallows.

"Oooh, you're such a sweetheart," she cried, throwing herself back onto the bed and catching Trevor up in a hug. "You make a perfect cup of coffee. Not only is it impeccably brewed, but you always get the cream and sugar part just right."

"Brits do the cream and sugar thing in tea too, you know. Mmm, Lara, you washed your hair in that lavender shampoo again." He began fondling her bare shoulders, nuzzling her neck, and unwinding the towel she'd draped over herself.

The same quick, insistent desire from the previous night built in her loins. "Oh no, you don't." She pulled away. "We've got to get something done today. When Lillian shows up, I'm going to ask her what she did to turn us into a couple randy teenagers."

"It'll only take few minutes, Lara." Throwing back the covers, he held out his arms. His body was so perfect she couldn't look away. He ran a hand lazily up his erection. "I say we take all of this we can get. It's not like we've spent the last twenty-something years screwing. I can think of lots of months we never touched one another." He smiled crookedly. "Come on, love, let's make up for some of that lost time."

Her nipples ached, and moisture slicked her nether regions, smoothing the way for him to join with her. Almost as if an unseen presence was pushing her, she gave in to desire turning her insides to molten heat. Gently moving Gunter over, she twined herself into Trevor's waiting arms and felt him slip inside her almost immediately…

"Told you it wouldn't take long." He smiled at her, the corners of his blue eyes crinkled with delight. A fine sheen of sweat beaded his fair skin. "If you want to take another run through the shower, I'll join you."

Giggling, Lara scooped up her damp towel, swallowed more coffee, and floated into their bathroom. Orgasms had often been a struggle for her, and here she'd had two doozies in less than twelve hours. A sense of well-being warmed her as she bent to turn on the water.

Got to focus on what I want to pack for this trip. If I keep thinking about sex, I'll head right back to bed.

Despite her good intentions, a soapy skirmish in the shower turned passionate and he entered her from behind, his breath hot against her neck as he drove himself into her.

Lara wasn't certain how, but she actually got a small bag packed while Trevor lathered up and washed his hair. He emerged from the bathroom with a towel draped around his slender hips, hair already fluffing around his strong-boned face. He grabbed an old pair of sweats off the edge of the bed, slid into them, and then gathered all their wet towels.

"Might as well start a load in the machine. Power seems to be cooperating so far today." He plonked the towels over the spiral staircase rail before coming back to collect the puppy. "See you downstairs. Good day for a bacon omelet." Lara heard him whistling as he tripped down the wooden risers.

Culling through her perpetually disorganized closet, she found a pair of black wool pants and a brightly colored silk sweater. A further search yielded a matching black wool jacket. Lara pocketed her phone and snapped up her dream journal, before following Trevor and Gunter downstairs.

"Mmm, I could almost eat the smell," she announced, as she walked into the kitchen. The puppy ran to greet her, yipping his delight that she'd miraculously reappeared. She patted his furry head. "Yes, yes, I've missed you too, snookums."

Turning away from the stove, Trevor came over to her and wrapped his arms around her. "I love you so much," he whispered against her hair. "I was worried after…well, after what I told you that I'd never be able to, uh…"

Pulling away, she cupped his face between her hands. "I understand perfectly. A lot of things will get easier now that you've kicked the closet full of skeletons open." She smiled and stroked the sides of his face. "You've got to trust someone. After all the time we've been together, it may as well be me." She smoothed stray curls away from his face. "Levity aside, dear, I'm honored you trust me. And I'm here, in case you decide you'd like to talk some more."

"I thought you weren't supposed to treat family members." He grinned happily back at her with the elfin smile she'd always adored.

"I'm not *treating* you. Merely listening, if you decide one of those skeletons needs a bit more airtime."

"Humph," he snorted. "So that's how you guys get around that one. Breakfast should be about ready." He turned back to the stove and flipped off the burners. "Fresh coffee's already on the table."

As she settled herself, Gunter jumped on her, clumsily placing his front paws on her thigh. "You want to be in my lap? Okay, sweetums. Here we go." She hoisted the growing puppy onto her pants-clad lap after placing a convenient dishtowel over the dark wool fabric. "Good thing he's black," she told Trevor, "otherwise I'd look a fright."

While she waited for breakfast, she jotted down the high points from the previous night's dream.

"What are you going to do when he weighs fifty pounds?" Trevor asked. "Or a hundred?"

Lara looked up from her journal. "We'll cross that bridge when we get to it. What are you doing today?"

"The safe is due to arrive. I need to get it situated. Besides, you won't be gone all that long. Didn't you say you'd be home by four or so?"

Lara nodded. "Uh-huh. Do you want some help with that?"

He'd begun bringing the omelet and toast to the table.

"Nope. That's everything." He sat down, frowning at her. "You're feeding him? Whilst he's in your lap?"

"Sure." She smiled gaily. "That's why he wanted up. Canines are quick learners."

He sighed. "Well, I guess we can un-spoil him once he's too big to hold."

"Ssht…" Lara placed a finger over her lips, then moved both hands to shield Gunter's ears. "Don't tell him he's going to grow up. All children need to believe in Never-Never Land, at least for a while."

Trevor gazed soberly at her. "Wish I'd been able to do that, even for a little bit of time."

"Yes, dear." She reached across the table and took his hand. "Me too."

CHAPTER 22

Three women sat on pillows scattered around the Oriental rug in Lara's office. She glanced from one to the other. Liz was a bulimic, whose primary form of purging was excessive exercise. Renée, an anorexic, spent every spare moment on the treadmill. The third group member, Theresa, was more of a binge-eater, who occasionally forced herself to vomit after particularly egregious episodes where she consumed thousands of calories and felt rotten about herself.

"Who's first today?" Lara asked. It felt cramped with all of them in the office, but the women wanted to form a group. They'd met three times so far. After some initial reticence, they were beginning to trust one another.

"I only binged twice this week," Liz announced proudly, coloring a bit as she delivered what was very good news for her.

"How much did you exercise?" Renée asked pointedly.

Liz's ruddy face turned even rosier. "Probably more than I should have," she admitted. She swatted a strand of coppery hair over her shoulder and mumbled, "Every day for a couple hours."

"That's nothing." Renée was dismissive. "I exercised at least five hours every day." Her porcelain skin contrasted with coal black hair and intense hazel eyes. "That was an improvement for me. Wasn't it, Doctor?" She raised defiant eyes to meet Lara's.

Lara ignored the question and asked, "Have you weighed yourself lately, Renée?"

The emaciated woman shook her head.

"Why not?" Lara persisted. "That's part of your commitment to the group."

"Too depressing," Renée replied.

No, too much cognitive dissonance between the low number on the scale and the fact you're convinced you're too fat, Lara added silently.

"I wish I was thinner." Theresa, a pudgy blonde with china-blue eyes sounded wistful. "You're all so slender." She eyed Lara, Renée, and Liz enviously.

Lara shifted gears. "Thanks, Theresa, for bringing that up. Let's talk about what it means to be thin in this culture, and how we feel we compare to the standard set by magazine and runway models. Not to mention actresses. Since you thought of it," Lara looked pointedly at Theresa, "Why don't you start?"

She gripped the sides of her cushion and muttered, "I'm a fat cow. It doesn't matter what I do, I'm still fat. Wish I could afford liposuction."

"Did you weigh yourself this week?" Lara asked. At Theresa's curt nod, Lara just looked at her and waited.

Finally, Liz jumped into the silence. "I weighted one hundred fifty-four yesterday morning."

"But you're thin!" Theresa wailed. "I weighed one-ninety." As soon as the words were out, a shocked look bloomed on her face, and she clapped a hand over her mouth.

Lara inclined her head and said, "See, that wasn't so hard."

"Yeah, right," Theresa groaned.

Lara nodded sympathetically. It was damned near impossible to get eating disordered patients to talk candidly about their weight. All of them had unrealistic expectations about so many things: their weight, other women's weights, how to establish and maintain a healthy body. Lara eyed Renée. "Do you have any idea how much you weigh this week?"

The dark-haired woman shifted uncomfortably on her pillow. "Um, maybe one-twenty?"

Lara looked hard at her. "One of our group rules is honesty. Would you like to try that one again?"

"Okay, okay, so I weighed ninety-eight this morning." Renée studied the floor intently.

"Thank you, Renée. Being honest with yourself is a great place to start. Regardless of how little you weigh, you always feel fat, though, don't you? Just like Theresa."

Renée's shoulders slumped. "Look," she plucked at some skin lying loosely on one of her stick-thin arms. "That's fat. And it won't go away."

"You don't have any subcutaneous fat anymore," Lara explained. "That's why some of your skin is looser than you might like. So you feel like you're fat, and Theresa feels like she's fat. What about you, Liz?"

The redhead blushed again. "Of course I'm fat," she said peevishly, as if she was explaining the obvious to a dim-witted listener. "I hate exercise, but if I didn't, well, I'd be up there at around two hundred right along with Theresa. In fact, I have been."

A muted tap sounded on the door. Lara swung her head around sharply. Arabel never interrupted her unless it was an emergency. She pushed to her feet. "I'll be back in a couple minutes. While I'm gone, talk about why you give the scale so much power over your lives."

Lara entered the small reception area. "What's up?" she asked, keeping her voice low.

Arabel handed her the telephone. "Think you should take this call."

"This is Dr. McInnis." Lara's pulse quickened as she gripped the receiver.

"Thank you so much for answering," a familiar voice said. "I interrupted one of your sessions, but this is the only opportunity I'll have to say thank you and goodbye."

"Bethany?"

"Yes, it's me. There's been some trouble at the shelter in Wenatchee. A fire. Anyway, they're moving me right after I hang up. I don't know quite where. But it's better if you don't know where I'm going next, if you know what I mean."

Lara's drew her brows together. "Promise me you'll try to stay safe. I do appreciate that you called." The shelter wouldn't have called her with any information. Battered women's shelters never divulged the whereabouts of their clients, even to their therapists. You either knew because you'd sent the woman there. Or you didn't.

"Don't mention it, Dr. McInnis. You and me, we have that special bond. Got to go." There was a hesitation. "I think the baby will come real soon. Then it will be easier for me to hide."

"Good luck to you, Beth—" but the line disconnected. Handing the phone back to Arabel, Lara shook her head to clear her thoughts of Bethany before she returned to her group.

An hour later, Lara emerged from her office and yanked her jacket from the coat tree. Arabel packed up to leave too. "That poor woman," she breathed. "Do you think she's gonna be all right?"

"I don't know," Lara said. "I just don't know. Remember, I won't be back in the office until Monday. Why don't you take those few days off too?"

"But I always come in on Wednesday," Arabel protested. "You teach your class and I git the billin' done for the week. If I went back to only billin' them insurance companies monthly, well we'd never git nothin' from 'em." She flashed her maternal smile. "Promise I'll stay away on Thursday and Friday, unless the service can't find you. Where you goin' to be again? Just in case somethin' happens."

Lara blew out a frazzled breath. That was one of the big problems with a private practice. You never really had any time that was truly protected from a potential patient crisis. She'd taken her pager to bed with her for so long it reminded her of an ever-present, but annoying, lover who wouldn't take the hint and go away. "We're going out of town. I'll have my phone and my pager, though. So it should be easy enough to find me."

Arabel nodded. "Let's hope I don't need to."

Yes, Lara thought as she opened the outer door of her office suite and walked into muted afternoon light, filtering through the stained glass panels in both stairwells. *Let's hope you don't need to.*

As she drove through Seattle, she opened the car window, breathing in the beauty of the Pacific Northwest. It had rained that morning, and sunlight created a glittering iridescent web, reflecting off all the damp greenery. Worry about Renée pricked at Lara. She was far too thin. Anorexia was almost impossible to treat on an outpatient basis, but when she'd suggested a live-in program, Renée ignored her.

Lara turned down her street and found a parking spot immediately. Smiling at the unexpected gift from the gods, she backed expertly into the empty slot and turned off the ignition. Plopping her phone and pager into her bag, she locked the car and bounded up the long front staircase. As she turned her key in the lock, she heard Gunter's excited yipping. "I'm home, guys," she cried, slamming the front door behind her.

"In here." Trevor called from somewhere near the kitchen. Leaving her bag in its accustomed place, she went to find him.

"Oh my God." Lara stopped dead and took in their new safe. "You weren't kidding when you said it was big. Jesus, how did they ever get it in here?"

"On a dolly. Say, love, could you take the pup out?"

"Sure. Back in a sec."

Gunter was getting much better at negotiating the few steps into the yard. He peed, then started sniffing next to the fence so she assumed he wasn't done. Lara walked to one of several rhododendron bushes growing in pots and absently plucked dead petals off the flowers.

"Ready to go back in?" she asked. Yipping excitedly, the puppy led the way.

Trevor was just dismantling an electric drill. "There." He piled up his remaining tools. "It's in there for keeps." He swung the heavy door shut, engaged the locking mechanism, and patted the metal side of the large box-like contraption. "We got a really decent deal on this," he said, wiping his hands on jean-clad legs. "Only six hundred dollars. It was used, of course, but this seemed to be the sort of thing one might buy used and not suffer any ill effects."

"I'm sure it will do the job." She wasn't quite sure what to say. The safe was an industrial green and ugly as sin. But she had to admit it would be a strong deterrent in case someone else broke into their home. "How'd the farm hunt go?"

"Fine. I spent some time with maps and the Internet and Realtor.com trying to get a few more ideas for where we might end up. Skykomish is another little burg we'll want to check out. It's west of the Cascade Crest, but there are farms in that area."

"Great." She blew a kiss his way. "All I need to do is go along for the ride. You can play tour guide. Do we have anything planned for dinner?" Peering around a corner, she glanced at the clock on the microwave. "Awk. Do we even have time for dinner? It's nearly four. Isn't Lillian supposed to show up around five?"

The electricity whirred strangely, and the house fell silent.

"Bollocks! Bloody hell," Trevor cursed and threw his hands in the air. "The day was going along so well. Yes, I did have something half-made for dinner, but it needs cooking. Guess I could fire up the grill."

"Let's do that. I missed lunch and I'm starving. I'll just run up and ditch my work clothes, then I'll be back down to help." She sprinted for the stairs. Gunter went after her, wailing piteously when she left him on the hardwood floor beneath the bottom riser. "Back in a minute, snookums. Momma loves you."

When she came through the laundry room on her way to the back yard, she noticed Trevor had left a pot of noodles balanced on the washing machine. She carried it to the barbeque where he'd just laid some thick-cut lamb chops over the flames.

"Gee, thanks. Had my hands full back there." He set the pot over the single burner hooked to the side of their outdoor grill.

"Were we having anything besides the lamb and fettuccini?"

"Yes. There's a salad made in the fridge. Radicchio, feta, olives, and those croutons you like."

"Yum! I'll just dash in and get it. We can eat out here." Lara returned with the salad, silverware, plates, and bowls piled atop a tray. "What do you want to drink?" she asked.

"How about beer?"

Nodding, she made another trip to the kitchen, emerging with two Sierra Nevada Pale Ales. "These okay?"

"Brilliant." Trevor held out a hand, grabbed one of the bottles and took a long swig. "Move over, I've got to get the pasta drained if we're going to have it al dente." He added grated parmesan, fresh grated pepper, and some sort of herb mixture he'd obviously prepared ahead of time to the noodles. Stirring briefly, he motioned for her to give him the plates. She heard him talking, half to himself, as he bent over the lamb.

After indulging in a single-minded attack on her dinner, Lara finally laid her fork down for the first time since she'd begun eating. "Another gourmet adventure," she proclaimed. "Hard to believe there's a food shortage."

"That's because I'm willing to pay through the nose so we can eat," he replied caustically just as Gunter started barking. "Must be Lillian." Trevor glanced at his watch. "She's right on time."

"I'll let her in." Lara stood. "I'm done eating, and you still have food on your plate."

Lara made her way to the door. The amulet emitted the same contented energy it had the previous night. Just to be safe, she peered through the viewing port. Lillian looked every bit as exotic as she always did. This time she wore a long, reddish-brown caftan, with enough gold jewelry to ransom a small kingdom. Or maybe a queendom.

"Are you going to let me in or not?" Lillian sounded irritated, her voice muted by the thick front door. "You've stood there for a full five minutes."

"Oops, sorry," Lara mumbled as she pulled the door open. "I don't know what I was thinking."

Lillian looked strangely at her. "Of course you do," she snapped. "You were immersed in wondering about all this." She gestured at the golden torc, golden bracelets, golden earrings, and golden threads adorning her gown. "And then you got lost wondering how I manage to get my hair done up in these braids."

"I suppose so." Lara smiled in what she hoped was a conciliatory fashion. "Would you like supper? We were just finishing, but there's food left."

"Thanks for the offer, but there's far too much work to be done to waste time eating."

Good thing we ate before she got here.

"We're in the back yard. Follow me." The minute Lara opened the back door, the puppy launched himself at Lillian. As she'd done the previous night, she squatted to pet the puppy, talking softly to him in a language Lara couldn't quite place. *Trevor might know what it is,* she mused, making a mental note to ask him.

Lara pulled out a chair for their guest and returned to hers. Trevor had finished eating while she was gone.

"Here," he volunteered, "I'll just take these dishes back to the kitchen." He stacked things on the tray Lara had used and disappeared inside the house.

Lillian turned to Lara. "He's a good one," she spoke in a matter-of-fact voice. "You got lucky. Not everyone listens when old blood calls to its kin."

"Yes," Lara agreed, wondering what on earth Lillian meant by *old blood.* "Trevor is a gem, but that's not what you want to talk about, is it?"

The corners of Lillian's mouth curved upward. "Of course it's not. I'm pleased you're wearing the amulet. Did you do any reading?"

"I tried. I'm afraid none of it made much sense, though. Isn't there another book? Perhaps one that comes before the one you suggested I start with?"

Lillian rolled her eyes. "You youngsters. How many years did you spend in school? Maybe twenty? Yet you can't understand a book written in your native language."

Irritation simmered. Lillian always kept her on the defensive. "There were a lot of terms I didn't understand. I tried looking a few of them up online both last night and today, but they don't seem to exist."

Lillian scraped her chair against the raised wooden patio, reorienting it so she faced Lara directly. Several moments passed before she chose to speak again. "You're in danger. It's not accidental you found the Institute closed to you, with Himmelschaun guarding the entrance like Cerberus at the gates of Hell. But we shall talk more of that later. You must discover which natural element will protect you. For me, it's trees."

"What are you?" Lara's voice was quiet.

"Why does that matter?"

"Because if I knew what you were, then maybe I could figure out if I'm like you, or something different."

Lillian laughed wryly. "A good answer, my dear. You *are* right, you know. There are many different types of magic wielders. I am one and you are, indeed, something different. Yet many of the same principles apply."

Trevor returned to the patio and slid into his chair as unobtrusively as possible. Meanwhile, the puppy had inveigled his way onto Lillian's lap. She stroked his fur, and a faraway look stole across her face. The other woman suddenly appeared unspeakably ancient and otherworldly, with such an eldritch cast that Lara's eyes widened. Recognition of something nagged just beyond the edges of consciousness.

"Settle in, children." Lillian's voice brooked no possibility of disagreement. "I have a tale to tell, and then we must decide what to do next. It is not accidental our paths have crossed."

CHAPTER 23

"At the Institute, they trained you in mythology, did they not?" Lillian eyed Lara, who nodded. "Which mythologies, child?"

"Greek and Roman," Lara replied. "Some Celtic influence also. We studied the Triple Goddess at length. Doctor Von Franz was still alive, and her primary interests—before she immersed herself in dreams of the dying—were archetypal presence in fairy tales and the Grail myth."

Lillian smiled wistfully. "The maiden, the mother, and the crone, yes? And Parsifal… Perhaps you won't have much trouble with what I have to tell you. Did you ever study the Tuatha Da Danaan?"

"Sure." It was Lara's turn to smile. "They were the people either of the Goddess Dana or Ana, depending which old translation you're reading. They fought the Mil after the first Gaels arrived in Ireland and lost. As I recall, that group were known as the Sidhe, or fairy folk. They were driven underground after losing that battle, but the myths claim they still live under the hills and barrows in Scotland and Ireland."

"I am Baen Sidhe." Lillian's voice was so quiet Lara thought she hadn't heard right. Trevor's quick intake of breath behind her, though, suggested otherwise.

"But that's scarcely possible." Lara stared at Lillian, her mouth agape. Catching movement out of the corner of one eye, she saw Trevor crook two fingers in a sign against evil.

Lillian saw it too and burst out laughing. "Look, son," she choked out, after getting her mirth under control, "save *that* for the other side. We were always blessed by the Goddess." Lillian skewered them with her glass-green eyes and continued. "I came over from the Old Country long ago. After a few skirmishes, I discovered I was less conspicuous as a Wiccan on this side of the Atlantic. Many of the beliefs are quite similar."

"How do you know Roxanne?" Lara asked.

"We're part of the same coven. There are only about a hundred Wiccans in this area. We all know one another, but I'm the only one with anything approximating real power. Roxanne is quite sensitive. She figured out my spells actually *do* something. I'm sure it's why she gave you my number when you came to her asking for a teacher."

Suddenly her seat was too confining. Lara rose and paced back and forth across the small yard. Stopping abruptly in front of Lillian, she settled her hands on her hips and asked, "What kinds of things can you do?"

"What would you like for me to be able to do?"

Touché! Lara winced. "Gee, that's the sort of answer I toss back to my patients when they ask me something I don't want to answer."

"Exactly. Takes one to know one." Lillian grinned enigmatically. "I've been many things in my lifetime. It was a wee bit early for psychology, but I did spend years as a local wise-woman, handing out advice."

"Can you foretell the future?" Trevor's voice sounded thin and strained.

"It depends. In this instance, it hardly takes any sort of precognitive ability to scry what's likely to happen to civilization over the next couple years. Even you figured it out, and while you have the old blood, you have little magical ability."

"What do you mean about *old blood*?" Trevor asked. Lara picked up a slight tremor just beneath the surface of his voice.

"You and she." Lillian crooked a finger in Lara's direction. "The both of you have old blood. What I mean by that is the blood of the Tuatha Da Danaan."

"Are you saying we're Sidhe?" Trevor's voice rose, cracking on the word *Sidhe*.

"Oh my, no. Merely that you have some Sidhe blood. It's far from pure. Like as not, that's how the two of you found one another. What did they tell you as a child about us," Lillian demanded, "that makes you so frightened?"

"That you steal children, and kill cattle, and wash the shirts of those who are about to die."

Lillian inclined her head. "Well, yes, we've done most all those things." Trevor opened his mouth to ask another question, but Lillian held up a peremptory hand. "Let me finish. The children we took had magical ability that needed attention. It would've been far more dangerous to simply let them be. Farmers prayed to us and left us offerings. Those who failed to leave us something lost cattle, which is as it should be. The Sidhe must command people's respect. That last about the shirt washing is simply unfounded. Do we know who's dying? Certainly. But I'm unsure just how that story came to be."

Trevor's eyes were huge. He lurched to his feet and stood next to Lara, taking her hand in his. "When you and I spoke earlier about children being encouraged to believe in Never-Never Land," he sputtered, "I didn't think for a moment that ...that ..." He swallowed hard. "Maybe what I'm trying to say is Grimm's Fairy Tales just chased me down, and it's nothing at all like I envisioned."

"Very little in this life—or any other—is quite what we expect." Lillian spoke quietly.

"What do you want with us?" Lara asked. "I do need to learn about my psychic side, and God knows I need protection from Himmelschaun, but what's happening here feels deeper than that."

"Times *have* changed." A small smile played about Lillian's full lips. "When I was learning my craft, I spent over a hundred years with my mentor. That wasn't unusual. Other than a sexual bond, I can scarcely think of a more intimate relationship than that between a teacher and her student.

"Philosophy aside, we have two immediate tasks. The first is to puzzle out that dream sending from the Goddess. Enough people have had it that it must mean something significant. The second is to give you enough tools to protect yourself.

"When you learned about the shadow," she went on, "you were taught nothing can exist without its opposite, that we need good for there to be evil." Lillian cleared her throat. "That hasn't stopped those on the other side from trying to wipe out everything they find that's pure. They're so stupid, they don't realize they, too, will cease to exist if they succeed in their quest to eradicate their opposite."

Lara opened her mouth, but Lillian waved her to silence.

"You," Lillian met Lara's gaze and held it, "have become both a target and a magnet for shadow. Your problems with the Institute are but one example. Those forces will continue to try to annihilate you. Without my help, they'll eventually succeed."

"Oh no they won't." Stepping between Lara and Lillian, Trevor sounded fierce.

Lillian flapped a tired hand at him. "Step down, Galahad. I told you before, I'm not the enemy. I've always worked on behalf of the Goddess. Tell me, young man, which languages do you speak?"

The question was so off-the-wall it caught Lara by surprise.

"Uh, French, German, Dutch, Italian, Latin, a bit of Greek, and a smattering of Mandarin Chinese," Trevor stammered. "Why?"

"How about Gaelic? Or Welsh?"

"I believe I can still read Gaelic. Never could speak it terribly well."

A warm smile lit Lillian's timeless face. Her freckles came alive, flowing into one another in intricate patterns. "I'd hoped as much."

She pulled a slender tome out of one of her pockets. "Translate this for Lara. Take good care of it. That book is very old."

"I'm not sure I want to touch it." Trevor just stared at the book without making a move to take it from Lillian's outstretched hand.

"What do you think will happen?" Lillian sounded amused. "If I wanted to turn you into a toad—or simply annihilate you—I wouldn't be sitting here. I don't need proximity to cause harm."

Trevor made a face as if he'd bitten into a rotten lemon, walked over to Lillian, and plucked the book from her grip.

"See now," she crooned. "That wasn't so bad. Open it and make sure you can puzzle through the dialect." Trevor nodded curtly and sat down. Thumbing through the small book, he bent close to the hand-written text, his curls framing his face, and his brow furrowed in concentration.

"Just how old is this?" he asked, looking up.

"Old. Can you read it?"

"Yes. The verb tenses are strange, but yes, I can figure it out."

Lillian returned her attention to Lara. "Now," she said, "about that dream—"

"Before we dissect the dream," Lara interrupted, "remember what you told me about Ken escaping from the hospital? I need to know if he managed to get out."

"Why?"

"I got a strange call today from his wife. There was a suspicious fire at the place where I sent her. She called to tell me she was being moved. I'm sure they're trying to protect the other residents."

Lillian cocked her head to one side as if she were listening to something, and closed her eyes. After a few moments, she opened them. "Pfffst," she hissed. "That scum did try to escape, but the attempt was foiled. He has a serious infection from his leg wound, but they've moved him to the King County Jail anyway, infection and all. That's good for us, likely bad for him. I can't believe medical care in jail is on a par with what he'd get in the hospital."

"How can you know those things?" The words tore out of Trevor.

He'd raised his hand to make a protective gesture again, but lowered it almost immediately. "Sorry," he mumbled. "Old habits."

"Because I can sense his energy." Lillian spoke evenly. "All I need to do is follow the strand that's him, and it gives me information. Of course it's not precise by modern standards, since I didn't believe his cronies would spring him until tomorrow."

"Could you kill him?" Lara's voice was low.

Lillian laughed wickedly, her wise old eyes brimming with barely suppressed power. "What a predatory question, my dear. Of course, but such has not been entrusted to me. I told you, I do the Goddess's bidding. You're better off with him alive. If he dies—and he may—his associates will become more aggressive. They live by a very old code. I'm sure you know it."

"An eye for an eye." Trevor spat on the ground and curled his fingers into fists.

"Roxanne told me Ken isn't aligned with any sort of paranormal forces," Lara offered feebly, realizing how ridiculous she sounded before the words were even out of her mouth.

Lillian looked speculatively at Lara. When she spoke, her tone was patient but pointed. "I already told you. Roxanne, while a sweet woman and a dear friend, has absolutely no psychic ability whatsoever. However in this instance, she's correct. Ken's a threat, but not because he's part of anything supernatural. Gradoxt's who you need to watch out for on that front. By the bye dear, the police seemed well-prepared for Ken's escape attempt. Did you talk with them?" At Lara's nod, she continued, "What exactly did you say?"

"Just to be vigilant because I expected he'd try to escape. The detective who's been working with us knows I'm psychic."

"You didn't tell him about me?"

"No. There was no reason to."

Lillian caught and held Lara's eyes. There was no possibility of looking away. She felt an odd tingling sensation, as if Lillian had entered her body and was sifting through her soul bit by bit, examining it minutely.

At length, Lillian blew out a tight breath and said, "Good. You've told me the truth. Never disclose my existence to anyone. Do you both understand that?"

Lara nodded. Trevor did too, after a pause.

"Enough about that Beauchamp scoundrel," Lillian said, her tone cold. "He may win yet by diverting us from our true purpose. What have you done so far with the dream? It's much more critical than that pesky human."

"Not much," Lara admitted.

"What would you usually do?" Lillian pressed.

"I'd separate the dream into parts. Then I'd free associate to each one. After that, I'd apply the images to specific parts of myself. Lastly, I'd match the dynamics to my inner life." She paused. "If I still had questions, I'd engage the parts of myself that were key elements of the dream in dialogue."

"Why haven't you done that for this dream?"

Well, why haven't I? After a well-considered pause, she answered both Lillian and her inner critic. "Several reasons. My patient had the dream first. So when I had it, it didn't feel like it was mine to interpret. I saw it as an archetypal dream, and a shared one at that. I refreshed what I know about the Senoi and their shared dreams, but it didn't help. When one of my students—and then Trevor—had the same dream, I felt overwhelmed. I tried to call the Institute but as you already know, something's very wrong there."

"Do you want to know what I see?" Lillian asked gently. "I'm not an expert on dream sendings, yet the Sidhe do use a place we call the *Dreaming* as an escape from the harsh realities of constant interactions with humankind."

"Sure." Lara nodded. "Tell me what you see, and I'll let you know if it resonates for me." Moving quickly, she pulled her chair across from Lillian's and sat back down.

"Very well. Don't interrupt. I must concentrate to get the spiritual sense of the sending." Lillian shifted her body in the wicker chair, folded her hands over Gunter's sleeping body, and began. "The guide in the dream is an instrument of Gaia. It appears differently to each dreamer. The tree is the Tree of Life. When the earth sustaining it collapses on one side, it's symbolic. When that tree fails, so will all life on Earth.

"The small creatures in the cavern represent species of animals. The one killed early on means we are losing some of them every day. When the dreamer gathers the little animals, it's a reminder we have a sacred duty to ensure the survival of life on this planet. As the hands and pockets fill with life, our task becomes harder, yet we are not excused from it. The golden object is Gaia's sacred temple, and the small black woman who crawls out and sits cross-legged in the palm of the dreamer's hand is Dana or Gaia. She's angry and demands to know what we're doing to rescue Her children and the planet supporting them."

As she listened to Lillian, Lara was filled with immense sadness, mirrored by doleful emanations from the amulet. Despair welled and threatened to drown her in a tide of hopelessness. Yet, the interpretation rang true.

Lara had learned early in her analytic training to listen to dreams with her intuition. Her sixth sense told her whether she was on the right track, as she wrestled with the arcane symbology of the world of the unconscious. Tears leaked from the corners of her eyes. Until she felt moisture, she wasn't aware she was crying.

Lillian watched Lara closely. "You must agree," she observed. "You can feel it, can't you?"

Nodding, Lara turned to glance at Trevor. His eyes were pinched with pain. "I didn't think much about that dream when I had it," he admitted, finally making eye contact with Lillian. "After listening to you, I feel guilty I dismissed it with so little thought."

"The Earth is our first mother." Lillian spoke sternly. "The last two hundred fifty years have devastated her. Gaia is reaching out, albeit at least a hundred years too late, to warn us. That's the essence of the dream."

"What can we do?" Lara's voice was stronger than she felt.

"I fear not much at this point." Lillian sounded grim. "You've recognized that and are beginning to prepare for a radically altered civilization once the natural resources supporting it are gone for good." As if it were sentient, the power whirred back into being. "Where are the two of you thinking about settling, anyway?"

"How did you know?" Trevor asked with a strangled gasp, before muttering, "Guess it's easy for you to see that sort of thing, huh?"

Rolling her eyes, Lillian replied, "Ask me a meaningful question, not a foolish one."

"Someplace in Washington, probably," Lara broke in. "Trev thinks we need to be in the mountains so we'll have access to good water. We'll also need to be able to grow food."

"Have either of you ever done anything like that before?"

"I have," Trevor replied curtly. Lara winced at the hurt in his voice, understanding he'd been stung by Lillian's assignment of the term *foolish* to his earlier query.

"It's not as easy as it looks," Lillian said.

"I know." Trevor's voice was a shade softer

"You two could live with me."

"I don't think that'd be a good idea." Lara spoke a shade too brightly, trying to be diplomatic.

"Maybe not. But you will need to be close enough to me to complete at least a minimal course of study."

"Hold up." Lara raised both hands, palms facing outward. "I'm not so certain we need to go anywhere anytime soon. I have a full practice, and I'm not going to shut it down unless I have to. We just thought we'd buy a small farm somewhere, so we'd have a place to retreat to if things did get bad."

"It's not if, but when," Lillian corrected her. "The crystal ball business has been a bit slow of late, but things might limp along for another couple years. It doesn't really matter. You will begin your lessons now, and we will continue until I think you're done."

"Why? Assuming we do go somewhere, won't I be safe then?" Lara felt confused—and annoyed—by Lillian's insistence on enrolling her as an acolyte.

"Once you've been targeted—and you have been—no place is safe. It's time I was going. You've got reading to do." She scratched the puppy tenderly behind his over-sized ears, murmuring to him in an arcane language before placing him gently on the patio. Gunter shook himself all over, ambled down the steps, and squatted in the grass.

"What's that language you use with him?" Lara asked.

"Ancient Gaelic. Same as in the book your intended has." Lillian shook out her skirts and pushed her heavy hair back over her shoulders. "I don't want to open another topic tonight, but you two need to solemnize your relationship. It's been open-ended for far too long. You're stronger as a couple than as individuals. Plan on a wedding during the Winter Solstice." Trevor started to rise, but Lillian said, "Don't bother, I can find my own way out. I'll be back soon."

"We're leaving town," Lara said. "Won't be back until Sunday."

Lillian turned and looked at her. "Fine. Stop by my house Sunday before you come home. I'll want to hear what you found in your travels."

CHAPTER 24

*L*ara stared after Lillian's retreating figure. She heard the front door snick shut from the distant recesses of the house. When she looked at Trevor, he had a stunned look on his face. "Guess I should go lock the door," Lara said and stumbled to her feet. "I didn't even notice it had gotten dark—until now."

"I'll come with you. Gunter's had enough back yard time for a while, and I need to pop those dishes into the washer since the power's back up."

"I'll help you," she said softly. "Then maybe we can make sense of what just happened. I'm having a hard time finding a place to catalogue all the things Lillian told us."

"That's because you don't have a logical spot for any of them. Here, pup." Trevor whistled, and Gunter trotted through open door, heading for the kitchen and his food dish.

Lara's mind raced as she helped Trevor clean up. She wiped water off the last of what hadn't gone into the dishwasher, folded the dishtowel, and asked, "How about we go sit in the library?"

"I'll get a bottle of Bordeaux. Be along in a moment."

Settled in one of two butter-colored leather chairs, she sipped thoughtfully at her wine. "Why don't you tell me what you know about the Baen Sidhe?"

"It's not all that much," he admitted. "What I think she means by that, though, is simply 'woman of the Sidhe,' as opposed to the more modern interpretation that's much narrower. Even you must have heard of Banshees who wail over the dead." At Lara's nod, he continued. "The Sidhe are the fairy folk. Supposedly, they live forever, and your best chance of seeing them is at dusk or dawn. Where I lived growing up, people still put out offerings to them so the crops wouldn't fail, and the cows would keep on giving milk."

"You grew up believing in spirits?"

Trevor gazed at her out of troubled blue eyes. Pushing his hair back in an unsuccessful attempt to get it out of his face, he shrugged. "I'm not so sure what I believed in back then. But there was a time or two as a small boy I was pretty sure I actually saw something that might have been a Sidhe. I tried to tell Mum, but she never paid any attention to me after the other babies started coming."

"Jung believed in the unseen world. So did Doctor Von Franz, especially after she started interviewing all those dying people. I was drawn to analytic psychology because I've always suspected there had to be more to humans than could be explained by a purely scientific approach." Lara set her wine glass on a side table and drew her brows together in thought, as she tried to puzzle through the mysteries of Lillian and the Sidhe.

"Damn!" Lara rolled her eyes. "She told us what she is, and inferred I was something different, but she never told me what she thinks I am. How could I possibly have forgotten to ask her about that?"

A corner of Trevor's mouth twitched upward. "You didn't ask because she wasn't prepared to answer that question. Lillian's orchestrating something here, and we're just playing along. What she wants from us will become clearer with time, and I don't think for a moment it only involves teaching you about whatever abilities you have."

"Gives me the willies. Any idea what her ulterior motives might be?" Lara shivered, despite the warmth of the room. When Trevor shook his head, she changed the subject. "Talk to me about the place you grew up. Remember, I used to nag you about wanting to go there, but you told me you didn't want to go back." Reaching out, she wove her fingers with his.

"Now you know why." He looked keenly at her. Lara felt him inspecting her innermost thoughts, dredging for the slightest bit of revulsion or disgust she might feel toward him. She met his gaze evenly, and after a time, he seemed satisfied.

He drained half his wine. "I grew up in Cumbria," he began. "Our place was a few miles out of Carlisle, not far from what's left of Hadrian's Wall. Historically, that spot of ground was sometimes Scottish and sometimes English, depending on who was in power. We were far closer to Glasgow and Edinburgh than London. The old Scottish folklore was alive and well in that part of Britain. I already told you about the witch-women who sold charms for everything from fertility to helping you get revenge against a neighbor for some slight." He hesitated. "I'm not sure what more you want to know."

"Neither am I." She smiled ruefully. "Wish I knew more about where my parents came from. I tried to quiz Aunt Mary, but she was so spooked by her psychic ability, she'd never talk about what she knew about our family. Now they're all dead, so there's not a soul left to ask. Ach, Trev—" Eyes wide, she pressed the heel of her hand against her forehead, and then she was gone.

The vision claimed her with vicious force, much like the previous one. The amulet sent out waves of warning, burning her skin, as she walked down the front steps to her car, dressed to go to work. She opened the car door as she'd done thousands of times and slid into the vehicle, fighting a sense of apprehension as she turned the key. An ear-shattering explosion deafened her; fire sprouted everywhere.

Lara coughed. Heat seared her as the interior of the BMW went up like a torch. Thick smoke narrowed her airway, and it became a struggle to breathe.

"Lara, Lara. It's okay. You're here. Wake up. Sodding hell, wake up, damn it." Trevor grabbed her shoulders and shook her violently, his voice frantic. Her eyes snapped open and she looked around, feeling trashed and still fighting to breathe. Trevor hugged her hard. "What happened? You were coughing and gagging and swatting at yourself."

The sudden jangling of their landline was shockingly loud. Reaching over Lara, Trevor picked it up. "Yes?" he said brusquely.

"It's Lillian," she said without preamble. "I need to warn you—"

"Let me give you Lara," he interrupted. "Whatever it is, I think we already know."

Lara grasped the receiver with nerveless fingers, finally steadied the handset with both hands, and said shakily, "Lillian?"

"Yes, dear, it's me. There's a bomb in your car."

"I know. I just saw it."

"Thank the Fates. The Goddess *is* watching out for you." Lillian sighed heavily. Lara could almost picture her tossing a heavy braid back over one shoulder. "There is better news, though. Your Mr. Beauchamp did something even his cohorts found unspeakable. He's been scamming his brethren in the Mexican Mafia. They found out, and they'll be taking care of him in their own way. This whole bomb thing happened just before they discovered he'd been stealing from them so, once you're done with that, you might be done with him *and* his fellow crooks."

"Ugh! He's not *my Mr. Beauchamp*. How did the Hernandez family find out what he'd been doing?" Lara asked, sensing Lillian might have had something to do with it.

"I have no idea, dearie. Better call the bomb squad. Tell them it's dynamite wired to the ignition." The line went dead.

Lara handed the phone back to Trevor. "What I saw," she said, "was my car exploding with me in it. But at least Himmelschaun wasn't lurking on the sidelines." Then she detailed what Lillian told her.

Trevor dialed Detective Archer's number from memory. He answered on the first ring with a crisp, "Archer here."

"It's Trevor Denoble, Detective. Lara's had another vision. We need you back out here."

"Can I talk with her?" Brad Archer asked. Trevor handed the phone to Lara.

"Hello," she said, her voice still trembling from the violence of her psychic sending.

"Evening, Doctor. Funny thing, but I actually had the phone in my hand to call you. First though, tell me what you saw." When she was done, he said gruffly, "Thanks. I'll have the squad out there soon. All we'll need is your key. You say that it's wired to the ignition. So we can open the door?"

"Yes, that's what I think."

"Ever considered doing police work, Dr. McInnis?"

"What?" she asked in a strangled voice.

"Police work. I told you we use psychics. It's rough out there. Crime's up five hundred percent since the rolling blackouts started two months ago. Homicides too. You seem more attuned than either of the other women we use. Anyway, think about it."

"Okay, I will. What was it you were getting ready to call me about?" she asked, her curiosity kindled in spite of herself.

"Huh? Oh yeah, thanks for the reminder. Seems there's been a little accident over at the jail. Beauchamp's dead. Not sure how it happened. His cell was locked, and the jailer for that pod is adamant he never heard a thing. Someone got in there, though, because his throat's been slit."

"Oh…" *Should I tell him what Lillian told me?* Lara decided there was no reason, since Beauchamp was already dead.

"Thought you'd see that as good news, Doctor. For that wife of his too."

"Of course," she replied mechanically. "Sorry, Detective, but I'm not sure what to say. Guess I'm not in the habit of cheering when someone dies, no matter how much I disliked them." Her voice trailed off, and she felt hollow inside.

"I'm sure you'll feel better about his untimely loss when you've had time to digest what it means," the detective replied sarcastically. "Got to go, Doc. I'll round up the boys and get them headed your way."

"Goodbye, Detective, and thanks." Shifting, she dropped the phone back into its cradle.

"Gee. He offered me a job." She rolled her eyes at Trevor. "And he corroborated what Lillian said, except I guess Beauchamp's really dead. Murdered in his cell."

"Hah! Past time for that scumbag. Good riddance." Trevor sprang to his feet, danced a little jig in place, and smiled broadly, before sitting back down.

Guess he doesn't share my ambivalence about pissing on Beauchamp's grave. She closed her eyes against an image of Ken and Bethany sitting in her office trading potshots. *That poor, poor man. Never mind he tried to kill me. He never had much of a chance. Some things that happen to children can never be undone.*

Ten minutes later Gunter barked sharply, just before the doorbell rang. "Must be the police." Trevor jumped up from his chair. "I'll give them your key."

After he left the room, Lara reached for the phone again and dialed Lillian's number. The now-familiar voice answered, "Yes, dear?"

"That vision I just had…" Lara launched into what nagged her. "It was so real, too real, actually. It was like I was in the car when it blew up. Can you die in visions?"

"Sometimes." Lillian's voice held a cautious note. "Depends who sent them. Since I believe the Goddess sent you this one, the answer to your question would be *no*. I didn't ask you, though, was Himmelschaun there?"

"No, but the rest of it was horrific, hideous," Lara murmured, squeezing her eyes shut against the memory. "Trevor had to shake me really hard to bring me back from wherever I went."

"It's better if he doesn't do that." Lillian sounded serious. "You could get trapped between the worlds."

"Where?"

"Never mind. The only way you might die in a vision is if it's one an enemy sent. Tell Trevor he shouldn't disturb you when you're in trance. Didn't the amulet warn you?"

"It might have. I'm not used to paying attention to it."

Lillian grunted derisively. "It's akin to an early warning system—for both good and bad. Is there anything else?"

"Yes, now that you mention it. You told us what you are, but what am I?" Lara closed her eyes. Another headache pounded behind her right temple.

"You'll have to figure it out for yourself. It wouldn't mean anything if I told you." She paused a beat. "Don't forget to have Trevor start translating the Gaelic book for you tonight. Do at least one chapter." She stopped again, then added, "It's encouraging Himmelschaun wasn't lurking about. Perhaps my presence in your last vision discouraged him, at least for a while." Lillian hung up before Lara could ask anything else.

She sat with her eyes shut, head thrown back against the headrest of her easy chair, when Trevor returned to the library, trailed by two officers in puffy bomb suits.

"Lara?" Trevor's voice was soft. "These gentlemen would like a word with you."

Nodding, she straightened in her chair and took a sip of her long-forgotten wine, hoping it would infuse some energy into her.

"It's curious, ma'am," one of the officers—R. Cunningham according to what was stenciled on his suit—said. "We found the wires, but whatever they went to had already been removed. Whoever did it was in a real big hurry. They cut the wires and took the explosives. If I were you, I'd let a mechanic dismantle your ignition to remove the rest of the wires. I'm sure your car is safe to drive, though."

"Are you positive the dynamite's gone?" she asked nervously.

"How did you know it was dynamite?" R. Cunningham looked strangely at her through narrowed eyes.

"Because I saw it in a vision," she said simply. "Your boss knows I'm psychic. Ask him if you don't believe me."

"We have one of the dogs with us, ma'am," the other officer said in response to her question. "He doesn't think there's a bomb anywhere near your car."

Lara closed her teeth over her bottom lip to stop it from trembling. Once she had herself under control, she murmured, "If he thinks I'm good to go, then I probably am. Sorry for the trouble." She got to her feet and extended her hand to both policemen.

"I'll walk them to the door and lock up," Trevor said. "See you upstairs."

CHAPTER 25

*L*ara gathered up their wine glasses and clucked to Gunter who followed her through the house and out the back door. Despite the brief time he'd lived with them, the puppy seemed to relish the small daily routines she and Trevor—well, mostly Trevor —had established for him. When he was done in the yard, she detoured through the kitchen to deposit the wine glasses in the sink, then headed for the stairs. Stooping, she gathered Gunter into her arms.

Trevor was already in bed, paging through the little book. He'd brought the puppy's kennel up. Unlatching the wire mesh door, she placed the dog inside where he immediately curled up on his rug.

"Come to bed," Trevor said abruptly. "I'd like to fulfill my part of the bargain with Lillian. It's courting disaster if you tell a Sidhe you're going to do something and then welsh on the deal."

"Okay. Let me run a washcloth over my face and brush my teeth." A few minutes later, she joined him, flicking off the overheads in favor of the muted lights recessed into their headboard.

Trevor cleared his throat and began reading to her in Gaelic. Contrary to his earlier protestations that he didn't read Gaelic well, Lara found the language intensely lyrical and moving. Closing her

241

eyes, she thought she could very nearly see the green hillocks of Scotland swathed in a sea of heather, with a fine mist rising off them. After a time, he switched to English with his mellow, lightly accented voice, and she continued to listen as he read about the ancient Sidhe and their reciprocal relationship with the Goddess Dana. Long before the Mil had overrun Scotland and Ireland, a separate strain of humankind had originated from *beyond the stars*. Whoever authored the historical account described these newcomers as *shining far more brightly than their earthly human counterparts, and possessed of powers not unlike ours.*

"Are you near the end of a chapter?"

"Very close. Only a couple more lines."

Settling deeper onto the pillows, she waited for him to finish and asked quietly, "Do you think that's what I am?"

He took her hand. "I don't know, Lara. Maybe we need to read all of it to figure that out. We finished about a fourth of it just now. The pages aren't numbered, but there can't be more than a hundred."

Something connected in her mind. Exhaustion dropped away and she leaped out of bed. The amulet thrummed excitedly.

"Where are you going?"

"To get my laptop. There's a journal article I want to look at."

Lara crawled back into bed with her computer and booted up. She entered the American Psychological Association's website, dutifully typing her username and password. When her account flared across the screen, she clicked on her journal subscriptions and picked the *Journal of Comparative and Physiological Psychology*. "There's this article Arabel was reading," she explained. "It's about a strain of humans with psychic abilities who came from somewhere else. Wish I'd paid more attention when she told me about it."

"Is that it?" He pointed to an article midway down the highlighted list on her screen.

Clicking, she brought it up. "Yes," she said excitedly. "That must be it. I only have the most recent issues at the office, and this was published four months ago. All the older ones are upstairs in my study."

Moving closer, Trevor draped an arm around her as they read. For a time, the only sounds in the room were Gunter's soft puppy yips as he dreamed of whatever puppies dream about, and the click of keys as Lara moved through the article. Trevor looked up when he was done and said, "Scroll back to the beginning so I can see when they did the research for this."

"You want the list of references, to see where they drew their data from," she pointed out. "They start here." She indicated a group of citations in ultra-fine print following the text of the article. Grumbling, Trevor turned away to filch a pair of reading glasses from his bedside table.

"Hardly ever have to use these," he complained, balancing them on the end of his nose as he looked at the reference list. "Humph. Everything in there is pretty modern as well. Interesting, given some of the conjectures they came up with in the main body of the article."

"It's not so different from that thousand-year-old book you were just reading from." Lara said. "Do you mind if I scroll back through to the beginning to see who the authors are?"

"Not at all."

The article, titled *Another Species of Human*, had been penned by a single author, one Guywright Tarryington M.D., Ph.D., who was affiliated with Dartmouth University. "Let's see what else we can come up with about him," she suggested as she exited from the APA site and moved to Google, where she entered Dr. Tarryington's name.

"Wow!" Trevor pointed to hundreds of hits that popped up. "Whoever he is, the guy's prolific."

"Let's see if intelligent aliens from space are his primary research topic." Lara worked her way down the first of the many Google pages associated with Dr. Tarryington, who happened to be an anthropologist as well as a medical doctor.

After a time, she glanced at Trevor. "Seen enough?" she asked. "Maybe I can order some of his other articles from either the APA or

University of Washington archives. Looks as if he wrote a book on the subject too. I'll order that right now." After a flurry of key clicks, she powered down the computer and reached over the side of their bed to place it gently on the floor.

"There have been stories for years," Trevor said pensively, "about spaceships landing here, disgorging humanlike creatures, and leaving. Look at *Chariots of the Gods* and *Behold a Pale Horse* and *Messages: World's Most Documented Extraterrestrial Contact Story*."

"Well, don't forget *Communion*." She smiled wryly. "That's quite an august group I've suddenly been elevated into. It must be near midnight, dear. We really should try to get some sleep. I'm not feeling as distraught as I was earlier. Who knows? Maybe all this will end up being helpful." She rolled over and held out her arms for a hug. "There's something I've been thinking about, though. If we do leave here, would you mind if we invited Arabel to come with us?"

Trevor turned out the lights and drew her into his arms. "I don't see why not. She's more like a combination mother and friend to you than anything else."

"Thank you," she whispered. "Thank you so much for understanding. If things really are going to hell—and I think they are —she'd be here all alone. She's an old lady. Must be close to eighty, though she's never told me her exact age. I'd worry about her. She doesn't have much family."

"I understand. I care about her too. Always have." He shifted positions slightly. "Can we talk about tomorrow for a couple minutes?"

"Mm-hum." Lara knew she'd be asleep soon. That wonderful warmth was stealing along her limbs, beckoning her to Psyche's realm.

"Did you talk to your broker?"

"Yes. I signed some papers he brought by the office, and he's supposed to call me. Guess we get cash, not gold."

"We need to convert most of the cash into gold. If the government fails, cash won't be worth anything. Anyway, I talked to a guy I've known for years who runs a coin shop and deals in gold bullion. He told me what to do and gave me the names of some firms we could buy gold from."

"If we get to where cash isn't worth anything, don't you think it might be hard to use gold as legal tender?" She snuggled closer. "Who'd be able to give us change for a bar of gold?"

"You've got a point," Trevor agreed. "I didn't want to get stuck with a lot of worthless cash, but we may well end up sitting on piles of gold that aren't much more useful. It's deucedly difficult to know the proper course."

"Yes it is, isn't it? Guess we should go ahead as planned, since it seems anything else would be even riskier." She yawned.

"Just a couple more minutes, love, then I'll get up and read. After we get the cash from the bank tomorrow, I'll leave you at the University."

"But I don't need Roxanne anymore," she reminded him. "At least not immediately. Never did make an appointment with her. So I can go with you, at least until it's time for my class."

"That would be wonderful." He held her close for another minute or two before slipping out of their bed and into his blue terrycloth robe. "'Night, Lara," he said, selected a book from the stack atop a dresser, and let himself out their bedroom door.

When Lara wakened, she wasn't surprised to find herself alone. Trevor really did keep unusual hours, with catnaps during the day to compensate for his lack of sleep at night. After showering, she dressed for the day in jeans, a brightly-colored sweater, and a lavender hoodie. Double checking her overnight bag, she clattered down the stairs in her slippers with the bag banging against the side of her leg. Finding the kitchen empty, she checked the coffee pot. It was full. Once she'd poured herself a cup, she hunted for Trevor and the puppy. When she didn't find them in the back yard, her heart rate accelerated. Where were they?

Did something happen while I was sleeping?

Lara threw the front door open and called Gunter. Squeaky puppy yips reached her ears, and she started breathing again. She took the steps to street level two at a time and traversed the half block to her car. Trevor was under it on a dolly doing something. The puppy was tied to a nearby streetlamp pole.

She bent to pet Gunter. "Trev? What are you up to? I was worried sick when I got up and couldn't find you anywhere in the house."

Slowly, the dolly slid from under the BMW. Grease splotched Trevor's cheek, and his hands were black. "Sorry, love, didn't mean to worry you. Wasn't planning on you being up for at least another hour. I'm getting the rest of those bloody wires out of there. 'Bout done. All I need to do is tighten the ignition from inside the cab."

"I could have taken it to the dealer," she protested. "You didn't need to get all dirty."

"We're taking this car today," he reminded her. "Probably wouldn't have been good to drive it any distance at all with those wires hanging down through the engine compartment. They might've gotten hot and caught fire."

"Thanks, dear. It's good you can take care of these things. You are going to wash up before you get into the car, aren't you?"

He started to laugh. "Oh, you think I should? Why might that be, lassie?"

His mirth was infectious and she giggled. "Never mind, laddie," she shot back. "See you upstairs when you're done." Untying Gunter's leash, she led him up the steps and into the house. A glance at the kitchen clock told her it was just past eight. Knowing Arabel was an early riser, and likely already at the office, Lara settled at the kitchen table with her coffee and dialed her office phone.

"Dr. McInnis's office."

"Arabel, it's me."

"Good mornin', Doc. What a nice surprise. I was just gittin' things in order from last week. What can I do for you?"

"What's the number for that Wenatchee shelter where we sent Bethany?" As Arabel read it off to her, Lara jotted it down. "Okay, thanks. The other thing I want might take a few minutes longer."

"Somethin's up. I can hear it in your voice."

Lara pictured Arabel sitting in her old secretarial chair, eyebrows raised quizzically, deep brown eyes shining with interest. "You know how we've talked about how bad things are getting?" she asked.

"Do I ever," The older woman replied emphatically. "Good thing I got my garden. Couldn't even git into Safeway last night. Went there at seven o'clock, and the place was shut up tighter'n a drum. Since when do the supermarkets close before nine or ten on a Tuesday night? Tell me that."

"That's terrible." Lara felt worried. The neighborhood Arabel lived in was well past its prime. "Did you have enough to eat last night?"

"Oh, I was all right, hon. Heated myself up some soup, and put some peas and tomatoes in along with it."

"Tell me what you wanted to buy. I'll bet Trevor could manage to come up with most of it."

"Thanks, Doc, but I stopped at that IGA just down from the office this mornin'. It was open early. Got what I needed there. But that's not what you wanted to talk with me 'bout, now is it? Here I've just been layin' my troubles at your feet. You go ahead, hon. I'm listenin'."

Lara took a deep breath. "Trevor and I are thinking about finding a little farm somewhere. If we do that we'll be leaving the city, likely for good. Would you like to come with us, dear?"

There was such a long silence Lara wondered if she'd somehow offended her old friend. She heard muffled crying. "Oh, Doc, that is just so kind of you to ask," Arabel snuffled. "But I'se an old woman. I'd just be in the way. You two young'uns wouldn't want to cart me along."

"Oh yes we would." Lara was both emphatic and insistent. "Trevor and I talked about it last night, and he's in full agreement. Please say *yes*. Besides I don't know the first thing about raising vegetables. All that knowledge you have about gardening would be a huge plus.

"Things aren't good here. I'd worry about you all alone in your little house. There are riots elsewhere in the country. It's only a matter of time before they start happening here. In fact, after what you just told me about the supermarket being closed, they'll likely be here before you know it."

Another long silence with more sniffling. Then Arabel's soft drawl came through the phone lines. "Yes. I would love to come with the two of you. I can't thank you enough for askin' me. I've thought you might be leavin', and I didn't know quite what I'd do. I'se too old to find me another job. Ain't nobody hirin' eighty-somethin'-year-old Black ladies. Actually, if you look in the papers, ain't nobody hirin' at all. White or Black. Young'uns or old'uns like me."

Lara smiled; fondness for Arabel welled up within her. "I'll keep you posted on what we find. That's what we're doing for the next few days: looking at property. Sweetie, if I could have picked a mother, I'd have wanted her to be just like you. Thanks for saying yes."

"Oh, hon," Arabel started crying all over again. "That was such a nice thing to tell me, 'cause if I'd had a daughter, I'd've wanted her to be just like you too." There was a pause, and Arabel blew her nose. "You can tell me 'bout what you found on Monday. Be sure to git land that's south facin', though. Makes all the difference in the world in terms of bein' able to grow crops. Got to go. The other line's ringin'."

Lara dialed the Wenatchee battered women's shelter and asked to speak to the director. When she got her on the phone, Lara explained she knew they'd moved Bethany. Next, she told the woman Bethany's abusive husband was dead, and the reason to fear reprisals from his Mexican-mafia kinfolk had evaporated.

"That's marvelous news," the director crowed. "It's so rare for any of our women to actually get to start fresh without having to constantly look back over their shoulders. I'll call where she is and let them know just as soon as we hang up." There was a hesitation. "I'm glad that bastard is dead," she growled, her voice low and frosty.

"Looking at what he did to her—and her so pregnant with his child—just made me ill. Thank you so much for thinking to call us."

"You're welcome. Of course I'd call. I've had quite a few domestic violence patients over the years—"

"That's very nice of you, Doctor." The shelter director broke coldly into Lara's explanation. "But unless you've been a victim yourself, you can't really understand. You only think you do."

The line went dead. *Touché*, Lara thought. *Why should domestic violence be any different from being stalked or robbed? Once it happened to me, I realized I didn't understand those two things, either.*

Maybe it would be a relief to stop being a psychologist after all these years. The front door opened. Yapping shamelessly, Gunter lunged at the puppy gate in an attempt to reach Trevor.

"How about cereal for breakfast today?" he asked as he stopped at the stainless steel sink to scrub ineffectually at his hands. "Need mechanics soap," he muttered, adding, "About ten more minutes and I'll be done."

"Cereal's fine," she agreed. "I'll cut up some fruit to put over it."

Trevor wiped his still-grease-stained hands on paper towels, nodded, and sprinted over the puppy gate on his way outside to finish fixing her car.

LARA GLANCED through her lecture notes for her afternoon class, while Trevor drove them across town. Although she suspected they'd mostly talk about Ryan's dream, she wanted to be prepared in case the dream didn't take up the full hour. Maybe she'd do a short lecture at the front end. At least that way she could pretend to cover the Orphan archetype. Give it a lick and a promise. That particular archetype was never easy to discuss because it mirrored her own life.

She'd been surprised to see two large suitcases in the rear hatch of the BMW when she loaded her overnight bag. "They're for our money," Trevor explained, and she felt stupid. Of course they'd need something to carry it in. Had she thought she'd stuff a few hundred thousand dollars—likely in twenties—into her purse?

"Hope this goes smoothly," he said, pulling the car into the bank parking lot. "Good thing the power's on this morning. Seems to lend everyone a false sense of security."

"Couldn't we just write the gold people a check?" she asked. "Wouldn't that have been easier?"

"That would have meant waiting," he replied. "They wouldn't give us the gold until the check cleared. For that amount, it'd be another ten days. Plus, they told me they prefer cash."

"I'll just bet they do, she muttered. "Good old invisible tax-free cash."

An hour later they walked out of the bank with both suitcases full of bills. Lara assumed they had the proper amount, but they'd counted bundled notes, as opposed to individual bills. *Eh, if they shorted us a thousand or two, it makes very little difference.* "Where to now?" she asked and grinned. "I feel like a bank robber. Want to play Clyde to my Bonnie?"

"Sure, love. I'll be most anything you'd like. We're going downtown to one of those new high-rises on the waterfront. They're expecting us. Gave me a price yesterday that seemed to match the going rate for gold."

"Math was never my strong suit. Tell me how much gold we'll be collecting for half that cash."

"Roughly eleven-and-a-quarter pounds."

"That's all? Somehow I thought it would be more than that. I still think it's wise to keep a chunk of it in cash since we can't spend gold."

"Yeah, I know." He chuckled. "Could have done with a smaller safe, huh?"

"Did you tell them we'd be coming by later to buy more?" She was curious.

"No."

"Maybe they'd have given us a price break."

"It doesn't work like that, love. Not for metals, or any commodity. You pay the market rate on a given day."

"Of course you're right," she murmured, reminded just how out-of-sync she was with modern life and lacking in practical skills to boot. "Good thing I have you, dear. I spend too much time in my head."

He blew a kiss her way. "Nice to be appreciated."

"It sure is." Lara reached across the console to stroke his shoulder. "I have good news. Arabel said she'd come with us when I talked to her this morning."

"That's great, Lara." Trevor beamed. "Just great."

"I had to twist her arm a bit. I think she really wanted to come, but she didn't want to be any sort of burden."

"That's not possible. Tell her she can be the mum I never had. Keep your eyes sharp for an open petrol station. I'd like to fill up sometime between now and when we leave town."

"Funny, I told her she would have been my pick for a mom too." Lara still felt warm inside from her earlier conversation with Arabel. "On a more practical note, I wonder if my broker can just transfer the ETF funds to these gold guys you found. That way we wouldn't have to bother carting cash around."

"That's a brilliant idea. Why don't you float it past them after we get there?"

CHAPTER 26

*I*t took far longer at the gold dealers than Lara imagined it would, since they *did* count the bills—individually. She gave them details regarding her ETF, and they hatched a plan from there. Trevor would stop by Monday to collect the remainder of what she hoped would be enough bullion to last the rest of their lives—assuming it was any more spendable than cash if things went to hell.

The extra time she'd anticipated having to prep for her class evaporated. Trevor dropped her off in front of Denny Hall a scant twenty minutes before her class and promised to not be more than a few minutes late picking her up.

"Not to worry. You're worth waiting for."

"Bet you say that to all the blokes."

"Nope. Just you." Giving him a quick kiss, she flew out of the car and up the well-worn steps of the psychology building. Lara had always loved Denny Hall with its Victorian architecture, and a bell tower right out of *The Hunchback of Notre Dame*. Since she had a couple minutes to spare, she stopped by Roxanne's office and knocked lightly at the closed door.

"Yes?"

"It's Lara McInnis. Are you busy?"

"Not at all. Be right there." The door popped open. Roxanne smiled at Lara, crooking a finger in an invitation to enter. The flamboyant professor was dressed in another flowing skirt. Today's eye shadow was teal green. "Lovely to see you. Did you and Lillian ever get together?"

"Yes." Lara smiled too. "Mostly I wanted to thank you. I have a class to teach in a couple minutes, but Lillian was a perfect referral. Just what I needed."

"I'm so glad. Good of you to let me know." Roxanne glanced down, and Lara saw glitter scattered atop the eye shadow. "Do you suppose you'll be along to any of our, um, festivals?" The professor looked up again, fielding Lara's dark gaze with a direct stare.

"You never know, Roxanne. You just never know. Got to run."

"Thanks for stopping by." Roxanne's softly-modulated voice tracked Lara down the long hallway. "One more thing. Whatever happened with that fellow you told me about?"

"He's not a problem any longer. Thanks for asking," Lara called over her shoulder, chiding herself for her loose tongue from a few days before. The less people knew about her connection with Ken Beauchamp, the better. Roxanne didn't have his name, but still.

"…When the Orphan is a predominant force in our lives, the world can seem quite hopeless," Lara lectured. The same queasy discomfort she always felt discussing this particular archetype twisted her gut into a knot.

"Abandoned by their parents—either actually, or metaphorically—Orphans attract other victims, who suck them dry or predators who take advantage of them. Orphans' emotional lives resemble a disconsolate infant, except the pain and loneliness never go away, because no one ever comes to rescue them. Where might salvation come from for this archetype?" Lara looked at her class—smaller today, with only eight students.

"Well," Natasha answered, her chin resting on an upraised hand, "don't they finally grow up when they give up on finding someone else to fix their pain and find ways to do it themselves?"

"That's correct. Any other thoughts?" Lara stood quietly, hands in her pockets.

Christina Yee raised her hand.

"You don't have to do that," Lara said. "We're small enough, you can just say whatever you'd like."

"When the Orphan takes control of someone's life, can they become more like a Warrior?"

"Camus—and Kolbenschlag too—talk about that," Lara agreed. "The gift of the Orphan archetype can be movement toward self-reliance, with a healthy give-and-take attitude. If Orphans free themselves from their dependence on external authority figures, they find a great deal of satisfaction helping others."

"Say more about Camus," Michael requested. "I've always been drawn to existentialism."

"I'd be glad to." Lara clasped her hands behind her back. "Then we need to make a choice about whether to delve more deeply into the Orphan archetype or move back to Ryan's dream from last week.

"According to Camus, when the Orphan becomes more of a Rebel by taking control of his own life, he might join with the Warrior archetype and really come into his own. Madonna Kolbenschlag, on the other hand, believes female Orphans are more likely to mature through an association with the Caregiver archetype."

"That seems old-fashioned," Natasha murmured. "Wasn't she supposed to be a feminist?"

"Yes, but she started doing research in the mid nineteen-fifties," Lara reminded her. "That's likely why Kolbenschlag's ideas feel a bit dated to you. What do you want to do next, more Orphan or Ryan's dream?"

Ryan looked around at the group. "I'm still interested in talking about it, but I'm not nearly as freaked out as I was last week."

Funny, Lara thought, since she was far more *freaked out*, to borrow Ryan's nomenclature, than she'd been the previous Wednesday. She settled on the edge of a soft chair and waited for her students to make up their minds.

"We did make a commitment to Ryan," Michael said. "We should honor it."

Despite his brave words from a few moments before, Ryan looked pathetically grateful. "Who wants to begin?" she asked. "Did any of you write down the elements of the dream and free associate to them?"

"I did," Ryan admitted. "At least until I got so scared I couldn't go on."

Lara narrowed her eyes and motioned for Ryan to keep talking.

"Guess I need to learn that technique, huh?" He made a weak joke. "All you had to do was waggle your fingers, and I understood exactly what you wanted."

"Years of experience, dear. But you're stalling. What frightened you? Close your eyes and reconstruct what happened."

He was silent for a time, his forehead crinkled deeply in thought. When he opened his hazel eyes, they still looked apprehensive, with faint dark smudges under them. "I'm not sure exactly, but the harder I looked at the dream, the surer I was the world was going to end. Is that crazy or what?" He laughed thinly to cover his discomfiture.

"What about the rest of you?" Lara asked. "Did you spend much time with Ryan's dream?"

Christina started to raise her hand, but then pulled it down. "I did." She swiveled in her chair to look at Ryan. "I got the same hit off it you did. The longer and harder I looked, the darker it got. I think the tree is supposed to be the Tree of Life. It's struggling for purchase after half its root structure fails, and all that dirt falls in. Scared the shit out of me to be honest."

Lara glanced at the clock in the back of the room. *I have time, but should I?* Swallowing hard, she made up her mind. "Let me run an interpretation by all of you. You can think about it between now and when we meet next." Stammering a bit at the beginning, she launched into Lillian's recitation about the dream. When she was done, the class looked thunderstruck. Rachel and Natasha wept quietly.

"It's just so hopeless," Rachel sniffed. "Coming from you, it sounded so…so real. What can we do, Dr. McInnis? Is it too late for all of us?" She reached out to Lara with solemn brown eyes, beseeching her to play mommy and say everything would be all right.

"I don't know, Rachel." Lara spoke slowly. "That interpretation rings true for me. Looking at all of you, I'd venture to guess it did for you as well. What that usually means is it's valid. As to what's to be done, I'm not sure where to start. We all have a personal responsibility to live conscientiously. If we could do that, it might help, but many variables are beyond our control." She looked at their young, stricken faces and felt horrible. "I wish I could say something more hopeful."

"Makes me want to go home," Natasha murmured. "If this will be the end of all things, I would like to be back in Russia."

"You couldn't get there." Ryan sounded defeated. "Two more airlines failed in the last couple weeks. They say there's no fuel for the planes."

"Huh! At least that should help the air pollution problem. Not sure for what, though. Sounds as if it's already too late," Michael said, angrily. "We're past the hour, and I've got another class. Not sure why I'm bothering at this point, except I don't know what else to do." Standing abruptly, he slung his backpack over one shoulder and stomped out of the faculty lounge. One by one, his classmates followed him, their heads bent in thought.

Lara realized she hadn't assigned an archetype to study for the following week. Shaking her head, she wondered if they'd even finish out the quarter before something hideous happened.

SHE SPIED the BMW in Trevor's favorite no parking zone. He had Gunter on a leash, and the puppy was sniffing the large trees lining the avenue in front of Denny Hall. As soon as he spied Lara, he yipped happily and tried to run to her, stopping short as he hit the end of his tether. Lara bent, murmuring her usual endearments, and he licked the tip of her nose.

She straightened and gave Trevor a quick hug. "You got here earlier than you thought. I'm glad. Class was hard. We talked about the dream."

"There wasn't much traffic," he explained. "Maybe the lack of petrol's finally catching up, and people aren't driving as much. It only took a couple minutes to put the money and gold in the safe, secure the house, and get him." He crooked a finger at Gunter. "Would have been even earlier, but Lillian called. There's a piece of property she wants us to look at. Told me how to get there and that someone, a Mr. Brighton, would be expecting us."

Lara raised her eyebrows, realizing she wasn't nearly as irritated by Lillian's interference as she would have been a few days before. "Where's it located?" she asked.

"You go to Skykomish. After that, it gets complicated. A forest road travels north for several miles, and then there's a turnoff near a place called Garland Hot Springs. Lillian said it would take a couple hours. Guess after you turn off the Interstate, the dirt road's slow going—"

The sound of angry voices split the still afternoon, and Lara spun, hunting for the source. "Oh my God, what's that?"

Trevor scooped up the puppy and sprinted for the car. "Run," he urged sharply. "Sounds like a demonstration. Lived through a bunch of those in the seventies. We've got to get out of here."

She barely made it to the BMW, slammed her door, and locked it, when a throng of angry students waving placards swept up the street, their arms linked. They shouted epithets and other things she couldn't make out. Craning her neck, Lara looked at the signage they carried. It all held some variant of an environmental message.

She clambered over the divider into the back seat and held out her hands for the dog. "I'll put him in his crate."

"Those riots in the rest of the country," Trevor said, his voice low. "They finally made it here."

She made her way back to her seat. "We should probably stay right here until the street's clear," she mumbled.

"No shit, Sherlock," he snapped, and then took her hand. "Sorry. I'm not mad at you, love. I'm mad at me. I knew this would happen. We should already be moved, not at the front end of hunting for somewhere to go. Hope they don't stone the car."

"Ach, I hadn't even thought about that." She shrank down in her seat, aiming for invisibility behind the BMW's tinted glass.

"It's us they're demonstrating against, love. We're the ones who were in charge, who should've known better." His voice developed a rough edge.

"I know, I know," she sputtered. "But it's hard for me to see *us* as the enemy." As she watched, horrified by a spectacle that reminded her of news footage from the nineteen sixties, the rowdy group passed them by. Errant fists banged on the roof of their car. She held her breath, jaw clenched tightly, waiting for the crash of breaking safety glass, but it never came. The roar of the BMW's engine caught at her attention, and she realized Trevor was backing out of his illegal parking spot, heading for Forty-Fifth Street.

"Get your University ID out," he instructed. "They probably won't wave us through this time."

"Before we get on the freeway, maybe we could swap drivers," she said, her voice unsteady. "I'd like you to read me more of that book from Lillian. It'll give me something else to think about. You did bring it?"

"It's tucked in my jacket pocket." He patted the front of his tan corduroy blazer.

She flashed her ID as they slowed down at the exit station, but true to Trevor's prediction, the guard motioned for them to stop. "Yes?" Lara leaned over the center console of the car and motioned to Trevor to activate the electronics to roll the window down.

"There's trouble on campus and in the University District. Hundreds of students demonstrating. Guess they're tired of the gas prices, or no gas at all. And a whole bunch of other stuff."

"We know," Lara said. "We saw some of them."

"It's a rowdy crew. Some are armed. Good night to get yourselves home and stay there." He lowered his voice. "I'm not supposed to tell you this, but it'll be on the news soon enough. A couple kids have been killed over at the Administration Building. I think it was only two, but there may have been more since my report came in." The man looked shaken. Lara imagined he rarely had to deal with violence in his University cop job.

"Thanks for the advice about going home." She smiled tightly and settled back against her seat. The guard, who seemed to want to continue unburdening himself, took the hint and finally motioned them through.

"What's the quickest way out of here?" Trevor asked through gritted teeth. His knuckles were white against the dark gray leather of the steering wheel.

"Left on Forty-Fifth, then another left on Fifteenth—"

"No, the fastest way to the Interstate."

"We're probably better off going left at the light up here, and then straight until we hit the freeway. It gets us farther from campus faster. Jesus, Trev, do you think this is the beginning of things falling apart here in Seattle, or just random events? Students do demonstrate. They always have. Screaming uber-liberal slogans is a really old refrain."

"Give me a break, Lara." His voice was thin, strained. "Look out there."

She did look and saw half a dozen groups of young people carrying signs, a variety of clubs, and the occasional rifle.

"It's definitely the beginning of something," he went on. "The only question is whether things will settle down before they get worse again."

"Scratch my suggestion about switching drivers," she muttered. "At least until we get out of town." He didn't answer. She could tell from the tight line of his jaw that he was willing the car to make the timed lights on Forty-Fifth. "Do you mind if I click on the radio?" she asked.

"Good idea." He pushed the knobs himself, using the search feature to find news. A scratchy announcer's voice filled the car with unsettling information.

"…and in South Seattle, we have six dead and ten wounded from an explosion at Wal-Mart. A gang war's broken out in the Wallingford District. Citizens are advised to go to their homes and lock their doors. Do not admit anyone you don't know. This just in from the University District. At least five hundred students are rioting. We have reports of two dead and at least a dozen trampled on campus this afternoon…"

Lara listened, appalled as the newscaster detailed mob violence in several other locations. Then he started in on traffic snarls. "We can't take the bridge," she said, feeling frantic. Sweat dripped down her sides, and fear chilled her. "They closed it after a two-car accident where one of the drivers pulled a gun and shot the other. Shit, the world's falling apart."

"I wasn't planning to go that way," he said in a voice that didn't sound very much like the Trevor she knew. "We'll go north through Bothell. That route's actually faster. By the way, I brought the shotgun. It's in the boot along with the other luggage."

Lara hugged herself, unable to stop trembling. She adjusted the temperature on her side of the car and zipped her hooded sweatshirt. "Heard enough?" she asked as she reached for the radio, since she couldn't stand to listen any longer.

He glanced at her. "It's not easy stuff to hear, but we need to leave it on, if only for the traffic updates, until we get out of town. Tell me about what happened in your class?"

As she recounted her afternoon, she felt progressively worse. Her head pounded, and her stomach felt unsettled. "Not much I can do about the dream—or my students. Let's refocus. We're not going to track down that property out of Skykomish tonight are we? It'll be dark in less than two hours, and I don't want to beat around on dirt roads at night hunting for a place that's probably haunted."

"Why would it be haunted?"

"Because Lillian's sending us there. Maybe haunted isn't exactly the right word. It's a sure bet the place won't be normal, though." She sighed brokenly. "Sorry, Trev. That demonstration really spooked me. I didn't mean to sound so harsh."

"It's okay." He reached over and took one of her hands. "What would you like to do once we clear the I-5 corridor?"

"Maybe find a nice pleasant supper somewhere, and a motel tucked away from the freeway. We both need to unwind."

"We can do that," he agreed. "Now that we're on the Interstate, traffic's been better than I expected. We'll be at the turnoff in just a few minutes. We'll look for a place to stay in Snohomish or Monroe. If nothing pans out, there're those three little towns on up the highway where I'm sure we'll be able to find what you're looking for."

"Sultan, Startup, and Gold Bar?"

"The same." He glanced at her. "Bet they haven't changed much in the two or three years since we've been out this way." He hesitated a beat. "You never take any time off."

"You're right. I should take more." She rubbed gingerly at her right temple, grateful her headache wasn't getting worse. "Buck up, dear," she grumbled dryly. "All my time will be off-time pretty soon here. No one will be able to pay me if things keep unraveling. Actually, other than the few cash-and-carry folk I see, the insurance companies are months in arrears now."

"You told me that a few nights ago." He chuckled wryly. "Good ploy on their part. Stall long enough and civilization implodes. Then they never have to pay you."

"That is so not funny."

"Didn't mean it to be."

They drove in silence for the next several minutes, listening to the crackly voice of the radio newscaster. "...this just in from Tacoma. Riots have closed the Narrows Bridge. Rioters on the bridge are throwing firebombs at stalled cars. Drivers are advised to take an alternate route. We'll repeat that for you. Riots on the Narrows Bridge have..."

"Could this really be happening so fast?" Lara's voice was so gravelly with worry she barely recognized it.

"Don't know why you're so surprised," he replied. "Seattle's starting to look like a lot of the rest of the country. Quite a lot of the social erosion the guy is chronicling on KIRO is just the normal bad stuff that happens every day. You miss an amazing amount when you ignore the news."

"Yes," she said faintly, "I suppose I do. After listening to people's problems all day, the last thing I want is to hear more of the same from the media." She laughed bitterly. "That's an indulgence I can't afford any longer, huh?"

"I don't know about that. If we truly end up leaving, there won't be any television, radio, newspapers, or Internet for you to disregard."

"A side benefit?"

"You could call it that. Try to relax, love. No point worrying over what we can't control."

CHAPTER 27

They found a cozy bed and breakfast inn that allowed pets just outside Monroe. As they strolled down a tree-lined street after a mediocre dinner at a Thai restaurant, Lara took Trevor's hand. It was shaping up to be a lovely sunset, the western horizon ablaze with pastel colors. Inhaling deeply, she felt far better than she had during their precipitous flight from the dissention-ridden campus.

"The world's sort of ordinary again, at least here," she said with an ironic smile. "Even though nothing's really changed. Hell, for all I know they could have gotten worse."

"Not much point in turning that over and over, now is there?" he replied thoughtfully. "It's pretty early yet. Would you like to go back to our room and spend some time with the Gaelic book?"

"Sure, Trev. Your language skills are such a plus."

Handing Lara the dog's leash, Trevor dug into a pocket until he came up with the room key. It was the old-fashioned kind: a real key, not an electronic card. He pushed the door open and motioned for her to go inside. "I'll double check the car's secure," he said. "You may not have noticed, but we're their only guests tonight, at least so far. Parking lot's empty."

"Do you want to bring the car closer to the room?"

"That's what I was planning." Trevor's engaging grin was back in place, but Lara sensed agitation and worry beneath the surface of his well-cultivated persona.

Over the next three hours, they finished the meager volume. Trevor's Gaelic was truly magical. Lara slipped into a pleasant trance almost as soon as he began to read.

The English translation wasn't nearly as relaxing, since she had to pay close attention. Listening, she pieced together that there'd been a series of spaceships leaving human-like creatures on Earth over a thousand year period. She wasn't sure of the time frame, since the translation for those particular Gaelic words was far from exact. The Sidhe, recognizing these humanoids were gifted, chose to mate with them. In doing so, they created a race of people with variable magical abilities, some of whom were nearly as powerful as themselves.

Laying the book on the quilted comforter, Trevor said, "Wow. It's one thing to read something modern like *Chariots of the Gods* where I can discount what I don't want to believe. It's quite another to read this book that's hand-written, and so old the pages are moldering away to dust. Gives me something to think about, particularly since this style of language died out before the Christian era. They hadn't heard of modern science, but it reads the same as that research article you pulled up online."

"Let's take the pup out." Lara got to her feet. "A walk would do us both good. My head's really full. Lillian must have loaned us that book because those people you were reading about are my ancestors. Christ, I wonder where my parents came from, and if it was just one of them or both of them, or—?"

Trevor stood and hugged her hard. "You'll probably never know." He clipped the leash to the wriggling puppy's collar. "Too bad we never had children. Whatever you have, well, they would have had it too."

Lara burst out laughing as she thought about the adolescents that had marched through her practice over the years. "Maybe it's good we didn't," she finally managed. "It's hard enough to raise kids. I can't even imagine how tough it would've been to raise one with magical ability." She giggled. "You've stuffed him in his room as a punishment, and he levitates out of there."

"Come on." Trevor's smile ran deeper than it had earlier. "It's starting to drizzle. If we hustle, we can get the dog walked and us back inside before it starts to pour."

They leaned into one another, drinking in the pastoral feel of rural western Washington, and rounded the end of the block. The dog had gotten better about not pulling on his leash.

"I suppose," Lara said after a time, "this place Lillian's directed us to is where we'll end up."

"Yeah, I'd figured as much too," he admitted. "The logistics of actually moving are overwhelming. We'd never be able to hire a truck, since it's best if no one knows where we're going. If things continue spiraling downward, we'd be the first place the movers would raid after they got hungry enough."

"My God, you're suggesting we'd do everything ourselves. You've got to be kidding." She stopped walking and just looked at him, her eyes wide with disbelief.

"Uh, no. I'm not. Not exactly, anyway." He draped an arm over her shoulders. "It's raining harder, let's turn around." Back in their room, he took off his damp jacket, shaking it briskly before hanging it over a chair. "I wasn't thinking we take all that much from the Queen Anne house," he explained. "You won't need any of those fancy work duds of yours. About all we'd need are some pots and pans, and a few dishes. It would be stupid to bring the crystal and china. A few books, lots of sturdy warm clothes, and that should do it.

"A lot of what you'll need, you don't even have yet. Like a few pairs of stout boots, rain gear, some long johns, and probably some down-stuffed outer garments."

"Hold up there, Thoreau." She sat on the edge of the bed to unlace her boots. "I assumed we'd hire a moving company, transport everything, and sort through it after we got situated."

"Think about it, Lara. That wouldn't be smart. Like with your clothes, we'll need lots of things we don't have yet. Not to mention farm equipment. And animals."

Heat crept up her neck. "Right you are. Again." Plumping the pillows, she lay on her stomach and rested her head on folded hands, elbows akimbo. "One problem is I haven't said goodbye to our old life yet. That's much harder than it ought to be. For Christ's sake, today should have pounded some sense into me, but apparently it didn't."

"Takes time, Lara. I've been thinking about this for longer than you have. Besides, you've got other things vying for your attention."

"Like the magical witch from Alpha Centuri, who was my great-great-great-great grandmother?" A corner of her mouth twitched.

"Yeah, her. Probably other stuff too, like your patients and your students. We've spent years building something together. It's not easy to walk away from. Doesn't matter if we know there's no other way out; we're bound to feel we're losing something. At least at first." He petted the puppy, who'd been pawing him for attention. "I love our home, Lara. Wish we could transplant it, but we can't."

"I love *you*, Trev. Come hold me."

"Can I bring my buddy?"

Gunter had his front paws on their bed and scrabbled for purchase with his rear legs, as he tried to climb onto the quilt. "Here you go, little guy. Go comfort Mum." He hoisted the rapidly-growing puppy up, and then joined Lara on the suddenly-too-small bed.

"Now that I know who I am," she said, her voice muffled against his shoulder, "The next thing is to discover what will protect me."

"Yes, that's what Lillian suggested."

"Mmph. Maybe I should have brought that other book along. The one I couldn't figure out before."

He repositioned himself, prying one hand from under her head to tenderly stroke her cheek. "We have it."

"But how? I left it at home."

"I thought you might want it after we finished the Gaelic book. So I popped it in my bag."

Lara kissed him lightly on the tip of his nose and murmured, "I'll take another crack at it tomorrow while we're on the road."

∾

THEY SAT over a lush breakfast of crepes, with strawberries, kiwis, blueberries, and clotted cream, Trevor scraped the plate with his fork. "Is there any more?" he asked hopefully.

"There certainly is." The innkeeper, a woman who looked to be in her seventies, smiled. "I always did like to see a man with a healthy appetite. Everyone's on a diet nowadays."

"Where did you get all this wonderful fruit?" Lara asked curiously.

"I've got a greenhouse out back. I'm Ruth, by the way. Told you that last night, but you might not have remembered. Nice to meet you both. We don't get much in the way of guests this time of year, but business should pick up again come spring."

"Do you really think so?" Lara bit her lower lip, wishing she could take the words back. Ruth didn't need a crash course in reality.

"Oh, you mean all that mess out there?" Ruth's pleasant smile twinkled at Lara, and she waved her hands expansively. "I don't pay it much mind. We've always had summer guests here. It's been over fifty years I've kept this place. I expect I'll have guests next summer, like always. If I don't, well, that'll be all right too. Mostly, I like the company."

Pouring herself another cup of truly excellent coffee to cover her embarrassment, Lara said, "I hope everything works out for you."

"Why, thank you. It's been lonely since my Timothy died last year. Not much chance of finding another husband at my age. Besides, not sure as I'd want one, even if a likely prospect did turn up."

Trevor glanced at his watch. "When you finish your coffee, Lara, we really ought to get moving. It's past nine."

"I know. Not sure why we slept so late."

"It's fair relaxing here." Ruth's blue eyes twinkled at her again.

"Most of my guests say they've never slept quite so deeply as they do here."

"Now that you mention it, I did sleep well." It had surprised her after the stress from the riot and the disquieting archetypal dream. Swallowing the last of her coffee, she turned to Ruth. "Thank you so much. Breakfast was wonderful. I'm sure we'll stay here again."

The old woman smiled knowingly. "I believe you will. I'm open all year. Just ring the bell out front."

It was still drizzling when they pulled out of the deserted parking lot of the Restful Inn. "We should top out the tank. Hope I can find a station," Trevor said.

"Looks like an open one right over there." Lara pointed up the street.

"Seven bucks a gallon! Never mind. At least they have some. Or their sign says they do."

"I'll drive after we fill up," she offered. "You're better with the maps. I can catch up with that book later."

It wasn't very far to the cutoff onto State Route Sixty-Five. After studying the map, Trevor determined that was far more expedient than the way Lillian suggested, and he directed Lara accordingly. "Guess she must be like me," Lara laughed. "No sensate ability."

"What exactly does that mean?" he asked, curious. "I've heard you say it before, but I never really understood it."

"Oh." She glanced over at him, a surprised look on her face. "It just means we're intuitive, rather than sensate. It's one of the elements in Jung's description of different personality types. Basically, I gather my information from inside myself, rather than using real world feedback. It's why you're so much better than me at the practical, real-world stuff. You're more evenly balanced on the intuitive-sensate continuum."

"Gee, that makes everything crystal clear." He smiled, the fine lines around his eyes crinkling with pleasure. "It's just lovely up here, don't you think?"

Lara gazed at the trees. Huge evergreens towered above the

winding country road. It was becoming progressively more difficult to picture the troubled world they'd left behind.

"I'm not sure I have Lillian's affinity for trees," she said, "but I've always found them comforting. I thought you needed open land to farm, though. This forest feels primeval. I don't see how we could clear enough of it to grow anything."

"Depends what you're farming," he replied. "We'll have at least a couple goats and several chickens. They can forage, but that takes space, as opposed to vegetables that we could raise in a green house. Slow down, our next turn is coming up soon."

"Oh my. Do you suppose that's it?" Braking hard, shortly after taking the side road Trevor indicated, she stopped the car abruptly and stared. The amulet throbbed encouragingly.

An unexpected clearing rose out of nowhere. Off to one side sat a rambling three-story wooden house—or lodge by the look of it—with a number of outbuildings scattered about. The lodge was crafted from enormous, rough-hewn logs; smoke curled lazily upward from both chimneys, one at either end. A wraparound porch held inviting chairs, arranged in groups of twos and threes.

Off to one side, a horse grazed behind paddock gates. Goats, sheep, and chickens wandered freely, with no fence to keep them from straying. A craggy peak rose right behind the house, and a rushing stream tumbled from unseen heights.

Maneuvering the car across a bridge that spanned the stream, Lara murmured, "Do you suppose this is where Lillian means for us to settle? It's wonderful."

"Well, it's certainly private, which solves one worry. Park the car. I want to get out and have a look-see." From the back, Gunter barked excitedly to let them know he wanted out too.

Lara released the hatch and went to free the puppy. "Do you think he'll chase the livestock?" she asked worriedly.

"Not a big deal if he does at this point. He's too slow and clumsy to catch anything. In fact, it might be good if one of those roosters nailed him with a spur. Teach him to leave the chickens alone."

Lara dropped the leash back into the car and breathed in the still air, entranced. The scent was reminiscent of the trees surrounding Lillian's house. Part musk, part rich loam, the heady odor filled her with hope. *Yes,* she thought wistfully, *an ingredient that's been lacking of late. I need Pandora and that box of hers.*

Laughing softly at her digression into mythology, she caught up to Trevor He'd walked to the stream so Gunter could get a drink, and the puppy was playing in the water. Silvery fish swam by, drawn downstream by the current.

"You two got here in good time," a voice said from behind them.

Startled, Lara spun and took in the tall, powerfully-built man with flowing waist-length black hair. He was dressed in mud-stained khakis, topped by a colorful shirt studded with runic symbols. A thick black beard fell halfway down his chest. Merry gray eyes, stark cheekbones, and a high-bridged nose lent him an arresting appearance.

"You must be Mr. Brighton," Trevor said. Striding forward, hand extended, he added, "Nice to meet you."

"Nice to meet you as well. Please, call me Raven."

"How did you know we were coming?" Lara asked, curious. "Surely you don't have phone service out here."

"I've known Lillian for a long time. She and I have a connection that doesn't require telephones. Would you like to come in? Or would you prefer to walk around out here? I can show you the different buildings. Garland Mineral Springs has been around for well over a hundred years. Most of it has been rebuilt many times since then, but there's still the original spring house. Much of the barn's original too."

"What do you think?" Trevor glanced at Lara. "I'd just as soon take the grand tour, so long as we're outside."

"Fine with me," she agreed. "How long have you lived here, Mr., uh, Raven?"

"Long enough," he replied in a tone that, while warm, didn't invite further questioning. "That's the spring house. It was built over a natural hot spring that never was all that warm. There's always had to be some sort of heating mechanism to ensure the water's actually hot enough to wash dishes or bathe once it gets to the main house…"

Over the next hour, they walked through the spring house, the barn, the root cellar, the tool shed—that included a blacksmith's bench—and a machine shop. A Model A Ford sat behind the shop. "Does it still run?" Trevor asked, excited as always by vintage machinery.

"Of course she still runs. And a lot easier to keep after than that fancy contraption you drove in here, I might add." Raven ran a hand lovingly over the highly polished hood.

"It would have to be," Trevor agreed. "Back when this was built, everyone was his own mechanic."

"The house?" Lara moved toward the main building. "When was it first constructed? Looks solid for how old it must be. Why do you want to sell this place, anyway?"

"I don't."

"What?" She turned to look at him. "Lillian sent us here because she knew we were looking for property to buy. So, naturally, I assumed this place was for sale."

"We don't believe in owning things, especially not parts of nature. Gaia is the rightful custodian of the natural world. We simply maintain it for Her. Come inside. We'll have a cup of tea and talk some more." Moving past her, Raven led the way up the broad front porch steps and into the house. "Come on, pup." Just as drawn to Raven as he'd been to Lillian, Gunter trotted into the lodge hard on Raven's heels.

CHAPTER 28

The interior of the structure had a turn-of-the-century feel. Kerosene lanterns hung on hooks and sat on several highly-polished wooden tables. The floors were planked wood, and the huge exterior logs had been meticulously cut away to accommodate unusually thick windows made out of a wavy fin-de-siècle glass. Off to one side Lara saw two staircases, one heading up and the other down.

Raven shepherded them through the single large room that made up the downstairs and gestured for them to sit at a circular table in the kitchen. A pump affair perched over the sink, and a vintage wood-fired stove took up most of one wall. Shelves and open cupboards held a variety of fresh and dried fruits, vegetables and herbs. Maybe it was the herbs, but the interior of the house had a dreamy aroma that wafted about them. Lara picked out lavender, mint, and rosemary, with undercurrents of other less familiar scents.

Trevor gawked at the old-fashioned kitchen and asked, "Don't you have problems with mice with all that open shelving? When I was growing up, we shut everything in bins, but the mice still got in."

"You have to make friends with them." Raven grinned. Very

straight, white teeth contrasted vividly with his midnight-dark beard. "I put the kettle on earlier. Might I brew you some tea?"

"That would be lovely. Anything I can do to help?" Trevor glanced at the stove.

"No. Just make yourself comfortable."

"Tea would be nice," Lara agreed. "But Raven, we don't want to waste your time. If this place isn't for sale, I'm not sure I understand why we're even here. It's not just the two of us that will be moving. We'll be bringing an older friend—well, she's really more like a family member—with us."

"I already know about that." Raven gestured at an antique china tea set in the center of the table. "Help yourself. There's goat's milk and honey in those containers."

"How could you possibly know about Arabel?" Lara demanded, feeling her muscles tense. "I didn't tell Lillian about her."

He cocked his head to one side. "You need to shield your thoughts if you don't want others in your mind." He sipped his tea. "You could learn easily enough."

"About this place." Trevor changed the subject abruptly, apparently even more uncomfortable than her with a world where shamans ranged freely.

"What about it?" Raven focused his storm-tossed gray eyes on Trevor and steepled his fingers together.

"Why are we here?" Trevor asked.

"That's simple enough. Lillian told me you two are leaving the city permanently. A good choice, by the way. Things are actually far worse than they appear."

"How do you know?" Lara stared at him. She balled her hands into fists, but the amulet radiated soothing warmth, in clear contradiction to her inner turmoil.

"Which do you want to hear about first?" He looked amused, eyes shining above his unruly facial hair. "This house, or the burgeoning civil unrest."

"I'd rather concentrate on the house," Trevor replied. "The rest doesn't really matter. At least not at the moment."

"Do you agree?" Raven looked closely at Lara. At her curt nod, he continued, "All right, we'll begin with the house. I am not here all that much. The animals and garden need tending, and as you may have noticed, there's plenty of space. You haven't looked through the upper floors, but there are close to twenty rooms. As things stand, I'm forced to return here more often than I'd like. My abilities are sorely needed in other locales, and that's not likely to change." Raven glanced from Trevor to Lara and back again.

"So you're looking for a tenant-farmer?" Trevor asked curiously. "That doesn't seem terribly secure. What if you don't think we're doing a good enough job?"

"Or what if we can't get along?" Lara chimed in.

Raven threw back his head and laughed. "Spoken like a true twenty-first century woman, my dear. Where I come from, people were packed into buildings far smaller than this one. While they worried about many things, whether they liked one another was pretty low on the list."

"Where did you come from?" she countered. "Since you brought it up."

"The same place as Lillian."

Lara waited, but it was clear he wasn't going to say anything further. "Are you Sidhe too?" she ventured.

"What do you think?" he asked mildly.

"Lara," Trevor laid a hand over hers, "I scarcely see where this is relevant. Let's circle back to the terms and conditions around this farm."

"There aren't any." Raven was still smiling.

"What? I must not have heard you right. Surely you'd want some sort of rent if we were to settle here." Trevor's blue eyes clouded with doubt, and he met and held Raven's gaze.

"Look," Raven explained patiently, "I already told you I don't own this place."

"Who does?" Lara was beginning to feel exasperated. "If it's not yours, how can you offer it to us?"

"This farm has been deserted since the nineteen-fifties. Checking the County Clerk's registry—which I did a very long time ago—there are no blood kin of the last owners, and no will. When that happens, things revert to the state. I've been here off and on for nigh onto sixty years, and no one's ever bothered me." Raven took another sip of tea. The cup looked odd, and out of place, dwarfed by his large-boned hand. "What's left of the government will fail soon enough. I'd say the ownership of these few acres is the least of anyone's concerns."

"But we'd want to pay you something," Lara protested.

"Why?" Raven raised his bushy dark brows. "Money's not worth much now. And it won't be worth anything soon. What would I do with your money? You'd be better off using it to stock this place with more animals, seeds, fencing materials, and some nineteenth century hand tools to help you manage."

The Alice in Wonderland adventure that began in Lillian's tree house rose to claim Lara, its hungry maw open and snapping. She dropped her head into her hands. *Wish I knew what to think. Can we trust him?*

The amulet thrummed warmly against her bare skin as if it were saying, "Yes. You can."

"We'll consider your offer." Trevor sounded subdued. "Maybe we could see the rest of the house? Then we'll leave to explore some of the other places I found betwixt here and Ellensburg."

Nodding, Raven rose to his feet. "You must promise you'll stop back by here before you return to Seattle. So you can tell me your decision."

"Certainly. It's the least we can do." Trevor said, retreating to an understated British graciousness.

"Come on." Raven gestured. "I want you to see the rest of the house. There's a rather unique room on the second floor that I think was designed especially for the two of you."

Trailing after their host—and Gunter, who'd permanently attached himself to Raven—they wandered through the rest of the rambling structure. Raven had been right about the spacious bedroom on the second floor, with a large picture window that looked out at the mountain she'd noticed when they first arrived. A cozy four-poster bed backed against the log wall, and a fireplace was recessed into a corner.

"This must be your room," Lara protested. "We wouldn't want to displace you."

"I don't sleep within walls." A corner of Raven's mouth crooked upward. "All the furniture here was left by previous residents. Other than airing it out, I haven't changed much. There's a tub behind that curtain there," he pointed toward an alcove. "You can coax a tepid bath out of it in a pinch. Or you can heat water on the stove downstairs and haul it up here if you'd like it a bit warmer. Or you could repair the heating mechanism in the spring house."

The top floor housed a series of small bedrooms, tucked under the slanting eaves. There'd been a few rooms on the second and third floors Raven hadn't shown them. Lara assumed that they were either empty or similar to the many rooms he opened up for them to view. The basement drew Lara's attention. Separated into many cubicles, each with a tub, it was apparent this must have been where the hot springs guests soaked.

"Water *is* a bit hotter down here," Raven said, confirming her impression. "At least it was when the heating contrivance in the spring house was operational. Anyway, I've not used this part of the house for anything." He hesitated before adding, "I don't care for being underground."

"Didn't the Sidhe mine for silver?" Trevor asked as they trooped up the stairs to the main floor.

"Who told you that?" Raven stared at Trevor, his grey eyes blazing with anger.

Trevor extended his hands in a placating gesture and mumbled, "Just an old wives tale, I'm sure."

"Old wives tale, indeed," Raven sputtered. "Silver is mortal poison

—to all of us. Goblins too. Unfortunate, since it means we can't wield it to wipe them out. Goddess curse them. Goblins always were a scourge."

"Is that why the Sidhe mated with humans? So their offspring *could* do things like that?" Lara looked sharply at their host and walked toward the front door.

"Ah, so you read the book?" His ill temper dispersed as quickly as it'd ignited, and Raven held out a hand. "Now that you mention it, I feel its presence. If you're done, might you return it to me? I'll see it finds its way back to Lillian."

Trevor pulled the slender tome from an inner jacket pocket and handed it carefully to Raven, who caressed the worn leather binding as if the book were a holy relic. *Who knows?* she mused. *Perhaps it is to the Sidhe.*

"You didn't answer my question," she persisted.

"Yes, child, I know. If you two settle here, there'll be more than enough time for all your questions. Time for teaching as well." Raven placed his thick index finger beneath Lara's chin and tipped her head upward so their eyes met. "You must be near to one of us for a time," he said, speaking deliberately. "You know next to nothing of what you can do."

"The other book—" She stammered, unable to look away from light glimmering deep within his eyes. "Since you knew about the Gaelic book, you must know about the other one too. If I brought it in here, could you answer some questions?"

Raven cocked his head to one side. "I'm not sure which book you're referring to, but by all means, go get it and let's have a look."

"I'll go," Trevor offered. "After I deliver the book, I want do some more poking around, if it's all right with you. The Gaelic book was intriguing, but I've had a peek at this one, and Lara's right. It's incredibly dense."

"Of course you can poke around. Get a good feel for the place," Raven said. "We'll be on the porch. It's still early in the day, but it's not too cold out."

"Thank you," Lara said and hurried outside, intent on retrieving the book from Trevor.

~

"Here," Lara pointed. "And on this page too. What does the reference to Hermes mean? I know he's the messenger of the gods, but it appears he has a far different role here, one I'm not at all familiar with." She and Raven had settled at one of the round tables on the generous front porch. They sat close together so they could both look at the book, and Lara felt an energy field emanating from him.

Intrigued, she opened herself to his aura. "Oh my," she gasped as multi-hued strands of light wove themselves about Raven's substantial form. For a moment, he looked numinous, both containing and reflecting all the colors of a prism.

"You chose to look," he quirked an eyebrow, "with your third eye."

Shaking her head, she shut her Earth eyes and looked again, but the psychedelic display intensified. Lara opened her eyes. "I've been reading auras for years, but I've never—"

He snapped the book closed and frowned. "Do you mind if I touch you? What I want to do is hold your head between my hands. It'll just take a moment."

"Why?"

"The reason the book appears obtuse is because it was written for different types of magic wielders. The parts that pertain to you would be clear, whereas the others are smokescreens. I must know more about you, though, to help you sort the dross from the gold."

"You can tell that by touching me?"

He nodded, his unnerving gray eyes never leaving her face.

What do I have to lose? If he meant me ill, I'd have sensed it.

"All right. Go ahead." The amulet warmed approvingly.

Lara shut her eyes again. She felt heat from Raven's hands before he actually touched her. Searing and soothing at the same time, his touch sent electric currents frittering along her nerve endings. After he withdrew, the day felt chillier, and she drew her sweatshirt closer around her.

"What happened?" She fought a dizzying disorientation, not unlike the aftermath of her visions.

"Breathe," he commanded. "Take nice deep breaths. Visualize bringing the mother into your body. That's better. A few more, now." He watched her closely.

After a time, he nodded as if satisfied. "What happened is you have a strong affinity for a place we call the *Dreaming*. I'd no sooner established contact than you were ready to use my body as a conduit to travel there. Sidhe blood runs strong in you, Lara. It would return to the *Dreaming* if it could." He coughed and then cleared his throat.

"What exactly does that mean," she demanded, feeling unnerved. "I don't understand. Would I get lost in the place you call the *Dreaming*? Couldn't I just visit there?"

He looked grave. "If you went there, you'd have no idea how to return. Don't worry," he added quickly, probably in response to anxiety streaming off her. "There's no possibility of you falling into the *Dreaming* on your own. Until you're much stronger in your magic, you'd be incapable of such a journey."

"This, whatever it is, it's always been in me?" Lara asked. At his nod, she went on, "What'd you discover when you touched me?" Her voice cracked over her last words. *Do I really want to know?*

"I can tell you some things. Others you must find out for yourself. You have already guessed at your origins. The parts of this book that will have meaning for you begin here." Raven plucked the book off the table. Thumbing through it, he pointed to a chapter heading about three-quarters of the way through.

"I never would've thought to start there," she admitted. "I doubt I'd have gotten that far. Are you sure?" She looked closely at him. "Lillian specifically told me to read here and here." She pointed out the two chapters much earlier in the book where Lillian had turned down pages.

"Yes, I'm sure." He looked uncomfortable. "Mayhap this is one of the books Lillian, um, inherited. I doubt she's actually read this one, or she wouldn't have made that error. This particular book is designed the way it is for a reason. In case it should fall into the wrong hands, the authors ensured that idle readers would do just as you did: feel confused, lay the book down, and forget its existence."

"What did you mean by *inherited?*"

"There's not time right now for lengthy explanations. Lillian was involved in an altercation many years ago. She lost some of her own books and was given those of another as replacements. This book is similar to one that was written hundreds of years before, except the earlier version was more straightforward. When the book was first written, few could read, so there was less danger of mischief. Later versions were penned by more cautious authors."

Lara started to ask just how many iterations of the book there'd been over time, but closed her mouth before words emerged. *Did he do something so I wouldn't ask any more about the book?*

"Our time grows short today. What else would you like to know?" Raven gazed at her, his eyes guileless.

"Lillian said something about finding a natural element that would protect me."

He looked at her appraisingly. "You'll find that information in the book, but I can tell you this much: your protection lies in the realm of minerals and with other people. Do you have any favorite jewelry?"

"For a long time, there was only this." She pointed to a gold medallion of the goddess Artemis hanging from a chain around her neck. The moonstone in the center of the pendant glittered with a pale incandescence in the afternoon light. "But then Lillian gave me this and told me to never take it off." She pulled the heavy amulet out from under her top to show him.

"Moonstones. They're as good a place to begin as any, I suppose," he said cryptically.

"Huh? What does that mean? Could you say more about people protecting me while you're at it?"

"Moonstones are your preferred gem. Another natural protection is your link to Trevor. There's a reason the two of you bonded, and even stronger reasons for you to wed. Have you noticed how he seems to *know* things? Often long afore you've figured them out."

"Lillian said the same thing." Lara met Raven's eyes with an impish grin. "I believe she's actually planning our wedding on the Winter Solstice. When is that? December twenty-first?"

"It could also be the twenty-second. Depends on the moon."

"Maybe you could show up to give the bride away." Lara drew back, horrified she'd been so forward with a stranger. "I'm sorry. I have no idea where that came from." She shook her head. "Don't mind me."

He laughed, but it held a somber undercurrent. "I'd be honored." Looking closely at her, he spoke solemnly, "There's at least one more question you need answered. Ask it. As I said, time grows short."

"Why does the moonstone amulet feel warmer when I'm next to you? The other moonstone pendant doesn't do that."

"Because it's a magic moonstone. Rather like a lodestone for power —of all sorts." The corners of Raven's eyes crinkled with merriment. "And it's just getting to know you."

Trevor bounded up the porch steps. "Are you about done?" he asked with a broad smile. Spots of color rode high on his cheeks, and he looked happier than he had in months.

"Thanks for your indulgence," Raven said. "We accomplished quite a bit." He stood and held out a hand to Lara. Clasping the book close, she rose and shook his outstretched hand.

"Thanks so much." Trevor shook Raven's hand too.

Lara turned to Trevor. "Think we'll be able to pry Gunter loose from here?"

"Maybe." Trevor clattered down the steps, whistling for the puppy. Yawning and stretching, the growing dog crawled from beneath Raven's chair and lurched sleepily down the steps after Trevor.

fternoon was wearing on toward evening. They'd looked at a couple places in the Skykomish area, and a few more on the eastern side of the Cascades just past Lake Wenatchee. In betwixt and between, they talked about Trevor's in-depth exploration of Garland Mineral Springs and Lara's sobering conversation with Raven. As they pulled into Leavenworth, Trevor glanced at the clock in the car. "Want to get an early dinner?" he asked. "We could sort out the properties we saw today."

Lara nodded, then noticed he wasn't looking at her, and said, "Sure. Sounds like a good idea. We haven't had much except crackers since breakfast. How about that little Tyrolean-looking place?"

He groaned. "We can look, but if there's Wiener Schnitzel on the menu, I'm walking out."

"Fair enough." She grinned. "I don't like fried food, either."

Despite the German decor, the restaurant served an Asian-rim cuisine with a couple Slavic dishes as specials. The proprietor seemed especially pleased to have customers. Seating them, he confided business had been terribly slow. "Must be the whole gasoline shortage problem," he theorized as he fluttered around them, placing napkins in their laps and unfolding their menus. "There're not as many tourists passing through. A cocktail before dinner, perhaps?"

"We'll order a bottle of wine once we've decided on an entrée," Trevor informed him. One side benefit of Trevor's long years as a flying waiter was he knew wines intimately, occasionally wincing at a choice Lara made. That mostly happened when one of them ordered fish, and the other beef. According to Trevor, it was close to impossible for a single varietal to blend with both items, unless it was some exotic vintage restaurants rarely stocked. To simplify things, she settled on a scallop dish with sea vegetables, after he'd told her he planned to order the Chilean Sea Bass with black bean sauce.

Lara swirled the last of her Chardonnay around the bottom of her wine glass, staring thoughtfully at the pale liquid. "We haven't talked at all about those properties we looked at today."

"We haven't," he agreed sheepishly. "Probably because none of them holds a candle to Raven's place."

"I hate to admit it, but I feel the same way. We could loop back and pick up I-90, like we planned originally, but I'm starting to believe it'll be a waste of gasoline and time."

"There're a couple more places between here and Wenatchee that we could check out tomorrow morning," he ventured. "I agree with you, though, about not bothering to drive an extra two hundred miles. One problem is modern farms all plant themselves right next to some highway. Makes it easier to bring supplies in, not to mention moving produce and livestock out. For our purposes we want to get as far off the beaten track as we can manage, or we'll be an easy target for the bands of ruffians that'll proliferate as staples become scarce."

She shuddered. The specter of masses of starving people roving through the countryside like locusts was unnerving "Want to spend the night here?" she asked in a subdued voice. "Maybe we could ask the restaurant owner for a suggestion."

"Brilliant idea, Lara." He motioned for the check. When the proprietor bustled over, Trevor asked about hotels.

"Are you looking for a little romantic getaway?" The white-coated man winked at Trevor. He was portly and middle-aged, with a mostly-bald head and warm brown eyes.

"Sure. Something off the highway would be perfect," Lara answered. Not quite sure what motivated her next question, she smiled at the man and asked, "Have you had problems here, yet?"

"A few." Spreading his hands in a self-deprecating gesture, he added, "But not so many you won't be safe here for the night. Now, down in Ellensburg…" He shook his head and frowned. "There's a college there. Students have been demonstrating something fierce. Weren't planning to go through there, now were you?"

"If we were, we'd alter our route." Trevor smiled crookedly as he peeled off a few bills and handed them to the man. "Keep the change."

The proprietor's eyes widened. "You didn't even look at the check. This is far too much. I can't keep all this." He tried to hand a twenty back to Trevor.

"You told us how slow things have been. The meal you served was quite good, and the Chardonnay was far better than what you charged for it." Trevor was adamant. "You might as well keep the money because I'm not taking it back. Come on, Lara." Rising, he extended a hand to her.

"At least let me get you the name of a motel. It might be exactly what you're looking for." The man reached into his jacket for a pen and paper. "Go right at the next light," he said jotting down directions. "Then down two blocks. The Bluebell Inn will be on your right. It's a bed and breakfast, and she's a mighty good cook."

"Guess that settles it," Lara said as she pulled her car door open. "The loop we planned through Ellensburg just got bounced right out of the equation. If I didn't know better, I'd believe the universe is herding us toward Raven." The puppy whined. "Whoops, little man." She pushed her car door shut again. "You need out before we try to find that motel."

"I'll get him." Trevor popped the hatch and snapped the leash to the puppy's collar. "To answer you, it certainly appears we're being prodded to tell Raven *yes* and just get on with things." He narrowed his eyes in sudden understanding and looked at her. "But of course," he muttered. "I feel quite the fool here."

"What?" Worry nibbled at the edges of her mind. Had they forgotten something critical?

"Lara," he spoke evenly, "If relocating to Raven's farm is where the Sidhe want us, then that's where we'll end up."

"They can't be *that* powerful," she protested. "I'd barely heard of them until a few days ago. When I studied the Tuatha Da Danaan, it was like studying any other lost people. Wouldn't you think if they're omniscient we'd have heard something about them these past few hundred years? Bet if I Googled them, I'd come up dry."

Turning slightly, Trevor shot her a knowing smile and started down the street with Gunter in tow.

As they strolled down Leavenworth's main street with its faux-German shop fronts, she wondered what it would be like to live in a computerless world. Next she considered picking through their accumulated possessions and walking away from most of them.

None of this will be easy.

"Look, Trev," she pointed. "A bookstore. It's open. Want to look for something about farming, and maybe animal husbandry?"

"What will we do with him?" Trevor pointed at the puppy.

"If things are as slow as the restaurant guy said, maybe they wouldn't mind if we brought him in." Pushing the glass-fronted door open, she craned her neck around, seeing nothing but deserted isles. "Yoo hoo," she called out.

"Yes?" A plump young woman with long black hair stuck her head out from behind a stack of books. "Can I help you?"

"Mind if we browse for a couple minutes? We have a puppy with us, but we could carry him."

The clerk hesitated. Then she looked at her empty shop. "Sure," she said. "Just be sure you keep him off the floor. Wouldn't want to have any accidents to clean up."

"Thanks." Lara flashed the young woman a sunny grin. "Where are your books on agriculture?"

"Here, I'll show you." She walked them to a long shelf at the back of the store. "This is what we have in stock, but we can order anything you want."

"Thanks." Lara nodded. The clerk gave her a thumbs up and left them to it.

"Hey!" Trevor gazed at the array. "We lucked out. This is a farming community, though. So I guess it makes sense they'd have lots to choose from."

"I'll take Gunter. You know what we're looking for." Scooting the wriggling puppy under one arm, she added, "I saw a bench right outside the door. We'll wait for you there."

After a long day of mostly sitting, she set the pup on the sidewalk. Lara stood next to the bench and gazed at the quiet, small-town street. A child detached herself from a clump of shadows beneath a grove of trees and sidled closer. Gunter sniffed, and then drew away whining softly.

The little girl couldn't have been more than six or seven. She was dirty, and a long scratch tracked down one side of her small, pinched face. Sparse, blonde hair was matted and grimy. "Spare a quarter, lady?" The child asked in a flute-like voice. "You looks like a nice lady, and I am fair hungry."

Having seen her share of child beggars in the slums of large cities, Lara's compassion kindled. She noticed a hamburger stand a couple doors down and smiled. "I won't give you money, but if you'd like I'll buy you a burger and a shake."

Disappointment and something else—was it fear?—flitted over the little girl's face. "That's right kind of you, ma'am, but just a quarter would do."

"You told me you were hungry," Lara pressed gently, while wondering about the amulet. It felt odd. Not exactly prickly, but its usual gentle warmth had departed. "If you don't like burgers, I'll get you anything you want from that restaurant down there. What's your name, child?"

"Tinni, ma'am." The girl's gaze darted this way and that, almost as if she were searching the shadows for something.

"Are you with someone?" Lara asked softly.

"No." The response was bitten off, terse. "I'm just with me."

"Where are your parents? You must have at least one." The waif was beginning to worry Lara. Visions of children sold into slavery nudged the edges of her mind.

"Sure you won't be givin' me that quarter?" Tinni sounded wistful.

"Yes, quite sure. But the offer for a meal stands."

"Lara? Oh, there you are." Trevor strode toward her weighted down with two large shopping bags bulging with books. "What are you doing all the way over here?"

"I was just talking with—" But when she looked to where she'd last seen the child, Tinni was gone. "That was weird," she murmured.

"What was? These books are heavy. Let's get back to the car."

"I'll take one of those bags," she offered holding out the hand that wasn't attached to Gunter. "There was this little beggar girl. I offered her food, but all she wanted was money. Her speech was peculiar. Almost like something out of the last century. Anyway, she left when you showed up, but she couldn't have gone far."

"Street urchins." He shook his head. "They're all the same, whether you're in Beijing or Cairo. There's always someone running them. Of course she wouldn't want food. The adult who's got her out here begging only wants money."

"But we're in America," Lara protested. "Not some third world country."

"Pretty soon that differentiation's going to wear thin. If it hasn't already. Let's put those books in the boot and go find the motel."

THE BLUEBELL INN was Lara's kind of place—feather beds, feather pillows, feather comforters, and lushly scented soaps. A cozy fireplace graced their room, and they lay in bed watching flames lick upward behind an ornamental black-mesh grate. Gunter had started out on the floor the previous night at the Restful Inn, but he'd whined so piteously they'd given up and put him between them where he'd instantly fallen asleep. Having commandeered a place between his human parents once, he clambered onto the bed, using his claws for purchase, and curled into a snug ball at Lara's feet.

After an epic breakfast of eggs benedict, fruited yogurt, and homemade cinnamon rolls, they piled into the car to go look at more of the farms on Trevor's list. Each was a small working ranch that had clearly seen better days. The owners had a desperate look about them, and even the farm animals seemed ill-kept and depressed.

"I give up." Slamming the car door in disgust, Lara looked at Trevor. "I can't believe that awful man wants over a million bucks for that trash heap of a dairy we just looked at. I'm going to have to wash my hair to get the stench out of it. Jesus, I'm *never* drinking milk again that isn't labeled organic."

"Cows looked pretty miserable, didn't they? Poor things." He started the car. "There's one more place. It's right across the highway and up a couple miles, but I'm sure it won't look much different."

"Why don't we spend another night at the Bluebell Inn? It's ridiculous to look at any more farms. Everything we've looked at is so inferior to what Raven's offering, it's a waste of time."

She smiled wistfully. "We could check in early, go for a run, and have a nice dinner. Tomorrow we can backtrack to Raven's and spend the night with him. I'd like to spend twenty-four hours there to get a better feel for the place. Once we make a commitment, we'll be stuck with it. I don't want to make a mistake."

"Neither do I, Lara, neither do I."

THEY WALKED out of the Leavenworth Steak House several hours later, arms twined around one another. Lara patted her too-full stomach. "My, that was good. I could get used to this traveling life. Wait. What was that?" Catching movement out of the corner of one eye, she stared into the darkness.

"What'd you see?"

"The little girl from last night." Continuing to rake the darkness with her eyes, Lara called gently, "Tinni, if it's you, come on out. We won't hurt you."

"Come on." Trevor tugged at her. "There's nothing good to be gained out of furthering your relationship with a beggar child."

"I suppose you're right." She paused, thinking. "There was something haunting about her. Like she was a very old soul locked into a child's body."

"Too much Cabernet, love. When you begin romanticizing the urchins of the world, you've had too much to drink." He opened the car door for her. As they sped off, she was almost certain she saw Tinni's skeletal features staring from the shadows of a large, withered oak tree. Touching the amulet, she searched for clues, but it rested quietly on her chest, exuding its usual soothing warmth.

Somewhere between the feather-filled duvet and the feather bed, they found one another during the night. Lara wasn't sure till morning, when she felt dried stickiness on her inner thighs, whether she'd dreamed making love. "So how was I?" she asked with a lopsided grin.

"If you don't know, I'm not going to tell you," he teased back. "You seemed half asleep. Guess you really were."

She swatted at him with a towel. "Shall we see what Mrs. Christopher's whipped up for breakfast this morning?"

"Sure. No lingering over coffee, though. I'd like to get an early start so we have plenty of daylight to explore things once we get back to Raven's."

"Did you get a chance to look through any of those books you bought?" At his nod, she went on, "What do you think? Will they be helpful?"

"Sure, Lara. When you start with nothing, anything's helpful."

"But you grew up on a farm."

"Yes, but I wasn't responsible for anything. I just did what Dad said. It's a whole lot different when you've got to figure out what to plant, when to harvest, how to take care of sick animals, how to recognize crop blight. And the beat goes on. There's a lot that goes into subsistence farming. Those books will be a big help. Wonder where we could get some of that antique farm machinery Raven mentioned?"

"Why don't we ask him?" she suggested, adding, "Arabel should be a big help too. She's had a garden most of her life."

"Speaking of books, since Raven told you which parts to read, have you opened that one from Lillian?"

Guilt, an all-too-familiar companion of late nagged uncomfortably. "Er, no." She sent a sidelong glance skittering his way. "I've been enjoying myself with you and the pup. Didn't want to ruin it by having to think too much."

Either I'm too disciplined, or not disciplined enough.

In her heart of hearts, she knew better. She groped for the amulet, and a flood of unwelcome thoughts marched across her mind. *Bullshit. Discipline has nothing to do with it. I'm scared of what I'll find in that damned book. I liked it a whole lot better when my link to the magical world didn't include the Sidhe. It's one thing to have a vision or two and read auras. Quite another to look at Raven and see light pouring through him. Or feel him touching me with those thousand-year-old hands.*

"Didn't mean to make you feel bad." Trevor's cheerful voice shattered her reverie. Thank God he didn't pick up on the extent of her inner turmoil. "Shower's hot. Let's get in before all the hot water runs down the drain."

After another stellar breakfast, they bid Mrs. Christopher goodbye and were in the car heading west before nine-thirty. Lara glanced out the BMW's windshield, gasped, and cried, "Stop the car."

"Why?"

"It's that girl. The one from two nights ago. Look. See that witchy-looking hag with the tangled gray hair. She's got Tinni by the shoulder, and she's practically dragging her down the street."

"I love you, Lara, but I'm not stopping this car. We're *not* getting involved. We have enough of our own problems without borrowing new ones."

"But—" Rolling down her window, she watched the little girl's retreating form. Almost as if Tinni felt Lara's eyes drilling into her back, the child wrenched free from her tormentor and turned to stare at Lara, her pale blue eyes pinched and sad. Moments later, the old woman gripped Tinni's bony shoulder with her claw-like hand and spun the child back around.

"Maybe I can call child protective services. There must be a local number." Lara picked up her phone and dialed information. "I won't interfere, Trev, but please pull over until I make this call. I don't want to chance losing my reception."

Ten minutes later, she hung up, feeling she'd done all she reasonably could, and motioned they could leave.

"Are you sure, Florence Nightingale? Guardian of the disenfranchised. What's that Statue of Liberty insignia? Give us your tired, your poor—"

"Stop it, Trevor," she hissed. "That child was being abused. I had to do *something* to intervene. The woman I talked with seemed somewhat interested, so perhaps mine's not the first report on that pair."

"Okay, okay. Thank you for not jumping out of the car and into the middle of something that would've turned ugly really fast." His voice was softer, the earlier sarcasm partially replaced by his usual kindheartedness.

"Thanks for realizing what I was about to do and stopping me." She smiled ruefully. "Wonder what I'm going to do when I only have goats, chickens, and tomatoes to watch over?"

"You can referee when one of the roosters goes after the other one. Don't forget the pole beans, they're always trying to choke one another out to see who can get closest to the sunlight." He chuckled as he maneuvered the car onto the highway.

Though the weather was generally drier east of the Cascades, storm clouds raced along in the jet stream. "Wonder if we'll get snow?" Lara eyed the deteriorating weather.

"This car can handle it." Trevor sounded confident. He'd been the one to insist she get a sports utility vehicle when her Honda Accord had died at two hundred eighty thousand miles. "I put chains in the boot just in case. And Lara…" He hesitated. When she looked over, a flush moved up from his open collar. "I got so upset earlier because I was jealous."

"Of that child?"

"No, of course not. Of the fact no one ever cared enough about me or Lizzie or Robbie to do anything. Here we are in a strange town, with a little girl where the only thing you knew about her was her name, and you cared enough to try to help her. That just struck me as so unfair."

Wordlessly, she unhooked her seat belt, reached over, and hugged him. Once she'd settled back into her seat, she said, "I wish there'd been someone like me around for your family too, dear."

They drove in silence until they crested Stevens Pass. The weather steadily worsened, and swirling snowflakes made patterns on the windshield. "What day is this?" he asked suddenly.

"Saturday. Why?"

"No, the date. Is this the thirty-first?"

"I think so." She picked up her phone. "Yes, tonight's Halloween."

Trevor rolled his eyes. "Great! We're about to spend Samhain with a Sidhe, or whatever he is. Guess if we survive that, we're fated to move in with him."

"I know it's a festival," she said slowly, "but could you fluff up its significance a bit for me? Isn't that when the spirits of the dead roam free?"

"We've got a bit of time, Lara. Let's stop here and give the pup a quick tour. When we get moving again, I'll tell you what I know."

"Think I'll stay in the car. Looks cold out there."

"Oh, come on. It'll feel good once you get moving. Just pop on your hat and gloves. You'll be fine."

She *did* feel refreshed after a jaunt up and down the highway in front of the Stevens Pass ski area. Deserted ski lifts, rising from the still-mostly-grass-covered slopes, looked like primordial dragons resting up for the winter to come. "How about Samhain?" she asked as soon as they were moving again.

"Once upon a time… Uh, no, that one's for the *good* fairy tales." He smiled wryly. "Seriously, I'm not sure I know all that much. But here goes. The Gaulish calendar was split into two halves: the light half that began in April and the dark half that began at Samhain, or the Celtic New Year. Unlike Halloween, Samhain actually lasts through either November first or second, depending which book you're looking at. Since it marked the beginning of the cold season, people took stock of their herds and grain supplies, and decided how many animals to slaughter so they'd have enough food to last the winter.

They built big bonfires and cast the bones of the slaughtered animals into them. Everyone began with a dark hearth in their own little hovel. They'd take a pot of fire from one of the common fires and use it to light their individual fireplaces. The ritual was supposed to bond the village families together."

"So far, it doesn't sound all that ominous," she said, glancing at him.

"Oh, it gets better. See, the Gaels thought the border between this world and the Otherworld thinned enough during Samhain to allow the deceased to reach through into the land of the living. Families set places for their dead relatives at the Samhain table, and told tales about their ancestors. Young men would dress up in costumes and masks to placate the spirits, and people carved large turnips into the faces of the saints as a hedge against evil."

"Turnips?'

"Yeah, they grow like wild seed all through the U.K. People would put these big hollowed-out turnips in the windowsill and place a candle inside."

"Did your family do that?" She asked, curious about customs he'd grown up with.

"Um, yeah. Mum used to bake this cake that looked like antlers too. It symbolized the Wild Hunt."

"I know about the Hunt," she said thoughtfully. "Hmm. We're about to spend the first night of Samhain with a shaman who travels freely in and out of the Otherworld."

"Not exactly." Trevor sent a sidelong glance her way, a slight frown on his face. "Fairy folk can be forced into the Summerland—Otherworld—but it's a place for the spirits of the dead. The Sidhe can't remain there long. They have other places. Under the mounds and hills, and a place they call the *Dreaming*. Raven talked with you about that, didn't he?"

"Sort of. It's like it is with Lillian, though. He talks in riddles. We need more books." She wrapped a lock of hair around a finger, then said, "Maybe I can find something at the University Bookstore next week."

"Better spend your time stocking up on practical clothes, love. You haven't got all that many. Oops. Just passed our turnoff. That sure came up fast."

CHAPTER 30

*I*f possible, the tree-shrouded dirt track was even more welcoming than it had been two days before. Snow flurries from the mountain pass gave way to a gentle, but persistent, rain. Lara chided herself for an over-active imagination, but she was almost positive the evergreens soughed a greeting as the silver BMW drove across the bridge and into the clearing. Before they'd even gotten Gunter out of his box, Raven strode toward them, a broad smile on his strong-boned face.

"You came back! Sooner than I would have hoped too." Looking closely at them with his shrewd, gray eyes, he added, "I trust this means you've come to a decision. And it's a favorable one."

"We're not quite there, in terms of a decision." Lara felt unaccountably flustered. *Probably because I still have more than my share of doubts— about everything.* "What we'd like to do is spend the night. To get more of a feel for what it might be like to actually live here." The amulet pulsed approvingly.

"Splendid! Tonight is All-Hallows Eve. And Samhain, which marks the start of a new year. An auspicious choice, indeed. Can I help you bring anything into the house?"

"Thanks, but no." Trevor extended a hand, grasping Raven's firmly.

"We're good here. I'd like to spend as much time outside as I can until we lose the light. You can show me where things are and how you've been managing." While he spoke, Trevor slipped a light waterproof shell over his jacket. He opened the crate in response to Gunter's escalating yips, and the puppy tumbled to the ground, making a beeline for Raven.

"He's sure growing fast," Trevor said. "Bet he's gained ten pounds since I brought him home."

"He'll be a beauty in a year or so." Raven bent to fondle the excited dog, and Gunter wiggled all over, licking and nipping at the mage's hands.

"I'll take our bags upstairs," Lara offered. "Is that second floor room all right for us to use?"

"More than all right." Raven beamed at her. "I even aired out the sheets."

"Then you knew we'd be returning? And for longer than it would take to tell you we were moving somewhere else?" She focused intently on the big, bearlike man, and tried to ascertain whether he'd played them like puppets.

"Whether I knew, or whether I only hoped…" He shrugged. "Sometimes it's difficult to tell the two apart. I am glad you're back, though. I feel in my bones that this is the right place for you." Raven's childlike enthusiasm, oddly out of place in such an ancient being, held a contagious element.

A TIGHT PLACE within her loosened, and her doubts faded as she stood in the grassy yard. When she smiled, it was genuine, not forced.

"Can I ask you about something?" she said hesitantly. When Raven nodded, she continued, "A little girl came up to me in Leavenworth. I'm not sure why she's still bothering me, but there was something quite strange about her…" She told Raven about Tinni and the old woman who'd grasped the child's thin shoulder.

"You say she wanted only coin from you?" Raven pursed his lips into a hard, straight line.

"Yes. I offered food, but she wasn't interested despite being much too thin."

"Describe her face again, please." Lara did, and Raven's troubled look intensified. "I cannot be certain," he said softly, "but she sounds like a Goblin. They have that otherworldly look. It makes sense she wouldn't want food, since they only eat uncooked meat. Had you given her something, it would've given her power over you, which is likely what the hag wanted." Raven fell silent, then added, "You have well-honed instincts. It's fortunate you refused her request."

Trevor, who'd been listening, chimed in, "I insisted we give the urchin a broad berth. Um, Raven, there's little enough left of the day as it is."

"Certainly, certainly. Follow me." Raven set off toward the barn. "We shan't be long," he called to Lara, and then jabbed a finger at Trevor. "See, I told you he *knows* things."

It took her a few trips to bring their overnight bags and books up to their room. As she ferried loads into the house, thoughts rioted through her head. In addition to all the problems Beauchamp had caused, Gradoxt still lurked in the wings. And now a Goblin had targeted her.

Culling through her memory, Lara dredged up Lillian's words. *I'm not sure why, but you've become known to dark forces. They'll continue to try to annihilate you. Without my help, they'll eventually succeed.*

Chilled by the implication, her throat suddenly dry, Lara wondered how she could roll back the clock to a simpler time when all she did was see patients and teach. *Not going to happen, and I know it.*

She pulled on a warmer sweater and set out to do a thorough job exploring what would likely be their new home. A narrow ladder-like staircase led to the long hallway running the length of the third floor. Driven by curiosity, she let herself into all the rooms. While most of them were the same, consisting of two single beds and a raised table with a basin and a ewer, the last room on the left held a surprise.

When she pulled the latch, it snicked open with a cheery little sound, and Lara walked into a well-appointed library. Floor to ceiling bookshelves lined the moderately-sized room, and windows looked over the front porch. A brazier between the windows was ready to light with a tidy pile of kindling and some larger logs on the hearth. Coming close, she gazed through titles and found that one entire wall was devoted to witchcraft and other arcane pursuits.

"Would've been premature buying books on those topics," she muttered. "Wonder if I'll be able to force myself to actually read any of them." She trailed her fingertips over book spines and jumped when she sensed muted energy vibrating from them.

Magic books hold magic. She rolled her eyes. *What a surprise.*

Back in the hallway, she located the main staircase almost immediately. Were there multiple ways to access each of the floors? Did they come and go depending on who was here? Could the structure be sentient?

If the books are, why not? While she'd paid lip service to a paranormal world, she'd never truly bought into it—or immersed herself in its possibilities. Shivering, she drew her sweater closer and zipped it.

She wandered through three other decent-sized bedrooms on the second floor, an old-fashioned water closet, its tank mounted high on the wall, and well-stocked linen cabinets.

Wall sconces for oil lamps dotted both the central hallways and the rooms themselves. Toward the end of the second floor hallway, she found a small room with a treadle sewing machine and a floor loom. Enchanted, Lara sat on a padded bench to examine the antique Singer. It was threaded, so she pulled a swath of fabric from a nearby wicker basket, fitted it under the presser foot, and pumped the foot pedal, pleased when everything worked.

She inspected the loom. It had a foot treadle too. A partially woven cloth hung from the warp bars. The shuttle with the weft yarn was stuck through at right angles. It looked as if the weaver had gone to get a cup of coffee and never returned. Lara glanced over her shoulder, half expecting the unknown craftsperson to reappear. Bobbins with every color of yarn imaginable were tossed in a nearby box.

By the time she finally made her way back to the first floor, the sun had dropped low on the horizon, sending sparkly highlights through the thick windows. The main floor was basically one large room, with an enormous stone hearth near one end. The kitchen, with its wood cook stove, lay at the other.

She had to hurry to complete her inspection before it got dark, and the only place left was the basement. Charging down the steps, she slowed almost immediately as gloom enveloped her.

Maybe I should go back for a flashlight.

Nah, I won't spend all that much time with spider's webs and old bathing tubs.

She made the bottom of the stairs and walked forward, flicking curtains aside to glance into the bathing enclosures. The deeper she moved into the basement, the creepier it felt. Something nagged her to retrace her steps, but the amulet was quiescent. "I'm being silly." She spoke to the gloom. "I'm going to see what's down here, and then I'll leave."

Another step. And then another. A pervasive wrongness wafted from the ghostly tubs like an evil miasma. *How close is it to sunset? Does sunset on Samhain matter?* Lara slowed her pace until she wasn't moving at all.

"Oh, to hell with it," she growled. After an abrupt about-face, she ran toward the stairs, taking them two at a time in her haste to be out of the unsettling space. Her heart pounded and her mouth was dry. Worse, she felt like an idiot. She'd never ascribed malevolent intent to inanimate objects. "Bah! That was just plain silly. Maybe I *should* get the flashlight and go back there. Just to prove it's only empty space."

Her brave words floated in the air, but the last thing she wanted to do was face the basement again. She focused on the amulet, searching for clues, but its energy field hadn't changed from when she was downstairs.

She stared at the basement steps for long minutes, and then went outside to look for Trevor. As soon as she stepped onto the porch, she saw him, along with Raven and Gunter, wandering up from the creek. The puppy was mud from stem to stern, and the men talked animatedly, their heads bent close together.

Trevor glanced up, spotted her, and waved. Lara ran back into the house to find a towel to wipe the mud-caked dog. By the time she got back to the porch, the men were already there. As she worked on Gunter, she asked, "Where's the washing machine, not that I'm going to do wash at this hour, but I don't recall seeing it?"

"In the basement," Raven replied. "This time of day you need a lantern, but there's a wringer washer down there. It's off to the left at the bottom of the stairs."

"I went down there." Lara looked away. "It was strange."

"What do you mean?" Raven, who'd pulled the front door open, stopped abruptly and turned to face her.

Feeling her face heat, she muttered, "It felt like something was down there. Something that wanted me to leave."

"Want me to have a look?" Raven furled his brows.

"If we're going to live here, there can't be places in the house that scare me half to death. I'd never be comfortable. So yes, but I want to come with you."

"Do you think I should come along?" Trevor sounded mildly worried. When Lara glanced at him, his eyes were alight over cheeks reddened from hours out-of-doors. He looked truly contented. In that moment, she grasped something: his boyish good looks had always provided an excellent smoke screen. He'd fashioned a comfortable niche with the airline—and with her—but the debris from his wretched childhood stood like a gargoyle at the gates, making certain he never got too secure, or expected too much.

Impulsively, she scooted over to Trevor and hugged him. "We'll be fine," she said. "I'm glad you had a good afternoon. Dog's clean enough. We can go inside."

Raven lit one of the many lanterns scattered about the room. "Ready?" he asked.

Determined, she marched back to the stairs. At the top riser, though, her courage failed, and she understood how scared she'd been. Moving aside, she mumbled, "How about if you go first?"

"I was about to suggest that. Those stairs will be easier for you to negotiate if I'm in front with the light, anyway."

Heart hammering in her chest, Lara made a herculean effort to calm herself. She'd feel really stupid if this turned out to be her imagination working overtime. Step by step, she trailed after Raven. He stopped at the bottom and set the lantern on a small table she hadn't noticed before. Steadying her breathing, she reached out with her sixth sense.

"Stop that." Raven spoke low. "It gets in the way."

"Sorry. We're too close to the stairs. Whatever I felt got worse over that way." She gestured. "The farther I got from the stairs, the worse it got."

"Stay here, next to the light." He moved away, silent as a spirit, into the gloom-shrouded interior of the cavernous basement. In a few minutes, she heard him call, "It's all right, Lara. Bring the light and come this way."

Snatching up the lantern bale, she willed herself to retrace her steps from earlier. *Yes. There it was.* That same sensation of something corrupt lying in wait for her.

"Keep coming. There's nothing here to hurt you." Raven's voice resonated in her mind.

She strode into the depths of the basement, feeling more and more anxious. Sweat slicked her hands and ran down her sides. Something brushed against her face and she jumped, her heart thrumming with fear, until she realized it was the long strand of a cobweb, hanging off one of the beams of the raftered ceiling. "This is ridiculous," she said out loud to steady herself. "Just walk to him."

"That's right. Come to me. Only another thirty feet or so." His voice was soothing, and she clung to it.

"What's down here that feels so putrid? And why doesn't it bother the amulet?" she asked as she sidled next to Raven's comforting bulk.

"Just ghosts, Lara. From what you described, I feared Goblins might have found a way in, but what you sense is the ghosts of two men. One lay in wait for the other down here when the hot springs was still in operation."

"What happened?"

"What you might expect. One had slept with the other's wife. The cuckold decided to murder his rival. Somehow, they both ended up dead." Weaving his hands together in a curious pattern, Raven chanted low in Gaelic. After a time, he asked, "Can you still sense them?"

She closed her eyes. "No. Not anymore." Picking up the lantern, she started forward to complete her tour of the basement. "What did you do?"

Low chuckling followed her as she found her way among the curtained cubicles. "I encouraged them to rest. What I did is far from a permanent solution. You'll find them down here again. One of the reasons they're so annoying just now is because it's Samhain and easier for them to pierce the veil between the worlds."

He hesitated. "The amulet didn't react because, as I've told you, it draws magic to itself. Ghosts aren't magical creatures. Also, you were never in danger. Had you been in peril, it would've triggered the moonstone."

"Who could teach me the spell you just cast?" she asked, recalling Lillian's adjuration about it already being almost too late for her to begin to learn much of anything.

"These things have a way of working out."

"Lillian said the amulet would warn me—" she began.

"It always responds in some way to magic," Raven broke in. "If magic isn't present, sometimes it will change, but its reaction isn't predictable unless you're in grave danger."

Though she waited, Raven didn't elaborate. "What you just said is I can't count on it." Lara eyed him.

He blew out a sharp breath. "No. I didn't say that at all." He shook his head. "I can't give you an exact formula, but a combination of the moonstone and your own magic are your strongest hedge against those who want to harm you."

"Why?" The word tore out of her. "Why'd I suddenly become a target?"

"I'm afraid I don't have an answer for you. Time to go upstairs." Raven pried the lantern out of her hands."

They found Trevor in the kitchen with the puppy. He'd apparently raided the cupboards and gathered enough ingredients to begin preparing supper, just like he did at home. Shirt sleeves rolled up, he glanced over his shoulder as they came into the room. With a few happy barks, Gunter lunged first at Lara, then at Raven.

"Did you get the bad guys?" Trevor grinned.

"Not exactly." Since she didn't feel like smiling back, she asked if there was anything she could do to help.

CHAPTER 31

Though their meal—a simple affair of brown rice and sautéed vegetables—had been over for hours, Lara, Trevor, and Raven still sat around the oak table in the kitchen. Raven poured fresh hot water over tea leaves and refreshed their cups. The puppy was asleep, curled on a braided rug in front of the wood cook stove.

"You seem to think we need to get ourselves up here just as soon as we can," Lara said, spinning the conversation back to Raven's exhortations that the civil unrest they'd encountered on Wednesday afternoon was a precursor of worse things to come.

"I did say that," he agreed. "Gather what you need. Time will grow short more quickly than you could possibly imagine."

"How can you know that?" Trevor asked. "Even Lillian said her crystal ball was a bit cloudy, and we might have another couple years yet."

"Did she really say that?" Raven looked interested—and troubled. He drew his thick eyebrows together so close they nearly touched. "Must be because she doesn't want to tear herself away from that tree house of hers."

"Why would she have to?" Lara, legs tucked beneath her in the generous kitchen table chair, was intrigued. "You can't even see that place unless the trees decide to let you in."

"It's water would be the problem," Raven replied, a worried look in his eyes. "There won't be any after the city system breaks down. And it will. Puget Sound is close, but that's salt water. She's talked about setting up cisterns—to take advantage of the rain—but I just don't see that as predictable enough."

"I'm not worried about Lillian. She strikes me as someone who can take care of herself." Trevor smiled and rested his chin on an upturned fist. "I suppose we could relocate here in a couple weeks—"

"Oh no, we couldn't." Lara looked thunderstruck. "I'd need at least a month to shut down my practice. Some of my more difficult patients might take even longer. And that doesn't begin to address how we'd manage to get our house sold. And my office."

Raven waved a hand impatiently. "Two weeks, four weeks. Not much difference, except two weeks *is* safer. You must come soon. If you don't, you'll find you're not able to get here at all." The mage nailed her with a ruthless expression, and the words that followed weren't much better. "No one will buy your home, or your office. Your thought patterns are still trapped in your old life. This is what's brought modern civilization to the brink of extinction: an intransigent unwillingness to change anything."

"What do you think is going to happen?" She gazed at him, searching for truth in his clear, gray eyes.

"The riots will worsen. Crime will escalate. Eventually, they'll ration fuel, if there's anything left to ration. Once that happens, unless you walk, you'll be stuck wherever you find yourselves. You," he jabbed a thick finger at Lara, "might learn to transport yourself by other means. But your friends here," he waved an arm to encompass Trevor and the sleeping puppy, "couldn't come along."

"Okay, okay. I get it. Maybe not the part about teleporting, or whatever you were talking about. But I get the rest of it." She rubbed at her temples. *Jesus, I feel old and tired.* "This is all fucking hard to accept."

"You have to move beyond that." Raven spoke brusquely. "Feeling sorry for yourself—and bemoaning your situation—is pointless. As is ignoring the book Lillian wants you to read."

"How could you know I haven't read any more of it?" Her voice wavered.

"We've been through this," he said, a weary edge sharpening his words. "Your mind is transparent."

"I'm not used to my thoughts being on display," she muttered angrily. "How can I keep you out of my head?"

"It's not me you need to worry about, but *them*," Raven supplied. "*They* know you're close to acknowledging the full extent of your powers and *they're* doing all *they* can to make sure that doesn't happen."

"What the fuck are you talking about?" She shrank back in her chair. It felt as if a small bird were trapped in her chest, trying to beat its way out. Who the hell was lying in wait for her?

Don't be coy. Lillian said pretty much the same thing.

"The Dark Ones. The Enemy. The Others. Doesn't matter what you call them. Those creatures living in the shadow of what Jung called the collective unconscious. You learned about them."

"Sure, but I always figured Jung made a lot of that stuff up. It just seemed so otherworldly, and impossible."

"It was all quite real." Raven gazed into the distance, chin atop his clasped hands. "Philemon was one of the Sidhe, sent to protect Jung after we noticed him venturing much too close to the boundary between the worlds."

Fragments of recollection from her years at the Institute clinked into place. Fascination displaced fear and she asked, "Can you tell me more?"

"Not right now. There's little enough time, and that would be a lengthy digression."

"Who was Philemon?" Trevor asked, his blue eyes alight with curiosity.

"Sort of like Jung's alter-ego," she replied. "A splinter part of him he could actually see, and walk with, and talk to. They even wrote letters back and forth to one another."

"I thought Raven said he was a Sidhe."

"Perhaps he was." She closed her teeth over her lower lip, thinking. "I suppose that would mean either Philemon never told Jung the truth, or he did and Jung chalked it up to ramblings from his unconscious."

"When will you begin reading the book?" Raven's deep voice held an unsettling edginess. "Once you immerse yourself in it, you will understand much. Especially since you're done with the Gaelic tome."

"Soon." She knew she was hedging. "How can you know it'll be more understandable than it was before?"

"I just do. The book will rally the forces of light. Akin to what you saw when you *really* looked at me the other day."

"Lillian said I'd likely waited too long as it is."

"Spare me," he roared and reared back onto his feet. His chair clattered against the wood floor as it tumbled backward. "Much as I love Lillian, I don't care what she's filled your head with. You must do as I say. Your survival depends on it. I can see all those pathetic little arguments lining up in your head. Stop thinking, woman. In my time, acolytes did as they were told because they knew how vulnerable they were before their magic had fully blossomed."

He stomped over to her, hunkered down, and took both her hands in his. The stark reality of his words, bolstered by legitimacy flowing from his touch, seared her soul. Gossamer curtains of self-deception fell away.

Find some humility and trust Psyche for chrissakes. She's a hell of a lot wiser than I am.

Trevor sprang to her other side. He looked uncertainly from Raven to her and then back again. Whining, Gunter crept from his place near the warm stove to be next to Trevor.

"It's all right, Trev." Her voice was low and had a catch as she struggled to find it again. "He's right. I've had lots of opportunities to read, and I've ignored every single one of them. I *am* ambivalent. I resent the hell out of the crucible we're caught up in. I'd like nothing better than to turn back the clock to before I told Ken and Bethany I'd take them as patients. Seems like that's where all the trouble started." She took a deep, shaky breath.

Raven still held her hands and nodded slowly. "Yes," he breathed, looking fixedly at her. "I'm sorry I raised my voice. It was necessary. You needed something to shake you out of your entrenched complacency." Releasing her, he rose and turned to Trevor, laying a heavy hand on his shoulder. "I would never hurt her. I hope you realize that. Not because you know me well. You don't. But because the old blood within you recognizes me for what I am. Once your people prayed to me."

"Who exactly are you?" Trevor asked nervously and shifted his weight from one foot to the other.

Raven eyed Trevor oddly. "Look within yourself, and you'll find the truth."

Trevor opened his mouth, then closed it, apparently thinking better of what he'd been about to ask. "It's getting late," he managed with a weak attempt at a smile. "Do you suppose we might light the Samhain bonfire?"

"You read my mind, human." Raven strode briskly toward the front door. "That's exactly what I was about to suggest. We must pay homage to the Goddess on this holiest of nights."

The night was chilly and clear, the dark sky riddled with thousands of stars. Lara detoured back into the house to grab her coat. Back outside, she followed the smell of burning wood around to where she found Trevor, Raven, and the puppy. Wood was just starting to catch in the large fire pit, and copper-red flames swirled upward into the night sky.

She settled into a relocated chair from the wraparound porch, breathing in night smells mingled with smoke. Taking stock, she felt different, somehow. A tight, broken place within her had come undone, opening a door to possibilities she'd never dreamed existed.

Whatever it is, it feels right. Trev's not the only one whose childhood kept him on the fringes of things.

Raven dropped lightly into a chair and said, "I won't be here when you return. In fact, I'm not sure when I'll be here next. Until it's time for me to go, there are things I would share with you." He smiled wryly. "I meant to tell you about them earlier, but sometimes my temper gets the better of me."

"I'm glad it did." Lara grinned back at him. "I needed a good swift kick in the ass."

Raven chuckled, smoothing his beard down. "Yes," he said simply. "You did."

"Not to change the subject, but how will we get in if you're not here? You'll have to be sure to leave us the keys." Trevor tossed another log on the fire.

Laughing, Raven replied, "The house isn't locked, son. In some ways, it's like Lillian's house, it lets you in if it wants to. Please, there's little enough in the way of time. If one or the other of you keeps interrupting, I won't get through this."

Raven clasped his hands together and hooked them around his crossed legs. "Outside of the old woman you're planning to bring with you, tell no one about your plans." He held up a hand when he saw Lara open her mouth. "Silence. If you've already told others, there's little enough that can be done about it. Don't tell them where. Better yet, if anyone inquires, tell them you changed your minds.

"You will, essentially, disappear. What that means is no protracted trips carrying things down those long stairs Lillian told me about. If you must, ferry things down very late at night when there will be fewer to watch. Bring a few things at a time, but leave most of it. Everything that's here will remain. Other than clothes and farming supplies, you won't need much at all.

"There are a few things you and I," he glanced meaningfully at Trevor, "talked about today. You may need to rent a trailer to move them here, or perhaps a truck. I know little enough of such things, since my travels in your world are sporadic. The cold season is upon us, so you'll have to bring staple foods to carry you through until spring when you can plant more of what you need and want.

"Once you've finished moving, throw away the keys to that car. You'll have no way of knowing how dangerous things have gotten in the world you left, and it'll be too much of a risk to leave here to find out. Lillian will visit here from time to time, as will I."

Something odd danced just beyond the edges of Lara's peripheral vision. Diminutive forms murmured softly, disappearing the moment she turned her head. She drew her brows together wondering what the hell they were and gazed upward to see if more of them appeared.

"Oh my God," she gasped, her mouth falling open. "Look! It must be the Hunt. What else could it be?" Horsemen and hounds traversed the darkness. Lara sucked in a ragged breath and smelled saddle leather and sweaty horseflesh. The throaty bay of hunting dogs mingled with the growl of hunting horns.

"It's midnight." Raven's voice boomed, deeper and louder than it was before. "I must leave you now, children. Make haste. Don't fall prey to your fears. There's no salvation to be found remaining in your old world."

He bolted to his feet and donned mail that lay in a shining pile next to the fire. Where had it come from? She could've sworn it hadn't been there a few minutes before. The air around Raven glowed strangely. Garbed as a medieval knight, he leaped into the ethereal world of the Wild Hunt.

Trevor shot to on his feet. "Wōden," he cried breathlessly. "Wōden. I adored you when I was a boy. I used to pray for you to rescue me from the madness in my home."

"And so I did, son," Raven yelled. "Only a few years late. Can hardly fault me for that. I told you your people used to pray to me."

Booming laughter and the din of hunting horns surrounded them, rising in intensity, as the Hunt swept across the sky.

Trevor yanked her to her feet and hugged her hard. His blue eyes glittered; twin points of light from the bonfire reflected in his inky pupils. "It's like the old tales come to life," he murmured. "This is a much better version of Never-Never land." He pulled her closer to him. "Much better."

Gunter nosed his way in, snuggling deep between them as he sought the warmth and reassurance of his human parents. Trevor bent to pet the pup before closing his arms around Lara again.

Her head spun. If the Wild Hunt was real, and if Philemon had been a Sidhe, then all the other Celtic myths were likely true as well. Since she didn't know what to think about any of it, she stopped trying to dredge any meaning, beyond the joy of being alive, out of Samhain eve.

"I love you, Trevor. What an amazing experience to share."

He stroked her hair and murmured in Gaelic. When she angled her head, he closed his mouth over hers. His lips were firm, demanding, and he sank his tongue inside her mouth. Heat kindled between her legs and her nipples hardened where they pressed against his chest. She felt the swell of him, hard against her belly, and her breath caught in her throat.

Trevor tore his mouth from hers. "I want you, Lara." His voice was rough with desire and he dragged cushions off the chairs, dropping them next to the fire.

"Yes." She ran her hands down his belly until they curved around his cock. "I want you too." Laughter bubbled from her as she sank onto the cushions and pulled him down with her.

CHAPTER 32

They made love and watched the fire burn until it was only a rosy bed of glowing coals. Because they hadn't gone to bed until close to dawn, they weren't up and moving until midmorning. The numinous wonder from the previous night clung to Lara. She gave Trevor a lingering kiss, then said, "Let's leave everything here. That'll be a few less things we need to bring."

"I already decided to leave my clothes and those books we bought," he replied. "And I'm wondering about the pup's crate. He's pretty good about accidents at this point, and it'd free up quite a bit of space in the boot."

"Let's just leave everything," Lara declared resolutely. "It'll be a symbol we're making a commitment to follow Raven's instructions and get back here as soon as we can."

"I could make a couple round trips a day," Trevor said thoughtfully. "One very early and the other quite late. I'll use the gate off the backyard that opens into the alleyway behind the house. No one ever uses it because there's no parking back there, so if I moved things out that way, it wouldn't be as noticeable. Good thing the gate's so overgrown. I didn't say anything at the time, but I was always concerned Beauchamp would discover he could get access to the house that way."

She frowned. "It's strange, but until you mentioned it, I'd absolutely forgotten about that gate. We've lived there for how many years, and I've never used it. Not even once. Good idea, though."

"I'll have to trim the hedge back, but that's easy enough. Likely the gate's not operable enough to get it fully open without at least a bit of work." He smiled at her, and her heart swelled. He looked truly happy, glowing actually. The brittle persona he'd hidden behind for so long wasn't there anymore.

Lara felt excited and joyful. Her other world—where she listened to tales of people's woe and nurtured graduate students—receded. As it did, she understood she hadn't led a particularly well-rounded life. *Maybe this will be an opportunity* to *do something for me—and for Trevor— instead of spending all my energy shoring up strangers.*

Psychology was an odd field. There'd always been village wise-women. You brought them a problem and left a dead chicken as payment. Psychotherapy in the westernized world had changed all that. The working theory was patients needed to keep coming for an indeterminate time, be stuffed full of psychiatric medications, and develop a dependence on the practitioner. That dependence even had a name: transference.

"Lara?" Trevor walked to her and draped an arm around her shoulders.

"What?"

"I've been talking to you, and it's like you can't hear me."

"Sorry. I was daydreaming about what things would be like up here. Then I started thinking about psychology, and—"

"Never mind. Do you want to catch a bite before we hit the road? There's some homemade granola, and I managed to persuade the goat to give me some milk. We should drink it since it won't keep till we're back permanently. The cooler in the spring house isn't nearly as efficient as a fridge."

"What's the goat going to do?" she asked. "Don't they need milking every day?"

"Actually, it's twice a day." Trevor smiled. "Raven told me some things. I didn't follow all of them, but I guess *these* goats will manage somehow. He told me to milk them when I came by. Said that'd be fine. Maybe they're Sidhe goats. Who knows?"

Lara clucked to the puppy. "It's a good idea to eat before we leave. That way, we won't have to stop anywhere for food. Since I don't have to pack, I'm done up here." Glancing around the bedroom, she added. "There's room for our mattress in this room. We wouldn't have to bring the whole headboard and frameset. Just the mattress since it's so comfortable. The other rooms on this floor are empty, so we could move this bedstead into one of them. Unless Arabel really wanted to bring her bed, she could use this one. I'll have to ask her."

She took Trevor's hand and chatted companionably, while they continued making plans. Their footsteps rattled down the wood flooring of the hallway until they descended the stairs.

TREVOR PULLED the car open for Lara. "Wonder what Arabel will want to bring? You'd mentioned the bed earlier. Even if she uses the one we just slept in, I'm sure she'll have lots of things she'd like to keep close. I'd be glad to help her move too."

"I'll let her know. I'm sure she'll appreciate any help we give her. Let's see," Lara glanced at the clock mounted in the center console, "It's past eleven. It'll take a couple hours—no less than that—to get back to town. I'd like to stop by that big outdoor store on lower Capitol Hill to stock up on clothes and boots. We promised Lillian we'd drop by her place before we went home. It'll be a busy afternoon."

"I assume you mean the main REI store?"

"Yeah, they always have a better selection than anywhere else." Lara reached for her seatbelt. "You could pick up some things too. You have more than I do, but a few more wool shirts and outdoor jackets and pants wouldn't hurt you, either. After whatever we buy wears out, we'll be stuck with what I can sew, knit, or pull out of that loom I told you about."

"Doesn't Arabel live in the same area as REI?"

"Yes, she does," Lara replied smiling at him. "Bet you were thinking of stopping by there once we're done shopping. It's a great idea. When I've got cell reception, I'll call her and let her know we're coming."

She called and called once they were back on the Interstate, but Arabel didn't answer. They turned on the radio and found Wednesday's madness had settled down. The news was still full of muggings, rapes, and murders, but the synchronous quality from the previous week's unrest had disappeared. Just out of Sultan, Lara settled into the book from Lillian. True to Raven's prediction, it *did* make sense as she read slowly, absorbing the complicated material. She looked up from its pages after Trevor stopped to buy fuel and was aghast the per-gallon price had risen to seven-fifty.

"Wonder how far it'll climb before there isn't any more?" she muttered.

"What?" Trevor was just getting back into the car. "How are you finding the book?"

"I was grousing about gas prices. To answer your question, the book's really, really interesting. It's about you as well as me. Or maybe it's about our link to one another."

"You'll have to tell me." He nodded encouragingly and fired the car's engine.

"I need to read it through first, so I can think about it," she said. "This isn't like anything I've ever read before. I have to feel the material in my guts. Reading with my eyes and brain doesn't seem to do it."

He reached over and patted one of her hands. "Whenever you're ready is fine. I'm relieved you're able to understand it, since both Lillian and Raven made such a big deal out of it."

"Yeah," she grinned. "Me too. Thank God that crippling

ambivalence dogging me disappeared. Who knows? Maybe it's another reason the book's accessible now, where it wasn't before."

"Settle in and read, love. It'll be another hour before we get into Seattle."

~

AFTER AN EXPENSIVE COUPLE HOURS, she and Trevor left REI, wheeling a cart full of overstuffed shopping bags. As they negotiated their way to the parking garage, she said, "We should stop by Arabel's anyway. Something's wrong that she's not answering her phone. Her answering machine's not picking up, either. Her house is only a few blocks from here up on Taylor North."

"Sure, Lara. We can stop. It's not even three yet. Doesn't take much time to spend a few thousand bucks." Smiling broadly, he hit the clicker, and the hatch popped open. After stowing their purchases, he helped the puppy jump down. "Five minutes and we'll go see what's up with Arabel. She's probably just taking advantage of the fact that it's not raining to work in that garden of hers."

As soon as they pulled up in front of the modest white clapboard home, Lara knew something had to be desperately wrong. The front door stood open behind the screen door, and Arabel's Toyota Avalon was missing. It didn't make sense for the door to be open and the car gone. She clutched at the amulet, but it lay quietly against her chest.

"I don't like this, Lara. You should stay in the car," Trevor said, his voice gruff with concern.

"No. I'm coming with you." Her stomach twisted into a knot, and saliva flooded her mouth. Reaching with her sixth sense, she saw a dark pall hanging over the house and she shivered. "Maybe you should bring the shotgun."

"Nah." Trevor shook his head. "Whoever was here, they're long gone. That's why her car's not here. Let's hope she's just tied to a chair."

They mounted the two steps to the front door. Trevor tried the screen, found it open, and gingerly pulled it away from the door frame so they could enter. Lara's breath caught in her throat. The living room had been ransacked. Every drawer had been pulled out, emptied, and discarded on the floor. The table that once held Arabel's television was empty, and her computer table sat naked as well.

"Arabel," she called out. "Arabel."

Silence ricocheted off the walls. Lara trod softly through the small dining area with chairs tipped on their sides. She swallowed hard before pushing the swinging door that led into the kitchen. It had been stripped of food, cupboards hanging open. When she looked out the terrarium window over the kitchen sink, Arabel's neat garden rows had been trampled into a muddy mush and stripped of anything edible.

Lara balled her hands into fists. "Crap. Aw, shit."

"Bloody hell, this just gets worse and worse," Trevor muttered. Looking shaken, he disappeared down the hall. Moments later a strangled shriek rose. "Mary, mother of God," battered her ears, followed by, "Bloody, fucking hell."

Back in the kitchen, pale as any of the ghostly riders from the previous night, Trevor said, "Don't come any farther. They shot her. Likely with her own gun, since you told me she had one. There's a lot of blood. Aw, Jesus. Poor Arabel." Tears gathered in the corners of his eyes, and he raised a trembling hand to his face.

"No. Noooooo," she moaned, her throat swelling with tears. "It's all my fault. We should have brought her with us, instead of just running away from the riots." Unbearable pain sluiced through her. Knees buckling, she fell heavily against Trevor. "Christ, ach Christ. How can I live in a world without her in it?"

Lara barely recognized the agonized sounds filling her ears as her own. Wrapping her arms around Trevor, she felt cold and desolate. She held her head against his sweatered chest, and he stroked her hair, but it didn't feel right.

"I need to tell her goodbye." Pushing away, she crept resolutely down the hall. There were only two bedrooms, Arabel's and a small neat guest room for when her sister came to visit. Fury at whoever had violated her friend's home gave way to wrenching grief, and her stomach lurched sourly.

Lara pushed the door to Arabel's room open and was confronted by a scene from Hell. It was obvious the old woman had struggled with her assailants. Blood was everywhere, streaked on the walls, pooling on the floor. An old-fashioned black telephone receiver lay close to her friend's hand, its cord cruelly cut. Wanting to go to Arabel, yet knowing it was wrong to disturb a crime scene, Lara hesitated.

Hot, bitter tears coursed down her face, and she keened like a wounded animal, sinking to the floor because her legs wouldn't hold her.

Trevor joined her. "I've called 911. They said not to touch anything and to wait for the officers."

It was well past dark when they crawled into the BMW. Lara had requested her old friend be cremated once the crime lab was done with its investigation. "At least I can bring something of her with us," Lara snuffled. "We should have invited her along this weekend. At least then, she'd have been safe."

"I talked to the Coroner for a bit." Trevor sounded devastated, his voice thin and drawn. "He believes she's been dead since sometime Thursday, but he told me he couldn't be sure until they complete the autopsy." Fishing a handkerchief out of his pocket, Trevor blotted his eyes. "He told me the riots were pretty much citywide, from the time we left town through Friday morning. Did you talk to any of the police? I'm sure you must have, it's just I wasn't paying very close attention."

"Yes. Remember, I asked for her ashes. And I told them I'd clean up here whenever they've cleared the crime scene," she replied, blowing her nose. "I want to box up what I can salvage for her sister. Did you look at the officers, Trev? I mean *really* look at them? Their eyes were dead, just like men out of Dostoevsky or Nietzsche. It's like they've seen too much and don't quite know what to do with themselves." Lara started crying again. "She was like a mother to me. And a friend. The secretarial part was the least of it. I don't know what I'll do without her."

Trevor handed his hankie over. "Do you still want to stop by Lillian's?"

"Not really. Maybe I can just call her." Dredging through her bag, she pulled out her phone, found Lillian's number in the call log, and hit send.

"I was just getting worried about you two." Lillian's voice crackled over the cellular network. "Are you still coming?" There was a silence and then, "Lara, why are you crying?"

In fits and starts, Lara told her about Arabel. Anguish poured out of her as Lillian listened. "This was my fault. We should've taken her with us. The whole timetable for leaving should've been moved up by a month. Never mind, I didn't understand we had to go until yesterday. Aw shit, I'm not making any sense." She dissolved into hiccupy sobs.

"My poor babe," Lillian crooned after Lara had run down. "You two go home. I'll come to you."

"Well?" Trevor asked. "Which way are we going?"

"Home. We're going home. Lillian said she'd meet us there."

He nodded. "Do you want anything to eat?"

"No. Not hungry. You?"

"Me, either." He took her hand. "I'm so sorry, Lara. I know how much Arabel meant to you." A hesitation, then, "We should've had her over more."

Lara wiped her streaming eyes with her sleeve. "Yeah. We should have. But you know, I'd invite her, and she'd usually have some excuse. I always thought it was because she was raised in the south when whites and blacks didn't go to the same schools or ride on the same busses. But she said it was because she didn't want to be a bother. Sort of like what she said when I asked her to come with us." Lara blew her nose again. "At the office it was different. It was *her* office, since she did everything. All I did was see the patients. So it was more of a level playing field, and her and me, we just appreciated each other.

"Ach, don't pay any attention to me. I'm blithering. I can't believe I'll go to work tomorrow, and she won't be there. I almost can't stand to think about it." Her voice broke and she started sobbing again.

"Maybe you don't have to go back to work," he suggested softly. "You'd have to go to clear out your files, sure. We could bring them home and burn them. But you could call all your patients. I know you've got a list of them."

"What would I tell them?" she asked, her voice small, broken.

"That you're closing for an indeterminate time because of Arabel."

"I'd have to refer them to someone."

"You could do that."

"I'll need to think about it, Trev. I'm supposed to hang onto records for seven years, but I don't suppose that matters all that much, since I doubt Seattle will still be standing seven years from now." She leaned her head back against the soft headrest, feeling her grief as if it were a living thing gnawing a raw, hollow place inside her.

"I'll go with you tomorrow, if you'd like," he offered.

"Thanks, dear. Can I sleep on that?" Closing her swollen, aching eyes, Lara started the process of bidding farewell to her oldest and dearest friend.

CHAPTER 33

*L*illian was waiting for them when they got home. She sat on the top step, with her feet settled against the next riser. "Can I help you bring anything up?" she asked.

"There's nothing to bring. We left it all at Raven's." Lara's words thudded dully against her ears. Gunter bounded around Lara and landed in Lillian's lap. Once there, he licked her face with abandon.

"There's a good boy," she murmured. "You've gone traveling, haven't you? You'll have to tell mother Lillian all about it." Petting and praising the small dog, as he wriggled with pleasure, Lillian rose, still holding the puppy. Wordlessly, she followed Lara and Trevor into their house before setting Gunter down.

Lara flicked on lights in the entry hall, unutterably grateful Lillian wasn't offering platitudes or other false comfort, since the effort of crafting polite responses felt beyond her.

"At least the place is still standing." Trevor sounded hollow and strained as he broke the silence. "I was worried it might've been trashed during all the rampaging after we left town."

"I hadn't even thought about that," Lara said, barely recognizing her own voice.

"Do you have candles?" Lillian shook her braids over her shoulders.

"Sure." Trevor looked mystified. "But why?"

"We need to bid farewell to your friend. The ritual requires three candles, and it's best done outdoors."

"I don't know if I can," Lara said brokenly. "I can't even stand to think about Arabel right now. It feels like I failed her. Like somehow this is m-my responsibility." Her voice cracked on the last word and sobs came again, great choking gasps of misery that snatched her breath away.

Lillian moved close and folded Lara into her arms. The Sidhe held her as if she were a small child, making comforting noises and stroking Lara's unbound hair. "There, there, child. I know how much you loved her. We shall honor her, and then you'll begin to accept her passing. She's gone to the Summerlands. It's not a cause for grief. You'll find her there someday when you pass through those gates."

"I've never believed that." Lara's voice was muffled against Lillian's shoulder. "They told us there was an afterlife at the Institute, but I never thought it could be true."

"I found the candles." Trevor called. "They're on the table in the backyard."

"Come along." Keeping a firm arm around Lara, Lillian led her through the laundry room and out the back door. "That's right. Just lean on me," she instructed kindly, as she guided Lara onto the porch and into a chair. Glancing at Trevor, she said, "Red wine. Bring an unopened bottle and four glasses."

Lillian arranged the candles in a circle. When she looked at them, they burst into flame. "How did you do that?" Lara asked. Part of her was curious, but a bigger part didn't care.

"Bringing fire is simple, dearie. Oh good, here's the wine." She took the bottle from Trevor, inspecting it to make sure it was still sealed, while he set the glasses on the table. "Do you want to take part in this?" Lillian looked sharply at him as she sat down.

"May I?"

"Of course. I expected you'd want to, but you must state you wish to be a part of this ceremony."

Clearing his throat a bit awkwardly, Trevor intoned, "Yes, I wish to be a part of this observance to honor Arabel Love's passing." He pulled a third chair to the table and dropped heavily into it.

"And you?" Lillian tapped Lara's shoulder gently.

"I also wish to be a part of this rite to honor Arabel Love," Lara answered around the lump in her throat.

Lillian scrabbled through several pockets in her ever-present long skirts and brought out a knife. Breaking the seal on the wine bottle, she dug out the cork, and then poured the claret-colored liquid into each of the four glasses, dividing it evenly. She placed a glass in front of Trevor, one in front of Lara, and took one for herself. Lillian's gaze swept the table, and she placed the last glass in front of the empty place before facing them.

"Now," she said simply, "We begin. Close your eyes, empty your minds. Breathe the blessing of the Goddess deep into your bellies..."

At some point, Lillian switched from English to Gaelic. Despite the unfamiliar language, Lara found she could understand it. Whether it was the rhythm and cadence of the strange words, or a sudden shift within her, she recognized what Lillian was doing and was moved beyond words as she recounted the story of Arabel's life, starting from her birth on a small farm in rural Alabama to a sharecropper and his wife. Once the gamut of Arabel's life played itself out, Lillian formally requested that she be granted succor in the Summerlands and commanded them to drink their wine.

Lara never knew whether Lillian's directive was in Gaelic or English, but she understood and drained her glass. "Yes." Lillian's voice softened. "It is done. Her spirit has found its home."

"How can you know?" Lara murmured.

Lillian gestured to the fourth glass, which stood half-empty. "The spirit accepts its last taste of earthly sustenance to speed its journey. Arabel was with us as we prayed for her and guided her. Now she is home."

Once Lara heard the words, she recognized truth in them. During the minutes—or was it hours?—Lillian chanted, Lara assumed the maternal energy flowing around her, comforting her, had been Lillian's, but she'd been wrong.

"How did you know all those things about her?" Lara asked. Wonder from the mystical ceremony filled her, warming desolate places in her soul.

"Because she told me. She was here with us." Lillian gazed at Lara, her green eyes soft with compassion. "Child, I know this is hard for you to accept. Two things helped us tonight. It's still Samhain where spirits roam more freely, and the violent nature of Arabel's death meant her soul was still unbound. Tonight gave you an opportunity to tell her goodbye, but it was a chance for her to bid farewell to those she loved also. I trusted she'd heed our call."

"She did." Awe carved deep in Trevor's words. "I felt her with us. I know I did." He got up and went to stand behind Lara, placing his hands on her shoulders. "Did you get a chance to say goodbye, love? You were closer to her than anyone."

"Yes." Lara's voice, far more her own now, was gentle. "I didn't realize it at first, but I did. Even now, she's still taking care of me." Turning to Lillian, she said, "Thank you for bringing peace to my closest friend."

"You're welcome, child." She hesitated. "Would the two of you share my wine? If not, I shall offer it to the Goddess."

Trevor took the still-full glass, drank, and handed it to Lara, while looking questioningly at Lillian. "You commanded us to drink, but you didn't?"

"I needed all my energies to hold the gates," she replied. "I told you before, alcohol dilutes my powers. We must talk more, but it's late. Do you mind if I make myself comfortable somewhere here?"

"Not at all." Lara turned toward Lillian. "Wherever you'd like is fine."

"I'll see you both in the morning." Lillian got to her feet and led the way into the house, disappearing into shadows as she turned toward the living room.

Later, lying in bed with Trevor and the puppy, Lara assumed that sleep—if it came at all—would carry a steep price. She feared the image of Arabel's body, lying broken and bloody, would rise up to haunt her nights for the rest of her life and wondered if she'd ever be able to close her eyes again.

"Can't sleep?" Trevor's voice rumbled against her hair.

"Not yet. I think I'll be able to soon, though. Something about what Lillian did was…" She blew out a breath and tried again. "I don't know exactly. It's like she took the part of me that was grieving and replaced the anguish with hope. My heart's still heavy, but I don't feel dead inside anymore. Maybe transcendent is the word I'm searching for. At least that's how I feel tonight. Maybe tomorrow will be different."

He folded her into his arms. "I understand. I was really looking forward to having Arabel live with us. I was only half-joking when I said to tell her she could be the mum I never had." Trevor was silent for a while, and Lara felt him hunting for words. "I think I knew," he went on. "The minute we pulled up outside that little house of hers. I just didn't want to believe it."

Nodding against his chest, she said. "And I knew when I kept trying to call her, and she didn't answer. She always went to her church on Sunday morning, but she spent Sunday afternoons at home. I deluded myself that maybe she'd gone out to lunch with one of her church friends, but I didn't reach out with *the sight* to check on her." Tears started again.

"It wouldn't have mattered. You have to stop blaming yourself, Lara. This wasn't anyone's fault. Just pure, blind, rotten luck. Sleep, love. Not much left of this night."

Twining her body around his and closing her gritty, swollen eyes, exhaustion claimed her. The drop into sleep was close to immediate.

~

Sunlight streamed through the windows as the three of them sat at the kitchen table sipping a fragrant amber herbal tea Lillian had brought with her. Conversation was sparse. Still lost in the mysteries from the previous night's ritual, and worried words might spoil her newfound sense of peace, Lara hadn't wanted to say much. Expecting to dream, she'd been surprised to waken with no recollection of any messages from Psyche.

"What will you do next?" Lillian's words were soft, almost like a gentle rain pattering through the room.

Trevor placed a hand over one of Lara's. "What do you want to do, love?" he asked as he squeezed her hand.

Raising her eyes to Lillian's, Lara said, "Raven told us there was a need for haste. You didn't seem to feel that way, at least last week. What do you think now? How much time is there? Or do you even know?"

Before Lara was done speaking, Lillian held up a hand. "My, what a lot of questions." She resettled in her chair, since Gunter was nestled on her lap, and exhaled sharply through pursed lips. "Raven and I are not in total agreement. After last week's tribulations though, I'm concerned I may have taken too sanguine an approach to a problem that's developing a life of its own. Raven's predictions appear to have greater accuracy than mine."

She shook her head and shrugged, an unusual gesture coming from her, then asked, "How soon could you leave?" Lillian's question startled Lara since it sounded more like something Raven might've asked. The Sidhe eyed them intently, waiting.

"I'm not sure." Lara spoke slowly. "If I offer a termination session to those patients that want one, maybe a couple weeks." She turned to Trevor. "Would you be okay with me giving the building to the architect and the CPA? They'll be here. And they can try to sell it. Or keep it. Or do whatever they want, since it'd be theirs."

"That's fine, Lara. It should be simple enough to have a transfer deed drawn up." He smiled. "We've gotten more than the worth out of that place as an ongoing depreciation on your taxes, anyway."

Trevor inhaled deeply. When he let his breath go in a whoosh, Lara noticed dark smudges etched beneath his eyes. "There are things," he began, looking at Lillian. "Things we'll need. I have no idea how hard they'll be to find. Mostly farm tools and implements, but hand tools as well. Everything either runs off batteries, electricity, or gas-powered motors nowadays. We can't use any of them. I suppose we could try to stock up on hundreds of gallons of petrol, assuming we could get a farm tank, but eventually it'd run dry. Best to start with what we'll have to work with." He sifted a hand through his hair. "Seeds might be a challenge too, seeing as how we're coming into winter."

"Start looking. If you need to have something shipped, better now than a month from now. Double up on seeds. Not all of them are viable," Lillian said briskly.

The peremptory tone that had grated on Lara when she first met the other woman was back in Lillian's voice. An authoritative twang simply assumed compliance with her directives. For some reason, Lara found it didn't bother her anymore. Lillian caught Lara's gaze, and her mouth relaxed into a smile. "Getting used to me, are you?"

"Guess so." Smiling back, Lara said, "It was really a nice thing you did last night. For all of us."

"Child." Compassion shone from Lillian's green eyes. "The demise of rituals eventually sounds the death knell for civilizations that depended upon them." She sipped her tea. "What we shared last night was a very old rite. None of us lives forever. Ceremonies surrounding the mystery of death used to be a central part of community life. Now it's mostly third world people who still honor Morrigan. Death isn't to be feared. It's merely the ending of one cycle and the start of another. How is it you don't know that?"

"I thought I did." Lara spoke slowly. "Perhaps not the link between rituals and civilizations failing, but on a smaller scale." Reflecting on how few rituals she had in her day-to-day life, realization dawned that she'd badly underestimated the sterility and isolation of twenty-first century America. No one developed anorexia in countries where there wasn't enough to eat. Probably no one struggled with agoraphobia, social phobias, depression, and a host of other mental health problems in societies where you didn't sit glued to an electronic box twenty hours a day.

"I asked you this once before," Lillian said. "Then I invited you to come live with me. This time, I am asking if you might consider having me stay with you. Not continually, mind you. But some of the time."

Lara glanced at Trevor and saw him nod. She twisted to meet Lillian's forthright gaze and said, "That would be fine. In fact, you'd be welcome. I suspect there's going to be more work up there than we can manage."

"Thank you. Both of you. It's good for me to have a link to humanity. And better for you," her gaze sought Lara again, "to have a teacher. I'm going to leave you now. There're things I must take care of." Whispering something to Gunter, she bent to put him down on the tile floor before standing and shaking out her clothes. The puppy whined softly and nipped at Lillian's long skirts. "You don't have to see me out." She smiled warmly at them. "I'll be in touch sooner than you might think."

They sat drinking tea after Lillian left. Lara was quiet, lost in her own thoughts. "Come on," Trevor finally said. "Gunter needs to go out. We need to talk a little before you leave for the office, and I swing by the gold brokers." Nodding, she picked up her cup and followed him into the back yard.

"Would you like me to stop by your office after I've gathered up the bullion? I offered yesterday, and you told me you needed to think about it."

"Sure, Trev. I'd like that. I'm going to begin closing things down. By the time you get there, I might actually have some files boxed up for you to bring home." She paused, biting at her lower lip. "You know that peacefulness from last night?"

He nodded.

"It feels pretty fragile. I suspect the minute I walk into my office and Arabel's not there, this is going to be way harder than I can get my mind around. I still can't fathom that she won't be sitting in her chair just like always." Lara's voice cracked.

He drew into his arms, and they stood like that for several minutes before he said, "What's percolating in that head of yours? Seems like it's more than Arabel."

She stepped away from his embrace, so she could really look at him and nodded. "There's so much, I scarcely know where to begin. If you'd asked me a month ago whether I'd be willing to dump our life and move on, I'd have told you that was nuts. In fact, if you'd pressed the matter, I probably would've urged you to go without me." Smiling sadly, she reached for his hand. "Sorry, dear, but I would have."

She shut her eyes and searched within herself. After she opened them, her next words came slowly. "This is tough to admit, but I've been attached to the wrong things. Way too invested in making money. And likely far too fond of my role as benevolent helper."

She looked at him ruefully, and a corner of her mouth turned downward. "Don't get me wrong. I believe I've done a far better job than that godforsaken crew who push psych meds and preach cognitive behavioral therapy to the exclusion of everything else, but just the same, I'm not feeling very good about how I've spent the last twenty-something years."

"Don't you think you're being a bit hard on yourself?" Trevor murmured. "I've spent those same years as a glorified waiter, for bloody fuck's sake. At least you were doing something a bit more significant than making sure Mr. Branford's tea water was the precise temperature that would brew Earl Gray to his liking."

Taking his hand, she spoke gently, picking her words with care. "We've never talked much about any of this. Some of it was you with your secrets, but a lot of it was me with my own sad, lonely childhood and abandonment issues. I've been hiding behind that Ph.D. ever since I earned it. Never mind the fact there was a part of me that never believed I actually deserved it."

"Sounds like a fresh start is long overdue." Though he spoke lightly, shadows flickered just behind his eyes. Pain for her, or for himself? Or, just maybe, for both of them.

"Come here, dear one." She opened her arms, inviting a hug. "That fresh start you mentioned is long overdue. And then some." She smiled at him. "But you know, I'm actually looking forward to it."

"So am I, love. So am I."

He stepped into her arms and wove his around her. They held one another tight until Gunter jumped on them, snapping and yipping. "Aw, he's feeling left out." Lara sank to the ground where the puppy could crawl into her lap.

Trevor lowered himself right behind her, cradling them both in his arms.

You've reached the end of Dark Prophecy. The Soul Storm Series continues in *Dark Pursuit*. An excerpt follows.

ABOUT THE AUTHOR

Ann Gimpel is a USA Today bestselling author. A lifelong aficionado of the unusual, she began writing speculative fiction a few years ago. Since then her short fiction has appeared in a number of webzines and anthologies. Her longer books run the gamut from urban fantasy to paranormal romance. Once upon a time, she nurtured clients, now she nurtures dark, gritty fantasy stories that push hard against reality. When she's not writing, she's in the backcountry getting down and dirty with her camera. She's published over 50 books to date, with several more planned for 2018 and beyond. A husband, grown children, grandchildren and wolf hybrids round out her family.

Keep up with her at www.anngimpel.com or http://anngimpel.blogspot.com

If you enjoyed what you read, get in line for special offers and pre-release special reads. Sign up for Ann's newsletter on her website or her blog.

DARK PURSUIT, CHAPTER ONE

*D*r. Lara McInnis began the day clinging to a slender island of solace. Hours later, waves of patients, errands, and phone calls had pounded against that island until it was nothing but a rubble heap.

Rubbing wearily at her eyes, Lara finally gave up and closed them. For a moment or two she thought she might get away with it, but then an image of Arabel, her long time receptionist, lying in a pool of her own blood rose out of some subterranean reservoir. The grizzly scene was so real, Lara's stomach clenched. Like an unwelcome tape loop, it played again. And again. Opening her eyes didn't help one whit. Arabel was just as bloody and just as dead. Over a week had passed, but the raw edges of her grief still cut deep.

Lara collapsed into the chair generally reserved for her patients. Outside her western window a scarlet sunset streaked the Seattle skyline, adding its bloody motif to the one already playing in her head. Disgusted with herself, she got to her feet and paced the length of her spacious office, burning a track in the Oriental rug. She should be boxing up client files, but couldn't force herself back to a task she was ambivalent about—at least not until she wrestled her emotions under better control.

The doorknob rattled. It startled her, and her heart jumped into overdrive. In her current state, the familiar sound was like a reproach. "How could I not have locked it with everything that's going on?" she muttered as she rushed into the outer office. Arabel's desk, another Oriental rug, and ornate Victorian furniture with floral upholstery flashed past the edges of her vision, but she focused on the door as she watched the knob slowly turning.

This is ridiculous. It's probably a pharmaceutical salesman thinking I'm a psychiatrist.

Or that demon that's been dogging me, a darker inner voice insinuated.

Since the only other option was throwing herself out a second story window and hoping for the best, Lara crossed the few feet to the door and yanked it open. A decidedly overweight woman jerked her hand away from the knob and eyed Lara balefully out of rheumy, blue eyes. Pale brown hair, going gray, was gathered into an untidy bun, and fat rolls bulged over too-tight jeans and under an inadequate T-shirt.

"Mrs. Stone." Lara tried to smile as she coaxed her heart back to a normal rhythm.

"Humph, surprised you remember me."

"Of course I do." Lara stepped aside, gesturing for the woman to enter. The last thing she wanted was another patient visit, but it would verge on the unethical—never mind the rude—to ask Myra Stone to go away without at least finding out what she wanted.

Lara waited while Myra stalked past her, looked inside the inner office, and circled back to stand in front of Lara, hands on her hips. "Guess she's not here," Myra snapped.

"If you're looking for Caren, no, she's not," Lara agreed, mystified. "Is your stepdaughter missing?"

The woman grunted. She still had an expression on her face that could curdle milk, but she knotted her fingers together and said, "How about if we sit down and you and me can have a little talk?"

"Okay." Lara kept her voice as neutral as she could, pulled the office door shut—taking care to lock it this time—and rolled Arabel's chair out. Her butt had barely grazed the seat cushion when the woman started talking.

"I don't think spending time here is helping Caren. Nope, not at all," Myra complained in an unpleasant, nasal twang. "I never know where she is. She's still taking what doesn't belong to her and that father of hers, well he's not any help at all. So it's just me." Accusatory eyes drilled into Lara. "All my *real* kids turned out fine. This one, she's just a bad seed." Rooting around in a battered handbag, Myra pulled out a cigarette. "Do you mind?"

"Uh, yes, I'd prefer you didn't smoke," Lara managed, struck by the gall of the woman and offended to hear her belittle her stepdaughter so blatantly. Caren had said Myra hated her, but Lara assumed it was just teenaged hyperbole.

Myra stuffed the cigarette into her T-shirt pocket and pushed her bulk upright. "Not much reason for me to stay," she muttered. "Really thought she'd be here. You're the only one she ever says anything good about."

If she felt like one of your real *kids, maybe she'd say good things about you—or feel safe enough to love you.* Discouraged by the woman's callousness—after all, Caren had been through hell in her sixteen years—Lara stood too. Trying for a positive spin, she said, "You must be concerned or you wouldn't have come looking for Caren. Would you like to make an appointment, Mrs. Stone? I already told you on the phone that I'm closing my practice, but I'd be glad to find a time slot for you in the next couple weeks. We could talk about some of the challenges of step-parenting and how hard it is for abused children to learn to trust—"

"Nah." Myra waved her to silence. "Hell, my uncle did me, and I didn't turn out like her. I didn't cut school or steal stuff. Or carve on myself." Shuffling to the door, she pulled it open and stalked out into the hall, the tiny chink in her armor replaced by a brittle, defensive anger.

"At least consider it," Lara persisted, addressing the woman's back as Myra headed for a stairwell. Lara drew the door shut, thinking Myra could do with a smattering of psychotherapy herself. *Yeah, like about ten years' worth.* Crimson from the sunset bled through stained-glass windows, casting her familiar furniture in an eerie light. Lara wrapped her arms around herself, seeking the warmth of her own body for comfort.

That poor child. From abusive kin to a stepmother who doesn't want her. Sorrow for Caren replaced the Arabel tape loop as color faded from the room. Lara decided it was an improvement, all in all, and she kicked a box over a few inches so she could open the lower drawer of her filing cabinet.

Lara pushed her long, red hair behind her shoulders and dumped banded files into the banker's box without any particular regard for order. The outer door of her office rattled again. This time, though, it was a key sound.

"Lara?"

"In here, Trev," she called back and straightened to greet her longtime boyfriend.

Trevor, his usually buoyant mood notably subdued, held out his arms. "'Lo, Lara. Sorry I'm a bit late but... Well, never mind, it'll keep." He scanned the room with his intensely blue eyes, taking in her half-finished packing job. "How much more?" he asked tentatively.

Shooting him a pain-laced look, she shook her head. "I don't know. I'm doing this as fast as I can in between seeing patients who want a last session or two. Thank God Arabel started calling all of them before..." She walked into his arms and buried her head against his shoulder.

He closed his arms around her, holding her close. "Doesn't matter, love. It'll be done eventually." Blond curls brushing against her face, he kneaded her shoulders with both hands. "Bloody hell, you're wound tighter than a spring."

The familiar clipped tones of his British accent washed over her, easing her anguish. "Feels heavenly," she breathed. "I didn't realize how tense I was..." Her voice trailed off. "Well, maybe I did, but I've been forcing myself not to pay attention.' She pulled away and flopped onto the floral couch spanning part of one wall. Exhaustion dragged at her.

Trevor pushed boxes out of the way and joined her. "I miss Arabel too, you know." His voice cracked with emotion, and he cleared his throat. "Any of those ready to take home?" he asked, pointing at the half dozen boxes littering the floor.

"Yeah, those three." She jabbed her index finger at a corner of the room. "They're records from patients I haven't seen in at least a couple years."

"What are you going to do with the others?" His tone was gentle, but he placed a finger under her chin, forcing her to look at him. "What are you saving them for?"

"Guess I can't very well keep any of them," she muttered. "It's not like we're even going to be here after a little while."

"No," he agreed solemnly. "It's not. And we're not."

Lara set her lips into a thin line and got to her feet. "Okay, then," she snapped, angry with a universe that was intent on stealing her life away. Pulling open file drawers, she grabbed a few charts and dumped them on her desk. "I need these since all of them have appointments, but all the rest can go."

Nodding, Trevor joined her in front of the twin horizontal files, and together they began to move twenty years of Lara's psychology practice into the waiting cartons. "You'll need more boxes," he noted after a few minutes. "Lots more."

"Thought we could fill these, dump them at home, and then I'd just bring the empties back tomorrow and begin all over."

"Ah, brilliant. Of course that's the obvious thing to do." Grunting, he shouldered a box and headed for the door. "I'll be back directly for another."

"Right behind you," she said, picking up a box. "I feel better when I'm doing something other than wallowing in my own misery."

"That's my girl," he shot back over his shoulder.

The minute Trevor opened the door of his old Mercedes

convertible, Gunter, their eleven-week-old German Shepherd lunged out of the car headed straight for Lara. The awkward black puppy yipped, whined, and launched himself at her, pulling at her wool skirt with his claws. "There, there, little man," she cooed and set her box down so she could unhook his feet from the fabric of her skirt. "Yes, I've missed you too."

As she fondled the puppy, she glanced at Trevor. Dressed in faded blue jeans, a green chambray shirt, and a tan corduroy blazer, his tall, lanky frame exuded its usual casual elegance. "How'd your day go?" she asked.

"Not bad," he replied, shoving his box of files into the car's small trunk and reaching for the one she'd set on the sidewalk. "We'll have to put the rest in your car, love. No more room in here." He slammed the car's boot. "I started really taking stock of what's in our house and making lists. Went down to the waterfront too." His lips curved wryly. "Didn't find much in the way of antique farm equipment, but I did get some leads. Bloke at the flea market looked at me as if I were daft."

She flashed him a weak smile. "Well, dear, I suppose it's not every day they get customers hunting for scythes, or whatever it was you asked for."

"Let's get those other boxes down here. Then we can walk the pup before we go home."

Lara inclined her head and turned to go back into her building *Lucky for us the electricity's not on the fritz. It's almost dark.* Power outages had been hit-and-miss. More often than not, she'd had to use a flashlight to find her way out of her building. Back in the office, she continued throwing files willy-nilly into the boxes. An orderly part of her rebelled when she looked at the files, no longer alphabetized, lying on their sides like beached whales. "It doesn't matter," she muttered fiercely. "All we're going to do is burn them."

She remembered something Raven had told her. *Your thought patterns are still trapped in your old life. That is what's brought modern civilization to the brink of extinction: an intransigent unwillingness to change anything.*

As she thought about Raven, a vision of the tall, broad-shouldered mage with his flowing black hair filled her mind. The amulet Lillian had given her, nestled between her breasts on its golden chain, thrummed approvingly. Lara grasped the moonstone through the fabric of her teal silk blouse, enjoying its warmth.

Raven and Lillian. Two ancient creatures, somehow alive and well in the early years of the twenty-first century. *Doesn't matter why or how, I'm just glad they're here, helping us.*

Trevor strode back into her inner office. "Got another box ready?" he asked.

"Uh-huh." She pointed. "That one. I'll just finish this one and cart it out. Then there'll only be two more to fill and we can head home."

∽

"Ugh," Trevor grunted as he shoved the last of the boxes into Lara's silver BMW. "Glad you only got six boxes. I don't think we could have crammed any more in with a shoehorn, since all that outdoor clothing we bought is still in there."

"Brrrr." She wrapped her arms around her upper body. "It's getting cold. Why don't you start for home? I'll be along soon."

"Right, then." He gathered her close. "No wonder you're cold, love." He fingered the silky fabric of her blouse. "Be sure to put your jumper on before you leave."

"Yes, Daddy." She smiled into the folds of his blazer, thinking how good it felt to be cared about.

He ruffled her hair, spun her round, and gave her a friendly swat on the butt. "Off with you, love. I'll have something started for supper by the time you get there. You *are* leaving directly behind me?"

"Right after I lock up."

Lara ran up the broad front steps of her Victorian office building, knowing she'd miss the old place with its unique stained glass windows. Pulling the front door shut and taking care to spin the deadbolt, she padded up the carpeted stairs to her office, opened the door, and stopped short.

Caren sat on the floor in the darkened reception area and shot a defiant glance Lara's way, but didn't say anything.

"Caren! How on earth did you get in here?"

"Back door was open." The teenager's voice was barely audible.

"I don't think so," Lara said and looked closely at her young client. "I distinctly remember locking it earlier."

"So I helped it along a little," the girl said, her voice rising in unspoken challenge.

"It's okay," Lara murmured. "However you managed to get in, it must have been important for you to find me."

"Yeah. I—I didn't believe what my stepmother told me. I thought she was just being mean. But it…it's true." Caren's voice broke and a low, keening moan escaped her. "I looked in there," she jerked a thumb toward the inner office where Lara saw her clients. "You're really leaving, aren't you? Just like everyone else has left me. You're leaving too." Reproachful blue eyes vilified Lara.

"Oh, sweetie—" Lara began.

"Don't *sweetie* me," the girl snarled. "You really had me going there, Doc. I thought you actually cared about me. But it was just a job, wasn't it? Just a fucking job, and now you're…you're…" Her face twisted into a rictus, and Caren began to cry. Soft little animal sounds tore out of her, as she turned her face to the wall.

Ach, what can I tell her that she'll believe? "Do you mind if I sit down?" Lara asked and drew the outer door of her office closed.

"I don't fucking care what you do," the girl choked out between sobs.

Nodding, Lara sank to the floor, but not too close to Caren. "I can see why you'd think I'm abandoning you." Lara reached toward her psychic side for help. Caren's aura reflected the girl's misery. Instead of lively colors, it had reverted to an opaque gray.

"You are."

"Well, I *am* leaving," Lara agreed, "but I'm not leaving to get away from you." Caren was silent, so Lara forged ahead, hoping against hope the girl would listen for long enough to not simply pigeonhole what was happening now into the long cavalcade of adults who'd let her down.

"My receptionist, Arabel, was murdered during the riots last week. She..." Lara swallowed hard. "She was like a mother to me, since my own mother died when I was very young. I— Well, Caren, I can't stand to be here without her. I know it's abrupt, and I would have liked to have had at least a month to tell all my patients goodbye, but..."

A tear dripped down her face, and Lara brushed it away. "I don't think I can keep on seeing people without Arabel's help. What I do is hard work. I can't do it if I'm empty inside."

"Oh." The girl's voice was small and wounded. "You didn't have a good mother, either?"

"Uh-uh. Not after mine died." Fishing around in her skirt pockets for a tissue, Lara wiped her eyes.

"That's why you understood. About me."

"Yes, dear. That's part of it." Lara glanced at her patient. Caren had straightened slightly from her slumped position, where she'd looked like a discarded rag doll. Her aura seemed a bit better too.

"But I don't want you to leave." The words tore out of the girl like shards of glass, painful to hear.

Lara held out her arms. "Come here," she invited. "Let me hold you. You look like you could use a hug. And I know I could." Figuring it was the last phrase that did it, Lara took a deep breath and closed her arms around the distraught teen, who'd scuttled across the floor, flinging herself into the offered embrace.

"This is so hard," Caren snuffled. "You're the first one I've trusted in years. Now you won't be here anymore."

"You'll carry the knowledge in your heart that you *can* trust someone," Lara murmured, stroking Caren's soft, dark hair. "And I'll carry you with me as well."

"You won't forget about me."

"Oh, sweetie, how could I?" Lara closed her eyes. Disclosing personal information ran against her professional grain, but what possible difference could the truth make at this point? Disentangling herself slightly from the trembling girl, Lara said, "Look at me. I want to tell you something."

When the girl's troubled eyes met hers, Lara let out a breath. "I could never forget you because you remind me so much of me when I was young."

Caren's eyes filled with tears. "You aren't just saying that. You really mean it."

"Yes, I really mean it. Now, when I called your stepmother, I asked her to find out if you wanted to come in for a last session or two. Did she tell you that?" Caren shook her head. "How about tomorrow after school?"

"I—I'd like that."

"Okay, let me take a peek at my schedule." Lara heaved herself to her feet, even more drained than when she'd been packing boxes. Silent fury at Myra Stone soured her stomach. Her cell phone trilled. Picking it up, she glanced at the number and then pushed the answer key. "Hi, Trev—" she began.

"Where in the bloody blazes are you?" he snapped. "Please, please tell me you've got a good reason for not being home."

"I'm almost out of here," she replied carefully, aware Caren was listening. "I'll call you from the car once I'm on my way. Don't worry. I'm okay."

His breath whistled through the cellular system. "Righto." His accent was very crisp, betraying his anxiety. "I'll wait for you to ring me back."

Of course he'd be worried after the riots and Arabel, never mind that patient of mine who tried to kill me. With her lips pursed together, Lara pulled up the calendar on her phone.

"Is your husband mad at you?" Caren asked tremulously.

"No dear, just worried. Would three-thirty work?" Lara looked questioningly at the teenager. At Caren's nod, Lara tapped buttons. "There," she said. "You're in. Do you have a ride home?"

"Yeah, I brought my car. It's in the, uh, alley."

"Next to my back door?"

Caren dropped her gaze to her hands. "Yeah."

"Okay, give me a sec, and I'll walk you out."

Lara slipped on a gray tweed wool jacket, grabbed her phone, pager, and purse, and shepherded Caren out of the office, down the stairs, and around to the back. "Is that it?" Lara asked, pointing to a yellow Volkswagen.

"Uh-huh."

"Are you better?"

Caren looked at her, bit her lower lip, and said, "Some. But I still wish you weren't going."

I wish I wasn't either. "Bye, dear. Drive safe." Locking up, she marveled that the unruly teen had managed to defeat a locking mechanism designed to stymie professional burglars. After setting the building alarm, she hit the speed dial digit on her phone that would connect her to home. Trevor picked up on the first ring.

"Well?" he said, still sounding half-sick with fear.

"It was one of my younger patients," she said as she walked to her car, "needing reassurance. She snuck in the back while we were loading boxes." Lara blew out a tense breath. "Anyway, she looked around the office, put two and two together, and panicked. I'm heading home now. Can I tell you the rest when I get there? I'm tapped out, and I don't want to talk and drive at the same time."

"Sure, love." His voice softened. "See you soon."

"I love you." She hit the end call button and engaged the ignition.

Lara shut her eyes for a few seconds to rest them before dealing with the glare from other cars' headlamps. She grimaced. Her eyes felt gritty, and she was so tired her bones ached.

Nothing's going to get better with me sitting here.

As she guided the car through light traffic on her way to the freeway, Lara thought about the last three weeks. Hard to believe it had only taken that short amount of time for life to collapse.

"Get a grip," she hissed. Her fingers clenched around the leather-clad wheel until they hurt. "It's not like Trev hasn't been warning me for months there wasn't enough gasoline or food, but I did my usual ostrich routine and didn't pay attention."

Her minded drifted to Lillian. After years of a love-hate relationship with her own psychic abilities, Lara had finally made an effort to find someone who could teach her about her magical side. "Heh! I got a tad more than I bargained for," she mumbled, finding enough energy to laugh ruefully.

Lara creased her forehead in thought. Everything that had happened since Ken Beauchamp accosted her on the front porch of her office, threatening her because she tried to help his abused wife, merged into a confusing maelstrom.

I can't think anymore. Maybe I could just do some breathing.

When she finally turned the car onto her street on Queen Anne Hill, she was painfully close to the end of her emotional tether. Relaxation breathing hadn't helped much, and she still felt like she was running on fumes. Her head throbbed dully. As she scanned the street for parking spots, she spotted one fairly close to the twenty-five stairs leading to their house and maneuvered into it. Shutting off the engine, she folded her hands together over the top of the steering wheel and rested her forehead on them. A sharp tap on her window made her jump.

"Lara?" Trevor's voice, muted by the thick safety glass, still sounded worried.

"Yeah, yeah. I'm coming." She pushed the door open and stumbled into the chill damp of a Seattle evening. He threaded his arms around her. "Bring what you need, love. Or I can get it for you."

"Bag, phone, pager." She drew in a shuddery breath. "Hell, Trev, I'm not that bad off. Nothing wrong with my body. I'm just emotionally drained, and my head hurts. If you hand that stuff to me, maybe you could haul one of those boxes upstairs."

He extracted the BMW's keys from her hand, then reached inside to gather her things. While he did that, Lara moved to the back of the car.

Got to stop feeling sorry for myself.

She straightened her shoulders and called, "Hit the hatch release, would you, since you've got my keys?" Once it was open, she reached inside and grasped one of the banker's boxes by its built-in handles.

Lara walked to the side of the car where Trevor stood, holding her things. "Just drop them on top of this box."

"Bloody bollocks, Lara. When you got out of the car, you looked like you could barely stand."

"Being home helps. Come on, dear. Please don't fight with me."

With an exasperated sigh, Trevor clipped her phone and pager to her bag, then laid all three atop the box she was carrying. "See you inside."

"No, you'll see me back out here in a couple minutes. We can eat after all those boxes are in the house. I can't leave them out here. They're confidential patient files. Burning them is one thing. Leaving them, even in a locked car, is quite another." Turning, she started up the steps to the front porch of their five story home.

"We could try one of those shredding services," he called after her.

Balancing the box carefully on a step, she trotted back over to him. "No, we couldn't," she said in a low voice. "Raven said it'd be dangerous for us if people know we're leaving. If we give hundreds of pounds of files to the shredders, someone's bound to get suspicious. Especially since they, of all people, would know I'm supposed to hang on to things for at least seven years."

Pulling the hatch closed, Trevor picked up two boxes, one atop the other. "Hmm, hadn't thought about it in quite that light, but they'd have to glance through the lot to search for dates and that doesn't seem likely."

She tugged a back door open and got another box. "Maybe I'm overreacting."

"No worries, love. Lead on, then. I'm just behind you."

www.ingramcontent.com/pod-product-compliance
Lightning Source LLC
Chambersburg PA
CBHW070822190726
48292CB00006B/2087